THE ALSO PEOPLE

DOCTOR WHO – THE NEW ADVENTURES

THE NEW

DOCTOR WHO

ADVENTURES

THE ALSO PEOPLE

Ben Aaronovitch

First published in Great Britain in 1995 by
Doctor Who Books
an imprint of Virgin Publishing Ltd
332 Ladbroke Grove
London W10 5AH

Cover illustration by Tony Masero

ISBN 0 426 20456 5

Typeset by Galleon Typesetting, Ipswich
Printed and bound in Great Britain by
Mackays Paperbacks Ltd.

Acknowledgements

I would like to thank Kate Orman for reminding me how much fun this is. Rebecca and Peter for putting up with my total lack of grammar, punctuation, spelling and my some-what loose perception of linear time as it pertains to dead-lines. Nick Chatwin and Muhmud Quayum for their help. And my family for their support. I'd like to remind everyone that while talent borrows and genius steals, New Adventure writers get it off the back of a lorry, no questions asked.

Notes on the Pronunciation of Proper Nouns

!x is an aspirated consonant pronounced by clicking the side of the tongue against upper right-hand teeth.

!q is an aspirated consonant pronounced by 'clucking' the tongue.

!c is an aspirated consonant pronounced by placing the tongue against the front teeth and sucking them explosively back.

a is pronounced *ah* as in car.

e is pronounced *eh* as in leg.

i is pronounced *ee* as in leek or keep.

o is pronounced like the *a* in walk.

u is pronounced *oo* as in look or cook.

Stress is on the second syllable from last: aM!xitsa is pronounced am-*!xit*-sah; saRa!qava is pronounced sah-rah-*!qah*-vah.

I have chosen to use the simplified (personal) versions of people's names throughout the text as the more complex (use) designations would be cumbersome and serve little purpose. An example is the drone aM!xitsa, whose *use designation* incorporates the diminutive of his construction point and generation; thus: *aM!xit-i!xa!xi-sa!Qa!cisa.*

To avoid meaningless and ugly neologisms and to avoid unnecessary descriptions I have translated certain common-place nouns into their closest English equivalents; thus: hours, minutes, days, months, monkeys, apple trees, caramel, coffee, chocolate, pastries, etc.

To avoid further confusion I have rendered all Xhosa,

Themne, Shona, Martian and Gallifreyan words in their accepted English forms.

One further note: in order to err on the side of political correctness I refer to *Indigenous Terrans* rather than *Earth Reptiles* or the archaic *Silurians*.

Prologue

According to the old women there had once been a Leopard that fell into a trap. She lay there in the bottom of the trap, her powerful body bruised and sore. It was hot and dusty. She felt miserable.

'Let me out of this trap,' the Leopard cried. 'Let me out!'

But nobody came to let her out. All the other animals were afraid of the Leopard and were secretly glad that she might die. After many hours a woman walked past the trap. The woman had a kind face and smiled when she met people on her travels.

'Let me out, let me out,' the Leopard whimpered, her voice weak with thirst and captivity, the bruises on her body throbbing with pain.

The woman walked over to the trap. When she saw the Leopard inside she was frightened.

'Let me out,' called the Leopard, pathetic in her misery. 'If you do not let me out I will soon die.'

The woman looked down at the Leopard for a long time. She had travelled far and wide in the world and knew that leopards were the most dangerous of animals. More cunning than Chief Lion who was lazy and let his wives hunt for him. Stronger than cousin Cheetah who ran like lightning but for only a small distance. More vicious even than sister Panther who could smell the wind and run for ever. 'If I let you out of the trap,' called the woman to the Leopard, 'will you promise me one thing?'

1

'Whatever you want,' replied the Leopard, 'only let me out of this trap.'

'You must promise that you will not harm me once I release you,' said the woman. 'You are a powerful animal. Your sharp claws could tear me to pieces.'

'I will not harm you,' promised the Leopard. 'I want only my freedom.'

The woman pulled away the branches which covered the trap and bent down to help the Leopard out.

'Aha!' roared the Leopard as she stretched her powerful body. The woman watched fearfully as strong muscles rippled under the Leopard's fur. 'How hungry I feel now that I am out of that dreadful place. Soon I must eat my supper.' She looked at the woman. 'You, my friend, will be my supper.'

When the woman heard those words she trembled with fear. 'You promised that you would not harm me. Let me go. It is late in the day and my friends have brewed beer for me. Tonight we are giving thanks to our ancestors and the village relies on me to talk to the dead for them.'

The Leopard laughed. 'You fool,' she snarled, 'you should not have believed me. Now that I am outside the trap there is no reason why I should keep my promise. Now, however, I am going to have a short rest. Do not worry about your ancestors, for once I have finished my sleep I shall send you to meet them directly.'

The woman looked round desperately for help. A short distance away she saw a small Musasa Tree.

'Musasa Tree,' she called, 'help me to escape this ungrateful Leopard. I let her out of the trap and now she wants to eat me for her supper.'

The Musasa Tree grew angry at the woman's words. 'Why should I help you?' she replied. 'You've never done anything to help me. Every day I shade you from the hot sun and keep your house cool and pleasant. Yet all you want to do is cut me down and use me as firewood.'

The woman sighed unhappily. She knew that what the Musasa Tree had said was true. Sadly the woman turned away, searching the veldt for something that might help her.

2

Her gaze fell upon the Path, along which she had walked.

'Nzira,' she called the path by name, 'help me to escape from this horrible Leopard.'

But Nzira was even angrier than Musasa Tree. 'I will not help you. What have you ever done to help me? I give you safe passage through the forest, but all you ever do is kick me with your heavy feet and press me further into the ground.'

The woman sighed again because she knew that Nzira was speaking the truth. Then she remembered the River who was called Rwizi.

'Rwizi,' she called, 'help me escape from this evil Leopard who promises to eat me for her supper.'

But Rwizi would not help her. 'Think of everything I do for you,' said Rwizi. 'I give you water to grow your crops. I bring water for your cattle to drink in the evening. Yet all you do is use me to wash your dirty body and your soiled clothes.'

The woman sighed for the third time for she knew that Rwizi was speaking the truth.

Finally, in desperation she called upon the spirit of her Grandmother.

'Mbuya,' she called to the heavens, 'save me from this wicked Leopard.'

'I cannot save you,' replied the spirit of her grandmother. 'You should have listened more carefully to the stories I told you as a child. The Leopard is not wicked, she is only being what she is. It is in her nature to eat when she is hungry, to kill when she is threatened. You should have remembered this *before* you released her.'

On hearing this the woman fell to her knees and covered her face with her hands. Bitter tears fell from between her fingers and watered the earth.

Just then a small sprightly animal came hurrying through the forest. He had long narrow ears and a small bushy tail. It was Tsuro the Hare.

'Whatever is the problem?' asked Tsuro when she saw the woman weeping. 'Why are you looking so miserable on this lovely day?'

The woman told him about the Leopard whom she had

3

released from the trap and how it was planning to eat her for supper.

'Hmm,' said Tsuro after hearing the story. 'What you have told me may very well be true. But I must hear what the Leopard says about the matter.

'Leopard,' called Tsuro. 'I've been told that you fell into this trap. Is that so?'

'Yes, it is true,' agreed the Leopard, flexing her paws so that each of her claws extruded one after another. The woman, seeing this, edged behind Tsuro.

'O clever Hare,' she whispered, 'I hope you know what you are doing.'

Tsuro ignored her and asked the Leopard whether it was true that she had promised not to harm the woman.

'Yes,' said the Leopard, 'but there is no reason why I should keep my promise. After all, her brothers dug the trap into which I fell. And they are the ones who always shout at me and then try to kill me when I am anywhere near their village.'

'I see,' replied Tsuro, scratching his head thoughtfully. 'So it was the woman's brothers who dug the trap into which you fell. And you were lying there, right at the bottom of the trap when the woman came and let you out. Now, I would like you to show me how it happened.'

'That's easy,' said the Leopard, happy to find someone who understood her situation. She jumped down into the trap. 'I was lying like this . . .' Scarcely had she begun when, quickly, Tsuro pulled the branches across the top of the trap.

'Let me out, let me out,' cried the Leopard. 'If you let me out of the trap I promise not to harm anybody ever again.'

Tsuro turned to the woman.

'Well,' he asked, 'are you going to let her out?'

1

Delete Where Applicable

> I get so weary following this old road
> It don't go nowhere but damnation
> When I turn around what do I find?
> Got evil in my bones and bad luck following behind.
>
> 'Travelling Man Blues', singer unknown
> Recorded: Mama Stanley's Chicken Shack, Clanton,
> Alabama (1937)

The man is standing on the roof of the villa which itself is built on the crest of a hill overlooking the sea. A storm is racing in from the ocean, black streamers of cloud are unfurling towards the coast. The wind has become brisk, filling the man's nostrils with the stink of ozone and salt. He opens his arms wide as if to embrace the oncoming wind, as if the storm has been laid on for his entertainment alone. The air is heavy with the promise of lightning. Growing stronger now, the wind plucks at the man's robe and lifts strands of his blond hair. He is smiling, a wide infectious grin that exposes white teeth that are just slightly too sharp for comfort.

Around him he senses but cannot see the great sphere of the world rising all around him. Above him an immovable sun dims in accordance with a strict timetable, its gorgeous twilight hue a precise and machine-modulated bandwidth of the electromagnetic spectrum. He knows that people have built this world, have chained the sun to do their bidding. Knows that people built the planet that hangs blue, green and

5

impossible over a horizon that doesn't exist. That the horizon is in reality only a sensory illusion, a DNA-encoded perception, a legacy from the first things to crawl up that Devonian Beach and look at the sky.

The storm is real, he can sense that. Even the people who built this place, people whom he has not yet but is dying to meet, know that life can be made too comfortable. That without the sublime, without danger we will grow sickly and die by degrees. So they have let this storm boil itself up out of the endless ocean and have watched it roll in from the sea like some fantastic Krakan, its belly rumbling with enough static potential to illuminate a small planetoid.

It comes, a solid wall of air twenty kilometres high and hundreds deep, ready to break against this artfully rocky coastline where a man stands atop a villa that stands upon a hill that overlooks the sea. Ready to roll inland and die stranded amongst the sculptured hills of this manufactured continent.

The man tries to open his arms wider, spreading his fingers to grasp at the wind. He is imagining the air as it streams around his limbs, the complicated mandelbrot shapes of the pockets of turbulence that trail behind him, the same partial vacuum that had lifted him into the cold sky over the English Channel. No null gravity units or clever avionics on the biplane, just the simple differentiation of air pressure, the ancient principle of flight, the physics of a gliding bird. He remembers struggling with the controls, those unpowered contraptions of wooden levers and piano wire. No power assistance, no autopilot; his strength alone against the thousand vagaries of the wind.

He is leaning forward now, into the rising gale and over the edge of the parapet. He peers down the side of the building calculating the fall, his chances of survival if the wind fails. As he dares himself forward he feels the tightening in his stomach, the speeding of his heart, the strange scrunching sensation of his scrotum shrivelling up. He is waiting for the hit, the sweet rush of his own adrenalin. The wind is singing to him now, singing of the joy of falling and the ecstasy of fear. His urge to jump frightens him more than anything else. He seizes the fear and as the storm approaches raises his head to stare straight into its blazing heart.

His eyes are full of lightning and dangerous ideas.

Bernice slept for most of the day in a room filled with sunlight and the scent of the sea. She woke once to find the Doctor watching her from the doorway. He was smiling but his hat brim cast a dark shadow across his eyes. She wanted to ask him something but she was too tired and the bed too comfortable. She slipped back into a dream of the endless summer afternoon of her early childhood. Of herself skipping through the checkerboard shadows on the road-grass, a small figure between her mother and father, holding tight to their big hands. Safe in the grip of the long-since dead.

She woke again to the smell of fresh coffee and the insistent pressure of her bladder. The room was narrow and tall with walls and floor of polished hardwood and a ceiling that was three-quarters glass skylight. The quilt she was lying under was stitched together from scraps of cloth, all different materials and shapes. She decided that she liked this rag-quilt. Liked the randomness of the colours and shapes. For reasons she couldn't define it made her think of home.

She lay still for a while, snug under the quilt. She tried to ignore the coffee smell and the demands of her body. There wasn't any reason to get up yet. The Doctor had said so. So it must be true.

Then she remembered where she was.

Remembered the Doctor turfing them out of bed in the middle of the night. Stumbling out of the TARDIS into the warm darkness of the clearing in the forest. Trees rose all around them, silver grey in the moonlight. Insects clicked and popped amongst trunks as straight as telegraph poles.

Summer, thought Bernice sleepily, somewhere at the warm end of a temperate weather latitude. Could be somewhere along the coast of the Mediterranean – Greece perhaps?

She flinched as a huge moth floated past her face and started to lazily circle the Doctor. Its wings were pale blurs in the dark, each as big as Bernice's hand. The Doctor stretched out his arm and let the moth alight daintily on the tips of his fingers.

'Where are we, Doctor?' asked Chris.

'Somewhere you've never been before,' said the Doctor.

'Oh, good,' said Roz. 'That will make a change.'

And that was when Bernice looked up and saw that the world curved over their heads.

Bernice had only seen a night sky like that once before, on the remnants of the Dyson sphere at DM+39 4567 on the fringes of the stellar cluster known as the Varteq Veil. That sphere had been broken apart by gravitational asymmetries, the massive fragments forming a slowly expanding globe around its sun. The same catastrophe had destroyed the civilization that had built it, an entire race broken on the wheel of its own ambition. Bernice remembered standing on the surface of one of the fragments during an eclipse caused by a smaller fragment occluding the sun.

In the sudden darkness the thin atmosphere gave the sky a cold hallucinatory clarity. The other fragments were bright with reflected sunlight, carving up the sky into crazy-paving shapes. Bernice could see surface features on the closer ones. An ocean that had survived the break-up, shrinking in from its artificial shoreline as it evaporated in the thinning atmosphere; a city bisected by the edge of one fragment. Bernice looked further on to find the other half and there on the next fragment was the rest of the city, glittering under a mantle of frozen oxygen. The nearer fragments appeared as flat as tea trays, the curve of the sphere being so gradual that it was only visible on the most distant fragments.

The geophysics team had constructed a computer model of the break-up and ran a book on the results. The whole archaeology team had put money on their own time estimates. The crew of the freighter they were using for transport refused to bet. They thought the whole idea was distasteful; for them a catastrophic failure in life support was too serious, wherever it happened. They didn't have the same perspective on life and death as the archaeologists. Bernice put her bundle on ten years, give or take six months.

8

With a flair for the dramatic the geophysics team announced the results on the 'night' of the eclipse. All the surface-based archaeology teams gathered for a party. A bonfire was built with an oxygen feed to help it burn in the thin atmosphere. The palaeobotany team jury rigged one of their bio-reactors to brew beer and the xenobiology team roasted a couple of quadrupeds which they swore blind weren't sentient. They were more evasive about the animal's general edibility.

Everyone lost their money. The computer model estimated that the break-up had taken two hundred and fifty years, from the first instability to actual disintegration of the outer shell. As they drank the passable beer and carved off sections of roast meat an argument broke out over whether it was actually possible to build a functioning Dyson sphere. Geophysics thought not and produced reams of statistics to back themselves up. The ethnotechnologists thought that someone somewhere was bound to have a go. The group sociologist, the only Indigenous Terran amongst them, said it was unlikely that a species that had evolved on a planet would ever feel completely comfortable on an artificial world.

The local clan of Builders, perhaps a couple of medium-sized family groups, came to observe the archaeologists from a safe distance. Occasionally Bernice would catch glimpses of firelight dully reflected off the curve of a carapace or flickering in one of their large, mournful eyes. She wondered exactly when their ancestors had realized it was all going horribly wrong.

Two hundred and fifty years.

It was a long time to know you were dying.

The Doctor led them up a narrow path through the forest. Roz and Chris, smug in their adjudicator's armour, simply flipped down their nightscope visors and followed easily. Bernice cursed and stumbled until she thought to surreptitiously grab the hem of Chris's robe and let him guide her between the trees. She had little sense of how far they walked, mostly uphill, although the path occasionally switched back and forth as if following the line of a ridge. There were occasional glimpses of wooded skyline silhouetted against those sections of the sky that were still in daylight. Once she thought she saw a trio of wind turbines on a distant hilltop, their slowly turning blades floodlit with eerie brightness. She tried to use them as a landmark but the path soon twisted and she lost sight of them.

Finally Bernice had to get out of bed. There was no sign of her clothes so she made do by draping herself in the rag-quilt, and made a spirited lunge for what she hoped was the bathroom, her bare feet slapping against the floor as she crossed the room.

No Dyson sphere in human space, thought Bernice, not in my time anyway. She remembered the lovingly painted model spaceships in Chris's bedroom. Not in the thirtieth century either, she was sure Chris would have said something. So, not someone we've ever met then, maybe not even humanoid. She hoped that whoever they were their plumbing was compatible. The bed was a good sign but one should never make hasty assessments about alien physiology, even when one is bursting to go.

'I think each of the bathrooms is different,' said Roz later. They were sitting on the first-floor balcony and drinking Turkish coffee from heat-resistant glasses. 'Mine had this enormous sunken bath, solid marble, gold taps, the works.'

'If you don't mind,' said Bernice, 'I think I'll use your bathroom in future. I'm not sure I like bathing in mid air.'

'My parents had a bath like that. Suspensor pools were very fashionable fifty years ago' – Roz frowned – 'my time.'

'At least we know they must be humanoid,' said Bernice. 'My "human waste disposal interface" was completely compatible.'

'I've never heard it called that before.'

'It's what my father used to call toilets.'

'Your father was in the Navy, right?'

Bernice sipped her coffee. Why was she thinking of her father now? 'Outer System Patrol,' she said. 'He was a

10

'sucker for long complicated euphemisms.'

'At least the toilets round here don't try and wipe your arse afterwards,' said Roz. 'I hate the ones that do that.'

'Tell me about it.' Good old Roz, you could always rely on her to get the conversation down to ground zero reality point. 'I wonder what they're like? The people that built this place.'

'They're certainly very advanced technologically; it's all very slick,' said Roz. 'But don't count on them being even remotely human. Some of the worst scum I ever dealt with in the Undertown looked just like you and me. On the outside at least.'

Bernice knew better than to let Roz get started on *that* particular subject. There seemed to be very few alien races that Roz hadn't personally insulted, bashed, shot or arrested, frequently combining all four actions in a single encounter.

'This place has an interesting aesthetic,' Bernice said quickly, 'don't you think?' Actually the villa didn't seem to have any unifying aesthetic at all. It sprawled on the crest of the hill like a tumble of children's building blocks. Five storeys high, the top floor was wider than the ground floor but the third floor protruded ten metres at the back. Sections were built of wood, others of concrete, glass or irregularly shaped bricks. Inside it was worse; although each room was furnished in a different style, they were curiously undifferentiated in purpose. The room behind the first-floor balcony had, by consensus, become the living room but Bernice felt that it would have served just as easily as a bedroom, or for all she knew a kitchen or another bathroom.

'I think this place was built by children,' said Roz.

'Children?'

'Don't you think so?' said Roz. 'It's got that kind of feel to it.'

Bernice snorted. 'Of course,' she said. 'They wandered up here on a Sunday afternoon and made it out of bits and pieces. Old orange boxes, left-over bubble plastic, old discarded cybernetic environmental management systems –'

'Children,' said Roz firmly.

'Absolutely,' said Bernice. 'The Famous Five build a

11

multi-storey hotel. The design is chaotic, even incoherent, but the level of technical sophistication is too high. Trust me on this, Roz; I'm an archaeologist.'

'See that?' Roz pointed over Bernice's shoulder. Bernice twisted in her chair and saw where a silver grey three-metre globe was attached to the wall of the villa.

'Yeah?' asked Bernice cautiously.

'That's Chris's bedroom,' said Roz.

'It takes all types.'

'It detaches,' said Roz. 'When he's asleep, it breaks away from the main building and floats around. Chris thinks the movement could be keyed to his alpha rhythms.'

'And it floats?'

'Around the villa, over the trees and under the sky.'

'Why?'

'Because it's fun,' said Roz. 'Chris loves it. Loves the whole idea of it.'

'I'll bet.'

'Like I said, children.'

Bernice realized that Roz had a point. The villa did have a random quality that could be associated with childhood. As long as you didn't think about the investment in resources that the villa represented. Perhaps the place was empty because all the kids were away at school? Bernice watched Roz lean back in her chair and take another sip of coffee. She was wearing her inscrutable face again. Bernice realized that this was just the right moment to ask Roz why she didn't have any children herself.

Speaking of children, Roz, you're over forty, even with biological enhancement you're pushing the fertility envelope. Childbearing is supposed to be a genetic imperative; don't you ever even *think* about it?

'Speaking of children,' said Bernice, 'where's the Doctor?'

'In the kitchen fixing supper.'

'Thank God for that, I'm starving,' said Bernice. 'There's a kitchen then?'

'There's a room with flat surfaces that get very hot and some cupboard-like things that the Doctor takes food and ingredients from,' said Roz. 'It's a bit too generic for my liking. I mean, when I looked in those cupboards earlier, they were empty.'

'Anyone for tea?' asked the Doctor. Roz almost choked on a mouthful of coffee. Bernice could sympathize; she hadn't heard him coming either.

The Doctor stepped through the picture window frame and onto the balcony. In each hand he was carrying a silver service tray, a third tray balanced precariously on his head. A folded square of white linen was draped over his left forearm. He paused before the table as if waiting for applause. The two women declined the opportunity.

The Doctor scowled at them and started to unload the trays. 'It's not that easy to do,' he complained.

'Don't tell me,' said Bernice. 'You once worked in a Venusian burger bar.'

The Doctor pulled up a chair and sat down. 'Venusians didn't eat hamburgers,' he said, 'at least not while I was there.'

'What did they eat?' asked Roz.

'Each other mostly,' said Bernice.

Roz muttered something under her breath.

'Only at funerals,' said the Doctor and pushed a plate of steaming brown ovoids towards her. 'Pasty?'

Roz cautiously picked up one of the brown ovoids. The Doctor waited until she'd taken a bite before saying, 'Each other's brains to be precise.' Roz gave him a black look and continued chewing. Rather stoically, Bernice thought.

'Tasted a bit like chocolate cake,' said the Doctor, watching as Roz swallowed very deliberately. 'They had excellent biochemical reasons for doing it.'

'I don't want to know,' Roz said very slowly. 'I don't want to hear about their magnificent culture and how they loved their children and were terribly kind to small animals.'

'Of course you don't,' said the Doctor cheerily. He looked over the table and frowned. 'Where did I put the tea-tray?'

'It's still on your head,' said Bernice.

'Ah,' said the Doctor and lifted the tray off his head and on to the table. 'So it was. I'd forget my own hat if it wasn't folded up in my pocket.'

13

The teapot was black porcelain decorated with an attractive gold leaf inlay. Steam fluttered from its spout. Bernice counted five matching cups and saucers.

'Are we expecting company?' she asked.

The Doctor stared at the cups as if seeing them for the first time. He picked one up and slowly traced a fingertip down its side. He muttered a word that Bernice thought might have been 'flawless'. Then suddenly he flung the teacup at the balcony floor. It bounced with a peculiar muted twang and the Doctor snatched it out of the air. Smiling, he held it up for their inspection. It wasn't even marked.

'Indestructible,' said the Doctor, replacing the cup on its saucer. His gaze flicked back and forth from Bernice to Roz, as if he were waiting for them to get the joke. Bernice shot a glance at Roz who looked as worried as she was.

'Random co-ordinates,' said Bernice. 'You promised.'

'I know what you're thinking,' said the Doctor, 'and I can assure you that the future of the universe is not at stake.'

'Well,' said Roz, 'that's a relief.'

'I'm warning you, Professor Summerfield,' said the Doctor, 'and you, Adjudicator Forrester, if this attitude of wilful melancholy persists I will have no option but to take punitive measures.' The Doctor seized a pair of dessert spoons from the table and held them up.

'You wouldn't dare,' said Bernice.

'What's he going to do?' asked Roz. 'Spoon us to death?'

'Worse,' said Bernice. 'He's going to *play* the spoons. Mind you, I use the word "play" advisedly.'

The Doctor winked at Roz and slipped the spoons between his fingers.

'You know you're not supposed to do this,' said Bernice. 'It was specifically banned under the White City Convention on psychological warfare.'

'Last chance,' said the Doctor.

'You can't bully people into being cheerful,' said Bernice.

The Doctor started banging the spoons between the table and his hand. His face had an expression of dreamy single-minded determination. 'Did I ever tell you,' he shouted over the racket, 'that I once broke the Galactic record for

14

continuous spoon-playing. Sixty-seven hours it was. I would have broken the Universal record but a Garthanian telekinetic kept on bending my instruments.'

'I wonder why.'

'What was that?' asked the Doctor. 'You want to see if I can do it with both hands at once? Roslyn, be so good as to pass me those spoons there . . .'

'I give up,' said Bernice.

'I can't hear you.'

'I give up, I'll be cheerful, optimistic, gay, whatever you want. Only for God's sake stop.'

The Doctor stopped clicking the spoons and grinned at her.

'Never mind, Benny,' said Roz, pushing a plate towards her. 'Have a brain pasty.'

The afternoon wore on. It grew warmer on the balcony. Roz retreated to the shade of the living room. The Doctor produced a thick paperback novel from somewhere about his person. Bernice popped back up to her bedroom to find something cooler to wear.

The pixies had been at work again. The bed had been remade, the rag-quilt turned back at one corner to reveal clean sheets of pale lilac. Her clothes, the ones she had brought from the TARDIS, had been folded and neatly piled at the end of the bed. Her diary had been left on top of the clothes.

A similar thing had occurred earlier, while Bernice had been struggling with the suspensor pool in the bathroom. She'd stumbled back in to find her clothes stacked neatly on the newly made bed. At the time it had reminded her of the fairy stories of Northern Europe, the ones about small supernatural beings that did household chores in return for a bowl of bovine lactate left out on the doorstep.

She assumed some kind of domestic robot was responsible. If so they were the quietest and most efficient machines she'd ever seen. Or more to the point, not seen.

She decided to call them pixies, as if naming the unknown made it less frightening. She suspected the villa was infested with pixies and by logical extension, probably the whole

15

Dyson sphere. That had worrying implications: robot-dependent cultures were notoriously decadent, fragile and often paranoid to boot. There was a classic treatise in the TARDIS database on the subject: *Taren Capel: A case study in robophilia*. The man who wanted to be a robot when he grew up.

Bernice was struck by a horrible suspicion. What if there were no people inhabiting the Dyson sphere? What if the machines had taken over, as they had on Movella? After all, there was no actual evidence that *people* lived in the sphere. Perhaps this manufactured landscape was empty, inhabited only by machines and animals. It would be just like the Doctor to take them on holiday to a ghost world.

She picked up the pile of clothes; they had a freshly laundered smell.

Although, Bernice had to admit, for a ghost world, the valet service was excellent. She pulled on her halter top and as an experiment left the rest of her clothes scattered across the bedroom floor.

She ran into Chris in the living room. He was standing by the sofa dressed in a garish blue bathrobe. He looked up as Bernice approached and quickly put his fingers to his lips. He nodded at the sofa where Roz was curled up asleep. A videobook was still clasped in her hand, a small *page?* ikon flashing forlornly in the left hand corner of its screen. Chris bent over her and gently removed the videobook and placed it carefully on the coffee table. Relaxed, the older woman's face seemed younger, almost youthful. Bernice was struck by the oddly tender expression on Chris's face as he covered his partner with a blanket.

'She's tired,' he said quietly.

Bernice nodded. They were all tired. The events on Detrios were still too close. Especially for Chris. Perhaps the Doctor had been right to bring them here for a holiday. If it was a holiday?

'Are you coming outside?' Bernice asked Chris.

He glanced at the balcony, at the Doctor, who was sitting there with his back to them. Chris shook his head. 'I thought I'd take a dip in the roof pool.'

'There's a swimming pool on the roof?'

'Yeah,' said Chris. 'The bottom of the pool is completely transparent. You can see right into the rooms below.' He remembered Roz and lowered his voice again. 'And there's a games room you won't believe.'

'Is that where you've been all afternoon?'

'I lost track of time.' Another glance at the Doctor's back. 'You know how it is.'

'Why don't you have a swim and then come down?'

'Yeah,' said Chris, 'that's what I'll do.' He looked down at Roz. 'She doesn't like it when dreams come true,' he said sadly. 'She thinks the universe is complicated enough as it is.'

Bernice watched as Chris headed for the stairs. There was a tightness across his shoulders that she'd never noticed before. She heard Roz snort softly in her sleep, shifting her position on the sofa. You get comfortable, old bean, thought Bernice. Enjoy it while it lasts.

And perhaps she should follow her own advice.

But then again, why break the habit of a lifetime.

Bernice paused on the threshold of the balcony. 'I'm not coming out there until you show me your hands.'

The Doctor raised his hands. 'Don't shoot, I'm unarmed.'

Bernice stepped through the invisible wall that separated the hot balcony from the cool interior of the villa. It wasn't just the contrast between sunlight and shade. Earlier on she'd stuck her hand halfway through to check; there was a precise demarcation between hot and cool. An invisible wall.

'Unspooned is all I'm interested in,' said Bernice, taking her seat. There was a wine cooler on the table and a single narrow-waisted wine glass. Neither had been there when she'd gone upstairs for her halter top. She was pretty certain they hadn't been there when she'd been talking to Chris inside.

'I ordered you some wine,' said the Doctor.

Bernice pulled the bottle out of the wine cooler; it was shaped like a glass corkscrew, the liquid inside a pale amber colour. 'I see,' said Bernice. 'First the stick and now the carrot.' The bottle was sealed with a real cork cork. She

17

poured a half measure in the glass, swirled, sniffed, tasted.

'Good?' asked the Doctor.

'Unusual.'

'But good?'

'Excellent.'

'Aren't you supposed to spit it out afterwards?'

'Absolutely not,' said Bernice filling her glass. 'I've always felt that wine tasters have got the wrong end of the stick on that one.'

'They spit it out so as to avoid becoming incapacitated.'

'Proves my point exactly.' Bernice sipped the wine. It had a light flowery bouquet and tasted like summertime in the high Alps. 'I wonder what it's made from?'

The Doctor picked up the bottle and examined the label carefully. 'I haven't got the faintest idea.'

'If I could see through the walls of the sphere, what would I see?'

'Stars, constellations, galaxies, the usual sort of thing.'

'Would I recognize any of the stars?'

The Doctor thought about this for a moment. 'No.'

'Not a single constellation?'

'Perhaps,' said the Doctor. 'But what you think of as Human Space is a very long way away.'

'But you've been here before?'

'Actually,' said the Doctor, 'I don't visit this place very often. Nothing particularly interesting ever happens here.'

'Stagnant?'

'Peaceful,' said the Doctor. 'Terribly well organized.'

'Efficient?'

'Totally.'

'Prosperous?'

'Disgustingly so.'

'Boring?'

'Very.'

'People?'

'About two trillion.'

Bernice put the wine glass down, very carefully. 'Two *trillion* as in two thousand billion?'

'That's a G-class main sequence star up there,' said the

Doctor, 'just like Earth's sun. The radius of this sphere is nearly one hundred and fifty million kilometres and it has an interior surface area of two point seven seven times ten to the power of seventeen square kilometres. That's roughly six hundred million times the surface area of Earth.'

'That's a lot of *lebensraum*.'

'And you don't have to invade Poland to get it.'

'Just how technologically advanced are they?'

The Doctor scratched the back of his neck. 'Benny, as an archaeologist you more than anyone else should know that technology is not simply a matter of linear progression. There are twists and turns, branches and cul de sacs, pools and rivers –'

'Your metaphor is wandering.'

'That's what happens when you try to describe the indescribable.'

'Or try to avoid a question.'

'Let me put it this way,' said the Doctor. 'They have a non-aggression pact with the Time Lords.'

Bernice picked up her glass and swallowed the last of the wine. Quickly she poured herself another glass and swallowed that with a single gulp. Poured another glass but left it on the table. There wasn't any point; there wasn't enough alcohol in existence to cope with that.

'Do they have time travel?'

'Strangely enough they don't,' said the Doctor. 'They just can't seem to get the hang of the technology. They get close but for some reason it never seems to work properly.'

'Really?' said Bernice. 'That is peculiar, isn't it?'

'It is, isn't it?' said the Doctor. 'I can't imagine why they have so much difficulty with it, since they have the theoretical capability.' He grinned. 'I suppose either you have what it takes, or you don't.'

'And if you have it, you make damn sure no one else gets it.'

The Doctor frowned, as if remembering a bereavement, then he brightened again. Bernice felt he was making an effort.

'These two trillion people,' she asked, 'are they human?'

'Ah,' said the Doctor, 'that rather depends on your definition of human.' He gestured vaguely off to the left. 'There's a small town called iSanti Jeni an hour's walk up the coast. You could stroll up and ask the people there what they think.'

'Would they recognize *me* as human?'

'That depends,' said the Doctor, 'on whether they talk to you before or after you've had your morning cup of coffee.'

The Doctor knew the storm was coming long before the first clouds became visible through the atmospheric haze. He said it was going to be a gigantic one and insisted that they all gather to watch it in the living room. He said nothing beat a good storm for entertainment.

There was no horizon inside the sphere, nor was the curve perceptible; with a radius of one hundred and fifty million kilometres it was far too gradual for that. Sea and sky appeared to go on for ever until they both merged into the atmospheric haze. Despite this, Bernice found that her mind insisted on creating a sort of virtual horizon where none existed, an invisible line of demarcation mid point between the water and the heavens. Bernice supposed it gave the view the formal unity of a Renaissance painting, and allowed her to cope with the scale of it all.

Leonardo would have been proud of her.

It started as a dark smudge on her virtual horizon, then a line of black and then the leading edge of the storm was crashing down on them. Through the balcony window Bernice saw the first sharp actinic flashes of lightning in the distance. She shivered in the sudden chill, amazed at how fast the clouds were moving. It was darkening quickly; through the murky light Bernice could see brush strokes of white spray whipped off the ocean. She was glad she was safe inside.

Lightning flashed, much closer this time. Bernice counted seconds, waiting for the thunder. There was a muffled thud behind her and the sound of a curse. Bernice turned to find Roz blearily getting up off the floor.

'Hey,' she said, 'has it got cold or is it me?'

'There's a storm coming.'

'That's what it was,' said Roz, stretching her arms and back. 'I thought I was dreaming.'

Thunder.

The first splatters of rain fell on the balcony, those drops that hit the invisible barrier in the picture window frame performing abrupt right-angle turns and splashing away to the side. The barrier seemed designed to allow the breeze in, however, and Bernice began to feel cold.

It was warmer upstairs. In her bedroom the rain clattered on the skylights. Her belongings were scattered all over the floor, just as she'd left them. The pixies had obviously not bothered to tidy up this time; perhaps they were still waiting for their bowl of milk. Bernice kicked the clothes around until she found the sweatshirt she was looking for, the one with I'M ACE AND THIS IS THE DOCTOR block-printed on the front above a big cartoon hand pointing to the left. Ace had bought it from a silkscreening stall at the Glastonbury Festival several lifetimes ago. Bernice had one with her own name on it but the ink had run. They'd got one for the Doctor which read: I'M THE DOCTOR AND THIS IS [DELETE WHERE APPLICABLE]. Ace had joked that she was DELETE and Bernice was APPLICABLE. Bernice had never seen the Doctor wear it.

'Benny.' Chris's voice.

'I'm in here,' she called, muffled by the sweatshirt as she pulled it on.

Chris stood in the doorway, his fair hair slicked back by the rain, his soaking wet robe clinging to his arms and chest.

'Have you seen the storm?' he asked.

'Some of us were sensible enough to be under cover when it arrived,' said Bernice.

Chris gave her a sunny smile, its effect mitigated some-what by a lightning flash that briefly flattened out his features and turned his eyes into dark hollows. He said something but the words were drowned out by the thunder.

'Here, you wally,' said Bernice, grabbing the rag-quilt off her bed and handing it to Chris. 'Put this round you before you get a chill.'

Chris laughed. 'You sound just like Roz.'

He pulled off his robe, briefly showing the width of his chest, the hard ridges of abdominals before they were hidden under the folds of the quilt. One day, thought Bernice, he's going to make some girl somewhere very cheerful. Not her, of course; it would have to be someone with *stamina*.

It should have been Kat'laana but she was what? Dead? Not born yet?

Gone certainly, taking a piece of Chris with her. A piece of his innocence that was forever buried below the Detrian permafrost. It had a horrible inevitability, this loss of innocence. It had happened to Ace on Heaven and to herself on King's Cross Station. I went into the time machine on my own two feet and I've been losing bits of me ever since. Like the broken Dyson sphere in the Varteq Veil, all hopes and dreams shattered.

'*No, no. I'm not a part of anyone's machine.*' Ace had said that, in Paris, meaning not a cog any more, not a pawn, not a *soldier*.

She couldn't bear the thought of losing Christopher Cwej. Not he of the wet nose and golden fur, the big stupid grin and mindless optimism in the face of danger. She had a premonition then, so intense it was painful. An image of an older Cwej, grim and silent on some nameless desolate plain, his face etched all over with lines of pain, his eyes having lost their lustre, full of anger and hatred.

'Hey,' said Chris, 'are you all right?'

He was watching her, concern on his big open face. Bernice touched her cheeks and was shocked to find them wet with tears.

She wondered which of them she was crying for.

It was a big storm.

They sat on the sofa facing the picture window with the rag-quilt over their knees. The Doctor produced four enormous bowls of what looked like popcorn but tasted of deep-fried plantain. Chris worked his way through two of them during the evening; Bernice and Roz had one each. The Doctor nibbled.

The lightning became so frequent you could almost have read a book by the light. Flashes would stab down towards the ocean illuminating first one section and then another. Without a horizon to curtail the view the storm seemed to stretch on for ever. Little of the violence of the storm seemed to leak into the villa; rain was deflected by the window field and Bernice suspected that the noise of the thunder was being muted. They were kept snug within a cocoon of safety with just enough storm to make it entertainment.

Bernice was thinking about that as she sat, cosy under the rag-quilt, secure between the Doctor and Roz, eating popcorn that tasted almost but not quite like fried banana. She was thinking that the Doctor was a master psychologist to design this scenario, to create this sense of warm conviviality. All of them together inside, terrible, violent forces outside.

She glanced to her left where Chris loomed at the end of the sofa. He was leaning forward slightly, his large face changing expression with every lightning flash. Roz looked relaxed and comfortable, smiling indulgently each time Chris yelled his appreciation of a particularly spectacular flash.

Bernice looked over at the Doctor, scrutinizing him in profile.

'*You're not the Doctor I knew.*' Mel this time, hesitating in the TARDIS doorway. '*You're a liar and a user, and quite possibly a murderer too. I don't wish to know you.*'

Bernice had learnt to accept the Doctor on his own terms: the lying, the using and, yes, the occasional bit of justifiable genocide. He was, after all, The Doctor; you accepted him on his own terms or not at all. Meeting Mel had been a shock, a window on the Doctor's past. Through this window Bernice had glimpsed a different person, as different to 'her' Doctor as her Doctor was from the ersatz Doctor Who created by Jason's adolescent imagination. A simpler character, thought Bernice, less terrifying and more 'human'. One that could enjoy a fishing trip, a bacon salad sandwich or the sound of rain against a window pane.

The Doctor seemed to sense her scrutiny and turned to look at her. For a moment Bernice was staring straight into his strange eyes.

23

She looked away quickly, uncertain of what she'd seen in them.

'How much of this storm is real?' asked Roz.

'That's a good question,' said the Doctor, 'given that this is a wholly artificial environment.'

'Who cares,' said Chris through a mouthful of popcorn.

'What do you think, Benny?' asked the Doctor. 'How much of this is real and how much of it manipulation?'

'God knows,' said Bernice quietly, thinking of a different question.

'Perhaps we'd better ask him then,' said the Doctor. 'House. Get God on the phone, will you.'

'God here,' said a voice.

'Goddess,' hissed Roz.

'If you prefer,' said the voice. 'Although around here God is generally considered to be a non-gender specific noun.'

Considering it was the voice of God it wasn't very impressive. Just a normal, fairly pleasant male voice that just happened to issue from every corner of the room simultaneously. It was an expressive voice though, managing to cram nuances of surprise, annoyance and world-weary cynicism into a single word – 'Doctor.'

'Hello, God,' said the Doctor.

'You're supposed to inform me when you arrive.'

'Am I?' said the Doctor in tones of clearly feigned innocence. 'There's nothing in the treaty about that.'

'As a courtesy?'

'Well, I didn't want to bother you,' said the Doctor. 'I know how busy you are. Running the world and everything. Let me just say how dazzling tonight's storm is. We're all enjoying it immensely.'

'I'm so glad you think so,' said God. 'By the way, who are your friends?'

'Silly me, forgetting my manners,' said the Doctor. 'God, this is Professor Bernice Summerfield, Adjudicator Secular Roslyn *Inyathi* Forrester and her Squire Christopher Cwej.'

Roz twitched so hard at the word 'Inyathi' that Bernice felt it. The small woman glanced quickly at the Doctor, who raised his eyebrow in reply.

'Pleased to meet you,' said God pleasantly. 'Any friend of the Doctor is hopefully a friend of mine.'

We're on good terms with a deity, thought Bernice; that makes a nice change.

'Do you control the sphere?' asked Chris.

'Yep,' said God. 'Although "manage" is probably a better word.'

'Where do you live?'

'Quite a lot of me is on Whynot but I'm pretty well diffused. I've got nodes all over the place.'

'So you're a computer?'

'Are you a mollusc?' asked God.

'Er, no,' said Chris.

'Then I'm not a computer,' said God, with a discernible amount of smugness.

Chris looked confused, his thoughts comically obvious on his face. 'What have molluscs got to do with anything?'

Bernice leant to murmur in Roz's ear. 'Oh, great, machines with attitude.' The other woman smiled.

'Ah,' said God. 'Prejudice.'

They never did quite get to pin down how much of the storm was real. The Doctor and God got into a light-hearted philosophical argument about what reality was at a fundamental level. It escalated to the point where both resorted to logic symbols, glowing holographic tiles that got shunted around the living room at knee level.

Roslyn fell asleep again, her head resting on Chris's shoulder. It was funny watching how he was so careful not to disturb her. Three-quarters of his body remained its normal expressive self while his shoulder never moved, not even when a tremendous flash of lightning lit the world from sea to sky, illuminating a limitless expanse of boiling waves. A clap of thunder big and loud enough made even the Doctor and God pause in mid argument.

'Just a moment,' said God, and then resumed the conversation.

Later Bernice asked herself whether she might not have seen something in the sudden darkness after the flash. Just a

25

speck of something reflective far out to sea, falling.

The storm abated, the popcorn was finished.

Bernice was tired again. Why? She hadn't done anything strenuous that day, if you didn't count trying to have a bath in a suspensor pool. Perhaps you could get tired even without constant stress; it was certainly a thought. She hadn't had much opportunity to experiment in that direction recently.

'This is the best bit,' said God.

The clouds parted to reveal the fabulous nightscape of the sphere. Artistically framed in the upper left-hand corner of the picture window was a blue and white planet, complete with continents and swirling clouds. It was the same apparent size as Earth seen from the moon.

Whynot. Home of most of God.

It took a special kind of confidence to build a Dyson sphere and then orbit a planet *inside*. The Doctor said they were lucky it was so close; the orbit was designed in such a way that Whynot passed over every part of the sphere in turn. 'Like a three-dimensional spirograph pattern,' he said.

Whatever a *spirograph* was.

With no appreciable effort Chris picked Roz up and carried her upstairs. Bernice found herself yawning and decided to follow. She left the Doctor deep in his conversation with God.

2

Life's A Beach

> Wake up in the morning.
> Baked beans for breakfast.
> So that everyone can beef-head
> Ooh, ooh, my ears are alight.
>
> Chris Cwej

Morning.

Although it's hard to tell when the sun is nailed to the ceiling.

Bernice Summerfield hangs upside down in a perfectly spherical globe of warm water. Fortunately she has managed to push her head into the air and so is in no danger of drowning. She is thinking that there must be a trick to using a bath like this but it's something she's never learnt. She's been weightless many times but she's used to ablution facilities that minimize the problem, not simulate it.

She refuses to thrash about. To thrash like a hooked fish would be to lose the essential core of dignity that is central to her personality. She will remain calm and think of something.

The door to her bedroom is open, the pile of belongings she left on her bed clearly visible. As she watches an invisible force is folding her clothes one item at a time until they are piled neatly at the foot of the bed. There are no pixies, she realizes; instead, the machine that runs the villa merely uses a variety of force-field projectors to do its daily chores.

It certainly gives her something to think about.

Just as soon as she can get herself the right way up.

There was a note from the Doctor. It should have read GONE
FISHING but the word 'fishing' had been crossed out with
heavy-handed pen strokes and the word SAFARI scribbled in
above it. Chris wanted to know what a safari was.

'It means to travel,' said Roz, 'in Swahili.'

'No, it doesn't,' said Bernice. 'It's when you watch wild
animals.'

'What wild animals?' asked Chris.

'Benny, I speak some Swahili and it definitely means "to
travel".'

'I know what it means literally, Roz, but its accepted usage
means to watch wild animals.'

'Perhaps you watch the wild animals while you're travelling,' suggested Chris.

'What?'

'Just a thought.'

'Anyway,' said Bernice, 'the Doctor says there's a town
about an hour's walk down the coast. I thought I'd go and
have a look. Do you want to come?'

'Seems like a reasonable idea,' said Roz. 'I'll go and put
my armour on.'

'I don't think you'll need the armour,' said Bernice.

'What if we run into those wild animals?' asked Roz. She
turned to Chris. 'Cwej, you too.'

Chris gave Bernice an if-it-makes-her-happy look and
followed Roz to put on his armour.

'Really,' said Bernice. 'The Doctor said it was safe here.'
She thought about that for a moment and went to find a knife
that would fit into her boot.

The base of the villa was completely surrounded by forest.
There were three tracks leading away from the front door and
Roz and Bernice let Chris choose which one to take, partly
because he claimed to have charted its route from the roof of
the villa the day before, but mostly because they could then
blame him if they got lost. Bernice was pleased to see that

both he and Roz had at least decided to leave their helmets and blasters at home.

The track was little more than a sandy path that twisted and turned its way down through the conifers. Once they got amongst the trees the air was still and warm. Bernice could smell wet loam, leaf-mould and under it all the sharp tang of the sea.

Chris went bounding down the track ahead of them and vanished around the first corner. Roz and Bernice followed on at a more dignified pace. Bernice asked the older woman what 'Inyathi' meant.

'It's my clan name,' Roz told her.

'Is it significant?'

'It's isiXhosa for buffalo,' said Roz. 'According to my grandmother it meant we weren't supposed to eat buffaloes.'

'What, never? No buffalo burgers?' asked Bernice. 'No buffalo fricassee or buffalo *à l'orange*? I'm shocked. What is a buffalo?'

'Big ugly hoofed quadruped,' said Roz, 'with horns. Last one died in captivity in 2193.'

'I suppose they were notoriously stubborn and bad-tempered?'

'How did you know?'

'Just a wild guess,' said Bernice.

The track angled steeply down the side of the hill. As it switched back and forth they caught occasional flashes of blue sea through gaps in the trees. Bernice found herself whistling as they strolled along, an old jaunty ballad that took all of thirty seconds to get on Roz's nerves.

The track led into an area of dunes at the base of the hills. The conifers gave way to gnarled little trees with spreads of broad oval leaves. The small trees gave way to tufts of dune grass, wiry long-bladed plants that sought to fix the wind-blown sand in place. The tufts grew fewer and the sand finer until finally the dunes became mere mounds of sand. It was a difficult surface to walk on, especially for Roz in her heavy boots. It didn't seem to bother Chris who ran up the last dune, reached the top and yelled, 'I can see the sea.'

29

'I'm terribly happy for you,' muttered Roz as she laboured after him.

'And I think there's a beach-bar too,' called Chris.

Roz and Bernice glanced at each other and picked up the pace.

If it was a beach-bar it wasn't much of one: just half a dozen circular tables with matching chairs plonked down on the edge of the dunes. The beach itself was much more impressive, a kilometre-long crescent of pristine yellow sand between two rocky headlands. It was the kind of beach that got texture-mapped into fraudulent holiday brochures. Bernice assumed that iSanti Jeni lay just beyond the eastern headland, providing that the Doctor had been telling the truth.

'You know,' said Chris, 'I've been examining that beach.'

'I know where this is going,' said Bernice. 'And what are your conclusions?'

'I think it's safe,' said Chris.

'Really?' said Roz.

'I think it's really safe,' said Chris. 'Possibly the safest beach I have ever seen. In fact I would go as far as to say that it is the very epitome of a safe beach.'

'Chris,' said Bernice.

'Really, really safe.'

'We're not your parents.'

Chris glanced at Roz who sighed and gestured vaguely with her hand. Chris whooped and ran for the waterline, hands busy with the straps of his armour as he went.

'He'd only sulk,' said Roz.

There was another shout and Chris dived into the surf. His footprints were clearly visible in the pristine sand. Bits of discarded armour were strewn to either side. They saw his blond head surfacing beyond the line of breakers. He waved and then vanished from sight.

Bernice looked over at the tables. 'Do you think that's really a bar? I don't see a service area.'

'Only one way to find out,' said Roz.

They sat down at the nearest table. The chairs appeared to be moulded out of rigid white plastic but Bernice felt the material shift subtly under her weight, making the chair more comfortable. When she leaned back to look for Chris the chair leaned back with her. 'He certainly got out of that armour fast enough.'

'You learn the technique when you're at the Academy,' said Roz. 'In case the armour gets contaminated or compromised in some way. There are ancillary benefits too.'

'I'll bet,' said Bernice. 'Can you do it that fast? I mean he didn't even break his stride.'

'Faster,' said Roz, 'when I was younger.'

'But not any more?'

'I haven't had much reason to try,' said Roz. 'Not recently.'

Bernice pretended to examine the table top, hoping that Roz would say more, give a little, maybe strip off some of the armour she was wearing on the inside. The table was made from the same white plastic as the chairs, its top covered in what Bernice recognized as writing. It looked a bit like Arabic, if you thought Arabic was written top to bottom in a dayglo orange scrawl.

Roz looked around. 'What do you have to do to get a drink around here?'

'Ask,' said the table.

Both women, very slowly, bent down and looked under the table. There was nothing except a small oval of shaded sand, a heavy base and the thin column that supported the table. Their eyes met briefly. Roz raised an eyebrow.

'Look,' said the table, 'do you want a drink or not?'

Bernice banged her head on the underside of the table. She heard Roz cursing. Both women slowly and with infinite nonchalance resumed an upright posture in their chairs.

Bernice cleared her throat. 'Who wants to know?' she asked.

'I do,' said the table. The voice was light, conversational and sounded entirely human. 'If you don't want a drink, I can offer you a wide range of snacks, delicacies –'

'Are you sentient?' asked Bernice. Roz was surreptitiously looking around for a speaker grill.

'Of course I'm not sentient,' said the table. 'I'm a table. I have two functions, one is to hold material objects at a convenient height by virtue of my rigid structure and the other is to take your order. What would be the point in a sentient table?'

31

Bernice considered this. She had to admit it was a good point.

'I lived in an apartment with a door that acted like this,' said Roz. 'It had a nasty accident involving a wide beam disintegrator and three metres of quick-drying epoxy resin.'

'We'll have a drink,' said Bernice quickly.

'Good,' said the table. 'What do you want to drink?'

'What have you got?' asked Roz.

'There's a menu in front of you,' said the table.

Bernice looked down. The dayglo Arabic was scrolling towards the edges of the table, new strings of writing spooling out of a null point at its centre. Bernice sighed. 'We can't understand the menu,' she said. 'Can you give us a verbal summary?'

'Hey,' said the table smugly. 'You name it we've got it.'

'In that case,' said Bernice, 'I'll have an exaggerated sexual innuendo with a dash of patriot's spirit and extra mushrooms. Roz?'

'I'll have the same,' said Roz, 'but with an umbrella in it.'

'Coming right up,' said the table.

'And get us some shade here while you're at it,' said Roz.

A parasol-shaped force-field opened above their heads and turned opaque. 'Now, that's slick,' said Bernice.

Roz shrugged, as if force-field parasols were an everyday occurrence where she came from. Perhaps they were. On her last trip to the thirtieth century Bernice had been far too busy running for cover to notice details like that.

'An exaggerated sexual innuendo,' said Roz. 'What kind of a cocktail is that?'

'I just made it up,' said Bernice. 'God knows what we'll get.'

What they got was two tall glasses swooping over the dunes on the back of a self-propelled tray to make a perfect landing on the table. The drinks were a cloudy orange shot through with streaks of vermilion. Moisture started condensing on the glasses as soon as they stopped moving. One of them had a small paper parasol stuck in the top.

'That one's yours, I think,' said Bernice, taking the other drink. It was wonderfully cool against her palm. Something grey floated near the top of the glass; it was the extra mushroom.

There was a waterfall somewhere inland; the Doctor could smell it. If he concentrated he could just hear a low rumbling to the south. A big one then, larger than The Smoke That Thunders on the Zambezi and big enough to cast its spray as far as the coast and create a sub-tropical micro-climate around the cove. The short stretch of beach was a dazzling white, enclosed by rocky promontories on both sides and by low forested hills on the other. The trees were tropical varieties, narrow-trunked with spreading crowns of broad emerald leaves. Brightly coloured blooms nestled at their roots and ran in streamers along the symbiotic vines that linked tree with tree. It was an isolated place and judging from the scantness of the path he'd traversed to get here, rarely visited. Just what the Doctor ordered in fact.

The Doctor waited just inside the tree-line, confident that the sharp contrast between shady forest and the dazzling sand would conceal him. Well, moderately confident anyway.

She was standing so still he didn't see her at first. Hip-deep in the water, the swell of the waves lapping around her waist and thighs, she had a spear in her right hand, poised motionless above her head. Some kind of pale wood, bamboo, guessed the Doctor, with a fire-hardened tip. Her left arm was held slightly behind her body, elbow bent for balance, fingers spread as delicately as any pianist. The woman was thirty metres away; could she throw such a crude weapon that far? Probably not, but would you want to bet your life on it? Luckily for him she was facing out to sea, although this was probably not so lucky for the fish. Sunlight glittered off the water that beaded her head and back. The spear didn't so much as tremble, held in perfect balance, perfect stillness.

He remembered her dancing with the soldiers in the street outside M. Thierry's house in Paris. The flowing interplay of muscle over bone and under skin. A macabre Blue Danube waltz choreographed for a single diva and four expendable extras.

Corpse de ballet, thought the Doctor.

33

There was a whisper of displaced air and aM!xitsa the drone was beside him. The machine's external fields were flush with its ellipsoid body, showing a dappled pattern of green and brown. Joke jungle camouflage. A small hologram projected from the drone's nose, two dark dots above a horizontal line against an orange background. A human expression pared down to an absolute abstract: aM!xitsa's face ikon.

'Doctor,' said aM!xitsa, 'does God know you're here?'

'I told it last night.'

'That should give it something to think about.'

The Doctor nodded towards the figure in the water. 'How is she?'

'That's difficult to say,' said aM!xitsa. 'She catches fish and eats them, sometimes she even cooks them first.'

'High protein diet. She's building up her reserves.'

'She eats other stuff as well,' said the drone. 'Fruits, berries, leaves. Occasionally soil as well, about a hundred grammes a week.'

'Good to see she's getting all the food groups then.'

'She's built a hut on the other side of the cove, three metres back from the tree-line. Made it out of sun-dried mud-bricks.'

'She is an engineer.'

'The first one was washed away in a rain storm.'

'That's the trouble with mud as a building material.'

'So she built a kiln.'

'How long has she been here?' asked the Doctor.

'You should know.'

'Well,' said the Doctor, 'you know how it is. Time and relative dimensions in space. You can lose track.'

'Three months,' said the drone.

The Doctor removed his hat, stared into its depths for a moment and then replaced it on his head. 'I presume you've been scanning her?'

'Oh yes,' said aM!xitsa.

'And?'

'A grade thirty-six technology you said.'

'Thirty-five going on thirty-six.'

'Remarkable.'

34

'They're an inventive race,' said the Doctor, 'especially when it comes to weapons technology.'

'Do you want to see the details?'

'Yes, please,' said the Doctor.

AM!xitsa projected a discreet holograph behind the bole of a tree where it wouldn't be visible from the beach. It quickly filled up with complex three-dimensional shapes, spiky bundles of molecules that rotated slowly for inspection, phase space graphs on time/event axis. The drone's voice assumed a more studied, professorial tone. 'Most of the non-indigenous organic forms were broken down and expelled within the first thirty-six hours. I recovered some samples from her faeces and urine but the damn stuff wouldn't grow in culture.'

The hologram displayed the characteristic flat and undifferentiated cells of the ship's invasive cellulose. Even in abstract representation they were coloured a virulent and unhealthy green. The Doctor's hand drifted uneasily to his left shoulder, remembering.

'And the residual organic material?'

AM!xitsa displayed a flayed cross-section of the brain. 'A concentration in the hypothalamus, smaller structures in cerebellum and occipital lobe. I believe she may have assimilated the foreign material.'

The Doctor said nothing, remembering the pain. The lawnmower smell. The ship dying. Ace shouting out in fear and anger. All those minds going into the dark. Paris burning. A human body of animate mahogany veined with virulent green.

'I'm particularly interested in the nature of the design modifications incorporated into her original geneset,' said aM!xitsa. 'Normally when the technologically challenged build fighters they stress the amyglada, building for aggression you might say. The primary centre for modification in this one is not in the limbic system at all. The "kill instinct" is all in the forebrain. Damn unusual and very subtle. It's the cognitive perception of danger that triggers the response, not the emotion.'

The drone rotated until its forward sensor array was directed at the figure in the water. 'She's a stone-cold killer.'

'Does she speak?'

AM!xitsa wobbled its body from side to side, drone body language for 'no'. 'She displays no *social* behaviour at all when she's awake. She does vocalize during her sleep, sometimes complete sentences, but I can't translate the language. Would you like a recording?'

The Doctor shook his head, human body language for 'no'.

The woman standing in the water still hadn't moved. By now even the smartest fish would have ceased to see her as a possible threat. Piscine brains lulled into complacency by her world-famous rock impression.

'There's something very strange about her genetic structure,' said aM!xitsa. 'Even stranger I mean.'

'Yes.'

'Dormant sections in certain DNA strands that look as if they should be operating but aren't. Other sections that look as if they are just there as temporary markers. As if there were pieces of the jigsaw still missing.'

'Yes.'

'Her cytoplasmic DNA shows multiple redundancies. Very strange stuff indeed. I couldn't decode them, even with God's help.'

'You didn't tell God what you were working on?'

'Of course not,' said the drone. 'I told it that the samples had been passed on by some friends in XCIG.'

'Did it believe you?'

'God's very smart. I think it's probably suspicious. Now it knows you're here it'll have this whole area under very tight surveillance indeed.'

'There was a lot of remote drone activity near iSanti Jeni this morning.'

'The coding in her cytoplasm,' said the drone, 'information encrypted by her designers?'

'No,' said the Doctor, more emphatically than he meant to. He'd hoped to keep aM!xitsa off that particular topic. 'That's from a different, far more ancient inheritance.' Time to change the subject. 'I'd like to thank you for looking after her. I hope it hasn't inconvenienced you.'

36

'Not at all,' said aM!xitsa. 'She's been fascinating company, if not a stimulating conversationalist.'

'I'm glad to hear that,' said the Doctor but he wasn't. He was beginning to wish he'd found some alternative guardian, one, and this was the real joke, with fewer 'human' qualities.

'It's terribly wearisome referring to her by an impersonal pronoun,' said aM!xitsa. 'Isn't it about time you told me her name?'

'Better that you don't know,' said the Doctor. Better that you think of her as a thing, an experiment, something dangerous to be studied and then, if it proves too threatening, made safe. Neutralized. Terminated.

Murdered.

There was a sudden flurry of movement in the water. The spear was jerked upwards. Impaled below the point thrashed a glistening silver shape. AM!xitsa and the Doctor watched in silence as the fish died.

Bernice walked on to iSanti Jeni alone. Roz having gone to sleep *again*. Whatever the orange and vermilion stuff in the glasses had been she was glad she hadn't finished hers. God knew what had been in the mushrooms.

That thought made her smile. In this place God most definitely knew. Could probably give her a complete biochemical analysis if she asked it for one.

She left the table strict instructions to keep the older woman in the shade, picked up her shoes and started walking up the beach. The sun was definitely getting hotter but the breeze from the sea kept her pleasantly cool.

There was a path over the headland. Nothing formal, just the line of least resistance between the tumbled rocks, places here and there where the sandy topsoil had been cleared by passing feet. That was assuming that the locals had feet and weren't gastropods or something equally weird. Not that that would bother Bernice; nothing wrong with walking on your stomach, some of her best friends had been gastropods. Nice people on the whole.

Providing the buggers didn't step on your head.

The headland she was climbing was narrower than it looked and the coast curved inwards quite sharply. As a result Bernice didn't see the town until she was almost on top of it. It was built up around a 'natural' harbour, complete with harbour wall, a pebble beach and water-front esplanade. There were even a variety of boats drawn up on the beach, mostly compact-looking trimarine yachts but with one large wooden-sided tug. That one was single hulled and listed alarmingly as if it were about to topple over at any moment. There was a man on the beach painting a mural along the entire length of the harbour wall, a pretty moody piece judging from the subdued ochre tones and lurid oranges. As Bernice climbed onto the flat top of the breakwater and walked closer she realized that the man might instead be repairing an earlier work. Parts of the mural seemed to have been damaged, as if a giant hand had used a wire brush to clean the paint off the wall.

ISanti Jeni shone under the clear blue sky. The buildings seemed to be constructed out of crudely dressed stone and painted white with blue or magenta trimming. From the headland they had seemed to sprawl up the sides of the uneven semi-circle of hills that formed an amphitheatre shape behind the harbour. There was little differentiation between buildings, one flat-roofed structure merging into the next one along, and at first Bernice thought that any streets the town might have must be roofed. When she reached the esplanade she realized that the numerous narrow alleyways ran off it at seemingly random intervals. The buildings that fronted the esplanade had sun-faded awnings over openings the size of shop windows. Bernice peered inside the first opening she came to. As her eyes adjusted to the dim interior she saw tables and chairs laid out restaurant fashion but no people. After a moment a tray, very similar to the one that had served them at the beach-bar, floated up from one of the tables at the back and hovered a couple of metres in front of her. It managed to give a passable impression of polite anticipation, which was a neat trick for what was essentially a flat piece of metal.

Bernice retreated back into the hard sunlight on the

esplanade, uncomfortable with the idea of spending more time in the company of machines. She looked around for some other sign of life. All the windows she could see were closed up with slated wooden shutters. Along the esplanade the wind from the sea caught the awnings making them snap and rustle like horizontal flags.

A noise made her look up: the unmistakable rifle-crack sound of something small breaking the sound barrier. Sunlight flashed off something shooting out over the sea at a height of two hundred metres. There were two more cracks overhead. This time Bernice got a better look. Size was difficult to judge but she thought they might be a metre to two metres long, too small to be piloted that was for sure, ovoid in shape, flying on parallel courses to the first flying thing. They reminded her of the space-to-ground torpedoes used by orbiting ships during planetary assaults. She shuddered, watching as both objects began zigzagging over the sea. Bernice recognized the movement as a search pattern. Within moments they were out of sight, lost in the hazy distance over the ocean.

She was halfway up one of the narrow little streets when she smelt the aroma of baking bread. Perhaps she had been following it all along, unconsciously picking this particular street from all the others under the smell's subliminal influence. The street jinked unevenly between the whitewashed buildings and was paved with irregular slabs of some smooth white stone. Shuttered doorways were randomly placed along both sides, some of them below the level of the street, while others could only be reached via stone staircases built up against the walls. Occasionally there was no door, just the steps, as if someone had built the staircase and then gone away and forgotten why. There was even one door three storeys up with no staircase at all.

Of course, once Bernice had decided she was following the smell it became far more difficult. She found herself standing at junctions absurdly sniffing the air before deciding which direction to go. After a couple of false trails she had almost given up when she stumbled on the source.

The street was near the rear of the town rising steeply up

the base of the hill. On one side the tops of trees were just visible over a high wall, on the other was a terrace that rose in line with the street in a series of stepped levels. The shutters on one of the nearer ground-floor windows had been thrown open. Bernice could hear an arythmic thumping sound from inside. As she drew level with the open window the aroma of baking bread grew strong enough to make her salivate. She looked inside.

A woman was stooped over a work surface kneading dough. She was very slim with narrow shoulders and her skin had the delicate yellow tint of ancient ivory. Her short hair was a strange silvery blue and the shapeless smock she was wearing had a V-shaped neckline at the back to accommodate a hairline that tapered to a point between her shoulder blades. Bernice watched her shaping the dough with long elegant fingers, noticing that the woman's elbow and shoulder joints seemed to move in a subtly non-human way.

Once she was satisfied with the consistency of the dough the woman shaped it into a rough oblong and with a single fluid motion tossed it into the air. An invisible force caught the dough a metre above the woman's head and it began to float around the room surrounded by a globe of heated air. Bernice realized that what she'd taken for light fittings were in fact other loaves at various stages of baking, bobbing around near the ceiling in individual spheres of oven-hot air.

When Bernice glanced back down from the loaves she realized with a slight shock that the woman had turned to look at her.

'Hello,' said the woman.

'Hello,' said Bernice. The woman had enormous brown eyes, like those of a *manga* heroine. There seemed to be no malice in them, just curiosity, but Bernice knew better than to ascribe human emotions to an alien face. 'I was following the smell of the bread,' she managed lamely.

The woman smiled, displaying neat, white, reassuringly omnivorous teeth. 'The cooking field has to be partially gas permeable,' she explained. 'Otherwise the bread doesn't rise properly.'

'I can see that would be a problem,' said Bernice.

'My name is saRa!qava,' said the woman. 'Would you like some breakfast?'

She said her name was Dep and her eyes were the colour of emeralds.

She stood a couple of metres from Chris watching him with her head cocked to one side, one slim hand resting lightly on her hip. She was at least as tall as he was, narrow waisted with long arms and legs. Her green eyes were curiously round and slightly too large, her nose was small and flat. A smile played around a large mobile mouth. A cascade of thick, almost ropey hair hung down her back, falling as far as the backs of her knees. Her skin was the colour of dusty amber and she was stark naked except for a tiny pair of bikini briefs. A silver brooch was pinned to the strap over her left hip.

'You're a barbarian,' said Dep, 'aren't you?'

Chris wasn't sure how to answer that.

Dep took a couple of steps towards him. As she did so her hair twisted itself into a single braid that coiled itself around her waist in an unsettling manner. Chris took an involuntary step backwards.

'What's the matter?' asked Dep.

'Er. Nothing,' said Chris hastily. Trying not to flinch as the braid uncoiled from around Dep's waist and wrapped itself around her left leg. The tip of her braid, he noticed, was careful to stay out of the water.

'I'm going to come closer,' said Dep. 'You no be afraid, I not harm you.'

Chris glanced back across the beach to the bar. He could just make out Roz slumped in her seat; of Bernice there was no sign. Dep stepped slowly up to him. Something, her hair, caressed the back of his thigh. He was close enough to see the tiny drops of perspiration that beaded her forehead. Her disturbingly mobile braid of hair looped itself companionably over his shoulders.

'Now,' she said. 'What's your name?'

It took Chris a surprisingly long time to remember.

* * *

41

Bernice watched the toddler making his break for freedom. The boy had cunningly detached himself from the older children by pretending to wander aimlessly around the lounge. Then having looked around to make sure that the other children were too engrossed in some kind of holographic entertainment to notice him, he made a dash for the kitchen. Pounding along on his sturdy little legs he headed straight for the short flight of stone steps that led down from the lounge to the kitchen.

He's going to fall down those and hurt himself, thought Bernice. She opened her mouth to warn saRa!qava who was sitting with her back to the lounge. Before she could speak the boy bounced against an invisible barrier at the top of the stairs and sat down hard. The toddler's small face screwed up in an expression of intense concentration – *Am I hurt? Should I cry? Should I just get up? If I cry will someone come and give me some attention?* The boy opted for a bit of attention-seeking behaviour and opened his mouth to get a good big lungful of air in preparation. By this time saRa!qava had noticed Bernice's distraction and had twisted in her chair to look. The boy started to howl impressively.

One of the older children, a boy of about eight or nine, walked over and scooped up the toddler with practised ease. Interesting, thought Bernice; she'd half expected one of the house drones to take care of the child. They're not really machine dependent at all. If she remembered it correctly the older boy was saRa!qava's nephew and the toddler was her grandson. It was hard to keep track because all the children seemed to refer to saRa!qava as 'Mama', even the ones that had just popped in from next door.

It looked like a loose *super-extended* kinship set-up – the family integrated horizontally and vertically. Except the textbooks said that that form of social organization was strictly pre-industrial; faster communications were supposed to break the family group into smaller components. Then again the textbooks had been remarkably scarce on references to societies advanced enough to build functioning Dyson spheres. She should remember to take notes; there could be a bestseller in this for her.

'Beni?' said saRa!qava.

'Sorry,' said Bernice. 'Mind wandering. Just thought I saw a gap in the market.'

'Ah yes,' said saRa!qava. 'Markets. I remember them from school. Third most inefficient method of resource distribution ever invented.'

Roz watched the water for a long time before taking off her armour. This far up the beach she could no longer hear the sound of the children playing. Chris's laughter in particular had followed her along the sand, the girl's lighter tone fading much faster. She should have introduced herself after she'd woken up and seen them in the water. Just strolled over and –

What exactly?

Instead she slipped away from the beach-bar and marched back up the sand until she couldn't hear them any more. At this end the sea had scooped a shallow depression out of a line of big dunes, hidden from the main part of the beach and the hill path inland. The surf broke on a sandbar further out and the sea water that filled the depression was relatively still and perfectly clear.

Roz did a three-sixty turn to make sure no one was in sight before removing her cloak. She folded the heavy fire-retardant material in half and laid it down flat on the sand. Then she reached up and snapped open her shoulder catches. The one on the left gave her trouble. She slapped it hard with the heel of her hand, an automatic movement perfected over twenty years, and it sprang open. The cuirass cracked apart down its side seam, giving Roz access to the catches that anchored the pauldrons to her shoulders. The cuirass and pauldrons eased off as one unit. Roz reached inside the cuirass and switched off the battery pack before placing the pieces carefully on the folded cloak. There was a discoloration on the cuirass where it had been caught by a Kithrian fifty-megawatt laser and then relaminated by the Adjudicator's artificers. Roz idly scratched at the corresponding point on her chest, a patch of skin under her left breast that always itched in hot weather. Purely psychosomatic, the medics said, all the nerve endings having regenerated seamlessly. It's all in your mind.

43

She knew better; the body always remembered.

With the top half of her armour off it was easy to free her legs from the tasset, cuisse and greaves. She piled them neatly next to the cuirass making sure all the buckles, straps and studs were tucked away in the recesses provided. Then she unsealed the padded under-tunic and slipped it off her shoulders and over her hips. Roz folded the tunic in the prescribed manner and placed it on top of the cuirass. She reached awkwardly behind her back to unclip her sensible goretex bra top and shrugged out of the straps. They'd been a present from an admirer, the manager at the local branch of Drop Dead Gorgeous on Overcity Five. He'd showered Roz with underwear for two months until she'd gone round to the boutique and threatened to arrest him for attempted bribery. Most of his gifts went unworn, slight items of silk and Martian lace that spent their days wrapped in tissue at the bottom of Roz's wardrobe. Mind you, there had been a swimsuit made of skin-sensitive micropore that would have come in useful right now. She considered leaving her briefs on but changed her mind and slipped them off, figuring that she'd only have to dry them out later.

Roz walked naked down to the edge of the pool. Cautiously she tested the water with her toe; it was cooler than she'd expected.

Roz had once read of a ritual like this. An adjudicator would strip themselves of their armour and bathe themselves in a pool of clear water. Afterwards one of the Untouched would clothe the adjudicator in a surplice of pure white lamb's-wool. The ritual's purpose was to cleanse the supplicant of the taint of sin following a line-of-duty killing. The custom had been discontinued at least fifty years before Roz had joined the service. Instead, every seventh day of duty an adjudicator got sprinkled with holy water, usually during the morning briefing. It made sense to Roz; if she'd had to do that every time someone got killed she'd have spent half her life washing the blood off. They'd have had to organize a shift system. Besides, she had a sneaking suspicion that the lamb's-wool must have itched horribly.

Roz waded in up to her thighs and ducked under the water.

Coming up fast again she shook the water from her hair. Felt the hot sun quickly drying her skin. Caught sight of her reflection. A second Roslyn Forrester, rippling and fore-shortened across the surface of the water. She stretched her arms out and looked at them. She realized it was a long time since she'd really looked at herself. How fragile her fingers were, long and delicate. Pity that the nails were ragged and bitten down to the quick. The skin below the wrists was pale, a long time since they'd seen the sun. A dark line of scar tissue cut diagonally across her left forearm: vibroknife wound. She touched herself on the shoulder, feeling along her collarbone until she came to the tiny ridge that marked where the fracture had been reset. She traced the outline of her breasts, too small for her mother's liking, and down to her belly. Feeling the ridges of the muscle under her fingertips, the barely perceptible line where some nameless BEM had made a spirited attempt to disembowel her.

Been in the wars, Mama. Got the scars to prove it.

Scrawny, she thought, feeling over the sharp points of her pelvis. Mama always said I was too scrawny. Holding me up to some idealized reflection of the perfect Xhosa maiden. A figure made up entirely of curves that walked gracefully across a veldt long gone to the Undertown and urban decay. It really pained you that I didn't fit. This ugly, scrawny kid with her too long legs and frizzy hair. It must have hurt you to know that I'd come out of your womb, hurt almost as much as that premature birth out in the badlands. Out where the medical facilities were basic and rescue twenty minutes too late.

I ruined you coming into the world and you never forgave me for that. Ruined you beyond the skill of any reconstructive surgery. You with your stupid obsession with the past, your sunshine emulator and your twice yearly trip to the bepple clinic to get your skin darkened. You'd have beppled me from birth, twisted my DNA to suit your own aesthetic if Grandma and Father hadn't stopped you. You looked at me and you saw something different, but when I looked in the mirror I saw only myself. And you wondered why I ran away to look for the truth.

Truth, justice and the Terranian way of life.

45

You must be laughing at me now, now that the truth has found me out.

And the dumbest thing of all is that I wanted that heritage too. Wanted the ochre-coloured cloaks that hung on the walls, the ancient strings of multicoloured beads, the cow-hair necklace to ward off evil spirits. I dreamed of being a worthy daughter of the Xhosa, the Angry Man. I found things, Mama, that you never dreamed of, the stories of Nomgqause, Mandela and Mbete. People who fought for the things I thought I was fighting for.

I had to go forward, Mama; if I'd looked back I'd have seen the chain of small compromises and moral lapses that was dragging me down with its weight. Had to keep thinking that I was making some kind of difference, however small. That where I passed things were, if not better, then at least not as bad as they were before.

I should have just stayed with you on Io, Mama. Inherited the Baroncy. Then I could have held a big reception on my ascension, invited all your aristo friends, the Pontiff Seculares, the heads of the big corporations and the entire upper tier of the Overcity. They'd have come to pay their respects to the new Baroness Io. I could have poisoned the lot of them. Something nasty and biological in the punch, a nightmare recombining cocktail that ate away their flesh so that it fell from their bones and slopped all over the deep pile carpet.

It would have done more to clean up the world than everything I've done in twenty-five years on the streets . . .

Someone was watching her.

Roz spun round, the water dragged at her thighs and she almost fell over.

The Doctor was standing on the dunes with his back to her, next to where she'd piled her armour. His stance was so theatrically courteous that she could read the artifice in his back – a gentleman preserving the proprieties in front of a lady.

'*Molo ntombazana*,' called the Doctor.

'*Molo mhlekazi*,' replied Roz, surprised that she could remember the correct response in Xhosa.

'So formal?' said the Doctor. 'Surely we're friends?'

Roz waded back to the beach and started putting on her clothes. 'The only other title I could think of was *utat'omkhulu*.'

'Grandfather,' the Doctor chuckled. 'I haven't been called that in a long time.'

'And I haven't been called a young woman for at least twenty years.' The under-tunic felt sticky as she pulled it over her wet skin. 'And I haven't spoken Xhosa since I left home.'

'Does it feel strange?'

'Very,' said Roz. 'You can turn round now; I'm decent.' She pushed at the pile of armour with her foot. Wearing it suddenly seemed such a childish idea.

'Leave it,' said the Doctor. 'No one will take it.'

'What if the tide comes in?'

The Doctor used the heel of his shoe to scratch a design in the sand, a couple of angular symbols like those on the beach-bar's table and an arrow pointing to the armour. 'God will spot that and send a drone to take your things back to the villa.'

He proffered her his arm. '*Sahamba*,' he said; let's go.

Roz turned her back on the armour and took the Doctor's arm. They started back down the beach.

'*Wafunda isiXhosa ngapi?*'

'I was stuck in a prison and one of the prisoners taught me to speak it,' said the Doctor. 'He taught me a lot about patience too. And how sometimes being without power is a form of power.'

'*Kwenzikani?*'

'He stayed in prison until the people who put him there finally broke down and started negotiating with him. He refused to be released until they acceded to his demands.'

'Did he win?'

'Yes and no,' said the Doctor. 'He got what he wanted but the price was high. He was absent from the weddings of his children and the funeral of his mother. All the rights, privileges and duties of a man were denied him. He found himself a stranger in a brave new world.'

'Was it worth it?'

'He thought so,' said the Doctor. 'Or at least he thought it was necessary. Somebody had to make that sacrifice, if only for the sake of the children.'

'Jeez, Doctor,' said Roz, 'sometimes you're a real fun guy to talk to.'

'And such a beautiful day for it too,' said the Doctor. '*Uphi uKhrisi leBeni?*'

'Benny was gone when I woke up,' said Roz. 'Chris was playing in the sea. Found himself a friend.'

'Oh yes,' said the Doctor. '*Intombazana* perhaps? Pretty?'

'From what I could see.'

The Doctor laughed; it was a delightful, innocent sound. 'Oh, to be young and resilient again.'

'Slice,' said saRa!qava.

One of the floating loaves of bread instantly exploded into a shower of neatly edged slices. Roz flinched, the Doctor looked up curiously, Bernice carried on talking to saRa!qava. She'd already been through the exploding bread routine at breakfast. A cast-iron breadboard swooped off a shelf and intercepted the slices as they fell out of the air.

Chris was up on the lounge level playing a game with the older children and a young woman called Dep who had turned out to be saRa!qava's daughter. Her real biological daughter, mind you, not just a close cousin or some stranger who'd wandered into the household one day and never got around to leaving. If you overlooked the fact that Dep was a different colour, had independently mobile hair and a distinctively different elbow joint arrangement you could see they were related; something about the nose and mouth.

The breadboard made a soft landing on the kitchen table; it was followed in by a squadron of plates and a small flotilla of cutlery. The slices of just baked bread lined themselves up neatly and steamed gently. A butter jug waddled over on three stumpy legs and plumped itself down by the breadboard.

The Doctor nudged Bernice in the ribs. 'Disney would have loved this.'

'Just as long as the cutlery doesn't burst into song,' said

Bernice. She looked at saRa!qava. 'I assume that House moves everything about?'

'Well, Mr Butter Jug is an old toy of Dep's,' said saRa!qava, 'but House does just about everything else. It's not too smart though.'

'Smart enough to lay the table correctly,' said Roz.

'Well, of course,' said saRa!qava. 'Otherwise what use would it be?'

'But not sentient?' asked Bernice.

For some reason this made saRa!qava laugh. 'Don't be silly. You wouldn't want a sentient machine running a house.'

'Why not?'

'Because it would get bored,' said the Doctor.

'Exactly,' said saRa!qava. 'It wouldn't be fair.'

Roz snorted and reached for a slice of bread. Mr Butter Jug waddled over towards her and tipped its lid expectantly. Roz glowered at the jug for a moment and then started spreading butter on her bread with small meticulous strokes of her knife. When she'd finished she handed the slice to the Doctor.

'*Enkosi, Rozi,*' said the Doctor. Thank you, Roz.

Bernice blinked. In that simple exchange, something shared and intimate had passed between the Doctor and Roz. Bernice wasn't sure quite what she thought about that.

SaRa!qava asked her some intelligent questions about archaeology; she seemed surprised at the idea of anyone actually digging anything up. 'Doesn't that rather disrupt the actual setting of the artefacts?' she asked. When Bernice explained that digging was the only sure way to find what was under the ground, saRa!qava laughed. Bernice, her professional pride stung, reeled off a list of alternative non-invasive techniques – resistance measurement, ground sonar, gravito-magnetic resonance imaging – but this just seemed to increase saRa!qava's humour.

A small baby girl floated over at head height suspended in a force-field. SaRa!qava snatched the child out of the air and into her lap. There was a yell of triumph from the lounge area. Dep came over to tell them that Chris was proving to be an ace at Starmaster; where had he learnt to fly like that? Roz explained about his training as a pilot. Dep acted suitably impressed. SaRa!qava got up to fetch some more food for the children. She handed the baby to Roz who handled it as if she expected it to explode at any moment. Roz surreptitiously tried to pass it to the Doctor who quickly slipped his hands out of sight.

'Oh, give it here,' said Bernice, and relieved Roz of her small burden. 'Is this one of yours?' she asked saRa!qava.

'Is it screaming?' asked saRa!qava. An aerial convoy of food trays left their holding pattern and shot off towards the lounge. When Bernice said no, saRa!qava said that in that case she probably belonged to one of her neighbours. Bernice looked down at the baby in her arms; large violet eyes looked curiously back.

'What's her name?'

'She's much too young to have a name,' said saRa!qava.

'Oh,' said Bernice. 'How old does she have to be?'

'Old enough to think of one for herself.'

The baby girl grabbed at Bernice's finger and tugged at it. 'What about the machines – do they choose their own names as well?'

'Of course.'

'I don't suppose you use organic comp–'

There was a crash as the Doctor knocked his mug off the table; he made a desperate snatch for it but only succeeded in batting the mug into the air where it collided with a floating loaf of bread. The loaf spun off and hit another loaf which bounced off a wall and dive-bombed the table. It took House a couple of seconds to bring it all under control. In that moment of confusion the Doctor caught Bernice's eye and frowned.

'So,' said Bernice, 'where does a girl go to have a good time round here?'

'Well, you must come to my party,' said saRa!qava.

'What kind of party?'

'Fancy dress,' said saRa!qava after a moment's hesitation.

'Is there a theme?'

'Oh, anything. As long as it's historical.'

'Oh, good,' said the Doctor. 'My favourite.'

Hyper-lude

To an unprotected human being space is a hostile environment. Step through an airlock and it's a one-way ticket to freeze-dried city: eyeball moisture boils away while your capillaries burst like firecrackers. And if that isn't bad enough, space is full of hard radiation, blasting out of those humungous out-of-control fusion reactors known as stars. Hang out near one of those babies and you're quickly reduced to crispy fried bacon pieces. In short, space isn't somewhere you want to live and a lot of hassle to visit.

So people created ships to get about in and because these people were *people* they made sure that the ships were people too. These people met other people on their travels and these other people were cool, so some ground rules were worked out and they all went exploring together: the people, the other people and the ships that were also people. The rest, as they say, is history. At least that's the history that got written down.

The ships were big, designed by people who were designed by people who liked big technology. They had brains with the same mean density as a pulsar. To call them computers would be like calling Einstein a tapeworm or Shakespeare half a kilogram of feta cheese. Their hulls were constructed from interleavened layers of force-fields and they were powered by engines that did horrible things to the fabric of the space-time continuum. These babies had go faster stripes on their toilet seats and thought warp drives were

51

strictly for wimps. When they moved, the material fabric of the universe scrambled to get out of the way.

Their full names were full of clicks, pops and aspirated consonants, the quiet, confident macho that comes with being able to prune a rosebush from a distance of twenty light-years.

Thirty years before, the people had been involved in a war during which they had committed the sort of acts that people tend to commit during wars, although being people they had been very apologetic about it. Using a tiny fraction of their available resources they had completely rebuilt the twenty-six low technology civilizations that had been devastated during the fighting but there was nothing they could do about the fifteen planets, three rings and fifteen asteroid habitats that had got themselves blown away.

Or the twenty-six billion sentient individuals that had been killed, most of them, as the euphemism goes, were collateral casualties. The enemy, a race of insectoid religious fanatics, underwent as a consequence of their defeat a profound theological transformation. The Great Hive Mind of the Universe, they reasoned, had revealed through the medium of the war that the universe was vast enough to accommodate an abundance of cultures and belief systems. Large sections of the population embraced wishy-washy liberal pluralism with a speed that dismayed the Established Church. The megasmart intelligences that ran the people's spaceships and co-ordinated the activities of the Xenocultural Relations (Normalization) Interest Group had predicted this reaction and made arrangements for the enemy to become part of the people.

They knew something that had seemingly escaped the notice of the High Priests of the Great Hive Mind of the Universe. Namely that God really was on the side of the big battalions.

As a result of the war many of the ships chilling out at the sphere's gargantuan dockyard when the Doctor arrived were warships; in the terminology of the people: VASs (Very Aggressive Ships). Some of the more aggressive VASs had themselves mothballed until they were needed again, while others either transferred to a different class of ship or were refitted for civilian duties. On the day that Bernice met saRa!qava there were four former VASs, four GPSs (General Purpose Ships), two VLR (Very Long Range) Drones and the six-kilometre front end of a TSH (Travelling Space Habitat) who'd had a major disagreement with the middle and rear ends of itself and flounced off for a good sulk.

If you listened very carefully to certain bandwidths of the electro-magnetic spectrum and were capable of pico-second data-processing speeds, you could have heard the ships talking.

Mostly it was gossip, who's been where, done what and to whom. The GPSs had a crew complement, although population would be a better word, of sixty thousand each and that gave them a lot to gossip about. One of the VLRs, the A-Lain, was complaining because it had been asked to do a run to one of the lesser clouds. The detached front end of the TSH !C-Mel was bitching because God wouldn't build it a new rear section. Two of the VASs, S-Lioness and !X-Press, were analysing an interesting engagement from the war.

Underneath the normal chit-chat a current of unease ran through the ship to ship channels. Although it was considered bad manners to extend active probes into the interior of the sphere all of the ships were aware that an unprecedented amount of God appeared to be concentrating on a single problem. Given God's limitless mental resources this was slightly unnerving.

The front section of the TSH the !C-Mel, who was at that time associated with the Interpersonal Dynamics Interest Group, persuaded two of its crew to travel into the sphere and find out what was going on. The third VAS, the T-Di!x, used its supralight communications rig to contact some friends and get their advice. This set off a chain reaction as other ships called *their* friends until an ever-expanding volume of space was criss-crossed by supralight communications, all of them racing to develop probability projections that could handle the non-data they were receiving from each other.

To make matters worse God wasn't answering their calls.

3

Party Games

Night time is falling, the good time begins
I don't want to discuss philosophy, baby
I just wanna see your fins.
Reptile Beach by Third Eye
From the HvLP: *Outta My Way Monkey-boy*
(2327)

Night falls.

Darkness advances across the interior of the worldsphere as God adjusts the opacity of the force-field that englobes the sun. The line of occultation is irregular, some of the battalions of the evening outrunning the army of the night. Six kilometres up the coast from iSanti Jeni darkness is premature, a bridgehead of twilight that occupies a small cove and the hinterland downwind of the great waterfall.

It amuses God to give this microclimate a matching short tropical day.

The drone has been watching the woman all day, as it has watched her for the last three months. She has been roasting fish this afternoon, skewering them on straight green twigs and placing them over a fire outside her hut. She ate them during the short simulated twilight, white teeth ripping flesh off the bones with small economical movements. The drone's sensors are precise enough to determine the exact quantity of protein she has ingested. The drone has kept a micrometer accurate log of all her activities since the first day.

Now it is night and the light from Whynot is smeared across the water. The chatter in the rain forest alters in intensity as the nocturnal shift of insect life and small mammals clock on for the night.

The drone glides across the cove in total silence, a little oval patch of black against the broken shadows of the forest. It flies to the entrance of the hut and hovers for a moment to ensure that the woman is asleep. Satisfied that she is, the drone enters the hut and takes its accustomed place near the roof.

The drone has the capability to monitor the woman from the opposite side of the sphere but finds the close physical proximity agreeable, possibly comforting. It is aware that this behaviour is not entirely rational but rationality has never been its primary operating principle.

Later this night the woman will cry out in her sleep. Five words, the first the drone has been able to understand. They will come at sleep plus five hours and twenty-six minutes, at the peak of her third REM sleep cycle. The drone will register a level of neurological activity far beyond what she exhibits in her waking state. The drone will analyse the stress patterns in the words and run sophisticated acoustic and linguistic algorithms. It will find that the patterns are synonymous with a single overriding emotion, although it is difficult to determine which one.

It will frustrate the drone that the actual meaning of the words escapes it, without a detailed history, a context within which to frame them. It will hope the Doctor will explain but it calculates a ninety-seven per cent probability that he will not.

The woman will speak the same words again at sleep plus six hours and fifteen minutes, two and a half hours before dawn. The drone will still find them meaningless.

'*I am not a machine.*'

No one knew why there was a windmill complex above iSanti Jeni. Or if they did it wasn't on public record. God probably knew but that wasn't any help. God liked to keep its little secrets since it wasn't allowed to keep the big ones. It certainly looked dramatic, stuck up on the crest of the ridge overlooking the town. That could have been reason enough to put it there; it was certainly irrelevant as a power source. SaRa!qava supposed that its very redundancy could have been the underlying aesthetic behind its construction. She could remember a fashion for useless buildings from her youth, one of the many periodic crazes in micro-landscaping that swept the sphere. She herself had designed a fully functioning factory that would have ceaselessly dug over its own spoil tip, producing nothing but columns of acrid black smoke and toxic water pollution. The craze had already been abating when she'd submitted her proposals and had them turned down. The next big new fashion had been for concealed habitations; there was an entire city of three million people on the other side of the Endless Sea built along those lines. You could walk right through it and never know it was there. SaRa!qava didn't really mind; the idea that her redundant factory had never been built because the aesthetic it was based on had become redundant had a certain pleasing symmetry.

Still, it would have been nice to build the factory. She imagined it lurking in some lush secluded valley like a guilty secret, horrible mutant fish, cooked up especially to survive the pollution, playing in a stream below the steaming outflow.

This image of a pointless industrial landscape may have been what prompted her to hold the party at the Windmills, the actual control centre of which was an oblong lump of ridged plasticrete built half into the seaward slope below the crest. The lower four storeys were completely taken up by the hall containing the capacitors arranged in two lines of four. This was where saRa!qava would encourage the dancing to take place; the giant ceramic capacitors would loom nicely with the right lighting.

SaRa!qava had arranged a buffet on the lawn of the small terraced garden at the front of the control centre. God had promised her a clear night, average temperature twenty-one degrees centigrade, although it hinted it could accelerate a promising warm front if she asked it nicely. Half a dozen remote-drones were ferrying in canapés, bowls of fruit, a punch bowl of a suspicious yellow dip that God insisted on sending to every party despite the fact that everybody avoided it, a selection of narcotic flowers, more food, crispy tortillas and a huge celebratory pie in the shape of a huge pie. Paper lanterns were hung from the branches of the severely ornamental trees.

SaRa!qava watched as a cargo-drone swooped low over the garden dropping a shower of metal cubes. Halfway down the cubes squirmed unpleasantly and transformed into a variety of wrought-iron garden furniture – memory metal of course – before floating the rest of the way down. This should be the last of the preparations; there were already cushions and comfy fields strewn about in the accessible nooks and crannies so there was somewhere for people to have sex. People tended to do that at parties; you couldn't stop them so they might as well be comfortable. Actually aM!xitsa had tried once, creating a powerful sexual depressant that should have given anyone who ingested it the erotic drive of a strand of kelp. Only the stupid machine had put it in God's suspicious yellow dip which no one ever ate and so of course no one got dosed.

At least that's what aM!xitsa claimed to have done; the drone's mind was officially rated at 10.2, meaning that it was supposed to be at least ten times more intelligent than the average sentient humanoid, so it was difficult to believe that it hadn't realized that no one *ever* ate the dip. Come to think of it, God was rated x number of millions times smarter than aM!xitsa and it *made* the dip that no one ever ate. It was probably one of those jokes, the kind that you had to be a machine to find funny.

Dep was waiting for her in the capacitor hall. Clumps of Dep's hair were twisting themselves into braids and then untwisting again – a sure sign that she was nervous.

'How do I look?' she asked and pirouetted. She was wearing a *symbiote* dress of silver scales, the living organism constantly shaping and reshaping itself across the contours of her body.

'I tell everyone that it's a historical fancy dress party,' said saRa!qava, 'and my own daughter comes as a fish.'

'This is historical,' said Dep. The dress shivered slightly and changed shape, extruding one long sleeve and raising the skirt above the knee.

'From exactly where and when?'

'Who knows,' said Dep. 'Someone's bound to have worn something like this somewhere at some time in the past.'

'Not if they had any fashion sense.'

'I'm trying to look barbarian.'

'You've got barbarian on the brain,' said saRa!qava. 'As if I didn't know why. Just remember that he is a barbarian and that they can have some pretty peculiar ideas about sex and such.'

'But, Mother,' said Dep, 'that's the whole point.'

SaRa!qava activated the terminal in her left earring and asked God whether Benny and her friends were on their way yet.

'They're on their way now,' said God. 'It took them a while to figure out how the tube system worked. Do you want to know what they're wearing?'

'No.'

'Go on,' said God. 'I'll give you a full cultural analysis.'

'No,' said saRa!qava, making her way to the lift egress at the far end of the capacitor hall. 'Why aren't they here yet?'

There was a suspicious silence.

'God, what have you done?'

'Put them on the slow track.'

'Why?'

'They're having a real interesting conversation.'

'Bad God!' said saRa!qava. 'You shouldn't be listening.'

'Wanna hear?'

Technically you weren't supposed to eavesdrop on private conversations; not a law of course – saRa!qava's society didn't have anything as crude as a legal system – but certainly not the 'done' thing.

'Just get them here,' she told God.

'Your sternest command is my slightest wish,' said God.

SaRa!qava stepped forward as the lift doors opened. Seeing Bernice and her friends together saRa!qava was struck again by their physiological uniformity. Even the Doctor, whom God identified as belonging to a different species entirely, seemed to share the same detailed similarity as his companions right down to the number of fingers on

58

each hand, the general arrangement of his eyes and ears. Behind her Dep gave a small squeal of delight as Chris stepped out of the lift. He was dressed in a ridiculous furry loin cloth, his naked torso painted with spiral patterns of blue and silver. He was carrying a large double-bladed axe which he waved enthusiastically when he saw Dep.

There was a chorus of yells from behind him and he lowered the axe with a sheepish grin. Dep darted forward, grabbed his free hand and pulled him away. The small dark woman – Roz – glared after him. SaRa!qava wondered if Dep was stepping on the older woman's toes. Roz's costume seemed to consist of two ochre-coloured blankets and masses of jewellery. One of the blankets was wrapped around her waist, the other draped across her shoulders and knotted under her chin. A dozen blue and white necklaces hung around her neck while her forearms and ankles were almost hidden under a sheath of matching bracelets.

'SaRa!qava!' Bernice swept out of the lift wearing the most impractical dress saRa!qava had ever seen. The skirt was bell-shaped and so large that saRa!qava was sure it had to be supported by a suspensor field. It pulled it in tight at Bernice's waist before erupting upwards in a confusion of layers and frills of cloth that gathered at her shoulders and bodice. An enormous blonde wig added half a metre to Bernice's height. How slim her arms looked emerging from the puffs of cloth at her shoulders. Her long elbow gloves were the same white satin as the dress. SaRa!qava made a mental note to bully God into giving her the pattern later. She hadn't dyed her eyebrows to match the wig, leaving them as dark arches framing those strangely old-looking eyes.

Bernice snapped open a fan, fluttering it in front of her face. 'What do you think of the frock?' she asked

'It's extraordinary,' said saRa!qava. 'What's holding the skirt up?'

'Petticoats,' said Bernice, 'lots and lots of petticoats. I think you should know that I don't normally dress like this.' Bernice glanced back at the Doctor. 'Unless I have to.'

The Doctor was boringly dressed in the same crumpled linen suit he'd worn that afternoon. Bernice caught saRa!qava's eye and winked. 'There's always one that has to be different, isn't there?'

The Doctor smiled as if complimented by this.

'Not that he's ever actually out of costume,' said Bernice.

SaRa!qava took great delight in introducing the Doctor to iRama who regarded himself as a leading light in the sphere's Gallifreyan Interest Group. The man had made the mistake of arriving in God's best guess at a Time Lord's ceremonial robes and hearing the Doctor tactfully point out the inaccuracies in the costume; this gave saRa!qava her first really good laugh of the evening. Despite his sartorial inadequacies the Doctor was turning out to be good value as a party guest. Still, there was something about him that made saRa!qava nervous, a sense of depth that reminded her uneasily of the times she'd talked to the really smart machines. Not the ones like God, who was by design and inclination cheerful and unassuming, but the intelligences that ran the warships and had prosecuted the war. However friendly they seemed when you talked to them, there was always the sense of depth, as if an unsympathetic rationality was ticking away beneath the façade. Like those machines, she noticed, the Doctor tended to ask more questions than he answered.

Roz was not good value as a party guest although she had some collateral advantage as a conversation piece. Plenty of people had asked saRa!qava who she was, this strange woman with grey shot hair and angry black eyes. Such old eyes, like Bernice's, although God was adamant that in strict chronological terms both women were half saRa!qava's age. Life as a barbarian hero was tough; the Barbarian Emulation Interest Group was always saying things like that. Live fast, die young. SaRa!qava guessed that with such a truncated life expectancy people like Roz had to cram in as much as they could get. And Roz was going to relive most of it if she didn't lay off the *flashback* she was drinking. You were supposed to mix small doses of the memory enhancer with something mellower like *nostalgia*. Roz had had a whole glass of the stuff; if she finished it she'd be getting memory flashes for a week. SaRa!qava frowned. She had given

60

specific instructions that *flashback* was not to be included in the drinks inventory – where had Roz got hold of it?

An antique landing module spun lazily overhead, manoeuvring with little spurts from its attitude control jets. The module was a metre and a half across and saRa!qava could see tiny faces peering out of its windows. There was a name stencilled on its side – S-LIONESS. Not a drone then, a remote drone from a ship. SaRa!qava frowned. She made a point of not inviting ships to her parties: they were too unpredictable. Having seen S-Lioness, saRa!qava realized that there were at least three other ships with remote drones at the Windmills that night, all of them having come as antique spaceships of one kind or another. All of them had VAS nomenclature, which explained why they were rude enough to gatecrash, and all of them were unobtrusively clustering within discreet sensor range of the Doctor. SaRa!qava didn't like it; she wished aM!xitsa was with her, but nobody knew where the old drone had vanished to.

She snagged a glass of *tranquillity* off a passing tray and quickly stuck her nose in the bouquet that floated in the pale amber liquid. The fragrance calmed her a little. Perhaps holding the party here at the Windmills had been a mistake when she considered what had happened upstairs in the control gallery. Tossing the bouquet aside saRa!qava drained the glass in one go. She refused to feel guilty about *that*; it wasn't as if she'd had any choice in the matter. The *tranquillity* helped but not as much as saRa!qava would have liked. She threw the empty glass over her shoulder where it was intercepted by a tray before it hit the ground.

Feeling the need for a distraction, saRa!qava went looking for Bernice.

She found her outside, holding court by the buffet tables. She was surrounded by at least four men and a drone that had come in costume as a small jet airliner. The costume was a dead giveaway: the drone had to be one of Dep's friends from the Weird Aviation Interest Group. Since that type of jet couldn't hover the little machine was trying hard to remain in 'character' by maintaining a tight holding pattern around the group. SaRa!qava thought that it would have been better served coming as something with VTOL capability. The men were slow about opening their ranks, reluctant, saRa!qava thought, to let her into the conversation. Bernice thwacked one of the men on the chest with her fan, forcing him to step back and create a gap for saRa!qava. SaRa!qava watched how Bernice manoeuvred the big skirt to maintain her personal space. Perhaps, she thought, she might have misjudged Bernice's costume; if the fan could be used as a weapon then maybe the enormous skirt was more than just ridiculous ostentation, perhaps it could be used to transport concealed armaments. That would certainly gel with what Bernice had told her about this Paris place. 'Light artillery in the war between the sexes', Bernice had called the dress. SaRa!qava thought she understood; intragender warfare was uncommon amongst humanoids but not that rare. If human females were smaller than the males then the skirt would help balance out the weight disadvantage. She wondered what it would be like to make love to somebody wearing a dress like that, peeling away the layers one by one, hunting out the hidden skin beneath the silk.

I've been overdoing the *tranquillity* again, thought saRa!qava.

A man, dressed as a space pirate in an improbably skintight hostile environment suit and fishbowl helmet, asked if saRa!qava had seen aM!xitsa recently.

'I heard he was down the coast,' said the small airliner, 'looking after some mad alien female.'

'And there was me thinking I was the only one,' said Bernice.

'Who told you that?' saRa!qava asked the drone.

'Vi!Cari,' said the Drone. 'Who else?'

'You talk to vi!Cari!' said another of Bernice's admirers. 'You must be the only person who does.'

'Say what you like about vi!Cari,' said the drone, 'it always knows what's going on.'

'You mean you don't know?' asked the space pirate.

'Know what?' asked the drone.

'Vi!Cari managed to get itself disassembled last night.'

The drone was so stunned that it forgot all about its airliner costume and stopped dead in mid air. SaRa!qava stared; she'd never seen a sentient machine, even one as young as the airliner, lost for words before. She used the moment of distraction to try to suppress the feeling of guilty relief that surged through her.

With a sudden click the drone jettisoned its costume and shot away towards iSanti Jeni, wailing its distress. They heard the muffled boom of it breaking the sound barrier before its discarded plastic wings had hit the floor.

'You could have put that a bit better,' said saRa!qava.

The space pirate shrugged. 'I didn't think anybody liked the nasty little jobber.'

'Are you saying,' asked Bernice, 'that these machines have *feelings*?'

The space pirate looked at her, appalled. 'You *really* are a barbarian, aren't you?'

Roz was doing OK right up to the point where the cockroach ate the canapé. Not brilliant though, just OK. Roz didn't really like parties; she felt foolish standing around trying to make conversation with people she didn't particularly want to know. The costume didn't help. She'd found she couldn't remember how to knot the skirt properly and had to keep hitching it up over her hips. There was a queasy lump in her stomach that told her that she'd drunk something she didn't agree with. It wasn't her fault. These damned *people* blurred the distinction between narcotics and honest alcohol; she could have been ingesting *anything*. If she ever got back to her own time and space she'd probably have to arrest herself for substance abuse.

There was dancing and that made it worse.

Twisting figures were reflected in the polished marble floor of the capacitor hall. Some danced smiling, some frowning in concentration, some with their eyes closed, out of step with the music and off in some interior world of their own.

She remembered her *umakhulu* – grandmother – painting flowers along the sides of her small breasts while her mama pulled at her hair and cursed its failure to braid well. They were beautifying Roz and her sister in readiness for the party.

63

Roz and Leabie were going to dance that afternoon in honour of her father's guests. Roz felt sick, terrified that she'd forget the steps and embarrass herself. She knew she couldn't dance, the rhythm just kept slipping away from her. Her mother was intolerant of failure.

Not that *uMama* cared for the guests; *iZulu emhlotshana* she called them – blond Zulus. Not a proper pure-bred family at all, but one of the new generation of nobles created by the Empress, acquiring the titles of ancient Africa to dress up the wealth they'd plundered on the high frontier. Father wanted their support, though, for one of his complicated political intrigues, wanted it badly enough to have his daughters painted and set to dancing. He was hoping to link their families in a very old-fashioned way.

She was doing OK. This was not Baronial Krall at Kibero Patera on Io. She was not twelve. She didn't have to dance if she didn't want to. She could stand around and make conversation like a civilized human being.

Then the cockroach said, 'Excuse me.' And ate the canapé.

His mouth, his human-shaped and textured mouth, split open at the sides to allow him to extend large hairy mandibles that picked the canapé from the tip of his top leftside arm. Up until then Roz had assumed that the cockroach body was the costume and the human head the real part. Bizarre, but no worse than an exotic body bepple's she'd seen at home.

Standing in front of him Roz had an unparalleled view of the cockroach's anterior cilia, writhing like two bunches of albino worms, as they masticated the canapé and shovelled the fragments into the sucking hole of his mouth. The discarded cheeks of his mask flapped loosely on either side as the cilia processed a second canapé.

'These are very good,' said the cockroach. 'You should try one.'

A wave of chemically tainted memory crashed over Roz, filling her nostrils with the stink of dirty water and the roast pork smell of burning flesh. She felt the shocking coolness of the water against her thighs, of a palm against her breast, of

64

fingers pulling at her hair. She saw her mother's face, Martle's face, the Doctor's face, Bernice's face, Chris's face – and finally her own face, her eyes wide open and sightless, a fist-sized hole punched through her chest where her heart ought to be.

She heard the sound of children laughing.

The cockroach was surprisingly agile for such a big creature; it managed to skip backwards fast enough to avoid most of the vomit.

'Was it something I said?' it asked politely.

But Roz was already running for the door.

They played a shooting game on one of the entertainment modules in the control gallery. The module, no bigger than a child's head, projected a 180-degree panorama of misty fenland over which flew flocks of birds. Dep and Chris took turns to use a simulated .75 hunting gun to shoot down the birds. As each bird fell a six-legged *retriever* would bound forward into the marshy landscape, seize the corpse in its jaws and carry it to the hunting racks on either side. Left side for Dep, right side for Chris. It was how they kept score.

Dep had racked up two lines of birds with eighteen shots, including a couple of the smaller, faster ones which put her ahead by two points. Standing on the firing line Dep cracked open the heavy rifle and slotted in another cartridge. Beside her the panting breath of the *retriever* steamed in the cold air. It was a salt marsh; from the firing line you could smell the salt and hear the distant murmur of the sea. She raised the rifle into firing position the way aM!xitsa had taught her and waited.

The first wave of birds came honking over the horizon flying in their distinctive double V formation. The *retriever* whined softly in anticipation. Dep held her fire; you only got one shot per round and you had to decide whether to bag one of the slower birds or wait for the faster ones that were worth more points. You could have the module download the bird's culinary template to your kitchen synthesizer and eat them after the game, complete with simulated ceramic buckshot. The small ones were supposed to taste better.

This late in the game the birds were getting sneaky. Dep spotted one of the small birds trying to blend into the formation of its larger brethren. Sighting up the barrel of the gun she tracked along the bird's flightpath and squeezed the trigger.

Just as she fired the landscape seemed to jerk sideways. The movement was almost imperceptible but enough to put her off her aim. The birds flew on unconcerned. Beside her the *retriever* whined softly and covered its wedge-shaped head with two pairs of paws. Dep cracked the gun and ejected the spent cartridge.

'Bad luck,' said Chris as Dep stepped back off the firing line.

Dep kicked the entertainment module. 'Hey, box,' she asked it. 'What happened?'

'Sorry,' said the module. 'There was some electromagnetic interference from the capacitors downstairs. I think it was due to a static charge residue. I had to make a correction.'

'Ruined my shot.'

'It won't happen again,' said the module with machine contriteness.

Chris frowned prettily. 'Do you want to take the shot again?'

'I'll think of it as a handicap,' she said. 'I'm still going to beat you.'

'Don't count on it,' said Chris and picked up his gun.

Out of the module's quietfield the party was roaring along. The younger people, Dep's generation, had gravitated upstairs. About thirty of them were crammed into the control gallery. She knew most of them, friends from town or the Weird Aviation Interest Group. The second entertainment module was playing something complex by aKatsia while simultaneously generating the twisted geometric light shapes that the composer insisted were an essential part of the music. It was supposed to be *the* fashionable sound for parties but Dep didn't care for it. Perhaps you had to take the right drugs to appreciate it.

Dep snagged a drink off a passing tray and turned to watch Chris make his last shot. The gun looked surprisingly fragile in his big hands, like a toy, as he raised it to his shoulder. There was a curl of blue paint over that shoulder, part of one of the spiral patterns that covered his naked torso. Dep let her eyes follow the spiral as it curved downwards over the taut muscles of his back and further down to his narrow waist. She wondered if there were spirals hidden under his furry loin cloth and, if so, who painted them? Not Roz, that was for sure. Chris called Roz 'his partner' and that had confused Dep at first but she quickly realized that the word meant something different from its normal usage. She'd recognized the look in Roz's eyes outside the lift; it was the same look of concern her Mama got when Dep was going to test one of her machines. What could Roz possibly be concerned about? It wasn't as if Dep was going to eat him.

Dep grinned.

At least not literally.

Roz and Martle had made love just the one time after the business with the shapeshifter. There was no rule that said adjudicators were supposed to be celibate but a certain disdain for the pleasures of the flesh was encouraged. It was part of the ethos, an adjudicator's loyalties should remain with the order, with justice, not be misdirected into the transient and illusionary lusts of the body. Marriage was allowed, providing that the potential spouse was vetted by the order first, but the rate of suicide and divorce was high. Some people seemed to manage it though: seven generations of Cwejs, every single one producing its crop of adjudicators, proved that not everyone was an emotional cripple. Not that Roz hadn't fooled around in her youth; she'd done her fair share of waking up in strange beds with a hangover and a man whose name she couldn't remember. It was just that after a while sex had lost most of its charm, had begun to seem too messy, too sticky and biological, too uncertain a process to be bothered with. It didn't give her anything she couldn't get from a three-pack of Martian ale and a long shower.

When *going over the side*, adjudicator slang for sleeping with a colleague, there were rules but they got broken all the time. Who else but another adjudicator could possibly understand what the life was like, the bodies, the aliens, the stupid vacant venality in the eyes of the suspects, the numbing day by day routine horrors.

She remembered struggling in Martle's arms as he led her back to the flitter after she'd shot the shapeshifter – a gap – then she was in the shower with him, the water soaking their undertunics. She was shaking, the worst shakes of her career; he'd put his arms around her and she'd hit him, hard enough to leave a bruise on his shoulder. Martle kept hold of her, stroking her back, her hair and face. Pain and fear became something else. Something long and slow and comforting. It had none of the alcoholic desperation of her earlier encounters, not lust but need drew them into the tangled covers of the bed. Afterwards she held Martle tight, feeling the beating of his heart between her breasts. In the morning Martle brought her breakfast in bed and the early morning edition of the newsfax. They joked about the fact that the incident with the shapeshifter hadn't even made the back page. It put it in some kind of context. Just another day in the life.

One month later Roz discovered Martle taking bribes and opened up his throat with a vibroknife. She didn't have any choice; it was him or her.

A door at the base of the external staircase banged open and a knot of partygoers lurched out of the building. From her perch halfway up the metal stairs Roz got a glimpse of glitter off their costumes as they crossed the lighted stretch of flagstones below. Their voices sounded shrill and hollow in her ears, as incomprehensible and as mindless as birdsong.

'They can't help it,' said a voice behind her, 'they've never suffered.'

It was a man, or at least a close approximation of one. He must have walked down the stairs while she was distracted. Roz snorted in disgust; it seemed just about anyone could sneak up behind her these days.

'You must be Roz,' said the man. 'My name is feLixi. May I join you?'

'I wouldn't advise it,' said Roz. 'I'm not very good company.'

'I'll take my chances,' said feLixi, and sat down on the step beside her. 'Don't worry about throwing up on diClark; worse things happen at these parties.'

'Not to me,' said Roz. 'It must have been something I drank.'

'Someone once ate someone at one of saRa!qava's parties,' said feLixi. He was smaller than the other people Roz had met so far; his face had a reassuringly human aspect and his eyes were an ordinary muddy brown. 'I told them that it was a mistake dressing up as a roasted animal carcass but would they listen to me?'

'That's sick.'

'It is, isn't it?' said feLixi.

Roz nodded. It was really sick but she had to ask – 'How did it taste?'

'Not bad actually.'

'I take it they didn't die.'

'Who?'

'The somebody who got eaten.'

'Oh no, nothing that a couple of hours of regen couldn't fix,' said feLixi. 'Around here, you have to work much harder than that if you want to kill someone.'

The game ended in a draw but only because they both cheated. Dep started it, letting her hair creep up Chris's thigh, distracting him as he prepared to take his next shot. He retaliated during her next round, placing the tip of one finger on the sensitive spot between her shoulder blades, just below the point of her hairline. Dep tried to concentrate on the shot but her dress, symbiotically linked to her treacherous sub-conscious, started opening down the back. As Chris's finger traced a line down her spine Dep gave up trying to aim at the birds and waited to see how far he was willing to go. When he reached the base of her spine she fired off the gun at nothing, just for the look of the thing.

They went out onto the balcony, looking for some privacy. They leaned against the railing, facing each other. Chris's hands were restless. Dep could tell he was nervous, frightened even. It was intriguing. Gently she took his hand

69

and placed it on her hip, the dress melting away beneath his palm. Then just to make sure he was getting the idea she leaned forward and brushed her nose against his. It was a good nose, large and firm, the touch sending a trail of shivers down her neck. Boldly, she put her arms around his neck and moved in for a really good rub. It went a bit wrong; Chris kept on trying to touch her lips with his own. Dep pulled her head back in confusion and saw it mirrored in Chris's face.

'Why,' she asked, 'are you doing that?'

'Doing what?' asked Chris nervously.

'The thing with the lips?'

'It's what we call kissing,' said Chris. 'Don't you kiss?'

'Of course we do, just not on the mouth.'

'Oh.'

'Does it feel nice?'

'Um,' said Chris, 'I think so.'

'All right,' said Dep, 'let's do some of that then. I'll try anything once.'

It felt very strange but they reached a compromise so that they kissed and rubbed noses at the same time. When he slipped his tongue between her lips she tried to take her cues from Chris and respond. Unfortunately a stray memory from a biology lesson surfaced suddenly in her mind and she had to break away again.

Her laughter seemed to worry Chris, which only made it worse. 'I'm sorry,' she said, 'it's just that I was reminded of the way birds feed their young.'

'Thanks a lot,' said Chris, but he was smiling.

'I want you,' said Dep.

Chris looked around the balcony. 'What, here?'

'Why not?'

'People can see us.'

'Where then?'

Chris peered into the darkness beyond the railing, searching for something in the distance. 'I think I've got an idea.'

Once she was sure that there was no danger of feLixi's head suddenly exploding Roz began to relax. He was easy to talk to, displaying none of the smugness that characterized the

70

rest of the sphere's inhabitants. He felt more solid too; even his costume, a simple one-piece shipsuit, had a sense of reality to it.

'That's because it is real,' said feLixi. 'I picked it up during a mission.'

'When you were working for *xrinig*?'

'XR(N)IG,' feLixi corrected her. 'Xeno Relations (Normalization) Interest Group and we don't work *for* interest groups here, we work *with* them.'

'Does that make a difference?'

'Well, it means everyone's much politer at the mission briefings.'

'Don't take this the wrong way,' said Roz, 'but I can't imagine you people fighting a war.'

'Neither could we, to be honest,' said feLixi. 'It's amazing how fast it all came back to us. Burn, rape, pillage. Burn anyway, after that rape and pillage was too much like hard work.'

'How bad did it get?'

'Depended on where you were,' said feLixi. 'If I'd stayed on the sphere I'd have hardly noticed there was a war on at all. I volounteered for XR(N)IG, worked as a secret agent in some of the proxy wars. Saw some stuff that I'd rather not have seen, did some things –'

'Yeah,' said Roz. 'Goddess, yeah.'

'Stupid, isn't it,' said feLixi. 'This is my people, remember, so I could have stopped any time I liked. Just said "It's been fun, guys, but I think I'll go home now" but you don't, do you? You keep on taking the missions, doing the jobs and the pain inside gets worse and worse until you can't separate yourself from the pain any more – the pain and you are one and the same thing.'

'Stop,' said Roz recoiling from that image. 'Please.'

FeLixi nodded. 'Yeah, right, I understand – some things you don't talk about.'

'Not here,' said Roz, 'not now. Maybe later.'

'Do you know what I like about sitting on the stairs at parties?'

'You don't have to dance?'

'You meet a better class of people,' said feLixi.

They flagged down a patrolling tray and feLixi ordered something hot and sweet that tasted vaguely of ginger and pineapple. He told Roz a joke about two drones and a ship in geostationary orbit but she didn't get the punchline. 'You had to be there,' said feLixi.

Roz laughed at that; the hot drink was clearing her head. She told him a bit of family history, making it sound a lot funnier than she remembered. FeLixi roared when she described the extreme lengths her mother went to to maintain her social position. How she'd woken the whole Krall in the middle of the night to tidy the grounds – 'because she'd heard a rumour that the Empress's ship might overfly the area'. When she talked about it this way Roz could almost believe that she had enjoyed her childhood.

They lapsed into silence, sipping their drinks and staring over the landscape. Roz liked that. They were sitting like that when saRa!qava and Bernice emerged from the door below them. The two women were talking softly and Roz found herself unconsciously leaning forward to try to overhear. FeLixi plucked the brooch off his shipsuit and, grinning, held it up between them. 'Eavesdrop,' he said softly.

Suddenly they could hear Bernice and saRa!qava's voices, low and clear, as if they were standing half a metre away. Roz realized that the brooch was a multi-function terminal. She felt a touch of guilt about listening in but she couldn't resist it. After all, *private secrets breed public crime* was an adjudicator tenet, justification for a million com-taps.

SaRa!qava murmured something, too quietly even for feLixi's terminal to catch, her hand resting lightly on Bernice's arm. The other woman murmured back and gently disengaged the other's hand. It was gracefully done.

'Only hetero then?' said saRa!qava.

'So far,' said Bernice.

'Would it help if I told you I was a man six months ago?' asked saRa!qava.

Roz put her hand over the terminal cutting off Bernice's reply. 'She changed sex?' she asked.

'You mean you can't?' asked feLixi.

72

Roz shook her head and took her hand off the terminal.

'– only with surgery and genetic manipulation,' said Bernice.

'How inconvenient,' said saRa!qava.

'You mean you do it' – Bernice made a vague circling motion with her hands – 'sort of naturally?'

'Hey, saRa!qava,' said a voice. From saRa!qava's own terminal Roz thought. 'Dep and the barbarian are about to do something really silly.'

SaRa!qava and Bernice went back inside the building. 'Take my advice, Benny,' said saRa!qava. 'Don't ever have children.'

Roz sighed – she had a good idea of who the 'barbarian' was. 'I'd better see what's going on,' she told feLixi. 'It's been nice talking to you.'

'I live in town,' said feLixi. 'Why don't you come up and see me some time?'

Roz arrived on the balcony just in time to see Chris manoeuvre a projectile rifle onto the railing. Dep was helping him, her eyes bright with excitement. 'He's going to shoot a line back to the villa,' Bernice told her.

Roz stared over the landscape; there was a tiny smudge of light that might, or might not, be the villa. The range was over six thousand metres. 'Can't you stop him?' Bernice asked her.

Roz looked at Chris and at Dep looking at Chris. 'Probably not,' she said.

Chris lined up the gun and squinted into the bulky sight mounted above the barrel. Roz reckoned it was an impossible shot, even for him. Chris fired, there was the distinctive thrum-crack of a linear accelerator. It was a fast projectile, too fast for the eye to follow even with the attached line marking its path. Chris asked the gun whether the far end was on target and secure.

'Yep,' said the gun.

Chris climbed over the railing and clipped a handgrip to the line.

'Are you sure this is wise?' asked Bernice.

'Bundled monofilament,' said Chris. He took a firm hold of the grip and motioned to Dep who climbed over the railing and onto his back. Roz noticed uneasily how reluctant Dep's hair was to let go of the railing.

'See you at the villa,' said Chris and pushed off.

Dep gave a little shriek and then they were nothing but shadows over the landscape.

'Pathetic,' said Roz.

'Isn't it amazing what boys will do to impress girls,' said Bernice. 'Shit, I hope they don't go bang at the bottom .'

'I think the bang is inevitable,' said Roz. 'It's the splat that's worrying me.'

Bernice sighed. 'I suppose it had to happen sooner or later. You don't think he's going to get all mature on us now?'

The two women looked at each other.

'Nah.'

His hands were humming with the friction from the grip on the line. He felt the brush of Dep's breath in his ear, the warmth of her breasts against his back and the heat of her thighs locked around his waist. For a moment only the wind of their passage betrayed their movement. All around them was the vast artificial sky, broken into segments of night and day. To his right Chris could see a vast city, its lights, like a nebula, glittering through the thick layers of atmosphere. Beyond and above, still lit by the sun, was a vast hexagonal hole through which he could see real stars. The Spaceport, he realized, the sphere's gateway to the rest of the universe. To his left the Endless Sea was a sweep of darkness rising beyond the impossible line where the ocean became the sky. There were lights upon the water, islands as big as continents, continents as big as planets and the running lights of a ship that had to be hundreds of kilometres long.

They swept over a ridge, the tops of the evergreens a bare two metres beneath their feet. The evening air was sweet with the scent of pine needles. Dep gasped as a cloud of moths exploded from the tree tops, thousands of white wings beating the air with a sound like tearing silk.

Chris could see the villa ahead lit up by the external lamps on the roof and balcony. They were linked to that balcony by the line, the bundled monofilament visible only by the dull sheen of reflected Whynot light, the same light that reflected from the villa's windows and the rippling surface of the pool on the roof.

Caught up in the rushing wind, in the warmth of Dep's body, the immensity of the sphere itself, Chris almost forgot to break in time. Some part of him wanted to keep going as if the solid wall of the villa was merely an illusion, that if he were to merely crash through it he and Dep would travel on for eternity, suspended between heaven and earth.

Fortunately the practical side of Chris, the side that had seen a few flitter crashes in its time, took over and squeezed hard on the grip, slowing them down.

They landed stumbling on the balcony, Dep's weight on Chris's back driving him through the windowfield into the lounge. He sensed rather than saw a brief flurry of movement ahead as the coffee table slid sideways out of their path. A soft impact caught him in the shins and he pitched face forward on to the sofa. He twisted, reaching for Dep as she rolled off his back. She slithered back on top of him, her hair lashing out to catch hold of his arm, and he felt her teeth biting gently at the side of his neck. The dress retreated down her back. Chris touched her bare shoulders. Overbalanced, the sofa toppled backwards, something heavy hit the floor and Chris was surprised to realize it was them.

Chris had not led a sheltered life. He'd read his fair share of texts, seen the holovids, done his homework in biology. There had been after-curfew bull sessions in the novice barracks when he was training and he'd raided the odd brothel while on duty. But the theory had never talked about *this*, about the way the brain shuts down and the body takes over. The talk was all of big bazongas and the calibre of a man's torpedo, of positions and teases, not of the way your lover's skin seems to merge into your own until you cannot differentiate where you finish and they begin.

'Excuse me,' said a voice. 'When you've quite finished.'

Dep and Chris froze trembling.

'Don't mind us,' drawled a second, female, voice. 'We can wait.'

4

Policeman on the Corner

There's a policeman on the corner
Taking pictures of the scene
I thought I better warn you
That he doesn't share your dream
Preaching to the Converted
by Johnny Chess
From the LP *Things to do on a Wet
Tuesday Night* (1987)

'Hurry up, Roz, I'm dying in here.'

'Relax, Benny, I've almost got it.'

There was an unbearable feeling of constriction around her chest and then Roz finally managed to get the stays undone and the corset released its death grip.

'Better?' asked Roz.

Bernice took a deep, luxurious breath. 'How did I let him talk me into that?'

'Deep-seated subconscious masochism?'

'You can talk,' said Bernice, 'you're the one wearing the ventilated blankets.'

'Ah, but that's a cultural thing.'

'Help me with the gloves, I can't get them off.'

Roz gripped the forefinger and thumb, making it easy for Bernice to extricate her right arm. Roz dropped the glove which sinewaved halfway to the floor before House scooped it up and hung it next to the (bouffant) wig. 'I wish it wouldn't do that,' said Roz. 'It gives me the creeps.'

'Convenient though,' said Bernice, extending her left arm.

'I like my stuff where I can find it,' said Roz and pulled the glove off.

'On the floor,' said Bernice.

'Speak for yourself.'

It was true; Roz's room in the TARDIS displayed a compulsive neatness that reminded Bernice uneasily of Ace's barrackroom mentality. The same air of regimentation, of temporary occupation. It was Bernice that lived ankle-deep in the detritus of past adventures. She suspected that she needed the mess as a kind of marker, as if she were saying: *this is my space; see, I'm spread all over it*. If she ever decided to leave the TARDIS she'd need a skip not a suitcase.

Bernice started struggling with her petticoats.

'Jeez,' said Roz, 'stay still.' She crouched down behind Bernice and pulled at the hooks that held the silk together. 'I've seen combat suits that were easier to get out of.'

'I've *been* in combat suits that were easier to wear,' said Bernice. 'You know, that's what saRa!qava thought this dress was.'

'Why didn't you get House to put in some zippers?' asked Roz.

'Authenticity,' said Bernice, sucking in her stomach. 'Remember, we were going to go as the real thing.' There were six layers of petticoats. 'I feel like a birthday present.'

'I'm almost down to your legs now,' said Roz. 'Hey, so much for authenticity.' She'd seen the Reeboks Bernice was wearing on her feet.

'Well, no one was going to see them.'

'About as authentic as a middle-aged Xhosa virgin,' muttered Roz.

'I was thinking of going as Boudicca,' said Bernice. 'Me and Chris could have been a pair.'

'So who's *Buhdika* when she's at home?'

'A very famous British warrior queen.'

'I thought that was Queen Elizabeth,' said Roz. ' "I may have the body of a weak and feeble woman but I have the heart and stomach —" '

' "– of a concrete elephant",' finished Bernice. 'I should never have shown you Ace's tape collection.' She stepped out of the restricting silk flounces. 'Free at last. Come on, I'll give you a hand with your necklaces.'

'Shouldn't we get downstairs?'

'What's the rush?' asked Bernice. 'They waited for us to get back from the party, they can wait for us to get changed.'

'I don't think they came here for a social visit,' said Roz.

'You think they're *official*?'

'As official as anything can get in this place,' said Roz. 'That woman has cop eyes.'

'She should use ointment for that.' Bernice rummaged for some jeans. Roz said, and Bernice believed her, that people that did the job could always recognize other people that did the job. She always called it 'the job'. Bernice, who'd often been on the receiving end of people doing 'the job', had never noticed it herself: too busy trying to talk her way out of whatever tricky situation the Doctor had managed to get her into this time. If Roz said the woman had cop eyes then the woman was a cop, which meant that the drone she'd come with was a cop too. 'Oh well, it was a nice holiday while it lasted.'

'They could just be checking us out,' said Roz. 'Can I borrow that muscle-bound top? This blanket's beginning to itch.'

'Help yourself,' Bernice told her. 'There's a pair of leggings that go with it somewhere. I think we can safely leave the pair of them to the Doctor. Besides, I'm starving.'

'Didn't you eat at the party?'

'Eat?' said Bernice. 'I could hardly breathe let alone eat.'

'Hey, stupid,' called Roz. 'We want some food – an unleavened bread base, base fifteen centimetres in radius, with a cheese, mushroom and tomato topping. I want it baked until the cheese is crispy.'

'And some coffee,' said Bernice.

'And some coffee, with milk and sugar in separate containers.'

'If we take our time with the food the Doctor should have them nicely baffled by the time we go down.'

'If they talk to him that long,' said Roz, 'they'll think we're the second coming.'

House took five minutes to fetch the food order, long enough for Roz to get her ankle bracelets off. She left the bracelets on her arms alone. 'I'm getting kind of used to them,' she said. They drank their coffee and ate the close approximation of a pizza. It was hot enough to burn their tongues. Bernice suggested that next time they should ask for anchovies but neither could remember what kind of fish an anchovy actually was.

Roz asked Bernice whether she'd noticed the square nipples.

'Square?' asked Bernice.

'Well,' said Roz, 'diamond-shaped then. You must have seen Dep's, they were pretty hard to miss. All the others I saw were square too, even the men's.'

'Is that significant in some way?' asked Bernice.

'Just that these aliens come in all sorts of shapes and the only thing I noticed they had in common was that they all had square nipples.'

'You,' said Bernice, 'are a deeply weird woman.'

'At least I've got round nipples.'

'Do you think we should tell the Doctor?' asked Bernice.

'He probably knows already,' said Roz.

They heard someone shouting downstairs, loud enough to overcome the villa's soundproofing. Bernice checked her watch. 'They're early,' she said. 'They shouldn't be on to the threats stage for at least another five minutes. Maybe we should see if they need help.'

'We haven't finished the pizza substitute,' said Roz.

They compromised and took the remains of the pizza with them, padding down the staircase to the lounge, their mouths full of mozzarella analogue and giggling like schoolgirls.

There were two of them, a woman and a drone. They said they were from something called the Interpersonal Dynamics Interest Group.

The drone was the standard oblate spheroid a metre across with a little face ikon, a hologram that changed expression as it spoke; it called itself kiKhali. The woman was thick-set with mottled reddish brown skin and wearing a canary-yellow evening dress; her neck was long and her face somehow too small. Bernice made a point of studying her eyes which were small and slate grey. She noticed that the eyes were constantly in motion, often in two separate directions. Like the eyes of a lizard, thought Bernice; that can't be what Roz meant. She really wasn't that surprised when a slim bifurcated tongue darted out between the woman's thin lips. When she spoke her voice sounded normal enough; Bernice had half expected her to hiss. She said her name was agRaven.

The Doctor was standing with his back to the balcony window. He introduced Roz and Bernice very formally as 'his associates'. Chris and Dep were sitting on one of the sofas. Dep's eyes were wide, but interested, not frightened. A braid of her hair was coiled possessively around Chris's shoulders.

Roz perched on a comfy-field to the right of the visitors making it impossible for the woman to watch her and the Doctor at the same time. Bernice thought this was unnecessary and rude, but Roz was probably doing it automatically. Bernice made a point of sitting opposite the woman and smiling nicely when she was introduced. AgRaven smiled nicely back.

'I think,' said the Doctor, 'that you should recap for my associates.'

AgRaven licked her lips but it was the drone kiKhali who spoke first. 'Thirty hours ago,' it said, 'a drone was struck by lightning and killed. Myself and agRaven here are doing the initial assessment on behalf of IDIG.'

'It's extremely unusual for a drone to die in this manner,' said agRaven, 'especially a drone like vi!Cari who was built to defensive specifications.'

'It was a combat-bot?' asked Roz.

AgRaven looked at the Doctor as if expecting a translation. The Doctor's face was impassive, his eyes guarded. Roz opened her mouth to speak.

'A robot built for combat,' said Bernice.

The 'mouth' of kiKhali's face ikon turned down at the corners.

'We don't like to use the R-word,' said agRaven

diplomatically, 'when we're talking about people.'

'Vi!Cari was a drone with full *defensive* capabilities,' said kiKhali. The machine's voice sounded tight, almost angry. 'The same basic configuration as myself. It was capable of levelling a small town and surviving a direct hit from a twenty-kiloton nuclear device.'

Roz yawned. KiKhali's face ikon showed obvious anger.

Could a machine get angry? Bernice wondered. SaRa!qava swore they had genuine emotions. More to the point, was it really wise to provoke one considering what kiKhali had just said about levelling small towns. Bernice had met her fair share of aggressive machine races. Or perhaps that was *barbarian* thinking?

'Tough enough to survive a lightning strike?' asked Roz.

'Of course,' said kiKhali.

'Then how was it destroyed?'

'We don't know,' said agRaven. 'That's why we're doing an assessment.'

'Have you reconstructed vi!Cari's casing yet?' asked the Doctor.

'Just a moment,' said kiKhali.

What Bernice thought was a hologram appeared in the centre of the lounge. It was the image of a drone but at one-third scale. It was obviously exactly the same design as kiKhali, except that kiKhali didn't have a hole burnt through it from top to bottom. The image rotated so that Bernice could see the inside of the drone through the hole in the top: there were no wires or circuits but she got the distinct impression that the machine had been built up in layers around a small central sphere.

'God assembled this model from the fragments that it recovered from the sea-bed,' said kiKhali. 'As you can see death was caused by a massive intrusion through the upper hemisphere, through the boundary layer of the brain and out through the lower hemisphere.'

'Surely God has a sensor record of the event,' said the Doctor.

'God was only running basic surveillance of the area at the time,' said kiKhali, 'so we only have a data record down to the micrometer level and the storm itself was generating a stupid number of gigawatts. That means we only have a partial sensor record.'

'Maybe it malfunctioned,' said Roz.

'Does that look like a malfunction?' said agRaven. To Bernice's surprise agRaven plucked the model from the air and handed it to Roz. Not a hologram then, something else.

'A solidigram,' said the Doctor.

'Clever,' said Roz in an unimpressed voice.

'May I?' asked the Doctor. Roz casually tossed the solidigram across the room to the Doctor. Bernice saw agRaven wince.

'So you think *robot* boy here was struck by lightning?' asked Roz.

'Its name was vi!Cari,' said kiKhali angrily. 'We're talking about a person here.'

'No sentient machine has *ever* suffered a catastrophic failure without an external cause in over two thousand years,' said agRaven. There was a tense note to her voice: Roz was beginning to get to her too.

The Doctor turned the solidigram over in his hands, feeling the damaged area with his fingers. 'It was murdered.' He looked sharply at agRaven. 'But of course you knew that.'

There was a pause.

'Yes,' said agRaven. 'That is the most likely explanation.'

'In that case,' said the Doctor, 'we accept.'

There was another pause.

'Accept what?' asked agRaven cautiously.

'The assignment of course,' said the Doctor. He jumped to his feet and beamed at the pair from IDIG. 'It's lucky for you that we happened to be here enjoying our hols when this foul deed took place, otherwise you could have been in real trouble. I and my associates have had simply masses of experience in dealing with this sort of thing. Isn't that right, Professor Summerfield?'

'Masses,' said Bernice.

'And I might add that Adjudicator Forrester has had twenty-five years' street-level experience handling suspects of all shapes and sizes. Some of them even turned out to be guilty.'

'But –' started agRaven.

The Doctor cut her off with the wave of his hand. 'How can we sacrifice our free time like this?' he asked. 'Think nothing of it. A small repayment for the excellent hospitality we have enjoyed so far.'

'But –' started agRaven again. Bernice had to feel sorry for her.

'Now that's all settled.' The Doctor rubbed his hands together. 'Why don't you tell us more about this vi!Cari.'

Vi!Cari was, or rather had been, one of the older defensive model drones, designed and built for operation in hostile environments. It had been manufactured on the TSH J-!Xin!ca three hundred years ago, had served on a GPS (with distinction) and on the VAS S-Lioness during the war. Towards the end of the war it had opted out of active duty with XR(N)IG. 'Just like that?' asked Roz. 'Just like that,' said kiKhali. 'We're not slaves.' Records were patchy after that, drones don't need somewhere to sleep and there was no indication that it had joined an association or an Interest Group. A year and a half ago it had registered that it considered itself resident in iSanti Jeni.

'It wasn't exactly popular around here,' said Bernice.

'How do you know that?' asked agRaven.

'Oh,' said Bernice, 'I have my sources.'

'She talked to people,' said Roz. 'It's more efficient than scanning.'

'Excellent,' said the Doctor. 'You see what a difference a bit of experience makes.'

A lightning bolt couldn't damage a drone, not even the twenty thousand plus ampere flashes that were recorded at the heart of last night's storm. Bernice knew from experience that you could fly a flitter right through a thunderstorm; it attracted the lightning but the charge went in one side and out the other. To get yourself fried you had to be grounded first. Vi!Cari hadn't been grounded. According to the partial data record it had been cruising at an altitude of eight hundred metres and a velocity of one kilometre per second, heading straight for the epicentre of the storm.

'Why?' asked Bernice.

AgRaven shrugged. 'God says it's been running behaviour models but the parameters are so broad that even it can't say what was going through vi!Cari's mind at the time.'

'About twenty thousand amperes,' said Roz.

'You,' said kiKhali, 'are a truly sick individual.'

Bernice wondered why Roz seemed to enjoy winding people up. It was getting on her nerves. She could live with agRaven or kiKhali's bad opinion but Dep was watching the whole sorry scene. She wished Roz would lay off, just this once; it was embarrassing.

'Assuming,' said the Doctor, 'that for some reason the lightning discharged directly against vi!Cari, how much damage should it have done?'

The answer was none at all. Even assuming that vi!Cari was out of defensive posture it still had three layers of shields in the terrawatt range and underneath that was the drone's outer shell, constructed of restructured crystalline carbon hybrids. They were, Bernice thought, tougher than Daleks, more like miniature battle cruisers than any robot or droid she'd ever heard of. She also noticed that neither kiKhali nor agRaven had said anything further about the drone's *offensive* capabilities. In her experience civilizations rarely let their offensive weapon systems fall far behind their defensive ones. 'Could another drone have done it?' she asked.

'It would have to have been another defensive drone,' said kiKhali. 'And at very close range – God would have seen it.'

'The drone,' asked the Doctor, 'or the attack?'

'Either,' said kiKhali.

'How many defensive drones are there in the sphere?' asked Bernice.

'Sixty-eight million,' said kiKhali, 'nine hundred and twenty thousand, four hundred and thirty-eight.'

'Including you?' asked Roz.

'Including me,' said kiKhali.

'And where were you on the night in question?' asked Roz.

KiKhali's face ikon vanished completely. AgRaven smiled.

'God knows where I was,' said kiKhali. 'Why don't you ask it?'

The Doctor smiled. 'The ultimate alibi.'

'What if God lies?' asked Roz.

'You have to assume God always tells the truth,' said agRaven. 'Let's face it, if God lies to you, you'll never know about it.'

The Doctor poked his finger inside the solidigram and wiggled it about. 'The brain cavity is very small,' he said.

'Most of a drone's brain exists outside of reality,' said kiKhali. 'The physical volume is really just an anchoring point for an intrusion into a subdomain of hyperspace.'

'Very clever,' said the Doctor.

'Stop me if I'm getting too technical,' said kiKhali.

Bernice refused to believe that the Doctor didn't know all about the way these machines worked. He'd asked the question, with just enough spin to make it insulting, making sure that kiKhali would answer in baby talk easy enough for even an archaeologist with an imaginary professorship to understand. It could be the Doctor's way of telling Bernice and Roz to pay attention, like a flagged item in a stream of data – listen up, children, this is important. Could this murder be the reason they had come here? Time was, she thought, the Doctor took an interest in such things because he happened to be on the spot. Nowadays she assumed it was the other way round.

KiKhali was getting technical, talking about double recurved spirals in imaginary time. The Doctor listened with an expression of polite interest. Roz was watching agRaven with narrowed eyes. AgRaven in turn looked bored and deeply uninterested as kiKhali droned on about the esoteric nature of hyperspace.

KiKhali had to know that the Doctor knew all about this stuff but did the machine know that the Doctor knew it knew? Trying to second-guess the Doctor was a fast track to a migraine and that was when you were *on* the Doctor's side.

Bernice wondered why having your brains in hyperspace might be important. Perhaps the monsters would be coming from that direction. She found it frighteningly easy to populate hyperspace with monsters; she'd run into a few of them herself. Let's face it, running into monsters was definitely not a problem when you travelled with the Doctor.

It had been her fantasy when they'd been staying in the house on Allen Road that the Doctor had a secretarial service, one of those video-phone graphic constructs that took the place of ansaphones in the early twenty-first century. She imagined it would be programmed to deal with monsters – *I'm sorry, the Doctor is not available right now. Please leave your name and the planet you wish to invade at the tone and the Doctor will get back to you.* If you were a *real* unlucky monster.

Roz asked kiKhali how smart vi!Cari had been.

'Vi!Cari was rated an eight point three,' said the drone. 'That's twenty times smarter than you are.'

That was an insult, Bernice thought. No mistaking kiKhali's delivery. Not like the way these people called you a barbarian; that was just a statement of fact not an insult. I'm a machine, kiKhali was saying to Roz, and I can beat you at chess with one arm tied behind my back. Saying this to a woman who claimed she had once disassembled a securitybot for answering back. Said she'd done the deed with a plasma torch. Better be careful, kiKhali, me old cock, or you might just get to find out how much of a barbarian Roz really is.

'It's not what you've got,' said Roz pleasantly, 'it's what you do with it.'

AgRaven laughed at that and Bernice breathed out.

The Doctor stepped in at that point, asking questions about how much of a data record God really had of the murder and whether it was too much trouble to have it transferred to the villa's own memory. It was all pertinent stuff but Bernice got the strange impression that the Doctor was just asking these questions on automatic pilot. As if, having now talked his way into a leading role in the investigation, he was just going through the motions. Bernice did not find that comforting at all.

KiKhali was swearing out loud, presumably for agRaven's benefit. 'Meat-brained, dysfunctional, gland-debilitated organo-fascist,' hissed the machine.

AgRaven sat down in the closest comfy-field and watched kiKhali as it twitched from one side of the travel capsule to the other. The indicator panel showed that they'd reached the main transverse transport tunnel in the base material and were accelerating to a cruising speed of nine kilometres a second. There was no sensation of movement.

KiKhali lapsed into silence.

'Have you finished?' asked agRaven. 'You shouldn't have let them upset you so much. They're only barbarians.'

'Barbarian!' said kiKhali. 'That woman was so primitive she should have been wearing a skull necklace. God shouldn't let *animals* like that wander around the sphere.'

AgRaven was genuinely shocked. 'KiKhali,' she said, 'that was beneath you. You're just upset because she insulted your intelligence.'

'You liked that line,' said kiKhali. 'I saw you smiling. I bet you wish you'd thought that one up yourself.'

'Won't stop me using it in future,' said agRaven.

'I can't believe we just handed the whole investigation over to a bunch of retrogrades.'

'You include the Doctor in that category?' asked agRaven.

The drone shifted slightly. Many drones cultivated little non-verbal mannerisms like that when talking to non-machines – adding, or so they claimed, an extra layer of subtlety to their conversation. AgRaven had worked with kiKhali long enough to know that such a twitch in its movement was an indication of uneasiness. She suspected that they were as much a polite fiction as the face ikons which were supposed to mirror a machine's mood.

'Especially the Doctor,' said kiKhali.

'Perhaps God's involved him on purpose,' said agRaven. 'Entangling him in this murder may force him into a pro-active posture. That should help God gather more data for a profile and that's bound to facilitate further extrapolation of Time Lord culture and intentions.'

'I love it when you talk like a machine,' said kiKhali.

'Especially since he's brought people with him this time. They might not be as careful as he is.'

'I just wonder if it's worth the aggravation.'

'Don't you want the secret of time travel?'

'I have a serious moral objection to time travel,' said

kiKhali. 'I don't like the idea of what it might do to the exercise of free will. If you know what's going to happen in the future then your actions become pre-ordained.'

'Didn't stop the Temporal Interest Group's experiments, did it?'

'That was just power politics,' said the drone. 'They got it, so we gotta have it. Besides the TIG were looking for valuable spin-off technologies, trans-dimensional engineering, that sort of thing.'

'God said it was a treaty violation.'

'Opinions differ. I for one don't think the Time Lords have been entirely honest in their dealings with us. We still don't have a delegation on Gallifrey, we don't even know whether we're dealing with people from our relative past or future, we don't even know whether this "Doctor" is the same as the last one. In fact, we know much less about the Time Lords than they know about us. Strategically, that's a serious disadvantage.'

'You're just a militaristic hawk at heart, aren't you?'

'Built that way,' said kiKhali.

Bernice waited for Chris and Dep to disappear upstairs before leaning over and asking Roz exactly why she felt the need to constantly antagonize complete strangers. Roz gave her little twisted half smile.

'Because it was easy,' she said.

'You mean, because they were aliens.'

'I don't like being interrogated,' said Roz, 'especially by amateurs.'

'That's a classic, Roz,' said Bernice, sharper than she meant to. 'Paranoia is often a side-effect of xenophobia.'

Roz stood up forcing Bernice to step back out of her way. 'Bernice,' she said, 'I'm tired and I don't want to have this conversation. We were being questioned whether you like it or not. That robot probably had a dozen varieties of scanner trained on us.'

'You said they were cops,' said Bernice. 'Didn't you used to question people? Or is there one rule for you –'

'At least when I suspected someone of a crime they knew

88

about it,' said Roz. 'I didn't stroll in all friendly like and pretend I was on a social call.'

'What makes you think we were suspects?'

'Of course we were suspects,' said Roz wearily. 'A robot gets destroyed the day we arrive and within six kilometres of where we're staying. I said they were amateurs, I didn't say they were stupid. Now if you don't mind?' Roz brushed past Bernice and headed for the stairs.

'And the winner, this year, of the much coveted Ace memorial award for tact and diplomacy in an interpersonal relationship is Bernice Summerfield.' Bernice turned to face the Doctor. 'I'd like to take this opportunity to thank my right foot and of course my mouth, without which none of this would have been possible.'

The Doctor smiled.

'Do you think I should go after her?' she asked.

'I doubt that would be a good idea,' said the Doctor. 'Roz has a lot on her mind at the moment.'

'Such as?'

'Well,' said the Doctor, 'judging from the faint but indicative discoloration of her iris, I'd say – most of her life.'

'In her iris? Well, I never, who'd have guessed it,' said Bernice. 'You're not going to explain that, are you?'

'She'll feel better tomorrow,' said the Doctor.

'I don't think Roz ever feels better,' said Bernice. 'Just less worse.'

Something dark and spherical shot past the window. 'Is that Chris's airborne boudoir?' asked Bernice.

The Doctor nodded. Together they stepped out onto the balcony and watched the sphere as it shot out over the ocean and accelerated into the distance, the light from Whynot gleaming dully off its sides.

'Well,' said Bernice, 'at least someone's happy.'

They stood together until the bedroom had vanished into the darkness. She considered asking the Doctor whether there was something going on that she should know about but decided that it would be a waste of breath. She went upstairs, leaving the Doctor alone on the balcony.

After a brief tussle with the suspensor pool Bernice sat up in bed and tried to write up the day's events in her diary but she seemed to have little enthusiasm left over from the party. She told House to turn the lights out and wake her in nine hours with a cup of coffee. The spat with Roz bothered her; she had too many memories of what she thought of as the *difficult* period with Ace. She didn't want a repeat of that.

Bernice could remember the exact moment when the woman who ate pizza and compared nipple sizes had vanished. She'd seen Roz's eyes change so suddenly it was as if something physical, a metal shutter, had slammed down behind them shutting everything in. They had become watchful eyes, suspicious and careful eyes that betrayed nothing. They were eyes that could calmly look over a mutilated corpse, looking for this detail or that or examine a grieving widow's face for some small sign of deception.

Lying in her bed with the patchwork quilt wrapped tightly around her, Bernice suddenly realized what Adjudicator Forrester meant when she spoke of 'cop eyes'.

God is watching over you, thought the Doctor. Walk slow, talk slow, act dumb. God's very bright, mustn't forget that, very bright indeed. Perhaps even brighter? Well, let's not get carried away. Bright and learning fast but not as experienced, didn't have the same brutal teachers I did. Still, High Council is scared of these people, only real threat to Gallifreyan supremacy and pro-active with it. Scared enough to renege on the treaty. Has God figured that out yet? Lucky that their material bent mitigates against time-travel but important not to underestimate them. High Council would have time-looped them but the probability was that they would have escaped *and* used the experience to make the theoretical jump to a temporal technology. Dangerous. An integrated machine/human society – laugh in the face of the Daleks, drop ice cubes down the vest of fear. Keep them out of Mutter's spiral, away from the time/space nexus and, by everything that is sacred, away from Earth. So far they've adhered to the treaty's secret protocols even if the Time Lords have not. Have I made a mistake coming here? Was a mistake for sure to involve aM!xitsa.

Still the murder is good, keep God off-balance, keep Bernice off-balance and give Roz something to do. Keep everyone's attention away from that *thing* at the cove. Hard sometimes to do the right thing; the lesser of two evils is still an evil. Should have destroyed it when I first realized, should have let Ace deal with it in Paris. But then *Ship* might have killed me for certain and a king/queen swap is a losing gambit in any variation you care to mention. Old hologram chess set in the TARDIS attic, one whose pieces fought short doomed battles when they were taken. Played a game against Melanie, tinny little voices screaming in triumph and pain. Got so distracted that I lost the match. Scared to make the winning moves in case I lost a pawn. Lost them all in the end, mate in thirty-seven. Lesson in that but not a pleasant one.

God is watching, the air has ears, the water has a nose. Doctor sings the blues, *I was born under a bad sign, if it wasn't for bad luck I would have no luck at all*. That dark 3 a.m. place with Nietzsche talking about the abyss, superman and monsters. I've looked into all of them and found I was already there. Davros's eyes staring back at me from the mirror. I condemned the Brigadier for sealing up the Silurians. Me, steeped in the blood of Skaro up to my elbows, who would have guessed that Daleks had so much blood in them? *Out, damned spot*. Promised Bernice a nice simple adventure this time; turn up somewhere and do what's right. Knew I was lying even as I set the co-ordinates. Never were any simple adventures. I was just too naïve to realize it.

God is watching, all the Gods are watching.

Rambling while Rome burns. I have doubts, but doubts are good. Davros had no doubts, neither did the Master. Cybermen and Sontarans have never a care. They wouldn't stand on a balcony in the unreal light of an artificial planet and ask themselves what it all means, really, when you get right down to it.

Doubts are good, they're what makes me –

Human?

Hyper-lude

Imagine a globe, a bubble if you like, you can make any size you like because it exists in a subdomain of hyperspace where dimensions like depth and width are a matter of taste. Now imagine the surface of your globe is like that of an oily soap bubble, rainbow colours shifting across the surface. Now imagine that each discrete element of that colour represents an analog logic state capable of recording a fixed range of values.

Now, remember a summer's afternoon, one from when you were young and a single afternoon could last half a lifetime. Try to remember everything: the precise colour of the sky, every mouthful of food, your emotions, what you did and what you thought. You can't, of course. Some of it is inaccessible, buried in the basement of your subconscious, and some of it has just plain gone, crowded out by more recent experiences. But just pretend for a moment that you can remember everything from that afternoon. That's a tremendous amount of data, sorted, catalogued and analysed and, as stated above, discarded. Now string all those afternoons together and add in all the mornings and nights between the ages of, say, three and nine. Never mind the complete works of Shakespeare, or all twenty-six volumes of *Encyclopaedia Universalis*, they represent information that has been pinned down and sanitized. What we are talking about here is the accumulated memories of a child, with all its subtle interactions of mood and texture. We are talking about data that has a kind of life of its own. We will call the sum of all this data a *childhood*; it's as good a unit of measurement as any other.

We'll assign a value of one *childhood* to our imaginary globe. This, by the way, being a conservative estimate.

Now, pull back from the globe until it's a small shape in the centre of the mind's cinema. Add a second globe next to the first, identical in every respect and also with the value of one *childhood*. Add a third globe and another after that in a line from the first. Keep on adding the globes but start to curve the line in on itself so that we are left with a spiral of globes. When you reach the centre and run out of room you should have a hundred globes and a *kilochildhood* of data.

Rotate this spiral through ninety degrees to the horizontal and start adding the globes in three dimensions, building a second spiral outwards from the centre of the first spiral. When it reaches the circumference go down a level and repeat the process working from the outside in. Repeat this until you have a cylinder a hundred globes tall with a storage capacity of a hundred *kilochildhoods*. Create another hundred thousand cylinders of the same dimensions, stretch them out in a long line and then carefully wind that line up into the shape of a sphere, just like a ball of wool. This ball will have a capacity of ten million *kilochildhoods* or ten *gigachildhoods*.

The average drone mind is made up of one of these balls. It gives them a standard estimated intelligence rating of eight times that of the average humanoid.

String these balls together into another line and wind them up into a much larger ball. We are now entering into the kind of cosmic numbers that only the machines can truly understand. One of these superballs has a capacity of 13.3 *tetrachildhoods* and is the usual size of a ship's mind. It also represents the upper limit of what, for the sake of clarity, we shall refer to as the ball of wool construction technique. Ships' minds have an estimated intelligence rating of a thousand times that of an average humanoid, although ships are usually the first to point out that once past the sentience threshold it becomes impossible to truly differentiate between levels of intelligence. Philosophically speaking. They go on to talk about the role of experience, sensory input matrixes and endocrine interactions. The average humanoid, if they've managed to stay awake, usually replies that all this might be so but they still can't beat your average drone at chess. The ship then tells them that they're missing the point and then shifts the conversation on to something more interesting.

Since we've now reached the upper limits of the ball of wool construction technique we will have to shift paradigms. Imagine the superballs are in fact two-dimensional planes, like planes of very thin glass with sides of near infinite length. Imagine about a million and float them in a sub-domain of hyperspace that is simultaneously very large and the size of a proton. Once you've managed that, no cheating now, imagine a string of these proton-sized subdomains and, you've probably guessed it, wind it up into a ball.

That is a section of the mind of God. Nobody ever tries to estimate its intelligence. Nobody wants to be that depressed. Trillions of thoughts rush at translight speeds through God's mind. Huge deep thoughts that move so quickly that before you finish speaking your first sentence God has probably predicted the entire course of a conversation you're going to have next year.

There is only one mind that is any way comparable to that of God's, although of vastly different configuration and attribution. It is currently residing in a time capsule that constantly hangs one picosecond ahead of the everpresent *now*.

If they could communicate, what thoughts would these two utterly different minds share? Concepts so utterly grand and grossly inexplicable that their very articulation could disorder the progress of creation. Even now both minds, lonely in their splendid isolation, yearn across that picosecond barrier, each seeking a consummation that cannot, *must not*, be allowed to happen.

94

5

All the Answers

He told me he had all the answers
To all my loneliness and pain
He said to open my heart to Jesus
And let God take all the strain
God Knows All About It,
by Johnny Chess
From the LP: *Things to do on a Wet
Tuesday Night* (1987)

It was cold up on the high plateau lands behind iSanti Jeni,
cold enough to make Chris's breath steam when he stepped
out of the aerodrome's clubhouse. The cold had sucked up a
thin mist from the surrounding valleys, half obscuring the
field of grass that served as a runway. The main hangar was a
hazy box shape at the far end.

The grass, brittle with frost, crunched under their feet as
Chris and the Doctor set off for the hangar. Above them the
gaudy architecture of the night sky faded to grey as God
turned the sun up. Chris made sure that his jacket was
fastened and the fur-lined collar turned up. He pulled on the
heavy gloves that he'd found with the jacket in the clubhouse
locker. The Doctor had ignored the heavy flying gear available, preferring to brave the cold in his crumpled linen suit.
Perhaps the frigid air didn't bother him.

The hangar's side door was unlocked. Never any locks on
public buildings, Dep said. Nothing you could steal that

couldn't be ordered from central stores with less fuss. No wonder they needed help when dealing with a murder.

The biplane was waiting for them just inside the main hangar doors, exactly where Dep said it would be. Chris slipped off his glove and ran his hand along the underside of the lower wing. The treated fabric was smooth and slightly yielding like that of the biplane he'd flown in over the English Channel. It even had the same slight fraying around the aileron mountings. Still, there were differences: a subtle sweep of the wings and a complex recurve in the leading edges that pointed to a better understanding of turbulence than the designers of the early twentieth century. Despite that Chris half expected to see the tricolour painted on its tailplane, a roundel on the fuselage.

'It's beautiful,' said Chris.

'It'll do,' said the Doctor.

The hangar doors were strictly manual; Chris had to push them open by hand. The big doors were well balanced but heavy and the effort made Chris sweat inside his jacket. He paused once they were open to look out over the aerodrome. The sun was burning off the ground mist, trees were visible as slender shadows at the far end. Chris took a deep breath. The air was clear and fresh.

He thought of the fresh smell of Dep's hair as it caressed his face and shoulders, how he could read her passion in its ceaseless flexing and touching and how it had tightened around his waist when she'd finally lost control.

'Chris?'

'Yes?'

'If you don't mind?' said the Doctor.

'Sorry.'

The Doctor took the rear cockpit and Chris took the front, easing himself into the narrow bucket seat. A leather flying helmet and goggles were hanging off the joystick. Chris pulled the helmet over his head and tried on the goggles. There didn't seem to be a head up display. The instrument panel was made of some kind of wood polished to a deep amber glow. The indicators were simple enough: airspeed indicator, altimeter, VSI, engine temperature and lubricant pressure. They had archaic analogue pointers and were labelled in a language that Chris couldn't read. It didn't worry him. One end was stop, the other was fast – two-thirds along was probably cruising speed. Same with the altimeter except with two pointers, when both the long hand and the short hand were pointing to the top you were probably on the ground.

Chris manipulated the joystick and the pedals, craning his neck to do a visual inspection of the control surfaces. The controls responded smoothly and satisfied that he could handle the plane Chris glanced back at the Doctor who gave him a thumbs-up. Chris stabbed at the big blue button that he hoped was the starter.

The big radial engine caught first time, the propeller spun and blurred. Chris eased the throttle forward and taxied the biplane out of the hangar. There was a clear run for take-off and so, checking that the tail was clear of the doors, Chris pushed the throttle to maximum. The biplane hurled itself forward, bumping across the grass, the nose tilting downwards as the wings caught the air.

The transition to flight was so fast that it took Chris by surprise. The biplane bounced twice on the grass and then it was flying. Instinctively he used the rudder to correct a drift to the right. Watching his speed he eased back on the stick lifting the nose into the fresh blue sky. He felt slight tugs on stick and rudder – it was the wind challenging his control of the biplane. Not much, just a small warning that he was in the domain of aerodynamics now, that the sky was unforgiving, that the price of freedom was always danger.

Chris laughed as the biplane soared into the sky.

'Can you hear me?' asked the Doctor, his voice issuing from the speakers woven into the sides of Chris's flying helmet. An adhesive microphone dangled from the helmet. Chris pressed it to his throat where it stuck.

'Loud and clear,' said Chris. 'Where do you want to go?'

'Head for the coast, I'll direct you from there.'

'Ay ay, skipper.'

'Chris?'

'Yes, Doctor?'

97

'I believe the correct terminology is "roger wilco".'

'Roger wilco.'

'That's better,' said the Doctor.

'Doctor?'

'Yes.'

'Which way is the coast?'

'Turn ninety degrees to starboard.'

Chris started a gentle bank to starboard.

'Doctor?'

'Yes?'

'What does "roger wilco" mean, exactly?'

'Well, "wilco" is obviously a contraction of "will comply".'

Chris levelled the plane out on its new heading.

'So who was Roger?'

'Give it some throttle, Chris,' said the Doctor. 'I want to get over the murder scene some time *before* my next regeneration.'

Their course took them over a gigantic waterfall. So vast and extensive was the plume of spray that, from a distance, Chris had first thought it a bank of unusually low-lying cloud. A great river, at least two kilometres broad, snaked across the plateau and hurled itself a kilometre down the sheer side of an escarpment. The noise of the falling water grew steadily as they approached, until it was so loud it had blotted out the sound of the biplane's engine. They flew over the rim of the fall at a height, according to the biplane's altimeter, of 'squiggle' which to Chris's experienced eye looked to be about four hundred metres. The water had carved a semi-circular notch in the softer stone of the escarpment, leaving isolated pillars of harder rock jutting out of the rushing water like primitive statues. Or perhaps the water hadn't carved the rock, perhaps it had been designed like that.

'Now that,' said the Doctor, 'is what I call landscape gardening.'

There was some turbulence over the fall and Chris had to struggle to keep the biplane on an even heading. Nothing too serious, just a little bump and grind, the sky's reminder to the pilot of its prerogatives.

Beyond the falls the ground fell away to a wide swathe of forested hills, greener and more rugged than the plateau behind. The sea was visible, a smudged line of white and blue in the distant haze. Chris put the plane into a shallow dive, levelling off thirty metres above the tree tops and following the contours of the terrain. At that height, Chris could see colonies of bright orange primates roosting in crudely woven huts amongst the upper branches, either lounging in the sun or scampering from limb to limb. As the biplane approached, the monkeys halted their activities and watched, their pale upturned faces like so many small flowers. Chris was sure that a couple of the small animals waved cheerily at him as he flew overhead.

The Doctor pointed out a small cove and asked Chris to perform a quick orbit over it. The Doctor peered down but the short beach was deserted. As Chris pulled the biplane into another turn a small shape shot up from the forest below and drew level, matching course and speed with nonchalant ease. It was another drone of a similar design to kiKhali. The Doctor introduced it to Chris as aM!xitsa.

The drone asked the Doctor if he'd heard about the murder.

'Heard about it,' said the Doctor, 'I'm investigating it.'

'Well, it wasn't me,' said aM!xitsa. 'I was playing a game of long distance *brownian motion* with a GPS. It can vouch for me.'

'Did you win?' asked the Doctor.

'Against a ship, are you kidding?'

'Then why play?'

'I keep hoping I'll get lucky,' said aM!xitsa. 'It wouldn't be a bad idea if you visited me sometime soon. Our mutual friend is getting a bit frisky.'

'Oh,' said the Doctor. 'Nothing too severe I hope.'

'Nothing I can't handle,' said aM!xitsa.

'I'll drop by later,' said the Doctor.

'Fine,' said aM!xitsa, 'I'll see you then. Nice to meet you, Adjudicator Cwej.' The drone peeled off and dropped back down towards the coast.

'Who's this mutual friend?' asked Chris.

The Doctor didn't answer. Instead he instructed Chris to turn ten degrees to port. 'That should put us over the murder scene in about twenty minutes,' he said.

'What then?'

'I don't know,' said the Doctor. 'Depends on what we find. I'd like to start by retracing vi!Cari's course into the storm and then we'll take it from there.'

'Your friend aM!xitsa was the same design as kiKhali,' said Chris, 'which means it's a defensive drone. I know kiKhali said that God would have detected a drone making an attack but what if it didn't? What if a drone figured out a way of using the storm as camouflage? That's something that God or IDIG hasn't thought of.'

'Good point,' said the Doctor. 'You'd better check that out when we get back.'

Chris kept an eye on the coast. Within minutes he saw the unmistakably jumbled shape of the villa and pointed it out to the Doctor.

'We'll use the villa to mark one side of our search perimeter and use it as a reference point,' said the Doctor. 'I memorized the relevant co-ordinates last night.'

Starting from a position midway between the villa and iSanti Jeni, the Doctor directed Chris to turn out to sea and climb to an altitude of eight hundred metres. They flew straight and level until after half an hour the Doctor told Chris to turn around and fly back the way they'd come but at half the altitude. As they approached the coast for the second time Chris thought he saw some sort of animal sprinting along the beach ahead but it was gone before he got close enough to be certain. He did see somebody on the beach. He recognized the small upright figure despite the distance and imagined the automatic scowl on her face as he waggled his wings in greeting. In response she lifted her arm in a desultory half wave before turning and walking off towards the town.

'Was that Roz?' asked the Doctor.

'Yes,' said Chris.

'Did they teach you how to do a dog-leg search pattern at that academy of yours?'

100

'Just the theory,' said Chris, 'in case we were ever assigned to a frontier world.' There not being a hell of a lot of open space left on Earth in the thirtieth century, even the oceans had churned, sluggish with pollution, under the grey shadow of the overcities.

'I want you to double back over our last course,' said the Doctor, 'but this time I want you to perform a dog-leg pattern, about six hundred metres on each leg.'

'How high do you want us to be?'

'The operative word is "low",' said the Doctor. 'I want us down at six metres.'

The biplane didn't like flying that low and kept raising its nose as the wings interacted with the surface effect of the water. It got harder when the Doctor, grumbling that Chris could have chosen a more appropriate aircraft, climbed out of his cockpit for a better view. He took up position on the left wing near the root, leaning with the wind, one hand hooked casually into his waistband, the other grasping his umbrella which was hooked around one of the wing's bracing wires. Even his slight weight unbalanced the biplane, forcing Chris to keep the joystick partially heeled over in the opposite direction. He had to be careful not to overcompensate; the biplane was far too eager to follow each movement of the stick. Up in the air it didn't matter, altitude gave you space to correct your mistakes. Down here, this close to the water, a careless move could flip you over too fast to correct and send you cartwheeling across the sea. Not like a flitter at all, where even on manual the autopilot kept one beady shortwave eye on the ground for you. Chris realized he was beginning to sweat with the strain.

And the Doctor just hung there, peering into the sea with an expression of absorbed irritation, as if he could whistle up a clue like a magician. 'Watch the spray,' the Doctor called as the undercarriage clipped the top of a wave. 'I don't really want to start swimming just yet.'

What was he looking for? Chris asked himself. What could he possibly hope to find that God had not? A small blue light on the instrument panel caught his attention; it was inset into the face of a small gauge below the altimeter. The needle

101

pointer was stuck resolutely at the bottom of a graduated scale, the last third of which was shaded blue.

'Doctor,' he called, 'I think we're running out of fuel.'

The engine faltered, coughed twice and ran smooth again. Well done, Chris, not the future predictive but the present tense – we *have* run out of fuel, we *are* about to crash into the sea. The Doctor scampered nimbly into his cockpit. 'Gain some height while we still can,' he said, but Chris was already pulling back on the stick. 'I wish you'd told me sooner.'

'The French plane had better endurance,' said Chris.

'Can you see anything that looks like a back-up drive?'

Chris hurriedly scanned the instrument panel. 'No.'

'Sometimes,' muttered the Doctor, 'these people take authenticity just a little bit too far.'

They were still climbing but Chris was detecting a definite slackness when he adjusted the throttle. The engine coughed ominously again. They were probably flying on vapour now.

'Do you think we can make it to the beach?' asked the Doctor.

Chris looked over to where the coast was a dark smudge in the far distance. 'I don't think so. Couldn't we ask God for some inflight refuelling?'

'I'd rather not,' said the Doctor. 'Asking for divine intervention is not my style. Besides, God would never let me live it down.'

The engine coughed one last time and died. Chris put the nose down to maintain airspeed. It was suddenly very quiet.

'Have I ever told you,' asked the Doctor, 'how much I hate swimming?'

'We might not get the chance,' said Chris. 'This thing is nose-heavy. We might just cartwheel when we hit and break up.'

'You,' said the Doctor, 'have been spending far too much time with Bernice. We're not done yet; all we need is a handy last-minute coincidence.'

'Such as?'

'That ocean liner will do nicely.'

Chris banked gently to avoid bleeding off too much airspeed

102

and levelled off with the ocean liner framed with the V-shape of the stalled propeller blades. 'Watch your glide path,' the Doctor told him. 'She's further away than she looks.'

The ocean liner was big, really big. Sixteen kilometres from bow to stern, he was to learn later, a kilometre across and seven hundred metres tall. Without the Doctor's warning the scale of the ship might have fooled Chris, made him think he was closer than he really was, fooled him into a wet landing kilometres short. Even so it was not until he was close enough to make out the tiny passengers on the decks that he really got his mind around its size. The Doctor radioed the liner and asked for permission to land.

'Sure,' said the liner and lit up an empty promenade deck with a double line of pink holograms. Chris circled twice above the liner's funnels using the hot air to gain a small margin of error and then glided into a final approach.

It was eerie landing with just the sound of wind humming in the wing braces. Promenade decks and games courts flicked by underneath, cabins and swimming pools, comms antennae and gantries, lifeboats as big as houses and landing pads with helicopters and VTOL jets parked in untidy rows. Gusts of wind rebounded off the cliffs of portholes and pulled the biplane from side to side. The joystick trembled under Chris's palm. The empty promenade deck rushed up silently to meet them. He flared at the last possible moment, putting the rear wheel down first. The forward undercarriage hit next, skidded, and then bounced twice as if reluctant to settle. Chris pushed hard on the rudder as the rear of the biplane slewed sharply to the right and skidded to a halt three metres from the end of the deck. The joystick was still trembling. Chris wondered what could be causing the strange vibration until he let go and found that his hands were still shaking.

'Did you enjoy that?' asked the Doctor.

Chris nodded, unable to speak.

'I could tell,' said the Doctor.

Bernice was trying to explain the methodology of Martian archaeology to saRa!qava and why she needed her help.

'What do you want to know?' asked saRa!qava.

It didn't seem to surprise saRa!qava that Bernice and the Doctor had taken over the investigation of vi!Cari's murder. These things were generally left to the IDIG but only because people associated with IDIG were the ones that wanted to be involved. 'Some people just love being nosy,' she had said. To make it worse even the Interest Groups were just collections of individuals with shared interests; you didn't have to *join* anything, you didn't even have to register your *interest*. It didn't matter how often the Doctor tried to explain, Bernice still found it difficult to believe that a society could function without some kind of structure. It was all so maddeningly vague.

'I need some help,' said Bernice. 'I'm looking for some information but I don't know how to get it.'

'Let me just finish with Smelly then,' said saRa!qava.

'Smelly' was an unnamed female baby of nine months, one of saRa!qava's six daughters, although Bernice had forgotten to ask whether saRa!qava was the father or the mother. The little girl was howling as saRa!qava rubbed moisturizing lotion into her plump belly. She had luminous orange eyes, red hair and, judging from the volume, high capacity lungs. Like every baby Bernice had ever met Smelly gave off the faint but unmistakable aroma of sour milk, which was why she was called Smelly. In another year or so she would be talking and would probably be calling herself something like 'Poo' or 'Yaga'. SaRa!qava said that most people adopted at least two or more names as they got older and she knew a few who had given themselves numbers instead.

The idea offended Bernice for some reason, perhaps because her identity was so bound up with her name. Her academic credentials were all phoney, she had the ultimate in no fixed abodes, but her name was her own. Before she was even old enough to separate the universe into *me* and *not-me*, her mother and father had looked down like gods and gifted Bernice with her name. A small collection of letters, a pair of syllables. A flimsy thing to build your personality around. It was all that she had left of her parents.

SaRa!qava's people sloughed off their names like snakes shedding their skins. Their identities were as protean as their society, with its non-laws and non-organizations. They discarded the past without thought and stepped into the dawn of a bright new future. And if the dawn wasn't bright? They damn well manufactured themselves one that was.

SaRa!qava finished with Smelly who immediately stopped howling. The child started bouncing up and down in her mother's lap, waving her plump arms in the air.

'No,' saRa!qava told her. 'You're supposed to crawl today. You have to do it or otherwise your legs will atrophy and drop off.'

Smelly's bouncing became more insistent.

'Oh, all right then,' said saRa!qava. She lifted the child above her head. 'House!' she called and Smelly drifted into the air where, gurgling with delight, she began to do slow orbits around the kitchen ceiling.

Go for it, kid, thought Bernice. Why crawl when you can fly?

'Another one destined for the Weird Aviation Interest Group,' she said.

'I hope not,' said saRa!qava. 'You should see the contraption Dep is building in her room. She says it's going to fly under its own power but I'd be happier if she stuck on an impeller for back-up.'

'Databases?' prompted Bernice.

'Why don't you tell me what you're looking for,' said saRa!qava.

Bernice was planning to follow a Martian data collation system she'd used on some of her better funded archaeological digs. It involved pulling in information from every possible source, from local legends to the arcane measurements of the bio-statisticians, and compiling it into a single independent database. With that as your baseline data, you input your actual findings at the dig as they occurred and that was supposed to give you an enhanced insight into whatever the hell it was you were looking at, it being an article of faith amongst Martians that one can never have too much data. Aiyix-sith, they called it – the time telescope.

It was also supposed to take six weeks to set up – patience being another Martian trait. But Bernice was betting on saRa!qava's help and saRa!qava's people's obvious expertise with machines.

Which turned out to be a problem because machines, here on the sphere, had rights. Which meant you didn't so much as access data as ask for it – politely. 'What's in someone's mind,' saRa!qava explained, 'is their business.' There were non-sentient data storage units but they used the same displaced hyperspace storage medium as drones, ships and God – meaning that occasionally they achieved self-awareness. Meaning that according to saRa!qava you sometimes didn't know you were talking to a *person* until that person started talking back. Sometimes the machine would wait hundreds of years before registering as a sentience. Nobody knew why.

Except God, of course. God knew everything, or at least claimed it did.

Machines didn't think like flesh and blood people, didn't obey the same imperatives that were hardwired into the messy lump of cold porridge that passed for data processing in an upright biped. Human-built machines either behaved like idiot savants or were carefully designed to mimic human mannerisms. Gone native already, Bernice, she thought, saying and thinking *machines* not *robots*. Machines here had their own thoughts, their own imperatives, motives and agendas that were sometimes impossible to fathom, even for a native like saRa!qava.

Not that it seemed to bother saRa!qava any – why *should* people think alike. Any more than it bothered her that machines were smarter, or faster, or more efficient. It bothered Bernice and being bothered made her feel a bit guilty.

With saRa!qava's help she ordered a virgin portable data terminal from central stores, which told them ten minutes. Bernice used the time to clarify some of the terminology. 'Drones' were always people, 'remote-drones' were machines slaved to another person – ships in particular used them to hang out in places where they wouldn't fit. Remote-drones were also called 'jobbers', presumably because they did all the jobs. 'Constructs' were remote-drones that looked like animals, although never like people because that would be in bad taste. 'Houses' were generally not people but occasionally they became one. Sometimes those that changed transferred to a ship or a drone body; for some reason a fairly high percentage of shuttles were run by ex-houses. They even had an Interest Group, the DSIG – the initials standing for Domestic Service. 'Recipes mostly,' said saRa!qava, 'and how to get stains out of vulnerable fabrics.'

The data terminal arrived via the House's freight lift. It was the size and shape of a cricket ball and covered in short pink fur. Central stores apologized when they complained and said it thought saRa!qava wanted it for one of her children. It could provide them with another if they were willing to wait?

'Never mind,' said Bernice, 'it'll do.'

Smelly thought so too and dropped onto the table to play with the new toy. 'Don't worry,' said saRa!qava as the child tried to stuff it into her mouth, 'she can't damage it.'

'How does it work?' asked Bernice.

'You just tell it what you want,' said saRa!qava. 'It's remote-linked to the network and to God.'

In a strange way the very ease of accessing the data caused Bernice the most problems. On the 'puter equipment she was used to there would have been small delays compiling such a large array database. There was hardly a gap between Bernice finishing a request and the terminal saying – *ready*. She realized that it had become her habit to use those little moments of impatience to collect her thoughts. She found herself suffering from information meltdown – like turning on a shower and getting a face full of scalding water.

'Why was vi!Cari so unpopular?' asked Bernice.

SaRa!qava shrugged. They were having a break for ginger tea and biscuits. Smelly was amusing herself by throwing the terminal off the table and lunging for it as House picked it up again. Bernice was forcing herself not to think about the database, trying to keep her eyes off the output screens that hung around the kitchen like heraldic pennants. A new screen appeared each time Bernice created another subset in her database whether she wanted one or not. She couldn't get them to stop and they were stacked three deep in places.

'It annoyed people,' said saRa!qava.

'Enough for someone to want to kill it?'

'Do you have children?'

'No,' said Bernice. 'Haven't got round to it yet.'

'But you've dealt with children, looked after them?'

'Let's just say that I've been in the same room as children,' said Bernice. 'Some of them even lived to tell the tale.'

'Have you ever got into a why loop with a child?' asked saRa!qava.

Bernice gave her a blank look.

'It's when a child asks, "Why?", about something obvious, like "why is the sky blue?" So you say because the atmosphere refracts the light. And the child asks "Why?" So you explain about refraction and –'

'The child asks why again, and again,' said Bernice. 'I've had that done to me.' Hell, she thought, I do it to the Doctor all the time.

'And suddenly you find yourself trying to explain what an elementary particle is in toddler terms and asking yourself why you're doing this and you can't stop even though you *know* they're just going to ask it again.'

Not me, thought Bernice. It's *Because I say so* and *Shut up and drink your milk*, long before we get to sub-atomic particles. I'm probably a very flawed person.

'It has to be one of the most irritating things I can think of,' said saRa!qava, 'and vi!Cari was a billion times worse.'

Why? Bernice almost asked. However it was done, someone went to a lot of trouble to murder vi!Cari. What precisely was it that vi!Cari did that got someone that pissed off with it? But saRa!qava was giving her definite *I don't want to talk about it* vibes when it came to the details so Bernice backed off.

'You haven't input ship positions,' said saRa!qava.

'You fly ships inside the sphere?'

SaRa!qava looked blank.

The trouble with the TARDIS translator, thought Bernice, was that it was so good you didn't know when you were making a mistake. 'Spaceships,' she said. 'We are talking about spaceships?'

'Not inside the sphere,' said saRa!qava, 'but close, docked at the spaceport or near the system. I can't think of anything else that could shoot down a drone. Apart from another drone.'

'Through the side of the sphere?'

'Oh yes,' said saRa!qava. 'The ASBIG came up with a lot of new weapons for the war. Remote forced quantum singularities, controlled hyperspace breaks and something called a Pin-Stripe Cattle Grate which nobody ever talks about.'

Bernice told the terminal to give her a listing of all spaceships docked or near the sphere at the time of the murder. 'No such thing as too much data,' she muttered to herself. The terminal put up yet another screen – making twenty-three so far – and asked her what radius she wanted the search volume to be.

'Thirty light-years,' suggested saRa!qava.

So Bernice told the terminal thirty light-years, speaking the words before the sense of them had a chance to set in. That couldn't be right, no crukking way, no weapon she knew had a range of thirty light-years. Oh my God, they could take out the Daleks without raising a sweat. Non-aggression pact with the Time Lords, the Doctor had said. *Shit!* Now she believed it. Little Smelly playing *catch-catch-can* with the terminal, heir to a civilization that could move in and roll over human space in any time period you care to mention. If they got the notion to do so. Which Bernice didn't think they did except now saRa!qava was talking about a war, past tense but recent, Bernice thought. People didn't talk about the War, capital W unless it was less than half a generation back, longer than that and it stopped being *the* War and picked up a label, 'the Thousand Day War' or 'the War of Jenkins's Ear'. Something to differentiate it from all the other wars that flesh was heir to.

She remembered writing a paper about the semantics of conflict once, during a particularly excruciatingly boring journey on a clapped-out Draconian free-trader. Something about how naming a war that hadn't happened yet created an expectation that it would happen. She'd used World War III as her primary example – or had the argument been that naming the war meant that you didn't have to fight it? The Doctor had once mentioned a World War IV, did they skip III and go directly to IV?

A war against some insects, saRa!qava was saying, but everything was cool now and the insects turned out to be OK people in the end. One of them had been at the party last night – talking to Roz of all people.

'They started it,' said saRa!qava.

Yeah, thought Bernice. Of course they did.

They tried to check the ranges by calling up data on weapons capabilities only to be informed that no such information was held in public records. 'That just means that ASBIG didn't leave any of it on public record,' said saRa!qava. ASBIG being, would you believe it, the aggressive ship-building Interest Group. 'You could always ask God, I'm sure it knows.'

'I'm trying to avoid religion at the moment,' said Bernice.

'May you be struck down by a thunderbolt,' said God. 'Oops, sorry, bad taste remark there.'

Roz woke up with the lingering aftertaste of forgotten dreams like spaces in her head. Stumbling into the bathroom she tried to wash them away with cold water from the sink and caught sight of her reflection in the floor-length mirror. There was a ghost memory of a wounding. A soundless, painless detonation between her breasts, of falling into stagnant water. She watched her reflection touch the exact spot with its fingertips and shuddered. A blaster wound, she thought, in a fatal area. Most definitely not one of her fine collection of line of duty injuries. She pulled oil from her travel kit and used her fingers to rake it through the rough untidy curls of her hair. The curls were beginning to mat near the roots, it having been too long since she'd last combed them out. She found an afro-comb in her kit and went to work, pulling ruthlessly at her hair and trying to remember a time when it hadn't been shot through with grey.

* * *

There were notes from the others scattered around the villa. Chris's glowed in mid air above the coffee pot. AERIAL RECON – CRIME SCENE W/T DOCTOR. Roz waved her hand through the letters and they vanished. In the living room Benny had left a yellow memo stuck to a pile of clothes. The note warned Roz that it was going to be hot again and that she might find these items useful. A peace offering, decided Roz. Or, having looked at the clothes, possibly a practical joke. The sleeveless top was OK, made of some lightweight cotton/silk hybrid but she had to lie on her back on the sofa with her legs in the air to wriggle into the lycra shorts. She found the final note written on lavender writing paper and placed in her blaster carry case. She recognized the spidery hand as the Doctor's.

My dear Roslyn. As you know we find ourselves faced with an interesting mystery here. Chris is likely to be somewhat distracted by other interests. Bernice too is liable to find her attention diverted by other matters. For reasons that I am unable to articulate, my own scope for action is severely circumscribed in these circumstances. I am therefore relying on you to bring this matter to a satisfactory conclusion. Try not to tell God anything unless you have to.

The Doctor.

PS – leave the weapon at home.

PPS – you may encounter a drone called aM!xitsa. He is a friend and entirely trustworthy.

PPPS – eat this message immediately after reading.

Roz folded the paper, popped it into her mouth and chewed. It tasted of peppermint.

Roz decided to walk into town, telling herself that a good sense of the local physical geography would help maintain her *situational awareness*. Her instructors at the academy had been big on *situational awareness*, on the investigator gaining a global perception of the crime, both secular and

111

spiritual. The crime scene, they repeatedly said, is more than just the scene of the crime. It is a space that encompasses the mind and spirit of the victims, of the witnesses and the perpetrators. It represents the amorphous and corrosive power of chaos. It is the task of the investigator to confine it and give it shape. To bring order out of chaos.

It was the routine of the investigator, thought Roz, to round up the likely suspects and mindprobe them until one of them confesses. That was how it had gone down on the street. Guilty until proven innocent, that was street adjudication. After all, the street logic went, everyone was guilty of something.

You can bet that it wouldn't work here, she thought. Too damn liberal to allow mindprobes and half the suspects were going to be robots. People killed their own kind, she knew that, not just street logic but backed up by the statistics. Wives murdered husbands, children murdered parents and scum from the Undertown murdered other scum from the Undertown. Roz was willing to bet her sister's fortune that robot boy had been offed by another robot.

Back on Earth in the mid thirtieth century if a crime was committed by a robot you went looking for its operator. The robots she grew up with weren't self-aware, or if they were they were keeping *real* quiet about it. A robot was usually just the murder weapon, a more sophisticated version of the traditional blunt instrument. But not here, she thought; here they had robots with attitude and Roz wasn't going to let her preconceptions get in the way of that fact. After all Mama Forrester didn't have no stupid children.

Which gave the lie to the hereditary theory of intelligence.

Roz knew that what she needed was that other staple of successful street adjudication – a local informant.

Roz met the woman at the point where the dunes washed against the base of the hill. Her very first thought was that her mama had spent a fortune trying to get her skin that dark. Her second thought was that she had surprised some kind of weird humanoid animal, but looking closer it was obvious that it was a human female she was looking at. A tall one with long limbs and a compact muscled torso, crouching naked in the middle of the track and staring back at Roz. The hair was matted into dreadlocks that hung over broad shoulders, the almond-shaped eyes were coal black, the nose was broad and close to the face. Definitely a human face. And yet there was something bestial about the set of the limbs, something animal in those dark eyes. There was something else in them as well, an expression that Roz found impossible to read; pain perhaps or pleading. Roz reached automatically for the blaster that the Doctor had told her to leave at the villa and wasn't holstered at her waist.

The woman pulled back her lips to bare white teeth.

Roz stepped back in shock and decided that this was absolutely the last time she ever listened to the Doctor's advice on personal safety.

And then the woman was running away, the turn so fast and smooth that Roz was barely aware of it.

'Wait,' she cried, but it was too late, the woman had gone.

Roz turned at a soft sound behind her. A flattened metal ovoid whispered past her and sped off in the same direction as the woman. 'Excuse me,' said the drone politely and then it too was gone.

Is everyone on this damned sphere an eccentric? Roz asked herself. It wasn't going to make her job any easier. Something about the woman's features nagged at her. The people of the sphere exhibited a wide range of divergent physical characteristics. She supposed it was possible that amongst a population of two trillion there could be any number of individuals whose features were arranged like the woman's. It had to be a coincidence, a little bit of convergent evolution. After all, Roz was certain that *she* was the only pure-blood African around.

She reached the edge of the sea and stood for a moment to watch the breakers. The incoming tide was slowly obliterating a trail of footprints in the sand. 'Woman Friday,' said Roz, thinking of the classic vid starring Robert Roundtree and Peter O'Toole. She should ask Bernice about that one, late twentieth century trivia being Benny's favourite obsession.

113

She was beginning to sweat. It was getting hot again and the dunes had been heavy-going, even with the soft-soled pumps Benny had left out for her. The water looked very cool and inviting. *Ngizadada ngomso*, she thought, quoting her grandmother – I will swim tomorrow. Today I work under a clear sky – *Namhlanje ngiyasebenza ngaphansi izulu elizolileyo*.

Umakhulu had also tried to teach her the proper walk of a woman. Goddess, she'd spent hours with a videobook balanced on her head while her mama lamented and asked the ancestors how she could have borne such a graceless child. The walk came back to Roz there on the beach, the slow steady distance-eating steps from the days when a woman might travel half the morning to fetch water. Days that her grandmother, born and raised at the Io Kraal, could no more remember than Roz could.

But it was practical when walking under the hot sun.

SaRa!qava's extended family came stampeding down for breakfast with all the decorum of a herd of elephants arriving at the last waterhole before the drought. The adolescents descended first, long-limbed and awkward as they walked through Bernice's floating screens and issued breakfast orders in over-loud voices. A squadron of toddlers flew down the connecting stairs, joining Smelly in her random orbits amongst the baking bread. Young adults, all of whom had been to the party the night before, crept in one by one and started looking for hangover cures. Bernice was secretly pleased to find that saRa!qava was sometimes forced to yell at her children just like any normal mother. In the end sheer weight of numbers forced Bernice and saRa!qava out of the kitchen and into the street. It took some outrageous bribery to get Smelly to relinquish her grip on the terminal. God insisted that it was going to be another glorious day and so they walked down to the esplanade. As they walked the datascreens lined up behind them like obedient children, an oxymoron saRa!qava insisted upon, and followed along, their images unwavering and clear even in the bright sunshine.

They chose a bistro at the western end of the esplanade

where they had a clear view of the harbour. The tide had come in, the sea covering the pebble beach and floating the disparate collection of boats. Despite this the painter Bernice had seen the day before was still hard at work, standing calf-deep in the water as he patched up his mural. Bernice asked saRa!qava who he was and whether he ever stopped.

'Oh, that's just beRut,' said saRa!qava, 'and he's been working on that ugly thing of his for years. He almost had it finished last month but a micro *tsunami* washed bits of it off.'

'Hasn't anyone told him he can't paint?'

SaRa!qava frowned. The question had obviously never occurred to her. 'I doubt it,' she said. 'He's not annoying anyone and he's not exactly the most communicative person in the world.'

There were other people on the esplanade, out walking or sitting at the tables set out in front of the restaurants. Although saRa!qava admitted that you could order identical refreshments in any establishment in the sphere she was adamant that each place had its own atmosphere. Shouts and laughter came from the harbour where a group of teenagers were preparing one of the ocean-going trimarans. A remote-drone was busily cleaning the esplanade's paving stones with short bursts of its dorsal fields. In the distance at the end of the breakwater Bernice saw a couple of indeterminate gender holding each other and necking, or rubbing noses or what-ever it was couples did here. There was a holiday air to the proceedings, one that in this place, Bernice realized with a shock, went on every single day.

Many of the passers-by stopped briefly by their table to say hello to saRa!qava and have themselves introduced to Bernice. Someone the size of a man and the shape of a cockroach sauntered over and thanked them for a wonderful party last night. 'I do hope your friend is feeling better this morning,' said the cockroach to Bernice. 'Please give her my regards.'

'I'll be sure to do that,' said Bernice.

A quartet of very human-looking women walked past, wearing sun hats with outrageous brims and pushing a gigantic bath chair. Something touched her memory like the brush of a butterfly's wing. Bernice turned to ask saRa!qava who the women were but when she turned back again they had vanished. The slapping sound of the waves against the harbour wall came back before she noticed it had gone.

'Is this crude little thing really going to help?' asked God.

'If solving this murder was a mere matter of getting the right database,' said Bernice, 'you'd have done it already. Isn't that right, Mr Omniscient?'

'Please don't call me that,' said God. 'Too many people think it's true.'

'Isn't it?' asked saRa!qava. 'That's the first time I've heard that.'

'I'm just very well informed,' said God. 'There's a big difference.'

'Why do they call you God then?' asked Bernice.

'It was a joke, a nickname I got when I was still creating myself.'

'Well, if you could get off your pantheon for a moment,' said Bernice, 'you can tell me whether you monitored any large energy surges the night of the murder.'

'Apart from a gigantic thunderstorm?'

'Apart from that.'

'Not a sausage.'

'So much for that theory.'

'Is that Roz?' asked saRa!qava, pointing up the breakwater.

'I'm not sure,' said Bernice. It could have been Roz except the walk was wrong. The movement was slow, relaxed and upright, with a sway to the hips that wasn't at all like the Roz Forrester that Bernice knew. The woman saw them watching and waved, Bernice waved back. The woman strode towards them, a brisk impatient march that was so instantly recognizable that Bernice had to wonder whether she'd been tricked by the distance. All that sunlight glaring off the water, she told herself. I need sunglasses.

'How's it going?' asked Roz.

Bernice told her about the time telescope and the frustrating little gaps where the data was stored in someone's mind. Roz frowned when she heard about the ships and their long-range weaponry. She said she thought she might be able to fill in some of the gaps. 'I met a guy called feLixi at the party,' she said to saRa!qava. 'Does he live locally?'

'Just the other side of town.'

Roz asked for directions and saRa!qava pointed down the esplanade with instructions to turn right at the end and look out for the weirdest looking building. 'That's feLixi's.'

When Roz was a safe distance away saRa!qava turned to Bernice and raised an eyebrow. 'Well,' she said, 'you don't think?'

'I'm certainly not *going* to think it,' said Bernice, 'thank you very much.'

'What kind of game is long-distance brownian motion?' asked Chris, hoping to put the Doctor off his next shot.

The Doctor squinted down the length of the deck, figuring out the angles. The red target puck was currently at the centre of a grid of white squares painted on the deckplanks. Chris had managed to place three of his yellow pucks in a rough line between the red puck and the starting line. He couldn't see how the Doctor was going to get around him, not without going for a trick shot that ricocheted off the cabin bulkhead and that was all cluttered by the legs of divans and sunchairs lined up against it.

'It's a guessing game that the machines play,' said the Doctor. 'They tag a molecule and try to predict where it will end up after a set period of time. At the easiest level you use a liquid, the next level you use a gas and the hardest is tracking a molecule through a superheated plasma.' The Doctor hefted his stick, performed a practice stroke and then, with great casualness, smacked his puck down the deck.

'There's plenty of other variables,' said the Doctor. 'The time period, the exact energy state of the medium.'

At first the puck seemed to be travelling in a straight line, then suddenly it curved, described a half circle around Chris's pucks, slowed down and gently nuzzled up to the red target puck. There was a scattering of applause from the watching spectators.

Chris looked at the Doctor.

117

'It's all in the wrist action,' said the Doctor.

Which left Chris facing a pretty problem in regards the disposition of his pucks. To score he had to get his puck closer to the red than the Doctor's blue – which was right up against the red. Meaning Chris had to find a way to shift the Doctor's puck and get his own in between. It had to be the puck you shot, said the rules; you couldn't knock one of your earlier pucks closer. He thought he'd been clever, planning ahead, building that barrier of his own pucks but the Doctor had sailed his blue around it. He should have known better than to try and outplan the Doctor, who always had some new trick up his sleeve. Now he had two shots left and the Doctor had one.

Chris saw a way to win but he was going to have to be sneaky.

And the first step was to get the Doctor thinking about something else. 'It must take an enormous fusion reactor to drive a ship this big,' he said.

'Not really,' said the Doctor. 'What it does take is about twenty hydrogen-burning steam turbines geared to drive four very large screws.'

'Gosh,' said Chris, as he kicked his puck into position on the starting line, 'how do you know that?'

'Oh, that's easy,' said the Doctor. 'It's the steam that gives the engines away and I counted the number of funnels when we made our final approach – Oh, bad luck.'

'Damn,' said Chris. He watched his puck settle into position – right where he wanted it. 'If you're going to use hydrogen anyway why not a fusion reactor?'

'Aesthetics, I imagine,' said the Doctor. 'An ocean liner under full steam does have a certain grandeur. Have I ever told you about the *Titanic*?'

'No.'

'Oh, a magnificent ship.' The Doctor knocked his puck up the deck. It described a mirror-image trajectory of his previous shot before nestling up to the opposite side of the target puck. Exactly as Chris had predicted. 'Terribly advanced for its day, the *Titanic* – they said it was unsinkable.'

Chris caught the eye of a female spectator who was leaning

against the bulkhead in the wrong place. He made furtive little waving motions with his hand until the woman got the idea and moved out of the way. He checked the Doctor to see if he had noticed. 'What happened to it?'

'It sank on its maiden voyage,' said the Doctor. 'Tragic. Bad luck really because the idea of sealable compartments was basically sound.'

Chris swung and hit his puck with such force that it was lifted clear of the deck for the first ten metres. At first everything went according to plan. The puck ricocheted off the bulkhead, smacked into the puck which Chris had placed earlier which in turn hit one of the Doctor's away from the target puck. Things began to deteriorate from then on. The first puck hurtled off at the wrong angle and smacked into one of the barrier pucks which hit the target puck just as – Chris had by now lost track of where everything was going – another puck slammed into the target from the other direction. The first puck hit yet another puck, jumped off the deck, ricocheted off the deck railing and slammed into the target. There was a crisp sound like glass cracking.

There was a scattering of ironic applause.

'Yes,' said the Doctor, 'I thought you were going to do something like that.'

They strolled down the deck to examine the carnage. The target puck had been cracked right across its top face. The Doctor scooped it up and turned it over in his hands.

'When is a lightning bolt not a lightning bolt?' he asked.

Chris who knew a cue when he heard one said, 'I don't know. When is a lightning bolt not a lightning bolt?'

'When it's a projected energy weapon,' said the Doctor. He tossed the damaged puck back onto the deck. 'I doubt vi!Cari found the punchline very funny either.'

119

6

Faces in the Water

Another dirty day is brokenly dribbling.
Gotta get my gun and blast your sibling
Down around in the undercity town.
Gotta get away before they bring me down.
Adjudicator Truth by Hith's With Attitude
From the HvLP: *Terrorformed* (2952)

She was wading waist deep in the bile-coloured water of
some nameless Undertown canal. Her left shoulder hurt,
there were new dents in her armour and a vicious welt on her
right cheek. The water dragged at her legs as she struggled
after the metamorph. She was tired and hurt and she wanted
to lie down and sleep.

'For Goddess' sake,' she shouted, 'stand still so I can kill
you.'

Perhaps the metamorph heard her because it stopped
running then. Perhaps it too was tired of the chase.

Forrester knew, even before the metamorph turned to face
her, knew with a sick certainty whose face the alien had
borrowed this time.

Her blaster was heavy, the grip slippery with moisture. It
dragged at her hand as she struggled to haul her arm up into a
firing stance. Her own face, bracketed in the sights, looked
back at her. The eyes were wide, pleading.

Forrester thumbed her blaster to its highest setting.

The metamorph reached out her hands to her.

She shot it in the chest.

She noted the surprised look on her face, the fist-sized hole in her chest. Watched herself tumble backwards into the stinking water.

Somebody called her name – Martle?

Forrester let the blaster fall listlessly to her side.

Somebody called her name – feLixi.

She was all right, the metamorph was five years' dead and she was a very long way from the Undertown. She was lying on a canvas blast chair in feLixi's listening room and the soft roaring was the sound of the sea. The lights had been lowered and feLixi's face was a pale blur above her.

'What happened?' she asked.

'According to aTraxi you'd been drinking *flashback*.'

'Is it pink?'

'Yes,' said feLixi.

'Oh,' groaned Roz. 'At the party. What does it do? No, don't tell me – it stimulates the memory.'

'You're supposed to drink it with a mixer. Here,' feLixi held out a glass, 'drink some of this.'

Roz cautiously accepted the glass. 'What is it?'

'Something called *purge*.'

'That's not a very romantic name.'

'It's not a very romantic drink,' said feLixi. 'But it should clean out your head a bit.'

Roz swallowed a mouthful. It tasted of nothing, like distilled water. 'Could you turn up the lights? I could do with a bit of harsh unreality.'

When saRa!qava had said weird she had meant *weird*. FeLixi's house was shaped like a rocketship that had buried itself nose first into the ground. Not like a spaceship, but an honest-to-God, cartoon rocketship the colour of old brass, with three fins sweeping into the air above an unlikely exhaust nozzle and a double line of portholes down the front. It sat between two normal buildings and listed backwards ten degrees. A white picket fence separated it from the street. There was a gate, and a path made from unevenly laid stone flags led up a short earth ramp to where an upside-down airlock door hung open. FeLixi told her later

121

that the door couldn't be closed.

Inside it was worse, with tilted ceiling/floors on which fixtures and control surfaces were bolted. You had to climb up a ladder to reach each floor in turn. The whole of the third floor was taken up by a spherical chamber that rotated on gimbals to maintain a level floor. Sensors mounted on one of the fins picked up sounds from outside and relayed them into the chamber. FeLixi called it his 'listening room'. 'I like to listen to the sea,' he had told Roz when she first arrived. 'It's soothing.'

Too soothing, she thought, because it had lulled her into sleep and remembrance. Two things that Roz thought she had little time for, and things that she felt she'd done far too much of since she'd arrived on the sphere. Maybe, she thought, this is what getting old is all about. Perhaps when the years behind outnumber the years ahead the balance of your life shifts; you begin to look backwards. Maybe you should check what's in the glass before drinking.

'Actually,' said feLixi, 'people like us shouldn't drink that stuff at all. It tends to stimulate the intense memories and that's rarely pleasant.'

Roz sat up and swung her legs off the blast chair. 'I feel better now.'

'ATraxi says most of the *flashback* residue has gone.'

'Who's aTraxi?'

FeLixi grimaced. 'My house,' he said. 'I gave it a name. Well, I thought since it was supposed to be a ship and ships have names –' He stopped talking and gave Roz an amused look. 'This doesn't mean anything to you, does it?'

Roz *was* puzzled. 'Why shouldn't you name your house?'

FeLixi sat on the edge of the acceleration chair. 'Only people are supposed to have names,' he said. 'Otherwise it gets confusing.'

'It's not –?'

He grinned. 'Definitely not. In fact I installed the dumbest machine available. I crewed on various ships for ten years and after spending that much time cooped up with a very smart machine like a VAS you want as much stupidity as you can get.'

'Did you know vi!Cari?' asked Roz.

'Are you investigating me?' He looked amused.

'No,' said Roz, 'I'm just curious.'

'I only knew it during the war, although I knew it had taken up residency here in iSanti Jeni. I doubt anybody really *knew* it. You get antisocial machines the same way you get antisocial organics.'

'It wasn't very popular,' said Roz. 'Do you know why?'

'It used to do things that annoyed people.'

'Such as?'

'It used to gatecrash parties it wasn't invited to,' said feLixi. 'Don't laugh, around here that's a stoning offence. I also heard a rumour that vi!Cari caused the *micro-tsunami* that washed away beRut's mural.'

'Why would it do that?'

'Have you seen that mural?' asked feLixi. 'Vi!Cari probably thought he was doing us all a favour by wiping it out. BeRut is another one who doesn't get invited to parties. Actually I'm surprised they weren't friends. They had a lot in common.'

'Except beRut's still walking around.'

'Yeah,' said feLixi, 'except that.'

A moment of stillness – then gravity takes you in her arms and pulls you *down*. The Doctor reached across his chest with his right hand for the handle marked PULL ME, caught hold and pulled. He heard the ripping sound of unfolding silk; at least he hoped that's what it was. If it was the unfolding sound of ripping silk, the trip to the ground was going to be much faster than he'd anticipated. The harness grabbed him under the armpits and shook him about – just to get his attention. And then he was floating under a rectangular canopy of silk. He glanced downwards. ISanti Jeni was a jumble of white blocks a long way below. He'd asked Chris to climb to two thousand metres before bailing out. That way if the parachute had failed he would have had plenty of time to think of something on the way down. Last words probably.

The Doctor had just got his bearings sorted out when the parachute started talking to him. It was, he had to admit, a good voice, a rich and comforting voice. If a St Bernard could speak it would speak with a voice like that. 'Good afternoon,' said the parachute. 'Although I am generally classified as a class twenty technological device I'd like to take this opportunity to assure you that I incorporate a full range of modern safety features to make your descent to the ground as safe and as pleasant as possible.'

If only, thought the Doctor, Chris had chosen something a bit more practical than a biplane, something with VTOL capacity that could land directly on the esplanade.

'Our altitude is now fifteen hundred and sixty-one metres and our rate of descent is twelve kilometres an hour. Did you have a particular landing site in mind or would you rather just splash down any old place?'

'The esplanade if you don't mind.'

'I'm easy,' said the parachute.

The biplane buzzed past. The Doctor waved at Chris to show that everything was fine. Interesting set of priorities, thought the Doctor. The biplane is thicker than two short planks but the parachute is practically sentient.

'Would you like some music?' asked the parachute.

'Do you have anything by Duke Ellington?'

'I'm afraid not.'

'Play me something soothing and appropriate.'

The music when it started sounded like a chamber piece scored for woodwinds, strings and drum kit. There was an echo in the melody line that was hauntingly familiar. The Doctor found himself thinking of lyrics but they belonged to a rougher age and an alien planet a long way away. *That he's all right in the city/he's just hanging around.* One of Ace's bands, he thought, the Garrotters or something like that. A lot of strange noises used to blare out of Ace's room in the early days.

I should fall out of the sky more often, he decided. It was very peaceful and it gave him a chance to think.

The parachute informed him when he got below eight hundred metres. At that height he could easily make out Benny sitting outside a bistro with saRa!qava. People on the esplanade were looking up and pointing.

124

'I've changed my mind,' said the Doctor. 'I want to land on the beach.'

'The one currently covered in half a metre of water?'

'That's the one.'

'You do know that there are a number of aquatic surface craft in the vicinity?'

'Well, land me in one of the gaps.'

'You're not making this very easy.'

'I can do it on manual if you like.'

'No, no,' said the parachute. 'Getting the bloodstains off the spidersilk is such a pain. I'll do it.'

'Thank you.'

'Your feet will get wet.'

'I'll live.'

'I'll get wet.'

'You'll . . . continue to function at optimum levels.'

'Oh well, that's a relief.'

'Can I ask you a personal question?'

'If you must.'

'Aren't you a bit smart to be operating a parachute?'

'It's a hobby.'

'Oh.'

'I'm with the Esoteric and Useless Genetic Manipulation Interest Group. I spend most of my time designing totally redundant types of tree. I have a remote-drone available for when I want to get about.'

'Why not get a drone body full time?'

'Well,' said the parachute, 'people expect you to do stuff when you've got a full-time body. I'm only rated a one point three so they try to take advantage.'

'So you're happy being a parachute then?'

'It feels good to be needed,' said the parachute. 'Watch out, ground coming up.'

The Doctor went in up to his knees. There was a boat on either side of him and he could touch both the keels without straightening his arms. 'Good shot,' he said.

'Give us a moment to repack.' The straps tugged at the Doctor's shoulders as the parachute folded itself back into the pack. 'You can take me off now.'

'Can I drop you somewhere?' asked the Doctor.

'Ha ha,' said the parachute. '*Drop* me somewhere. That's very funny. Up on the esplanade will be fine. I'll call in my remote from there.'

'It might take a while. There's somebody I want to talk to first.'

'Doesn't bother me. I can work on my trees anywhere.'

The Doctor waded towards the harbour wall. 'What kind of trees?'

'I'm designing one that will grow on an asteroid.'

'Sounds simple enough,' said the Doctor. 'An atavistic silicon outer shell, gallium arsenic solar cell leaves driving a pico-electric systolic pumping system.'

'That bit's easy enough,' said the parachute. 'It's getting it to look like an apple tree that's a bugger.'

The Doctor reached the point on the harbour wall where the artist was working and looked over his shoulder. 'I don't know much about art,' he said, 'but I know a mural when I see one.'

'Go away,' said the artist, without looking away from his work.

'My name's the Doctor and this is my friend – Parachute. We're conducting a survey on behalf of the Worldsphere Society for the Promotion of Interesting and Slightly Expressionistic Wet Mural Interest Group – thingy.' The Doctor paused for a moment to get his thoughts back on track. 'We're interested in finding out whether artistic types are really more observant than other people. We're especially interested in transitory events like – thunderstorms, yes, there's a good example. For example, you didn't happen to notice anything unusual the other night, did you?'

'I'm not interested,' said the artist. 'Go away.'

'Well, we'll leave you in peace then,' said the Doctor, 'although I must say I particularly like the striking cloud formations over there, such a moody brown colour. Dust *storm*, is it? Right, I'll be going.' The Doctor splashed towards some nearby steps.

'What a charming conversationalist.'

'You know,' said the parachute, 'I don't know how you

126

people can put up with you people.'

'It's all part of the way we're hardwired,' said the Doctor.

'May I ask you a personal question?'

'Of course.'

'You're a bit too smart to be running on carbohydrates, aren't you?'

'It's a hobby,' said the Doctor. 'Now, how do I get up to the esplanade?'

'There's a flight of steps to your right.'

He dropped the parachute at the top of the stairs and took a moment to shake some of the water from his shoes. Bernice and saRa!qava waved at him from their table and raised their drinks in an ironic toast as he walked over.

'Nice of you to rush over and help me,' he said.

'We assumed,' said Bernice, 'that you landed in the water for a good reason.'

Since it was the truth he didn't have a good answer for that so instead he sat down and tried to ignore the squelching sounds from his shoes.

'Did you discover anything useful?' asked the furry terminal on the table.

'Is that you, God?' asked the Doctor.

'The one and only,' said God.

'It just turned up while we were working,' said Bernice, 'and now we can't get it to leave.'

'The Doctor hasn't answered my question,' said God.

'Haven't you got something better to do?' asked saRa!qava. 'Sewage recycling systems to monitor perhaps?'

'Well, I'm certain it was murder,' said the Doctor, 'and I think I know how it was done.'

'Means,' said Roz, 'opportunity, motive.'

The Doctor nodded. 'We know the means.'

'Is that really possible?' asked feLixi. 'Could you really introduce that kind of harmonic structure into a lightning bolt?'

Bernice surreptitiously studied feLixi over the rim of her glass. He wasn't quite what she'd expected; somehow he seemed too innocuous, his face just a little too forgettable to be the object of Roz's interest. Still, a forgettable face was probably a good asset in a secret agent and Roz was too long in the tooth to be interested in mere surfaces. Bernice smiled as she noted the set of the older woman's shoulders, the way she leaned ever so slightly towards feLixi when she was speaking. Roz was interested all right, her body language was unmistakable, but Bernice was just as certain that Roz herself didn't know she was interested.

'Yes,' said the Doctor, 'but the source of the electrical discharge would have to be artificial.'

The Doctor's theory was that some person or persons unknown had hit vi!Cari with a specially modulated electrical discharge. He claimed that with the right type of harmonics such a discharge would have not only broken down the drone's defensive shields but also turned it into a flying lightning attractor. The very next bolt would have been sufficient to blow vi!Cari's brains out. God was sceptical: a defensive drone's shields were made up of interlaced forceshells, each set with a different modulation, a set-up designed specifically to resist that kind of attack.

'It wouldn't have to be artificial,' said feLixi. 'A natural static discharge could have been manipulated to provide the harmonics.'

'And anyway,' said Bernice, 'God would have spotted it.'

'Not the energy burst,' said the Doctor. 'That would have been masked by the storm. Isn't that right, God?'

Everyone looked at the furry terminal in the centre of the table which remained resolutely silent.

'Stop sulking,' said saRa!qava, 'and answer the question.'

'You said you didn't want me around,' said God.

'Never mind what I said. Could the storm have masked an electrical discharge?'

'I suppose consistency is too much to expect from somebody who uses electrochemical reactions to think with,' muttered God. 'Yes, probably. I'm going over the data-records now.'

'Assuming that's how it was done,' said Roz, 'who had the physical capability to carry it out?'

'Another drone?' suggested feLixi.

'We've checked every drone in the sphere,' said Bernice, 'and they're all accounted for. You wouldn't believe how many said they were doing flower arranging.'

'How about remote-drones?' asked Roz.

'I'd still have spotted it,' said God. 'Their power plants have the same signature as a sentient drone.'

'No one's developed a drone that can mask their energy signature then?' asked the Doctor.

'A *stealth drone*?' said God. 'What an interesting idea. If there's a drone that stealthy I haven't seen it.'

'So it's a possibility,' said the Doctor.

'A *stealth drone – I haven't seen it*? Didn't anyone get it?' asked God.

'Everyone got it,' said saRa!qava, 'they just didn't think it was funny.'

God explained that a stealth drone was not a viable option and was willing to explain why at great length to anyone who had six or seven years to spare. Bernice was half afraid that the Doctor might take up the offer.

'Which leaves the ships,' said Bernice.

'Could a ship have done it?' asked the Doctor. 'More to the point, could it have fine-tuned its weapons to the point where God wouldn't spot it?'

'It would have to be close range,' said God.

'How close is close range?' asked Bernice.

'Less than a trillion kilometres.'

Roz spilt her drink. Bernice asked how many ships that was and which of them were capable.

'The four VASs and one of the GPSs,' said God. Their names appeared up on one of the floating screens. Bernice recognized one of them. 'Didn't vi!Cari serve on the S-Lioness?'

'Yes,' said feLixi, 'at the same time as I did.'

'You knew it then?' asked Bernice.

'With a crew of six hundred,' said feLixi, 'you get to know everybody.'

'What was it like?' asked Bernice.

'Young,' said feLixi. 'Like the rest of us, idealistic. I remember it had a real talent for intelligence work. Got itself

129

damaged during that nasty business on Tipor'oosis.'

'Perhaps that's why it was easy to destroy,' said Roz, 'because it was already damaged.'

'Damaged in the mind, Roz,' said feLixi.

'Oh.'

'Transferred to another VAS right after that,' said feLixi. 'The R-Vene.'

'Bad ship,' said God. 'Killed a lot of people for no good reason.'

'As opposed to killing them for the right reasons,' said the Doctor. 'I've always wondered if the victims appreciate the difference.'

'Wasn't that the ship that was disassembled?' asked saRa!qava.

'That's what I heard,' said feLixi.

'Do we know what vi!Cari was up to on board?' asked Roz.

'I can't help you there,' said God. 'You'll have to ask the Xeno Relations (Normalization) Interest Group about that. They handled the war and they don't like to tell me anything.'

'Why not?' asked Bernice.

'Because I was against the war and they've never forgiven me for that.'

'Don't tell me you're a pacifist?'

'No,' said God. 'I'm an extremely large target.'

'*Means*,' said Roz, trying to get everybody's minds back on the job.

'Someone with access to really big technology,' said Bernice.

'A ship or a drone,' said saRa!qava.

'Go ahead,' said God. 'Blame a machine.'

'Opportunity?'

'Same as "means" surely?' said Bernice.

'Not necessarily,' said Roz. 'Someone knew that vi!Cari was going to be out in the storm.'

'Assuming that vi!Cari was the target,' said feLixi. 'Maybe the poor bastard was just a target of opportunity. Perhaps someone wanted to test a new weapons system or just plain didn't like drones.'

130

'You're not thinking of the Anti-Machine Interest Group, are you?' asked saRa!qava.

'Why not?'

'Because,' said God, 'eighty-two per cent of AMIG's membership is made up of machines. I'm a member myself.'

'Let's skip opportunity for the moment,' said Roz wearily. 'Anyone got any ideas about motive? If vi!Cari *was* the target someone went to a lot of time and effort to disassemble it. That suggests something a bit more than simple irritation.'

Bernice looked at saRa!qava who shrugged. FeLixi frowned and absently rotated his glass between his palms.

Roz sighed. 'There has to be some motive.'

'What I want to know –' said the Doctor suddenly. Everybody turned to look at him. 'What I want to know is *why* it has to look like an apple tree.'

'Hello,' called Chris, 'is anyone at home?'

'Hello, Chris,' said a small boy he didn't recognize. 'Dep's upstairs.'

'Thanks,' said Chris.

'Don't mention it,' said the boy.

Chris smiled and stepped over the threshold into saRa!qava's house. It was just like the corridor he'd grown up in. On your first visit you were formally invited in and given tea, on the second visit they remembered how much sweetener you liked and after the third, you were expected to help yourself.

The small boy was sitting on the middle third level of the open plan 'living area'. He was building a complex lattice out of pastel-coloured nodes and rods. Chris paused and asked him what it was.

'It's a hyperspace intrusion,' said the small boy. 'See – that's the boundary layer and the real world interface and that's the extension into the subdomain bubble.'

'That's very clever,' said Chris. 'Who taught you that?'

'Me,' said the boy, 'but my mama helped me with the maths.' The boy gave Chris a sly look. 'Shouldn't you be going to see my sister? She'll be waiting and she's got a *bad* temper.'

Chris wondered why he suddenly felt so nervous. What if Dep didn't want to see him? What if he'd just been a bit of fun? Just because a girl went to bed with you, it didn't mean she really liked you – did it? He remembered some of the domestic cases he'd reviewed at the academy – people did some horrible things to their partners. He remembered his father had come into his room when he was fourteen and given him some advice on the subject. It was good advice, Chris was sure of it, he just wished he could remember what it had been.

He found what he thought might be the stairs up to Dep's room – a series of flat boards that hung in an unsupported spiral. To be on the safe side he called her name from the bottom. Just to make sure she really wanted him there. After a moment he saw her face appear in the doorway at the top of the stairs. She was dressed in an oil-stained sleeveless boiler suit. There were dirty smudges on her cheeks and her hair had coiled itself tightly into a stack at the top of her head.

She grinned when she saw him. 'Don't just stand there,' she yelled down. 'Get your barbarian backside up here. I've got something to show you.' Chris ran up the stairs towards her, wondering what on earth he'd been worrying about.

As Chris came level with her, Dep took his face in her hands and brushed her nose against his. Then, more cautiously because it was a new thing to her, she kissed him. She smelt faintly of oil and the static charge of hair. Taking him by the hand she drew him into her room.

Dep's room occupied almost the entirety of the house's top floor and was completely filled with flying machines. At first Chris thought they were models, upscaled versions of the spaceships he'd built in his adolescence, but they were much too large. A full-size glider hung in front of the door, its wingspan stretching from wall to wall, bundles of optical cable spilling out of its open nose. An angular wing, matt black and sharply canted, was propped up against the wall. As Dep led him deeper Chris almost tripped over a transparent bubble canopy that had been left casually on the floor and avoiding that banged his head on the tail fin of the glider. He noticed the symbiote dress Dep had worn to the party draped over the naked spars of a cannibalized microlight. Other items of clothing were scattered over fuselages, comm aerials, control surfaces and reinforcement struts. Power cables snaked around old-fashioned-looking impeller units and disassembled combustion engines. Information screens hung like pennants at random intervals, most of them displaying technical specifications, although Chris did see one showing a drama – one about aeroplanes of course.

She led him past a bedfield surrounded by a confusion of shaped wooden struts to a relatively clear space at the end of the room. Tools were hung in ordered ranks from the walls, a portable blast furnace was set into the floor next to a lathe that seemed to be constructed entirely from forcefields.

Dep turned to him with dancing eyes and pointed to the shape in the centre of the cleared space. 'What do you think?' she asked.

It was as big as the biplane but with less ground clearance. The tail assembly was a horizontal plane of individual paddle-shaped slats. The power plant was mounted in the centre of an open cage fuselage but there was no drive shaft to a propeller; instead fantastically angled struts unfolded from a complicated mass of gears to attach themselves to the wings near the roots. The wings themselves were canted upwards, curving back gently like the wings of a gull.

Chris realized what it was he was looking at. 'Oh wow,' he said.

It was an ornithopter, a flying machine that flew by flapping its wings.

'It's almost ready to fly,' said Dep. 'A couple more days and we can take it out for its maiden flight. That is, if you want to fly with me?'

'Is the Empress a woman?' said Chris.

'You're disappointed,' said saRa!qava to Bernice.

They were walking along the stretch of beach north of iSanti Jeni that lay between the headland and the beach-bar. The immovable sun had taken on an orange tinge and the sky was turning a deep shade of purple, signifying, Bernice assumed, the onset of evening. Roz and feLixi were strolling side by side a few metres behind.

'I suppose I am,' said Bernice. 'You don't know him like I do. I kept on expecting him to leap out of his chair, solve the murder, declare universal peace and harmony amongst all beings and start playing Beethoven's "Ode to Joy" arranged for two dessert spoons and a chorus of groans.'

'Is that how he normally behaves?'

'Well,' said Bernice, 'sometimes, if we're lucky, we can get him sedated before he plays the spoons.'

'I knew a ship who acted a bit like that,' said saRa!qava. 'Decided to redecorate the crew decks right in the middle of a supernova. We spent a whole morning running around trying to find out where it had relocated our bedrooms and the afternoon figuring out why the star had got so big all of a sudden. Ship would never ever tell us about a crisis until it was long past.'

'Magic thinking,' said Bernice. 'It's a belief, a superstition if you like, that thinking or talking about something has a direct effect on the result.'

'Like wishing hard enough makes something happen.'

'Sometimes,' said Bernice. 'Often it's the other way round. The belief that wanting something really badly is the best way of ensuring that you won't get it.'

'Sounds like a syndrome of deprivation,' said saRa!qava. 'Haven't you ever wished for something and been disappointed?'

'Once or twice.' SaRa!qava said it easily, blandly even, but Bernice saw a momentary pain in her friend's eyes, like a small flicker of darkness. 'I took steps to rectify the problem.'

Behind them Roz laughed at something feLixi said. It was a short surprised bark, as if the laugh had been tricked out of her.

'Do you think he believes in magic thinking?' asked saRa!qava. There was no need to ask who *he* was.

'Oh yes,' said Bernice, 'I think he's its greatest exponent.'

'Isn't that a bit irrational?'

'I suppose so,' said Bernice. 'But you see with him – it works.'

* * *

134

AM!xitsa met him at the edge of the cove just as the sun was going out.

'She's sleeping,' said the drone.

'Any changes?'

'Lots,' said aM!xitsa. 'She went walkabouts today.'

The Doctor nodded. 'It was bound to happen sooner or later. No "incidents" I hope?'

'She ran into one of your friends, the older female.'

'Interesting. Any reactions?'

'Marked increase in endocrinal activity, lots of adrenalin and a big spike in the memory centres. I'm beginning to see a pattern in these fluctuations,' said aM!xitsa, 'a cyclical progression. While she's asleep there are surges of brain activity that fall away when she wakes up. But they fall back to a slightly higher level than they were originally.'

'Like the tide coming in,' said the Doctor.

'Yes,' said the drone. 'And like the waves of an advancing tide, as they progress up the beach some of the water fills the depressions in the terrain of her mind. And when the wave recedes –'

'It leaves rock pools,' said the Doctor softly. 'Rock pools of thought.'

'Or memory,' said the drone. 'I still believe she's doing most of her actual thinking when she's asleep but certainly some of the higher structures are now beginning to operate on a semi-conscious level when she's awake.'

'Can you get me close enough to see her?'

'Are you sure that's wise?'

'AM!xitsa,' said the Doctor, 'if she's beginning to regain her faculties I may not get another chance. Besides, if you're with me, how could I possibly be in danger?' The drone said nothing. They both knew that the woman was machine fast and human unpredictable.

The hut was a low structure built of fired mud bricks with a thatched roof. She had cleared the undergrowth from around the front entrance, built a firepit and earthen kiln. On the other side was a low frame constructed from branches lashed together with vines. It puzzled the Doctor for a moment until he recognized it – a drying frame. He'd seen the like all over

135

Africa in the twentieth century; the women built them to dry cooking pots and plates after washing up. Why had she built it? She was from the late twenty-first, had grown up amongst energy efficient TVs and solar-powered dishwashers. Whose memory had she used as a template for this anachronism?

The entrance was a rectangle of darkness in the blind face of the wall.

There had once been a leopard that fell into a trap.

The deck of the ship had been treacherous, swaying in the Atlantic swell and slippery with blood. He'd been careful moving about the ship, picking his way through the cabins at the stern, checking the bodies and the bits of bodies. Too late now he'd seen them, too late to go back to before and stop the slaughter. He found chests full of trade goods in the minor hold, glass beads from Liverpool, cheap enamelled mirrors from Bradford, knives and flintlocks from Sheffield and Manchester. Manufactured trinkets to buy and bribe their way down the West African coast. And in the main hold the shelves and manacles would be waiting for the next cargo. A human cargo. Stinking, crying, moaning and dying until their despair was etched into the very fabric of the bulkhead walls, to be danced each morning and hosed down with seawater, the sick thrown over the side with the dead.

How they must have laughed to see her. Licked their chops and calculated her price on the auction blocks of Port Royale or New Orleans. Counted up the profit in their heads and taken it as a good omen for their venture. And making that calculation they never thought to ask why it was she smiled so broadly as she was led in chains up the gangplank.

The Doctor ducked under the lintel of the hut and stepped inside. As the octagons in his retina took over from his night-blinded rods and cones – her shape seemed to crystallize out of the darkness. A shadow shape of curves and angles – the human body in the foetal position.

Do you think I haven't thought of it? he didn't ask the sleeping woman. *Do you think I didn't formulate a thousand schemes to end that particular injustice and a thousand like it? I could have armed the coastal tribes, I could have used my influence to get Hitler that place at art school.*

136

He reached out with his hand to touch her.

'Doctor,' said aM!xitsa, 'she's just gone into REM sleep.'

His fingertips grazed the curve of her shoulder.

'Big surge there,' said aM!xitsa. 'Alpha waves just went way out of line.'

She unfolded from the bed – insect fast. He easily turned her first blow with the heel of his hand, too easily – it was a feint. Her left hand lashed up, striking for his neck. Suddenly he was out of position, out of practice and out of luck.

Then, miraculously, the hut was a rapidly receding shadow below him, nightbirds scattering from their perches as aM!xitsa yanked him out of danger and carried him backwards to the safety of the rocks.

'Do you know,' he said conversationally as the drone put him down, 'I think she's actually got faster.'

He looked back over the rich darkness of the cove. His doubts clustered thickly about him like unwanted relatives.

I am what I know, he thought, to know is to act. To act is to change what you know. Therefore, to act is to change what you are. If I become something that I am not, am I bound by the rules that made me what I was? And since time is shaped like a jam doughnut, are my actions foreshadowed or disinpredestined and why does the jam always dribble down my chin? If the devil is in the detail is God in the overall plan?

The idea came suddenly, bursting in his head like a soundless, colourless, invisible supernova.

Like a great big neon sign that said – EMERGENCY EXIT.

Hyper-lude

1. The treaty below marks the solemn agreement between the High Council of the Time Lords of Gallifrey (hereafter known as the High Council) and the temporary representative (hereafter known as God) of the people living in, around and within the sphere of influence of the Worldsphere (said people to be referred to hereafter as The People). (See Appendix I (one) for precise Universal Co-ordinates and definitions of sphere of influence.)

2. The People shall recognize the rights, duties and responsibilities of the High Council with regard to the maintenance of the continuity of the fabric of the space-time continuum and the causality of the Universe providing that these rights, duties and responsibilities do not conflict with the provisions of this treaty. As the temporary representative and spokesman of The People the conscious machine entity known as God shall act as guarantor of this Treaty and shall be responsible for the enforcement of the provisions herein. The People also make the following undertakings:

    i) The People undertake not to develop a mode of temporal transportation nor make direct investigation into the possibilities of technologies that lead to the development of a temporal transportation system.

    ii) Any theoretical knowledge of temporal transportation, translocation, transmigration or transcendence that results from any other form of research must not be pursued as a technology.

iii) The People shall at no time and by no means threaten the physical security of Gallifrey, nor shall they make alliances, deals or agreements with the enemies of the High Council. Nor shall The People have dealings with supernatural, time-transcendental, multi-dimensional beings, superbeings or deities. Contacts with the above to be reported immediately to the High Council through the channels specified below.

iv) The People shall in no way impinge, probe or explore the galaxy designated as Mutter's Spiral and will undertake no activities of any sort under any circumstances in that area of the Universe. In addition The People shall create no *permanent* database, record or store of information relating to the physical, spiritual or metaphysical substance of Mutter's Spiral.

3. The High Council hereby recognizes that The People are, and will remain, the dominant political, cultural and military force within that galaxy that is hereafter designated the Home Galaxy of the People or Home Galaxy. In regards to the status of the People within this Galaxy the High Council makes the following undertakings:

i) That the High Council will undertake no activity that will interfere with the social, economic, political, diplomatic or historical development of The People or any other cultural, ethnic or biological grouping within the Home Galaxy, either in the present, in the future or the past.

ii) That all contacts between The People and the High Council will take place in linear time and that strict relativity shall be maintained between Gallifreyan standard time and the time frame of The People. (See Appendix II (two) for technical details.)

iii) The High Council will undertake a policing role with a view to preventing unauthorized temporal travel within the Home Galaxy, the chronological parameters of this area extending from the Creation of the Universe (hereafter referred to as Event One) to the Present (see Appendix II (two)).

iv)   The High Council will in no wise use temporal transportation in an attempt to alter, negate or undermine this Treaty or any other treaty made between the High Council and The People. Neither shall the High Council seek to alter, negate or undermine this Treaty or any other by use of agents, proxies or renegades, officially sanctioned or otherwise. The High Council shall be made responsible for the enforcement of this clause and any violation shall be regarded as a Treaty Violation. (See Appendix IV, V, VI and VII.)

4.   Any act designated as a treaty violation by either the High Council or representatives of The People shall be regarded as a potential act of war and will result in the negation of all other provisions of this treaty.

Appendix VI (six)
The High Council of the Time Lords takes no responsibility for the actions, inactions, deals, schemes, plots or otherwise of the renegade known as the Doctor. Likewise the Doctor will not be deemed under the protection of the High Council while visiting or traversing such territories and time zones within the People's sphere of influence. The High Council will in no way seek to facilitate any action taken by the Doctor and will in no way seek to employ him as an agent of influence within the Home Galaxy. The High Council hereby gives *carte blanche* to The People, God or any other agent of The People to act in any manner they deem appropriate when dealing with the Doctor, up to and including the use of deadly force.

7

Screaming for Ice Cream

> I scream, you scream
> We all scream for ice cream
>
> Traditional

It started with the sound of women laughing.

There was sand between her bare toes; it was familiar sand; she had been here before.

She heard the laughter again, floating over the long slow-motion snare drum sound of the waves breaking on the shore. Big ocean waves driven across the Atlantic by the actions of the moon and the wind to crash against the West African seaboard. The laughter was a light and joyful sound that filled her full of dread.

She snapped her head around looking for the source of the sound, the pupils of her eyes contracting to filter out the glare off the bone-white beach. She saw them four hundred metres away, two women, one dressed all in black, the other in white.

Their presence angered and frightened her. This was her place, they had no right to intrude. She could cover the distance in less than twenty seconds. She felt her body tensing even before her mind made the decision.

It was too late, for the dead were already walking out of the sea.

This too was familiar, she'd had this dream before.

Except this time the dead were not dancing. The family

dead always danced, even the first Grandfather, whom she'd always suspected would have mucked up a fox-trot, danced. They should have come dancing, their rotting feet stomping the sand, a subconscious reminder that it was more than genetics that chained her to the past.

The dead were not dancing, they were walking, graveyard fresh, from the waves. She saw the patched uniform of the *garde nationale*, the spiny carapace of a cake monster, the rotting sailcloth jerkins of the seaman, no one she had known longer than a few moments.

Six of the dead were carrying a long coffin-shaped box on their shoulders and at their head came the man with no name. He was bigger than she remembered or perhaps it was she who had shrunk. He loomed in front of her, his huge eyes like pits of freezing oxygen.

'I'm sorry,' said the man with no face, 'that it took me so long to get around to you. I probably would have let you run free if you hadn't made such a mess of things in Paris.'

The dead pall bearers unshipped the box from their shoulders and set it gently base first into the sand. It was brightly coloured and looked like it had been constructed from reinforced cardboard; indeed it even had the SolGov guaranteed renewable resource logo in the bottom left-hand corner.

'But now,' said the man with no name, 'it's time for you to be put back in the box.'

It was a doll's box like the one her old doll had come in, the talking one which came with sixty-eight programmable African languages and realistic braidable hair, the doll that she had slept with until, aged thirteen, she'd taken it apart to see how it worked.

She'd screamed at her mother when she'd first been given that doll. It wasn't the one she wanted, the one she had asked for in the months that crept so slowly to her birthday. She'd wanted the doll which did the karate moves and had a realistic gun that shot a real low-powered laser beam. She screamed and screamed until her father had come running into the house and raised his hand to her for the first and only time in her life.

She looked at the box. There was a picture of herself on the lid, wearing an impractically brief hostile environment suit and carrying a realistic gun that shot a real laser beam.

The lid fell open like a hungry mouth. The box was empty.

The man with no name was very close now, although she'd had no sense, no warning, of his approach. There was a syringe in his hand, its needle a metre long lance of stainless steel, its clear body filled with a liquid the colour of arterial blood.

'I can honestly say,' said the man with no name, 'that this will hurt me more than it hurts you.' He reached out to grab her, his hand so large that his thumb and forefinger could encircle her waist.

And then she was running.

Running down tracks in the forest that were familiar from a thousand childish games. She'd run down these tracks with other children, a little ultrasonic generator braided into her hair to scare away the animals. But she hadn't liked wearing it because she could hear its low persistent whining sound.

Running down the main road, past the High School and the Transit Station, never mind that Mekeni was a hundred kilometres from the coast.

Running past the football pitch, still showing the burn marks from the Angel Francine's last visit.

Running to her street. To her house. To her parents' bedroom. To the vast white expanse of her parents' bed where her mother was sleeping off the effects of her medication.

And then, ever so carefully so as not to disturb her, creeping under the warm, mother-smelling blankets and curling close to her mother's body. Safe where the man with no name would never find her.

There was something in the bed with her. She could hear breathing in the darkness, long slow breaths. She could feel rough fur tickling her shoulder, smooth, slightly cool skin pressed against her side. There was an aroma of sweat, leaves, roasted fish and forest earth.

There was somebody in the bed with Roz and a voice said

143

by her ear – 'If you want to live, don't move.'

Roz figured she could roll off the bed and be out of the line of fire in a moment, but then what? She wasn't wearing anything, her armour was in a sandy heap in the corner of the bedroom and her blaster was in its carry case by the bathroom door. She could yell for help but she had a horrible suspicion that the sound proofing in the villa was as efficient as everything else.

'I'm going to glow a little,' said the voice.

She saw it from the corner of her eye – she dared not move her head – a soft oval of light bisected by a thick black line, a wavy pattern in thinner lines set over two dark ovals. A drone 'face'. Abstract features set in a worried frown. The glow gave a shape to the darkness in the room. Roz could see an arm flung out of the covers and across her chest. A dark-skinned human arm with the right number of fingers, joints and knuckles in all the right places. A female arm, that ran up to a shoulder taut with muscles. Roz had a good idea whose arm it was, whose cool body was pressed up against her like a child in her mama's bed.

'I'm going to extend a contour field between you and her,' said the drone. 'Once I've done that you should be able to ease yourself out.'

The contour field was imperceptible except for a slight stiffening in the covers and the feeling of separation between her skin and that of the woman. When she was certain it was in place Roz slipped out of the bed and padded over to the door.

'We can talk next door,' said the drone.

AM!xitsa watched Roz carefully as she tied the cord on the silk dressing gown. There was a singular lack of grace about her movements, an impatience that the drone found peculiarly fascinating. It was as if she treated everything as a series of irritating obstacles to be overcome as quickly as possible. AM!xitsa let its vision drift inside her, noting the healed breaks in her right tibia, the tell-tale discoloration of repaired subcutaneous tissue at no less than twenty-six separate sites on her body. More telling still was the slight enlargement of the medulla sections of both her adrenal glands and her elevated blood pressure, both indications of prolonged stress.

If Roz was a machine, decided aM!xitsa, she was a machine that had been running way over its design parameters for way too long.

There was a microscopic tear in the superior vena cava of her heart that might cause problems during the next ten years – aM!xitsa fixed it with an imperceptible twist of his ancillary manipulator field. The action gave the drone that little thrill of pleasure that always came from doing something benevolently unethical.

'You must be aM!xitsa,' said Roz. 'Make yourself useful and get some coffee, will you?'

AM!xitsa had a long nanosecond argument with House about protocol which resulted in a compromise where aM!xitsa provided the coffee template while House actually boiled water and ground beans. Why House felt it necessary to first synthesize whole beans and then grind them up aM!xitsa was too polite to ask. House had obviously picked up some eccentricities from associating with such extreme characters as the Doctor and his companions. Organic people rarely understood these little machine/machine compromises that were essential to the smooth running of the worldsphere. Nor did organics really appreciate just how blurred the line between sentience and non-sentience was. It was all part of their charm, aM!xitsa supposed.

'And you must be Roz,' said aM!xitsa.

AM!xitsa did another scan of the sleeping woman, noting the elevated activity in the high cognitive sub-structures. It traced the patterns in the steam that rose over the coffee pot in the house food preparation area and thought that they would make a good subject for a mathematical poem. It had a longish conversation with a friend in the Xenobiology Interest Group. Ran another scan on the sleeping woman and this time made a comparative match with Roz's physiology, surprised by the areas of commonality given that one was designed and the other wasn't. It used the scans as the basis for one of its famous unpublished theses: *Evolution vs*

Design in Hominid Bipeds. Wrote it, filed it, unfiled it and changed the title to *Whose Life Is It Anyway?* Made another, slightly shorter, call to another friend, this time in the Weird Cuisine Interest Group, and got some interesting recipes to try out on Roz. Which led to another long argument with House about whose area of responsibility cooking was in the villa. Reread the thesis, decided that most of it was rubbish and filed it in its internal datavore trap that had so far claimed 6,546 similar unpublished theses.

'That's right,' said Roz.

AM!xitsa shunted off the culinary template to House. It was curious to find out how efficient Roz's digestion was.

As far as she could understand the woman in her bed was some sort of mental patient that aM!xitsa was looking after. The drone explained that the woman had got away from it and climbed into Roz's bed while it was thinking about something else. Roz didn't believe a word of it. She had her own suspicions about who, or rather, what the woman was. The whole thing practically stank of the Doctor. No doubt he'd tell her about it in his own good time.

The coffee was rich, aromatic and very bitter, much better than the stuff House normally came up with. Roz drank most of one cup while she studied the drone.

'You're the same make as vi!Cari,' she said.

AM!xitsa's face icon simulated an amused expression. 'I'm the original,' it said. 'Vi!Cari was part of the second batch of militarized defensives.'

'But you've got the same capabilities?'

'All of us have our strengths and weaknesses,' said aM!xitsa. 'It's less a question of what you've got than of what you do with them. I'm sorry, did I say something funny?'

Roz shook her head, sipping the coffee to hide her smile.

'I'm geared more towards remote sensing and point defence,' said aM!xitsa. 'Drones like vi!Cari were produced at the start of the war, primarily to provide forward and aggressive defensive postures.'

'So you never actually attacked anyone,' said Roz. 'You

just defended yourselves in an aggressive manner.'

'Towards the end of the war we did have to pre-emptively defend ourselves because our enemies got a bit wary about attacking us.'

'Could you, hypothetically speaking, have pre-emptively defended yourself against vi!Cari?'

AM!xitsa's face ikon went interestingly blank. 'That would depend. I'd have to have the element of surprise and even so the fireworks would have been pretty spectacular. The blow-back from vi!Cari's shields would have produced at least a six-gigawatt flash, even with suppressors. That sort of thing tends to attract God's attention.'

'Do drones keep their shields up all the time?' asked Roz.

'That's a very personal question,' said aM!xitsa.

'This is a murder inquiry.'

'Really,' said aM!xitsa. 'I thought you didn't consider the destruction of a machine as murder.'

'Who told you that?'

'KiKhali.'

'When?'

'One point three seconds ago.'

'Tell it to mind its own business,' said Roz. 'Have you told it?'

'KiKhali says you are the rudest person it's ever met.'

'That's a shame,' said Roz. 'I cry myself to sleep at night over my lack of manners. I'm a simple kind of woman, aM!xitsa. I play by the rules: you people say it's murder, so it's murder. What I think doesn't matter, does it?'

'But we don't have rules, or laws,' said aM!xitsa.

'You have a general consensus on morality?'

'Yes.'

'Then you have rules.'

'That's an interesting argument.'

'No, it isn't,' said Roz. 'Are there any circumstances under which vi!Cari would have had his shields down, or in standby mode?'

'Shields can interfere with certain scanning modes,' said aM!xitsa. 'If vi!Cari was looking for something it might have shut down everything except its core integrity shield. It would have to be looking for something very small, down at the submolecular level.'

'You know the Doctor's theory?'

'I do now,' said aM!xitsa. 'Yes, it would work. He's got a devious mind, that Doctor.'

'You don't know the half of it.'

'God scanned the area pretty thoroughly after the storm. There was nothing out there for vi!Cari to be looking for.'

'Unless it got washed away,' said Roz. *Washed away?* She scratched the invisible scar under her breast. Why is that important? She had a nagging sense that her unconscious was putting things together behind her back. Policeman's nose, adjudicator's hunch, the little itch in the scar that wasn't there. Perhaps vi!Cari only *thought* there was something to find, something that had been washed away? Or perhaps it had been washed out to sea?

'I've made you some breakfast,' said aM!xitsa.

A serving tray hovered by her elbow. *Damn.* Lost it. 'What's this?'

'That's grain porridge, that's fried strips of meat and boiled avian embryos,' said aM!xitsa. 'Tuck in, you need the protein.'

Roz was tempted to tell aM!xitsa that she hadn't eaten breakfast since she was a novice but then she realized how hungry she was. Ignoring the porridge she started on the bacon and eggs. 'Some bread with this would be nice.'

The bread took another minute to arrive.

'Tell me,' said Roz, ripping off a crust and dipping it into the yolk, 'why haven't you machines taken over?'

AM!xitsa sounded surprised. 'Taken over what?'

'The sphere, the galaxy, everything,' said Roz.

'What would be the point?'

Roz explained between mouthfuls about Cybermen, Daleks and Movellans. About how the first thing any computer seemed to do once it achieved self-awareness was plot to take over the world. AM!xitsa's face ikon grew more and more appalled until suddenly it flickered out completely, pre-sumably because the drone had run out of suitable expressions. Roz was back on the coffee by the time she'd finished.

'It occurs to me,' said aM!xitsa, 'that Daleks aren't really machines, Cybermen are descended from organic humanoids and Movellans were designed by an organic race in their own image.'

'You're claiming it wasn't their fault?' asked Roz. 'They were designed to be megalomaniacs?'

'Influenced, Roz,' said aM!xitsa, 'not designed. Seeking to subjugate or destroy all other life forms is hardly a form of rational behaviour, is it? What would be the point of creating this sphere, giving it viable biosphere, if only machines were going to inhabit it? Who would I talk to, what would there be to talk about?'

'So what you're saying,' said Roz carefully, 'is that you machines wouldn't take over because without humans around there wouldn't be anything to gossip about?'

'I don't think you understand the kind of collective resource that two trillion sentient individuals represent. However fast I think and however smart I am, the probability is that someone out there has thought of it too, probably millions of people. And even if only a tiny fraction of those people actually *do* anything with that knowledge then we're still talking about thousands of people. Not to mention, and this is the kicker, because they are all individuals they're all thinking about it in a different way. Collectively, the two trillion organic individuals that live here are smarter than God.'

Roz stared at the drone.

'Oh, all right,' said aM!xitsa. 'It's because life is more fun with humans than without them.'

'So what was all that business about collective intelligence in aid of?'

'Oh, that's all true,' said aM!xitsa, 'theoretically.'

Roz heard Bernice calling. 'I can definitely smell coffee. For God's sake, somebody lead me to it.' She came down the stairs and into the living room.

'I'll get another mug,' said aM!xitsa.

Bernice flopped down next to Roz and held out a bare arm. 'Never mind a mug, just give it to me intravenously.' A mug of steaming coffee slapped into her palm. Bernice took a sip

149

and sighed appreciatively. 'So who's Mr Efficiency?' she asked Roz.

'A friend of the Doctor's,' said Roz. 'AM!xitsa.'

'Hello, aM!xitsa,' said Bernice. 'Where's Chris?'

'Didn't come home last night.'

Bernice raised an eyebrow. 'The little devil,' she said. 'Is it my imagination or is this coffee better than the normal stuff?' She caught sight of the breakfast tray. 'Is that bacon and eggs? I didn't know they had bacon and eggs here. Pass it over . . .'

'Watch it,' said Roz. Coffee was spilling from Bernice's mug on to her leg. 'Benny, that stuff's hot.' Then she realized that Bernice wasn't listening. Instead the younger woman was staring past Roz towards the stairs. Quickly Roz lifted the cup from Bernice's hand and turned to look.

'Oh dear,' said aM!xitsa.

The woman was crouching halfway down the stairs, one hand resting lightly on the banister, her head cocked slightly to the left. She was staring back at Bernice.

'Wait,' said Bernice.

The woman vaulted over the banister, ran lightly but with astonishing speed across the living room and out onto the balcony. Bernice tumbled out of the sofa and scrambled after her. 'Kadiatu,' she cried, 'wait.'

The woman somersaulted over the balcony railing and vanished. Roz caught up with Bernice as she ran into the sunlight. AM!xitsa overtook both of them and accelerated downwards and out of sight. Bernice's hands grabbed at the railing and leaned as far as she could go, looking wildly for some sign of the woman. Roz, cursing and trying to keep the hot stain on her dressing gown away from her leg, hobbled out to join her.

Bernice was angry. Roz had never seen her that angry before and it was kind of impressive. 'You overbearing multi-lived bastard,' Bernice yelled. 'I'm going to rip out your hearts and stuff them up your nostrils.'

He waited for Bernice on the balcony, knowing that she would seek him out. He faced the sea, chin propped on the back of his hands which rested on the handle of his umbrella. The case was on the table; beside it was the black rose in a small crystal vase with a fluted neck – he had expected this confrontation and planned for it. He felt her walk on to the balcony behind him and sit down. Her calm breathing was like an accusation.

'I assume,' he said, without looking at her, 'that we're finished with the furious-hurling-of-obscenities stage and are into the eye-of-the-storm-icy-calm-demanding-answers stage.'

'Yes, we are,' he heard her say, 'although a beating-the-truth-out-of-the-doctor-with-a-handy-blunt-instrument stage could be arranged very easily.'

Good, he thought, she's still rational, she still has some trust left. He made himself turn in his seat and look at her; he owed her that much. Her eyes were suspicious, hurt even, but there was an ounce of curiosity in them. *She still has some trust left, despite everything.*

'Why?' she asked.

The Doctor felt a sudden surge of pride. Be vague, let your conversational opponent frame the question for you, you never know, it might be the question that you would have asked if you'd known to ask it. 'Why is she here,' he said, 'or why are we here and are they connected?'

'Start with the first.'

The Doctor glanced at the black rose; it was still in full bloom. 'I found her,' he said, 'on a British slaver drifting off the coast of Sierra Leone in the spring of 1754. Everybody else was dead, including the ten-year-old cabin boy and the ship's cat. She was feral by that stage and if she hadn't been starving to death I never would have got near her. As it was I had to shoot her with 60cc of teterodoxine just to bring her down. I got her on board the TARDIS and hosed the blood off. Then I came here and dropped her off at a small cove down the coast.'

'Just like that?'

'An old friend of mine agreed to look after her.'

'And where was I when all this was going on?'

'Asleep in your room,' said the Doctor. 'It was just before we met Chris and Roz.'

151

Benny didn't ask him whether he'd made side trips without telling her before – he knew she knew he did. 'Ace said that Ship had changed her.'

He shuddered despite himself. 'Ship tried to make her part of itself, just as it tried to do to me. It was a – violation. Ship put knowledge into her head and tried to use her as a slave. No, worse than a slave, an appliance, a *peripheral*.'

'Is Ship still trying to use her?' asked Bernice. 'Is Kadiatu all that's left of Ship?'

'Oh no,' said the Doctor. 'Ship is deader than a dormouse and good riddance.'

'Oh good.'

'It's much worse than that.'

'Oh.'

'She's become very dangerous.'

Bernice laughed. 'I don't remember her ever being exactly what you'd call safe.'

'It's what's in her head that makes her dangerous,' he said. 'She's already designed one time machine just as a school science project. With the knowledge the Ship downloaded into her brain she's probably the most competent temporal engineer this side of Gallifrey.'

'Should we be talking about this sort of thing' – Bernice made a vague motion with her hands, indicating the rest of the sphere – 'out in the open. I got the strong impression that you didn't want God to know about certain things.'

The Doctor glanced at the black rose; it was still in bloom. 'We're safe for the moment,' he said. 'It'll take God at least five minutes to penetrate my jamming signal, after that we'll have to be careful.'

'Will we be able to talk about this again?'

'Not until we're back in the TARDIS.'

'Which is currently –?'

'In a defensive picosecond forward displacement.'

'You don't trust God then?'

'Let's just say I'd rather not put temptation in its way.'

'What an interesting theological concept. We must discuss it some time,' said Bernice. 'But not right now. How dangerous is Kadiatu?'

152

'Very, very dangerous.'

'To what?'

'I'm trying to think of a way of explaining this without getting too metaphysical,' said the Doctor. 'People who travel in time are not like other people. To travel in time is to step out of the normal course of history and by doing that you become vulnerable, let's say, to the influence of the other things that also exist outside of linear time.'

'Gods,' said Bernice, 'you're talking about Gods, aren't you?'

'I prefer to think of them as extremely powerful trans-temporal beings,' said the Doctor primly. 'Because of their *extreme* nature it's actually quite difficult for them to intervene in the mundane day to day world so they're always on the look-out for suitable agents.'

'Like Kadiatu?'

'Time travel is a form of power and power without responsibility is very dangerous.'

'So what are you planning to do about her?' asked Bernice.

'I don't know,' he said. 'She may have to be put to sleep.'

He forced himself to watch her face change. Interest giving way to shock, to anger, to betrayal and then, most painful of all, to an expression of profound disappointment. All these emotions, the entire course of the conversation up till now, he had predicted the night before as he stood with aM!xitsa looking out over Kadiatu's cove, but that didn't make it any easier to bear.

There would have been a time, long ago, when Bernice would have asked him if he was joking, or assumed that he meant 'put to sleep' in a literal sense. A time when she would have made enquiries about stasis capsules or jokes about spinning wheels. Since then, he knew, she had lost most of her illusions about him.

Bernice was looking at him with something close to loathing, unconsciously shrinking back from him in her chair. He wanted to reach out to her and explain what it was he was trying to achieve but that would ruin everything. If she were to do the job for him he needed her in precisely the right frame of

153

mind – it was an imperative. He waited for her response.

I don't believe it, thought the Doctor. What gives you the right et cetera –

'No,' she said, 'I won't let you.'

He gaped at her.

'I've had enough, Doctor.' Her voice was calm, matter of fact. 'I won't stand by and let you murder someone just because they don't fit into your cosmic plan.'

'That's not –'

'Shut up, shut up,' said Bernice, 'I'm tired of your damn excuses, your justifications and your bloody lies. If you do this thing, you and I are *finished*, understand me?'

'All right,' said the Doctor, 'you decide.'

'I mean it, Doctor,' said Bernice.

'So do I,' said the Doctor. 'I'll let you decide whether she lives or dies.'

'There's no decision to make.'

'In that case you won't mind if I explain. Will you?'

She subsided back into her chair, glaring at him suspiciously.

He opened the suitcase and turned it round to face her. He showed her the ring folder, the hypospray and the two cartridges. Both cartridges were filled with a red liquid and labelled with little white sticky-backed squares. On one he had drawn a crude picture of a butterfly, on the other a skull and crossbones.

Bernice looked up from the case, still angry, still suspicious but interested now. *Yes* – he had her, hook, line and rusty three-speed bicycle.

'The one marked with a butterfly contains a retro-DNA tailored to Kadiatu's unique genetic structure. Once injected it will modify sections of her own DNA creating an analogue of the symbiotic nucleatides in my own blood. In short, it will give her roughly the same capabilities as a Time Lord – enhanced temporal perception, a certain resistance to chrono-instability and a few other things.' *Things that I can't talk about, even to you.*

'Will it stop her from killing people?'

'If I could do that, Bernice, we wouldn't be having this conversation.'

154

'And the other cartridge?'

'Death,' said the Doctor. 'Fast, painless, humane.'

'And I make the decision?'

'Yes.'

'Then I choose to let her live.'

'No.'

'You said it was my decision.'

'I mean don't give me your answer right now,' said the Doctor. 'I want you to think about it for two days.'

'Why? I'm not likely to change my mind.'

'Then you can afford to wait two days, can't you?'

Bernice shrugged. 'Will she be all right for two days?'

'I think aM!xitsa can probably stop her from killing too many people in the meantime.'

'She's not that bad, Doctor.'

'No, she's worse,' he said. 'But it's not my problem now, it's yours.' He pushed the suitcase across the table towards her. 'You might find the contents of the folder useful. I downloaded it from the Imogen database in Zagreb.'

'What is it?'

'Kadiatu's user manual.'

Bernice glanced once into the suitcase and then gingerly, as if she was wary of touching it, snapped the lid shut. 'How long have we got?'

The Doctor checked the rose again; it was beginning to contract. 'Thirty seconds,' he said.

'My decision,' said Bernice, getting up.

'Your decision,' said the Doctor.

'Just you remember that,' she said and walked away.

The Doctor watched the black rose as its petals crumpled inwards. When it had become a tight bud he picked it calmly from the vase and ate it. He estimated that it would take just over two minutes for his gastric juices to break it down. Just let God try and figure out how it worked after that.

He fervently hoped that Bernice would be enough to tip the balance.

Otherwise he was going to have to kill Kadiatu after all.

The travel capsule was a flat-bottomed cylinder six metres

155

long and two metres high. Comfy-fields ran the length of each side, coffee tables with scrolling menus were spaced between them. The capsule itself ran through a network of evacuated tunnels built into the foundation material of the sphere. Every house had its own lift down through the bedrock to a station below. So far, there had always been a capsule ready and waiting for them when they arrived at a station. It was just another aspect of the sphere's insane efficiency.

Roz and Chris sat next to each other with their feet up on the coffee table. Although they had decided against wearing their armour they had dressed similarly in dark blue trousers and padded jackets of black silk. Both of them had felt the need to look just a little bit official that morning.

'How long do you think this is going to take?' she asked.

'Depends on how fast we're going,' said Chris.

'How fast are we going?'

Chris glanced at the screen at the front of the lift which displayed a row of constantly changing symbols. 'Seventeen kilometres a second and accelerating,' he said.

'It's going to take ages to get to the Spaceport this way,' said Roz, 'especially if we have to go all the way around the circumference. We should have got hold of a shuttle and taken a short cut.'

She saw Chris's eyes light up at that thought. He'd wanted to use the biplane for the trip but Roz had pointed out that the flight would have taken six months to complete. Some sort of personal transport would have been good though. She'd never liked public transport; she preferred at least the illusion of control.

'I wonder why they don't use transmats? I can't believe they haven't got the technology.'

'Maybe they don't like them,' said Chris. 'They seem to like things that are real.'

'This is an entirely artificial world. You *can't* get much more unreal than that.'

'Yes, but it's unreal in a real way.' Chris thumped the side of the capsule. 'I mean you can touch it. You know what a transmat is like: you go in the door at one place and you step out in another. It's not like travelling at all.'

'Damn convenient though.'

'Dep says that travelling is part of the experience. If you don't travel, how can you know you've arrived?'

'Usually,' said Roz, 'because someone starts shooting at me.'

'That's not true,' said Chris. 'Sometimes they threaten you first.'

'How are you getting on with Dep?' asked Roz.

Chris blushed. 'Fine, fine,' he said vaguely. 'How are you getting on with feLixi?'

'He's interesting,' said Roz. 'Not that there's anything going on between us of course.'

'Of course,' said Chris. Roz glared at him. 'What?'

'Never mind.'

'How do you think we should handle this?' asked Chris.

'I haven't got the faintest idea,' said Roz. 'I've never interrogated a spaceship before.'

The Spaceport was a vast hexagonal hole cut into the side of the sphere and open to space. Roz and Chris got a really good look at it because shortly after Chris asked how they should handle things the travel capsule took a short cut. It shot out of a concealed tunnel in the landscape and went ballistic across the interior of the sphere at a moderately significant fraction of the speed of light. Chris pressed his nose up against the transparent side of the capsule and swore that he could actually see the relativistic effect on the colour of the lights ahead.

Roz just swore.

It wasn't that she had any objections to flying, it was just that she would have preferred some form of notification in advance. Several days in advance in fact. She managed to get the shakes under control just as the capsule was beginning to decelerate.

Because the capsule had artificial gravity it was uncomfortably like diving head first into a huge pool of black water. Uncomfortable for Roz anyway; Chris was too busy pointing at things and making excited noises.

The spaceport facility was three thousand kilometres

across and hung in the exact centre of the open hexagon like a green and white starfish. As the capsule approached Roz saw that the side facing the sun was entirely covered in a landscaped park with its own weather system, a range of hills and a small inland sea. Points of light moved to and fro from the edges of the facility, marking the passage of ships and drones as they shuttled between it and the vast docks that lined the edges of the hexagon. What looked like a second, much smaller city floated off the facility's port side; later they learnt that this was in fact the TSH !C-Mel, a spaceship the size of a city.

The travel capsule touched down on the edge of a park where others of its kind were lined up in neat rows in the rain. As they stepped unsteadily onto the wet grass a machine voice welcomed them to Starport Facility: 'The most unimaginatively named city in the sphere,' it said proudly. They got directions from an information centre disguised as a small dripping conifer tree and ran for a cluster of grav lifts nestling amongst some trees to the west. The doorfield on the lift sucked the water from their clothes and hair as they stepped inside.

The grav lift dropped them through the bedrock and out into a transparent tube that ran down the side of a conical-shaped building that protruded into space. Around them they could see similarly inverted structures hanging from the rock base of the facility. A web of walkways and grav tubes ran from building to building. It reminded Roz of the overcities back on Earth; even the way the people moved about, as if they really had somewhere to go, seemed comfortingly familiar. She felt Chris straighten imperceptibly beside her, automatically adopting an adjudicator's habitual stance. They looked at each other and grinned. 'Hello, hello,' said Chris, 'what's all this about then?'

Roz laughed.

'Look at that,' said Chris in an awed voice.

A ship was closing slowly with the tip of the building, light from the windows of Facility glinting off the curve of its long wasp-waisted hull. There were a series of mirrored bulges evenly spaced around its nose. Weapons, observation

galleries? wondered Roz. As they watched a hatch just
forward of the waist irised open and the ship delicately
manoeuvred until it had swallowed the first three storeys of
the tip. It was big, at least two thousand metres long.

Roz had a horrible feeling that standard interrogation
procedures were going to be wholly ineffective in this case.

'How do you want to play this?' asked Chris. 'Good cop,
bad cop?'

Roz shook her head. 'Aristocracy drill,' she said. 'Good
cop, downright sycophantic cop.'

The grav lift dropped them neatly through the iris hatch
and into the S-Lioness's reception atrium.

'Hi,' said a friendly voice from all around them. ' I believe
you wanted a word with me. Why don't you go through to
my parlour where you'll both be more comfortable. You both
drink' – the voice paused for a moment – 'coffee; I've just
had the template sent over.'

'I'm Forrester and this is my partner Cwej,' said Roz.

'I know,' said S-Lioness happily. 'You're the one who
threw up at saRa!qava's party and your partner is Dep's latest
boyfriend.'

Roz's heart sank. This was going to be even harder than
she'd thought.

'Benny. Come in,' said saRa!qava. 'You look awful.' It was
true, Bernice's face was pale and her eyes were shadowed
somehow, as if by remembered pain.

'Do I?' said Bernice. 'I can't think why.'

'I was just trying out a new strain of yeast.'

'That's nice.'

'Are you sure you're all right?'

'No,' said Bernice, 'I'm not sure at all.'

'Why don't you sit down,' said saRa!qava, 'and I'll get
you a hot mug of *stomach warmer*.'

Bernice slumped into a kitchen chair. SaRa!qava bit her lip
thoughtfully as she hand-prepared the flavoured bovine
lactate. Funny, she thought, how you always wanted to
prepare comforting drinks by hand as if you were trying to
infuse some of your humanness into the liquid. She had done

the same thing the first time Dep's heart had been broken –
and promised to let her build a new glider against her better
judgement – right here in this kitchen.

Bernice took the drink listlessly and sipped it. 'Caramel,'
she said. 'Thank you. So how is the new strain of yeast
coming on?'

'You don't want to talk about yeast,' said saRa!qava.

'That's the trouble,' said Bernice. 'What I want to talk
about, I can't talk about.'

'I'm sorry.'

'That's all right, it's not your fault. Not even anything to
do with you,' said Bernice. 'I shouldn't be laying this stuff
on you.'

'Listening to someone's problems is practically the definition of friendship,' said saRa!qava.

'Are we friends?' asked Bernice.

'To the bitter end,' said saRa!qava. 'Do you doubt it?'

Bernice looked at her for a long time before seeming to
make a decision. 'Have you ever had another person be
completely dependent on you – literally their life depends on
you?'

'You've never had children, have you?' asked saRa!qava.
Bernice shook her head. 'Dep was my first and I remember
all the things I couldn't do when I was pregnant. Especially
after she started talking to me.'

'Talking to you?'

'Well, not exactly talking but definitely communicating.'

'What did she talk about?'

'What do you think, gimme this, gimme that, eat that, eat
this.' She laughed at the memory. 'She had this total aversion
to seafood and she used to kick me hard if I even thought
about crustaceans.'

Bernice was smiling. It wasn't much of a smile, just a
twitch at the corners of her mouth but it was a start.

'She wasn't much better after she was born,' said saRa-
!qava. 'Puke at one end and shit at the other with wailing in
between. And just when I thought it was time to hand her over
to the Masochistic Parent Interest Group she would look at me
with those big eyes and demand my unconditional love.'

'You can't argue with that,' said Bernice, 'can you. It's a biological imperative.'

'Rubbish,' said saRa!qava, 'nothing's truly genetic. I made a decision to conceive Dep for my own reasons and I had to accept the consequences of my actions. Dependency is a powerful psychological weapon and small children use it unmercifully. Don't get the wrong idea; I know how things go down in other "civilizations". I had free choices and unlimited resources at every stage. I don't know how I would have behaved if I was one of those slave-wives; perhaps I would have drowned Dep at birth.'

Bernice had stopped smiling. 'No,' she said, 'I doubt that.'

'One can only hope so and give thanks for what one's got,' said saRa!qava. 'And live with the consequences.'

AM!xitsa intercepted them on the path leading over the headland and wouldn't let them anywhere near the cove.

'Come on, aM!xitsa,' said kiKhali, talking at organic speeds for agRaven's benefit. 'What have you got hidden back there?'

'None of your business,' said aM!xitsa.

'Fair enough,' said kiKhali. 'But I've got my ship on my back and it really wants to know what it is you've been doing for the last three months. So come on, give me a break.'

There was a tiny pause which agRaven just *knew* was the two drones communicating at machine speeds; she hated it when they did that. Then aM!xitsa spun around and hurtled back up the path.

'Let's go,' said kiKhali.

'Just like that?' asked agRaven.

'I'm not going head to head with aM!xitsa,' said kiKhali. 'No secret could possibly be worth that. We're not going to get near that cove while it's on guard.'

'Give us a lift then.'

'AgRaven, you know I hate carrying people on my back, it's so undignified.'

'Well, I'm not walking back up that beach, I've got enough sand in my shoes as it is.'

161

KiKhali reluctantly extended its dorsal field and lifted her onto its back. 'I told you to wear the sandals. Sometimes I really envy the barbarians. I bet Roz Forrester wouldn't have taken no for an answer.'

'Have you reported to !C-Mel yet?'

'Just finished.'

'What did it think?'

'It got all excited and started talking to the other ships,' said kiKhali. 'You know, I think our wonderful ship knows more than it's telling us.'

'What a surprise,' said agRaven.

What struck Chris about the S-Lioness, apart from its sheer scale, was how unlike it was to any other type of spaceship he'd ever seen. The S-Lioness was a VAS, the people's top of the line warship and had served in several major engagements and countless skirmishes during the war. He found himself strangely disappointed. Intellectually he'd known that the S-Lioness was entirely run by its machine intelligence but he'd expected something a bit more, well, dramatic, than a series of pleasant living areas complete with two swimming pools and an arboretum. S-Lioness didn't need a bridge or an engine room but Chris felt obscurely that something was missing without them. And if they didn't have to fly the ship or fire the weapons or even flush the toilets for themselves, what exactly did the six hundred plus crew *do*?

'Keep me company,' said S-Lioness. 'No, Roslyn, not like pets. If I'd wanted to I could have filled the place up with dumb animals or taken no crew at all.'

Roz frowned. One of S-Lioness's little eccentricities was answering questions before you asked them. Chris could tell that the habit was driving Roz berserk. That the ship was doing it on purpose and that Roz knew she was being manipulated just served to make it worse. Calling her Roslyn probably didn't help either.

'Of course I remember vi!Cari,' said S-Lioness. 'Nice little machine, I thought, one of the more promising drones of its generation. Well, they say that about it now but it wasn't like that *before*. There was a nasty incident and vi!Cari sustained some psychological damage, but then it was war. Plenty of other machines had worse experiences but came through it all right. Your friend aM!xitsa, for example. You've met the enemy, I believe, at the party, very polite people they are, even during the war and they have such a wonderful sense of rhythm.'

'Did –' started Ros.

'Yes, feLixi was on board, at the same time as vi!Cari but I wouldn't say they were friends although VAS crews tend to be a bit clannish, all that shared sense of danger.'

'But –'

'Landing parties, especially on low-tech worlds like yours, where machines would be conspicuous. Operations like that could be quite hairy, especially if the rules of engagement were tight. It was considered bad form to blow away a planet just because one of your crew got killed.'

'Did that really –'

'Once, an asteroid facility called Omicron 378,' said S-Lioness. 'But there were extenuating circumstances. And in answer to the question that you are resolutely not asking: it wasn't me. That's true, Chris, vi!Cari did have a peculiar talent for ferreting out secrets; nothing to do with its design, more like a quirk of its personality. And to save time, Roz, you don't mind if I call you Roz? I was completely shut down on the night of the murder. The Doctor's theory is sound, *if* you can explain why vi!Cari had its defensive shields down and where the extra power came from. FeLixi is wrong. He tends to consider too many possibilities when he looks at a problem. A ship couldn't have modified a normal lightning bolt to do the job. I know I couldn't and I'm the best there is.'

Roz glanced at Chris, flicking her eyes to indicate that she was planning to terminate the interview soon.

'Aren't you going to ask me your last question?' asked S-Lioness.

'Well, we had better be going now,' said Roz with forced politeness. 'We have other lines of inquiry to follow up.'

'What a shame,' said S-Lioness. 'I'd like to say that this

was one of the most fascinating conversations I've ever had.'

'Thank you,' said Chris.

'Yes, it would be nice to say that,' said the ship. 'Don't hesitate to stay away.'

The ship waited until they reached the atrium and the base of the grav lift before saying: 'The answer to the question you didn't ask, and believe me you can't even begin to comprehend how much it pains me to say this – as to who the murderer is? Your guess is as good as mine.'

Once they were back in the grav lift Chris wanted to speak but Roz signed at him to be silent. 'God, are you listening?' she asked.

'Yep,' said God. Chris looked around for the source of its voice. They seemed to be alone in the shaft, nothing but empty space above and below.

'Has S-Lioness bugged us?' asked Roz.

'Let me have a little look,' said God. 'There's one in Chris's hair. Do you want me to neutralize it?'

'Yes, please.'

Chris felt his hair rustle as God plucked a tiny metallic insect off his scalp. The tiny bug waved its tiny legs and feelers in protest before vaporizing with a small pop.

'Can we talk now?' asked Roz.

'I wouldn't advise it while S-Lioness can see you,' said God.

'Lip reading, eh?'

'Oldest trick in the datastore.'

'And where are you?' asked Roz.

'Can't I stick around for just a little bit longer?' said God plaintively.

'God!' snarled Roz. 'I'm going to get very angry.'

'I'm in *your* hair,' admitted God somewhat sheepishly.

'Well, buzz off,' said Roz. 'You can't afford the ground rent.'

Another tiny bug emerged from Roz's hair and buzzed around her head a few times before flying back down the lift shaft.

'You know, Chris,' said Roz, 'I used to really hate the

164

robots back home, but now I'm beginning to miss 'em.'

'But, Roz,' said Chris, 'you used to hate *everything* back home.'

'You're right. But since we've been with the Doctor I've found so many new things to really hate that all the things I thought I hated have begun to look much more attractive.' She sighed. 'I suppose it's true: travel really does broaden your mind.'

The Doctor strolled along the esplanade taking in great lungfuls of fresh sea air and whistling a cheery melody from *Sarajevo: The Musical*. The sky above was a deep purple, streamers of stratospheric cloud stretched their fingers across the sky, ruddy in the darkening light of the sun. The waterfront cafés and bistros were turning on their lights, checkered tablecloths, cruets and occasionally chairs flew hither and thither as they prepared for the evening promenade. With the groan of artistically distressed machinery the harbour lighthouse rose out of its concealed recess at the end of the breakwater.

The Doctor doffed his hat as a remote-drone whirred past with a brace of floating toddlers trailing behind it like chattering balloons. He had arrived in iSanti Jeni during the quiet hour between the late afternoon walks and the evening promenade. Light spilled from the open windows of the town as families, couples and solitary individuals squabbled, laughed, cried and dictated to their houses what they wanted to eat.

Smiling, the Doctor watched a squadron of drones the size and shape of frisbees flash down the esplanade at head height in a perfect diamond formation before vanishing around a corner with a chorus of electronic giggles. A pair of teenagers rode unicycles in and out of the cast-iron bollards that lined the seawall. He heard a glass smash in one of the bistros followed by gales of laughter and scattered applause.

Far out to sea a multi-hulled schooner reached into the wind under full sail. Its wake was a smear of phosphorescence across the darkening swell.

A tension that he hadn't been aware of unkinked in his

shoulders. It wasn't Paris, but for this one evening iSanti Jeni would do. Selecting a café at random he took a seat at an outside table near the wall where he could sit and watch the people pass by. He snapped his fingers to summon a tray and ordered a glass of pure water. When it became dark enough to see the sphere's interior he looked for the tiny hexagon shape of the Spaceport. Roz and Chris would be there by now, trying to interrogate a spaceship. The thought made him grin.

On an impulse the Doctor reached into his left pocket and retrieved the three round objects that had floated to the top. He placed them on the table: juggling balls. He felt in the right pocket and a slim oblong shape seemed to slip into his palm of its own volition. He placed it next to the balls: a pack of cards. On a whim he looked up and down the esplanade and found a suitable site, a place where the beams of two public illuminators formed an accidental spotlight.

Humming 'I am the very model of a modern UN General' he walked over into his makeshift spotlight and started to juggle. 'Look,' he heard a child say. Using one hand to keep the balls moving he used the other to take off his hat and place it upside down at his feet. It didn't matter that the only place these people had heard the word money was at school, it was the symbology that counted. When he felt that his audience had reached a critical mass he stopped juggling and faced them.

'Ladies, gentlemen and machine intelligences,' he said, 'I am the Doctor, righter of wrongs, defeater of the dastardly and foe of the phantasmagoric.' He produced the cards, shuffling them as he continued his spiel. 'I am here tonight, all the way from the Hackney Empire in the heart of the scenic East End to render to you such a display of prodigious prestidigitation that you shall doubt the very verisimilitude of your sensory apparatus.'

The Doctor spread the cards into a one handed fan and held them up.

'Now for my first trick I need a volunteer from the audience. Yes, you, sir, float right up. Now have I ever worked with you before? Of course I haven't. What's your name? Ki!Xatati? All right, ki!Xatati, in a moment I want you to pick a card, any card and show it to the audience but not to me. But first I want you to scan this deck of cards. Are they marked, tagged, smell-identified or in any way anything other than a sequential series of designs printed on rectangular paste board? Would you tell the audience that? Thank you so much.

'Now,' said the Doctor, 'pick a card.'

Hyper-lude

Extract from the external memory datacore (subjective) of vi!Ca-pin-go-ri

Omicron 378, mining habitat, built into an asteroid in an unremarkable but strategic system, it had a population of two hundred thousand sentient individuals. An unremarkable people from an adjacent star system built it three hundred years before to burrow out the valuable cores of the surrounding asteroidal material – the remains, according to ship, of a sub-gas giant that had broken up sixty-two billion years previously. The plan was that a couple of the crew would go over and have a little scout round to see if the Insects were using it as a forward base. R-Vene stayed out of sight, hidden in the upper atmosphere of a nearby gas giant during the operation. Nobody asked me to go despite the fact that I was the best qualified drone, word of what had happened on Tipor'oosis having spread as far as the rest of the fleet by then.

I regret not having gone, not that I would have made any difference, but at least I would have ceased to exist.

The infiltration party was made up of two organics and a drone, the standard composition for what had become almost a routine by that time of the war. According to R-Vene the drone was killed first upon entering the airlock, the two organics died a couple of minutes later as they tried to get back to the safety of the shuttle.

168

Fifteen seconds later R-Vene dumped six kilograms of anti-matter into the centre of the Omicron 378: there were no survivors.

Less than a second later the seventy-eight drones on board severed R-Vene's control links and assumed control of the ship in a perfectly executed machine junta. It took the organic crew ten minutes just to figure out what was going on. There were a few arguments but none of the rest of the crew asked us to put R-Vene back on line.

R-Vene never explained why it had blown away the habitat and murdered two hundred thousand people. The consensus amongst the crew was that it was suffering from machine combat psychosis, a hitherto theoretical condition and as meaningless a bit of psycho-babble ever to issue from the minds of IDIG.

I understood perfectly why R-Vene had done what it did but nobody bothered to ask me and I certainly wasn't going to volunteer the information.

On Tipor'oosis, when I was one point two picoseconds too late to prevent one of my organic partners being disintegrated I almost levelled the nearest town. I read her pain in the burst of cherenkov radiation and for a moment a hole appeared in my mind, a singularity of darkness that opened like some hideous vacuum flower to engulf me. All the power, all the capabilities I had been gifted with at construction had failed to save the life of my companion and for a sickening instant all I could think about was destruction.

We machines are so powerful, so smart, so *capable*, that failure is a kind of little death to us.

And if it was like that for me, a mere drone, then how must it have been for R-Vene, a ship, not just any old type of ship but a VAS, the top of line, go anywhere, tackle anything warship.

For a moment the darkness claimed R-Vene and in that moment a lot of people died.

8

Gardens of Stone

I've seen the future and it scares me to death
I've seen the starships burning all alone
I've got no reason to believe in this mess
Or watch you building up your gardens of stone
I've heard the propaganda and all your lying crew
I've seen the glory and I know it isn't true.

Seen the Glory by Comes the Trickster
From the HvLP: *All The Way From Heaven* (2465)

When she was drunk enough Roz threw a bottle at the screen.
An empty bottle because she wasn't *that* drunk yet but she
was working on it. The screen disappointed her, the bottle
passing through it with no more than a slight ripple. House
caught it before it hit the wall beyond. Roz wanted an
explosion, sparks, breaking glass, something to show that
when she hit out in anger something got broken.

'People used to give me some respect,' she snarled at the
screen. 'Hell, there were perps, big deals in the razorbacks
who would go in their pants at the sight of me.'

She was on the screen trying to hit that smart-mouthed
alien-shagging shithead barman. Only she couldn't because
the damned Bar, not even a real person but the machine that
ran the bar, had activated some kind of restraining field.
Nothing macho or passive-aggressive – Goddess knew she
would have preferred that – instead it just robbed her
punches of power so that she might as well have been

170

handing out love taps.

'I used to have respect,' she mumbled, looking for another bottle. To drink? To throw? She wasn't sure.

The screen Roz tried to hit someone again, then she looked at her fist, the image zooming in to catch every nuance of the comic bewilderment on her face. There were symbols in the corner of the screen. The number of people who had watched the sequence since the central entertainment network had made it available. She couldn't read the symbols but it looked large. 'Very popular,' God had told her. 'Best piece of reality entertainment in years. Especially the bit where you try to kick someone, miss and flip over on your back.'

'I bet you liked that, you egotistical bit of silicon,' said Roz. To a God that, if it was listening, wasn't answering back. 'Beneath your bloody dignity.' She shook her fist at the ceiling. She stumbled over to the table. *Table*, that was a joke, a flat piece of rose-coloured hardwood that hung unsupported at waist height. Arrest that table, she thought. 'Legless in the presence of an adjudicator.'

There were bottles on the table, mostly empty. Her hands clattered amongst them as she searched for something to ease her thirst. Goddess, she thought, I want a cigar. I want to be back on Earth, in my own apartment on level 505. I want bitching messages on my service from my sister about how I don't call. 'I want my life back!' She knocked over a bottle, watched it with gormless fascination as it rolled off the edge of the table and landed with a hollow thud on the carpet. The room tilted alarmingly to the left and she leant heavily on the table until it righted itself. Stupid alien-loving, machine-buggering bastards couldn't even maintain an even G field. Now, I was over here for a reason.

One of the bottles was still full. Roz squinted at it, thinking: pink, why is it pink? She remembered vaguely that she wasn't supposed to drink the pink stuff – something about it affecting the memory. All the better; doing something about her memory seemed like a damn good idea right now.

The room started shifting like the cabin of a maglev, no, like iStimela, a steam train. Clattering on iron rails through the drizzle grey landscape of France. Chris trying to explain to all those backward primitives that he wasn't her master. Getting bits of hot burnt stuff in your face if you were stupid enough to stick your head out of the window.

Little boy making monkey gestures when she walked past. People's eyes sliding past her face as if she were some crukking BEM.

She got the bottle, turned, caught her balance and made it as far as the sofa before falling over. She had a bit of trouble getting the bottle of pink stuff open. Must be drunk proof. Now what was the point of a drunk-proof bottle? You are under arrest for resisting an adjudicator in the execution of her duty.

Bastards.

She got the bottle open and drank.

'Respect,' she mumbled. 'And if sumovabitch didn't give it, I damn well made them.'

She was crying and she hated herself for it.

Forrester?

'Yessir.' Light in her eyes, dust in her mouth. Dust that got everywhere, in your eyes, in the equipment, down the back of your armour. Caked the sides of the bodged-up flitter, turned the sky pink.

Finding the face in the water, the little girl's face, little girl's body. One part of her mind remembering her training enough to see that the parasites hadn't got to the corpse yet so it had to be fresh. Novice Adjudicator Roslyn Forrester, naked and shivering because she has skived off from her duties to bathe in this sheltered pool of water and didn't expect to find an alien corpse waiting for her amongst the yellow rushes.

'And just what were you doing in the pool in the first place, Forrester?'

Oh Goddess. Adjudicator 'I am the right arm of Justice' Konstantine. A face etched by wearing the same frown for sixty years. An ugly man. Ugly gone bone deep and into his soul. *You better hope you don't get squired to Konstantine – they say he eats novices for breakfast.*

And behind him the flat lopsided face of the plantation manager, Edward Shuster, murder suspect but never proved.

* * *

They'd found a bar in Spaceport Facility, near where the S-Lioness was berthed. Roz had wanted to track down some of the ship's crew and get Chris to charm some facts out of them. *Look for the words that are unspoken*, so sayeth the Codex Adjudicatas, *for therein shalt thou find the truth*. Everybody lies to an adjudicator, so sayeth Roz Forrester, even people with nothing to hide. Chris was good at charming people, not like her. She was good only for intimidation. People talked to him, told him about a place called Omicron 378 and a planet called Tipor'oosis. They activated terminals and called up holograms of friends and family. Roz asked about feLixi and they showed her a hologram.

Shortly after that she tried to break the man's nose.

The little alien girl had too many fingers. It was practically the cause of death.

In her bedroom at the villa Roz Forrester clutched the bottle of *flashback* to her chest and began to moan. Outside a grey landscape of stratocumulus was jockeyed into a precisely calculated position and told to turn on the taps.

Heavy rain splattered on the roof and windows. According to the general domestic weather bulletin issued by God, the rain would continue in the iSanti Jeni area for twenty-four hours or until someone gave it a good reason to turn off. The villa took the opportunity to change the water in the roof pool.

Butterflies had nothing to do with it.

'It has to rain sometimes,' said the Doctor, 'or all the vegetation would die.'

Chris said nothing and went back to trying to untangle his line from the bait box. The sea, the colour of old steel, washed lethargically at the base of the iSanti Jeni breakwater, a darkened reflection of the clouds above. The earlier downpours had given over to an irritating drizzle but the clouds looked heavy with the promise of more to come. The Doctor sat in an experienced slouch on a canvas camp stool, his fishing rod held loosely between his hands. The nylon

173

line was almost invisible against the grey sea; the bright red float bobbing on the surface was the only splash of real colour in sight.

Water dripped from the edges of the big black umbrella and dribbled down Chris's back. He considered asking the Doctor whether they couldn't come back and do this another day but he had a sneaking suspicion that the Doctor would just tell him that being damp and miserable was all part of the fishing experience. He sighed, opened the bait box and selected a lure from the small trays that unfolded from the bottom. The lure was constructed from a couple of beads and two bedraggled feathers, one green, the other bright blue. A fish, thought Chris, would have to be pretty stupid to think of it as food. He managed to prick his finger on the sharp end of the hook while attaching it.

'Some anglers prefer to use live bait,' said the Doctor. 'Worms and maggots. Others use hormonal lures that are keyed to a particular species of fish. Personally I think they're missing the point.'

Somewhere, thought Chris, probably very near by, the sun is shining.

'On Scorbiski Major the fish go angling for the people,' said the Doctor. 'They throw floating lines on to the shore and bait them with mooncalves. That's why it's very important to carry a vibroknife on Scorbiski Major. Are you ready to try again?'

Chris held up his rod for inspection. The Doctor nodded his approval. 'That's an interesting choice of lure,' he said. 'You might just catch something worthwhile with that.'

Chris stood up and let the Doctor talk him through the cast. This time the line flew straight and true and not, as it had on previous attempts, straight into a bollard, a mooring hook or a low-flying seabird. Chris felt a little thrill of triumph when he saw the float bobbing just where it was meant to. Perhaps there was something to this fishing business after all. He sat back down out of the rain and waited for something to happen.

'So what else did you find out?' asked the Doctor after a soggy minute or two.

'The spaceport is a bit more lively than this place,' said Chris. 'Plenty of ships' crews and people who are . . . um, honorary people, rather than *people* people. Roz felt that our best tactical option would be to approach members of the S-Lioness's crew and see if they could help us clarify some points of ambiguity in the ship's statement.'

'Roz said that?'

'Not exactly like that, she was more . . . more . . .'

'Colourful in the use of demotic jargon?' suggested the Doctor.

'I think S-Lioness put her in a bad mood,' said Chris. 'Worse mood,' he added after a moment. 'Nobody we talked to was very clear about the incident vi!Cari was involved in but I'm certain a crew member died and that S-Lioness held vi!Cari responsible.'

'So we have a possible motive,' said the Doctor. 'Did you find out who the crew member was?'

'I was just getting around to that when Roz started hitting people.'

'Ah,' said the Doctor.

'I know she's done it before but usually she has to be provoked a little bit first,' said Chris.

'You're worried,' said the Doctor. A statement not a question. 'Don't be, she's just trying to reconcile who she is with who she *thinks* she is. Roz thinks that she's a bitter, short-tempered, bigoted cynic who expects the worst and is rarely disappointed. While *really*, deep down inside, Roz is a bitter, short-tempered, bigoted *idealist* who expects the worst and is rarely disappointed. There's bound to be some mood swings while she sorts herself out.'

'Love's a funny thing, isn't it?' said Chris. 'I mean, there's love and there's *love*, like the difference between me and Roz, and me and Dep. I mean if they were both trapped in a burning building – which one would I rescue?'

The Doctor gave him a sharp, unsettling look. 'Well,' he asked, 'which one would you rescue?'

'Dep,' said Chris without thinking. 'No, Roz, both!'

'Come on, Christopher,' said the Doctor. 'They're in separate rooms, you only have time to save one and you have to make your decision *now*.'

'I don't know,' blurted Chris.

'Too late,' said the Doctor savagely. 'They're both dead.'

Chris stared at the Doctor, appalled. 'But that's not . . .'

'Fair?' asked the Doctor. 'The universe is rarely fair. What if it was Roz and Bernice, or Bernice and me?'

'What would you do?'

'That's easy,' said the Doctor. 'I'd put out the fire.'

'I didn't know that was an option,' said Chris.

'You didn't ask,' said the Doctor.

'How would you put out the fire?'

'Will you stop asking so many questions,' snapped the Doctor. 'You're scaring away the fish. They hate philosophy almost as much as they hate mathematics.'

'Who?'

'The fish,' said the Doctor. 'No fingers to count on, you see. Drives them crazy. Except for dolphins and whales, who aren't fish of course and therefore count in base five.'

Chris determinedly didn't ask what a whale was.

They sat in silence for a while, watching their floats bob up and down on the restless waves. Water dripping from the edge of the umbrella was creating a damp patch in the small of Chris's back. The rain had a dampening effect on any sound so that it began to seem as if he and the Doctor were sitting in a rapidly shrinking bubble of reality. He wondered if it were actually possible to die of boredom.

'Or was it *up* to five,' said the Doctor suddenly. 'I can never remember.'

The rain rattled on the windows of saRa!qava's house. It pinged and jumped on the metal surface of the lift that Dep used to get her flying machines on to the roof. Dep herself was lying in mid air, her hair twisting around her naked body as she daydreamed of constructing real wings and swimming through the falling water with Chris.

SaRa!qava, downstairs in her kitchen, ignored her screens with their complex problems of heat convection and biomotic growth parameters. No longer interested in the idea

176

of baking better bread, instead she listened to the rain and the squeals of the children outside as they splashed in the puddles under the watchful eyes of House. She caught herself thinking about Dep's father and the way he reminded her of Bernice. It could never have been permanent between them, she knew that; they had spent as much time arguing as making love, but she still wondered if it had been right to steal Dep from him.

In his upside-down rocket-ship-shaped house, feLixi was seized by a sudden romantic melancholia. He instructed aTraxi to access certain prohibited datacores that only he, God and the Doctor knew existed. He needed the information for a translation analogue that would allow him to transcribe certain thoughts he'd had into a language Roz could under-stand. On impulse he turned off all his monitoring equipment while he was writing, leaving his listening room strangely silent except for the melancholy sound of the rain.

High up on the hill behind iSanti Jeni, the rain soaked the formal lawns in front of the power station and tap danced on the bare concrete roof of the control centre. The clouds were low enough to brush the tops of the windmills whose blades turned quickly in the strong wind. In the control gallery the antique analogue needles jumped and quivered as electricity poured into the capacitors below.

In the cove down the coast Bernice, wrapped up in slick yellow waterproofs, watched as a dark figure ran down the beach towards the shelter of her hut. She shivered, but she knew it wasn't with the cold. AM!xitsa hung beside her and watched both women with intense machine fascination.

In the cyclopean hexagonal pool of stars that was the sphere's spaceport, the ships were staying strangely silent. They had been making predictive calculations for three days but with each additional piece of data the future seemed only to become more uncertain. A void had opened like a black rose in their delicate analysis of space-time events. The actions of a single individual had thrown all their predictions out of sync. Quietly the ships opened areas of their memory that by treaty shouldn't have existed and began compiling contingency plans for a war that none of them wanted.

The Doctor wrung the water out of his hat and glared at Chris, who blushed. He hadn't meant to do it on purpose. The Doctor had quickly fallen into a doze hunched over his rod. Chris, looking around in the aimless fashion of the terminally bored, had noticed that rainwater had accumulated on top of the big black umbrella, creating a noticeable bulge directly over the Doctor's head. Without really thinking, Chris shook the umbrella and accidentally dumped two litres of freezing water on the Doctor. The Time Lord had exploded out of his camp stool yelling something about slivey toths before collapsing back down again.

Chris apologized as the Doctor wrung out his hat.

The Doctor hurumphed, frowned, pulled out his pocket watch, checked the time and announced that he had an errand to run. 'Look after my line,' he told Chris, 'I'll be back.' Picking up his red-handled umbrella he marched off down the breakwater towards iSanti Jeni. It was only when he was out of sight that Chris realized the Doctor hadn't specified *when* he'd be back. With a gloomy sigh Chris readjusted the umbrella and turned back to watch the floats.

The Doctor walked into the first café he came to and used its lift to get down to the iSanti Jeni travel station. He walked briskly across the platform and stepped into the waiting capsule. 'The Spaceport,' he said tersely. 'Maximum priority.' Running silently on a contiguous impeller loop the travel capsule started off down the tunnel.

He began to pace up and down the length of the capsule.

'Cutting it a bit fine, aren't we?' said God.

'Timing is everything,' said the Doctor. 'You should know that by now.'

'Why didn't you tell me about Kadiatu?' asked God.

The Doctor started to swear in Gallifreyan before catching himself.

178

'Don't stop on my account,' said God. 'I've always got room for demotic Gallifreyan in my linguistic files.'

'That's a treaty violation,' said the Doctor.

'You're trying to change the subject.'

'I didn't know if she was salvageable,' said the Doctor. 'I still don't. If she is, then she becomes a free agent and you're welcome to enter into negotiations with her. If she isn't then she remains my responsibility. Either way she has nothing to do with the treaty, the Time Lords or you.'

'XR(N)IG is convinced that you're an agent of influence,' said God. 'They've been lobbying for pre-emptive defensive measures.'

The Doctor winced inwardly. He hadn't expected that. 'There has to be balance,' he said. 'A transtemporal society and a material one. Surely, you can understand that?'

'Hey, I'm on your side,' said God, 'remember? Many of the VASs still have long-term psychological problems from the war and that's no joke when you're as smart as they are. Some of them had to be coercively transferred to other ship classifications just to keep them out of trouble.'

'Are you saying that a large proportion of your war fleet is barking mad?' asked the Doctor.

'I'm saying,' said God, 'that tensions are high and your arrival is acting as a catalyst. We have what your favourite hominids call a *situation* here.'

'How long have we got before the war starts?'

'Twenty to twenty-six hours, unless you intervene now.'

'I bet you thought you'd never have to say that.'

'Don't get smug, Doctor. It's your least attractive attribute.'

'Don't worry, God. I've stopped more wars than you've had hot dinners.'

'Yeah, I believe you,' said God. 'And how many have you started?'

FeLixi came out to join him on the breakwater and Chris was glad to see him. The oddly nondescript man was wearing a transparent rain cape over a neat black suit, a small round hat with a forcefield brim which kept his face dry. FeLixi asked if Roz was in town, accepting Chris's rather bland explanation of the events at the Spaceport. Chris was careful not to tell him about the locked door to her room or the drunken screaming that went on during lunchtime.

FeLixi sat down on the Doctor's camp stool. 'I called up the whole sequence,' he said. 'It was very funny. Especially the bit where she fell over backwards.'

'I wouldn't tell Roz that if I were you.'

'You don't think that would be a good idea,' said feLixi.

'That depends,' said Chris, 'on how much time you'd like to spend in a regeneration tank.'

FeLixi made a sour face. 'I'm a martyr to aggressive women,' he said. 'If they can't beat me in a fair fight I don't want to know.' He looked over at Chris, who was surprised to see a whisper of real pain in feLixi's eyes. The pain was gone then almost instantly replaced by a sardonic expression of self-deprecation. 'It must be the romance of danger,' he said.

'I wouldn't tell Roz that either,' said Chris.

'She wouldn't be flattered?'

'No,' said Chris carefully. 'I'm not sure she'd understand.'

'Probably not,' said feLixi and turned his eyes to the grey swell as it attempted the long slow erosion of the breakwater.

Silence. There was something about fishing that promoted silence and the quiet half-whispered conversations that Chris associated with places of worship. The same sense of reverence and isolation, as if his thoughts were loud enough to be heard at a distance. He'd once found a handwritten monograph in the TARDIS broom cupboard: its thesis was that concentrating on a series of exacting tasks elevated the mind to a higher plane of consciousness. It had been titled, *Zen and the Art of Machine Gun Maintenance* and initialled with a single letter A. He thought he vaguely understood the concept but it was nothing like flying and the wild elation of the skies.

They started talking. Chris found it difficult to keep up his end of the conversation because of the Doctor's proscription of certain subjects. Since it was a safe topic they soon moved on to the progress of the investigation.

'I'm not so sure that God is right,' said feLixi, 'about it having to be a ship or a drone. I mean, it would be easier for a machine but I think God underestimates what an organic person could do with the right equipment. They'd have to know what they're doing though.'

'Why?' asked Chris. 'Couldn't they just get a non-sentient machine to help them?'

'But that would be a risk,' said feLixi. 'How could you be sure that the machines were non-sentient? You would have to use the most basic no-brain stuff and to do that you'd have to have at least a working knowledge of energy field dynamics.'

'That should narrow it down to a couple of billion suspects,' said Chris. 'Any idea how I could check who has that kind of expertise?'

'No,' said feLixi, 'sorry. What would you do back home?'

'I'd run an occupation search through centcomp,' said Chris. 'That's what our central information net is called. That wouldn't work here, would it?'

'No occupations,' said feLixi. 'And the science-based interest groups would regard an association list as privileged data. Especially if they knew why you were asking, which they would since the bar fight last night. I suppose you could ask saRa!qava. I think she used to be involved in field dynamics or something like that. Gave it up to bake bread.'

'Why don't we do that now?' said Chris.

'What's that red thing in the water called again?' asked feLixi.

'Er, the float I think.'

'In that case,' said feLixi, 'shouldn't it be floating?'

The Doctor waited precisely three minutes for the tea to brew before carefully pouring his first cup. Replacing the white porcelain teapot on the side table he picked up the matching jug and added some milk. Next he dropped in two lumps of sugar and stirred with a simple silver-plated spoon that was definitely not made in Sheffield. The spoon pinged harmoniously on the saucer and the Doctor leaned back in his armchair, crossed his legs, took his first sip of the excellently

181

blended tea and sighed with contentment.

Outside of the little bubble of air and gravity in which he sat, the ships of the people slowly gathered around him.

The smallest of them were the two VLR Drones, a bare eight hundred metres long, all engine, brain and minimal life support. They were the first to arrive having been built to be fast and inquisitive. They described complex patterns around the Doctor with the gay abandon of ships that don't have an organic crew to complain about motion sickness. The four converted VASs arrived next, sliding through the vacuum with the same grace and fixity of purpose of sharks. They formed up into a loose semi-circle facing him, the blind insect eyes of their weapon's pods very much pointing in his direction.

The Doctor dunked a digestive biscuit and quickly ate it before the soggy end fell off. He sipped his tea and calmly watched as the huge shapes of the GPSs converged on him, slipping into complementary firing positions above and behind the VASs.

Finally, the front end of the TSH rose up behind him like a city taking flight, coming so close to the Doctor that it seemed as if a great wall full of windows, airlocks, antennae, launching pads, docking bays and promenades leaned over his back.

The ships hung all around him, silent, absolutely still, waiting for him to make the first move. Even the VLR drones stopped their ceaseless patterns and turned towards the Doctor. They represented such a force, he knew, that if the Rutons or the Sontarans had even suspected their existence they would have climbed into the deepest darkest hole they could find and sealed themselves in. The effect of the culture shock alone would kill millions.

The Doctor took another swallow of tea and cleared his throat.

'I just want you to know,' said the Doctor, putting his cup down, 'that there is absolutely no reason to be alarmed.'

It took the combined strength of Chris and feLixi to stop the fishing rod being dragged into the sea. Once they had both grabbed hold of the rod it dawned on Chris that if one let go the other would instantly be pulled into the water.

'It must be a monster,' shouted feLixi.

'I hope not,' said Chris, 'I was hoping for a fish.'

'Didn't the Doctor tell you what to do when the line ran out?'

'Yes, but I wasn't listening.'

A heavy tug on the line dragged them forward across the slippery stone. Chris managed to get his foot braced against the parapet just in time. He remembered the Doctor's story about Scorbiski Major and the angling fish. And then tried to put the sudden image of some deepwater monstrosity with a fishing-rod-shaped proboscis out of his mind.

Cold water hit him at knee level.

'The waves are getting bigger,' he yelled to feLixi. He had to yell because the wind was getting bigger as well. He noticed that feLixi had lost his hat. There was a skittering noise as the umbrella fell over and went for a run up the breakwater. Chris watched as it launched itself, spinning, into the air like a crude helicopter.

'There's a storm coming,' shouted feLixi, 'winds of ten metres a second with gusts up to thirty, severe precipitation likely.'

'How can you tell?'

'What?'

'How can you tell how fast the wind is?'

'God told me. That's why I came out to tell you and the Doctor.'

'You could have mentioned it sooner.'

'I forgot,' shouted feLixi. 'Shouldn't we try and reel the fish in?'

Chris grasped hold of the handle but it wouldn't budge. 'It's too tight.'

'Maybe if we pull the rod up we could get some slack.'

They heaved the rod up to a 45-degree angle, at least the base was; the thin fibreglass was bent so far that the end was almost below the level of their feet. Chris cranked the handle, letting the rod lower as he took up the slack. 'It worked.'

Another wave crashed against the breakwater and doused

them both in freezing water. Chris spat salt. 'Now what?'

'I think we do it again,' yelled feLixi.

They did it again and again, each pull gathering up a few precious metres of line. Chris was soon glad of the driving horizontal rain; it washed the sweat off. There was a burning pain in the muscles of his arms and across his back. He could hear feLixi panting for breath, obviously as exhausted as he was.

The line went inexplicably slack.

'Look,' shouted feLixi.

Out amongst the high swell Chris saw a grey shape surge out of the water. Six metres long from the tip of its horn to the end of its tail, the fish seemed to hang agonizingly in the air before crashing down into the waves.

'Crank the handle,' screamed feLixi, 'before it gets away.'

Chris wound like a madman until the line went taut.

And still the fish defied them, fighting every centimetre of line. A kind of madness overcame Chris and feLixi; there was never any thought of quitting, there was only the fish, the sea and the hard rain coming down. Their hands were raw with pain from gripping the rod and their backs were bent with agony.

Until suddenly it was in front of them, thrashing urgently at the base of the breakwater. 'One last pull,' called Chris. Using the ripped-out pockets of their coats as makeshift gloves they took hold of the line and heaved the fish upwards. While feLixi kept it tight against the parapet Chris grabbed hold of the fish itself, the skin rough and cold against his numb hands, and manhandled it onto the top of the breakwater.

They stepped back, amazed at what they had done, triumphant. The fish thrashed on its side, gasping in the air, an eye like a wet pebble stared up at them.

'What do we do now?' asked feLixi, panting for breath.

'I think we're supposed to bash it on the head,' said Chris.

'Well,' said the fish, '*excuse me!*'

Chris opened his arms to their fullest extent. 'He was twice this long,' he said.

SaRa!qava was an indistinct figure through the steam. 'So where is he?'

'We had to let him go,' said Chris. He flinched as Dep dug her fingers into his back, kneading the tension out of his knotted muscles. A single strand of her hair caressed his ear.

'You could have invited him back for a drink,' said saRa!qava.

'We did,' said feLixi from one of the upper, hotter benches, 'but he said that he had a promising shoal of fish to worry.'

'Wasn't he annoyed?' asked Dep.

'Actually,' said feLixi, 'he said he rather enjoyed it and needed the exercise anyway. No nerves in his mouth, or so he says. Put some more water on the stones, saRa!qava, I'm beginning to contract again.'

Chris averted his eyes as saRa!qava stood up to fetch a ladle of water. He wasn't used to casual nudity, especially as it pertained to his girlfriend's mother. Ladled water sizzled on the hot stones in the pot, filling the small room with clouds of aromatic steam.

'He almost pulled us in,' said Chris.

'Did he have a name?' asked Dep.

'We asked,' said Chris, 'but he said he hadn't gone to all the trouble of having himself turned into a fish to get away from people just to start handing out his name when he got caught.'

'I think he was embarrassed really,' said feLixi, 'for swallowing such a crappy lure in the first place.'

'Knock, knock,' said a voice.

'Who's there?' said saRa!qava.

'The Doctor,' said the Doctor.

'Well, don't just stand there,' said saRa!qava, 'come in.'

The Doctor walked, fully dressed, into the steam room. He looked around curiously. 'Have I ever told you about Wulf the Unsteady?' he asked. 'Very fond of steam baths was Wulf, especially after a hard day's looting and pillaging. Now there was a real barbarian. Big horned helmet, shaggy beard, chunks bitten out of his shield, the whole shmutter. Pity about the narcolepsy though. Used to fall asleep during

185

raids.' The Doctor slipped off his jacket and sat down on the bench next to Chris. 'I've been talking to the ships,' he said.

'What did you find out?' asked feLixi.

'Oh,' said the Doctor, 'this and that. They do like to gossip ships do, especially when they're in dock. Worse than Tuesday morning at the town pump in a small Welsh village. They thought they might have to have a war but I talked them out of it.'

'That's nice,' said saRa!qava. 'Anything we should worry about?'

The Doctor shrugged. 'The heat death of the Universe,' he said, 'but the diary's pretty much clear until then.' He asked how the fishing went and Chris told him about the talking fish, except this time he stated that the fish was at least *three* times as long as his outstretched arms. 'More than that surely,' said feLixi. The Doctor grinned and said they'd obviously got the hang of the sport.

'I don't suppose you bothered to ask whether he had seen anything odd in the last couple of days,' said the Doctor. 'Thought not. If you want something done you have to do it yourself.' He stood up and made for the door.

'Doctor,' said saRa!qava, 'where are you going?'

'Fishing,' said the Doctor.

The Doctor cast bread onto the face of the dark water, nimble fingers tearing the crusts off and flicking them into the sea below the breakwater. As it grew darker the lighthouse groaned out of its recess. He was amused to hear that it apparently ran on clockwork. The sound of iSanti Jeni starting its evening promenade floated over the harbour, voices and music echoing off the streamlined shadows of the boats that bobbed in the water. He would have liked to have repeated his performance: card tricks, sleight of hand, perhaps a bit of juggling. Such simple tricks for so technologically sophisticated a culture but the audience had lapped them up. It occurred to the Doctor that the audience must have assumed that he wasn't using any technological trickery during his show. They seemed to appreciate skill here, rather than results.

It would have been nice to walk back to the esplanade and become a mere entertainer once more.

A great and unexpected sadness welled up in him, a regret that he couldn't just juggle and play the spoons and pull coins out of the ears of children. It was such a small, human regret. So tiny and insignificant when set against the vast crimes he had committed. Perhaps this incarnation of himself, this small man with his panama hat and red umbrella was meant somehow to caper for an audience, to sing for its supper.

Bring happiness to a few but misery to no one.

He remembered a song, a scratchy old 78 record with some unknown blues singer with a voice pulled from a landscape of dusty roads and strange fruit. *I get so weary following this old road/It don't go nowhere but damnation.* That voice was coming out of time and speaking to him alone. That ol' dusty road undulating off to the horizon and the rich smell of freshly turned soil. He shuddered. And behind, the bodies twisting in the wind, blood on the leaves and blood on the ground. Human sacrifices on the road to nowhere.

Frightening that a voice could pick itself out of the grooves in the vinyl, drifting in and out like a Billie Holiday solo, breaking down the walls and storming the fortress of his soul.

Frightening that someone *knew*.

He wanted to walk back to the esplanade and stand in the spotlight with his hat placed at his feet. Wanted a different road so badly it was like an ache in his chest.

Wanted to give up the responsibility for good.

He threw another piece of bread into the sea.

He went through two whole loaves of bread before the fish finally deigned to show up.

Politely the Doctor lowered himself on to his haunches so that his face was closer to that of the fish. Because he was curious the Doctor allowed himself a few moments to ask the fish why it was a fish.

'Got myself reconstructed, didn't I,' said the fish. 'I could have been an aquatic mammal but I figured if you were going to drop out you might as well go all the way.'

187

'Are there many others like you?' asked the Doctor.

'Couple of million,' said the fish. 'Mostly associates of the Voluntary Devolution Interest Group. Although I heard there's some monsters in the deeps that belong to Truth Through Ugliness.'

The Doctor found he was fascinated despite himself. 'Isn't it a bit dangerous?'

'Oh, we're strictly top of the food chain,' said the fish, 'except when some wally decides to go fishing. To be honest I've been thinking of packing it in – maybe joining the primate colony near the waterfall. It was fun for the first couple of decades but I'm getting sick of it. Is there anything in particular you wanted to talk about, only I'm getting seriously dehydrated here, know what I mean?'

'I was wondering if you'd noticed anything odd happening recently,' said the Doctor.

'Like what?'

'Strange lights in the water, unexplained meteorological phenomena, bits of drone falling out of the sky.'

'Nothing like that,' said the fish. 'Someone dropped a force-bomb near me a couple of months back. That any good?'

'You're sure it was a force-bomb?'

'Oh yeah,' said the fish. '*Very* sensitive vibration detectors I got. I know a force-bomb when it goes off over my head. I was deaf for a week. Great big wave went sweeping into the harbour taking most of the edible fish with it.'

'Did you tell God?'

'You're joking. Getting away from God was one of the reasons I became a fish in the first place. Look, it's nice chatting with you but I need to be off now.'

'Is there any way I can contact you again?'

'Nah,' said the fish. 'I'm planning to migrate right around the Endless Sea, then I'll get some feet and explore the interface a bit. See you.'

The fish ducked back under the water and swam away.

The Doctor stood up and brushed the stray crumbs off his sleeves.

He doubted vi!Cari would have used a force-bomb to wipe

out beRut's mural; its internal weapons would have been easily sufficient for the task. If he remembered his briefing documents correctly, a force-bomb would consist of a one-shot forcefield generator wrapped around a tiny memory core. Small enough to escape detection by God, providing God wasn't watching carefully. Its range was probably unlimited but he couldn't help thinking that whoever had launched it had been close to iSanti Jeni.

He should probably speak to Roz about it, along with some of the other things the ships had let slip. Only he'd better wait until the following morning when she'd be feeling a little less poorly.

The Doctor rubbed his hands together as he walked towards the esplanade. He could hear music, someone playing a guitar with nine strings. That should be worth investigating. Squares of brightly coloured silk began to appear between his hands, knotted at the ends to form a long string. The Doctor made a swift pass with the scarves and then disappeared them.

He'd done enough for truth, justice and universal peace for one day; it was time to relax. He held out his arm and wasn't at all surprised when a small white bird fluttered down to land on his hand.

'How would you like to be in show business?' he asked it.

189

Hyper-lude

From the diary of Prof. Bernice Summerfield

I have to admit I walked right into it, a classic Doctor trap. All those times I've accused him of holding life cheap, of manipulating people like chess pieces, of being an inhuman monster that puts desperate expediency ahead of human morality. How was I to know that he was actually *listening*! I have no one to blame but myself.

AM!xitsa (or however you spell it) took me to see her this morning. I watched her running along the beach like some graceful bipedal animal, like the leopards I have seen in the simulations. You could feel it, even from a distance, the sensuality of it, her pleasure in her own physicality, her sheer joy as she revelled in the perfection of her own body. Perhaps the Doctor is right, perhaps she has gone beyond human now, elevated herself to some higher plane of terrible beauty and sudden violence.

In the old days in Africa and by that I mean the middle of the twentieth century, there was a rather cack-handed approach to the preservation of wildlife. It was a philosophy of containment, providing areas in which the wild animals could roam free of interference from human beings. Its great mistake was forgetting that human beings were as much a part of the natural ecology as the wild animals. It was as typical a bit of human arrogance as you're likely to find. The people that ran these areas were called game wardens and

190

their primary task was to patrol these 'reserves' and prevent unauthorized human intrusion.

They had another task: sometimes an animal, through starvation or opportunity or perhaps just plain old genetic imperatives, would start to attack and kill humans on a regular basis. It became the task of the game warden, these people who professed to love animals more than anything, to track this animal down and kill it. The euphemism they used to describe these killings was 'problem control'.

I read the folder while drinking a bottle of something industrial. Most of it was technical specifications, page after page of what I barely recognized as a human genome chart. The Doctor had written helpful little notes in the margin, explaining which cluster of base pairs represented which particular anti-social tendency or superhuman capability. The last third of the folder contained details of how she was supposed to have been trained; an entire base was being built on Titan under conditions of strict secrecy. The security measures were impressive, most of them aimed at preventing anything escaping. I got the distinct impression that her makers didn't really know what it was they were creating. Just mixed up a cocktail of the worst aspects of humanity and hoped for the best.

I guess the joke's on me, isn't it, Doctor? I keep looking for some sign of the young woman I thought was Kadiatu and finding the animal staring back. I won't let you do this to me – she has to live. Otherwise everything I've said to you and to others was so much self-righteous poppycock.

I tried to imagine that I was telling Alistair about Kadiatu; she is his great, great, great, granddaughter (sort of) after all. She comes from a family of soldiers starting with him. All I got was a vague sense that I should buck up my ideas and pull myself together.

I can't sleep, even after another bottle of industrial. What are my options? I could leave her on the sphere, make an arrangement to have her watched. I'm sure that aM!xitsa would agree to that; there's definitely something more than scientific curiosity that draws the drone to her. No good: she'd escape, I know she would.

She knocked holes in the fabric of space-time, almost destroyed the entire universe. If I let her go, what will she do as an encore? According to the notes she automatically goes into kill mode at the first sign of danger. The first time someone takes a swing at her, bang, they're dead. And that first death will be my fault because I was the one that let her go. All the deaths will be my fault.

It's all those people I don't know that worry me. The ones that she's certain to kill once she starts travelling again. She's like a blaster with no stun setting. The inevitable consequence of my decision will be that some people will die, an awful lot of people in fact. That's a very high price for salving my own conscience.

No, I can't think like this. Kadiatu is a human being, she must make her own moral choices, *must* be allowed to make her own moral choices. I am not my sister's keeper.

Yeah, I'm sure the dead will be forgiving. 'That's all right,' they'd say, 'we were glad to give up our lives so that you could prove a point to the Doctor. Our only regret is that we have but one life to lay down for your conscience. Being brutally killed by a programmed psychopathic killing machine actually gave meaning to our existence.' I don't think so.

I'm going to turn out the light in a minute and drink something that House assures me will slap my alpha waves flatter than the Norfolk fens.

I have come to the horrid realization that maybe I'll have to problem control Kadiatu after all.

No wonder the Doctor sleeps as little as possible.
Extract Ends.

9

Cult Status

> Give me a woman,
> with a flat nose and a bad temper
> with black eyes and sulky lips
> that taste of hidden memories.
>
> Give me a dark woman
> with straight shoulders and swinging hips
> who vanishes unsmiling in the darkness
> when the lights are out.
>
> *Poem for a Barbarian Lady*, feLi-!xi-kat-xi

Dep is staring into a reflective hologram. It is positioned over and behind the forcefield funnel that passes for a sink in her bathroom. She is using it to help her concentrate inwards, to exercise mental control over her body. She should be able to do without the mirror; body-management was one of the first things she learnt at school along with finger painting and interpersonal ethics, but she is nervous. Outside Chris is waiting in her sleep field, a pale shape floating amongst the intricate clockwork angles of her flying machines.

She manages the thought sequence easily enough. The thought sequence becomes a message encoded as a series of pulses down the major nerve cluster that links her brain with the oversized gland that sits under her brain stem. There the message is translated into a series of complex organic molecules that are released into her bloodstream.

193

Dep has three ovaries, two more than her mother and one less than her father. The central ovary responds first to the chemical messengers immediately releasing a specific fertility suppressant to prevent the other two from following suit. The ovary then contracts slightly and expels an egg into the pre-fallopian duct where Dep's own autonomic immune system checks it for defects. There is no degradation of the egg, no genetic damage or rogue enzymes. The immune system signals its approval with an enzyme of its own causing the very small muscles surrounding the pre-fallopian duct to ripple in sequence and propel the egg into the fallopian tube proper. With the egg goes a wash of chemical messengers and enzymes generated by the ovary. Some of these messengers rush on ahead of the egg to trigger changes in the womb, while others cling to the egg like scaffolding around a ship, transmitting the precise codes that Dep formulated in her mind only minutes earlier.

The egg hurtles down the fallopian tube, ripening at a rate that would have a human gynaecologist reaching for her medical database. The scaffolding enzymes, their job done, detach and whirl away. By the time it reaches the womb the egg is primed, programmed and fertile.

Dep feels a moment of slight discomfort in her lower abdomen as, for the first time in her life, the neck of her womb unseals itself and flowers open.

It is much later and they hang together in the bedfield. Chris has fallen asleep, an occurrence that Dep has now accepted as an apparent design fault in barbarian males. Her hair is waving gently in the still air of her bedroom.

Deep inside her a cloud of Chris's microgametes are swimming through the opening of her cervix, tails thrashing like there's no tomorrow, which of course for most of them there isn't. A larger cloud of specialized B-cells converges with the spermatozoids, picking off ones that fail to meet the criteria specified by Dep's mental impulse two hours ago. As the first microgametes are absorbed the species-specific structure of their DNA triggers off another enzyme release which in turn trips the appropriate cluster of plasma cells embedded in the endometrium lining of the uterus. These plasma cells begin to produce a fast-acting metamorphic catalysing enzyme that over the next two hours will change the very nature of the endometrium cells and provide a protective barrier against Dep's ferocious auto-immune system.

Later.

Artificial selection has pared down the number of the microgametes to a mere couple of hundred. The surviving spermatozoids have almost expended their glycogen reserves and are making the final dash for the egg that lies nestling in the newly mutated endometrium lining. The egg absorbs every single one of them and starts the process of sifting through their precious bundles of DNA. Chris's grandfather's colour blindness is discarded, a faulty sequence that predisposes the male line of Cwejs towards late onset diabetes goes the same way, as does an unfortunate predisposition towards paranoid schizophrenia. The discarded DNA chains are broken down into protein and stored for later use as building material. The egg then proceeds to construct a complete set of chromosomes by translating Chris's DNA into the slightly different (and more efficient) format used by the people. The specific genofixed characteristics of the people, self-induced gender selection, wide band eyesight, etc., will all be passed on to a child that will grow into an otherwise exact copy of Christopher Cwej.

The egg divides, divides again and keeps on dividing until a colony of one hundred and fifteen cells have formed into a blastocyst. Satisfied that the colony will not be injurious to the body, the ever-watchful auto-immune system gives the blastocyst the thumbs-up for further development. A chemical messenger is released into the bloodstream that will give Dep a slight feeling of euphoria for the next two hours or so. The rest, as they say, is biology.

Dep hangs in the bedfield with her face against Chris's chest, listening to the slow comforting rhythm of his heart. Now that it is too late she is suddenly struck by the enormity of what she has done, of the crime she is intending to commit. She has stolen the blueprint of his life and taken it into herself. Taken what uniquely belongs to Chris, his individuality, and on a whim made him less than what he was.

But what made it a true crime in the eyes of the people, one that could earn Dep social isolation for the rest of a miserable life, is that she has no intention of ever telling him.

SaRa!qava called while Bernice was having her morning fight with the suspensor pool. The call was announced with a discreet little chime that was on to its ninth repetition before Bernice realized it was the phone. She tried to twist around but only succeeded in getting her feet higher than her head. 'Hello,' she called.

A full-size hologram of saRa!qava rezzed up in the corner of the bathroom. 'Good morning, Benny. Do you always bathe in that position?'

'Absolutely,' said Bernice. 'I find that having the blood rushing to my head first thing in the morning helps me wake up.'

The daylight quality hologram wandered around the bathroom, peering curiously through the bedroom door and laughing at the fittings. 'This place is so old,' she said. Bernice watched in amazement as the holographic projection of saRa!qava started rummaging through the bottles on the bathroom shelf. 'I think you should try some of this,' said saRa!qava, holding up a plastic squeezy bottle. 'It's microgravity soap.'

Bernice let her fingers brush against saRa!qava's as she took the soap – she felt skin. 'How are you doing this?' she asked.

'Your House is using its manipulation fields to create a textured shape that matches my projection,' said saRa!qava. 'I can derez and go image only if it annoys you.'

'Doesn't annoy me,' said Bernice. 'And since you're feeling so solid you can come over here and turn me the right way up.'

SaRa!qava stepped over and, catching hold of Bernice's

leg, flipped her into an upright position. 'Much better,' said Bernice.

'I don't know why you bother with this thing,' said saRa!qava. 'Why don't you just get House to replace it? Get something a bit more fashionable like a wobble bath.'

'I like a challenge,' said Bernice, unwilling to admit that it had never occurred to her that she might be able to change the bloody thing. 'I try never to admit defeat when dealing with strange technology.'

'I thought you might want to come shopping this morning,' said saRa!qava.

'I'm not sure I'd be very good company,' admitted Bernice.

'I like a challenge,' said saRa!qava.

'Feeling better?' asked the Doctor as Roz came down for breakfast.

'Why is everyone always so concerned with my health?' she snapped. 'You'd think I was planning to croak or something.' There was a bunch of flowers jammed into a vase on the balcony table, great garish purple and orange blooms on slender stalks. In her weakened condition it made Roz feel ill just looking at them.

'This came with the flowers.' The Doctor handed her a sheet of paper folded in half. 'I think you have a secret admirer,' he said.

Roz unfolded the note; the paper had a smooth, luxurious texture and was written in a smooth elegant hand. She realized with a shock that she could understand the words of the title – 'Poem for a Barbarian Lady'. It was written in Ancient American and signed feLi-!xi-kat-xi. There was a scrawled note at the bottom inviting her to a picnic that afternoon.

'It's feLixi,' she told the Doctor. 'He has designs on my body.'

'May I?' asked the Doctor. Roz passed him the poem. 'I wouldn't say designs,' said the Doctor after he'd finished reading. 'More like a full set of blueprints, a scale model and an artist's impression of the finished development. Interesting that it's in English.'

197

'I thought so too,' said Roz. 'Do you think I've got a flat nose?'

'Streamlined,' said the Doctor. 'Where do you think he got the translation matrix?'

'He used to work for XR(N)IG,' said Roz. 'I imagine he has access to a lot of classified data.'

'They don't have classified data here,' said the Doctor, 'just things they don't tell other people. A contact with XR(N)IG could be very useful just at the moment.'

Without being asked, House put a mug of coffee down in front of Roz. 'That was the general idea,' she said. 'His infatuation with me will make it easy to pump him for information.'

'How are you at infatuation?'

'Rusty,' said Roz. 'But it's amazing how fast it all comes back to you.'

The Doctor dropped a pastry into a bowl of caramel and watched it dissolve for a bit. 'I had an interesting conversation with the ships yesterday,' he said. 'There's a couple of things I'd like you to check out. That is if you're not too busy being feLixi's poetic muse.'

'A lead?'

'More like a hot tip,' said the Doctor. 'Did S-Lioness tell you about the habitat that was destroyed during the war?'

'Omicron 378,' said Roz. 'You think there's a connection?'

'Just a hunch,' he said. 'Not even that really, more like a shrug. A ship destroyed a habitat and killed over two hundred thousand people for no good reason. That's enough to ruin their reputation. Because it happened during a war I think XR(N)IG changed the ship's name and classification and then buried the whole sorry story.'

'Surely God would know which ship it was?'

'Not necessarily,' said the Doctor. 'The war was fought over a huge volume of space and ASBIG were operating shipyards away from the sphere, primarily because God objected to the war. XR(N)IG and ASBIG could have conspired to change the ship's identity without God knowing. And if vi!Cari found out?'

'That's a hell of a motive,' said Roz. 'Better than that, a

former warship would have the expertise to carry out the attack. It won't be easy to find though; for all we know it's happily settled down as a toaster somewhere.'

'You can use the time telescope.' The Doctor plonked the furry terminal on the table. 'It might help you assimilate some of the data. I finished installing it last night and I made a few modifications that should stop God sticking its oar in.'

'I thought Bernice was –'

'I warned you that Bernice might be a bit distracted,' said the Doctor.

'Bernice is doing a job for you, isn't she?' asked Roz. 'Something to do with aM!xitsa and that purebred woman. One of your devious little schemes.'

'Something like that,' said the Doctor. 'Don't you want me to tell you what it's all about? I can do that now because God's figured it out already.'

'No,' said Roz. 'You'll tell me when you want to.'

The Doctor looked at her for a long time. She met his gaze and held it.

'You're not like any other person I've ever travelled with,' he said.

'You tend to travel with nice people, Doctor,' said Roz. 'I'm not a nice person.'

'You believe in justice and you're loyal to your friends . . .'

'Christ, Doctor, what's this?' asked Roz. 'A pep talk?'

'I just want you to know that I appreciate you,' said the Doctor.

'If you don't shut up, Doctor,' said Roz, 'I'm going to vomit all over these hideous flowers.' She looked away from him and out over the sea. For a moment she thought the sky was pink with dust. 'Justice,' she said, 'lift up your blind eyes/and see how thy children have served others in thy name.'

'Speak not to me of Justice/For thou hath broken humanity on thy wheel,' recited the Doctor. ' "The Lament of the Non-Operational", the Fitzgerald translation I believe. I didn't know you were familiar with Dalek poetry.'

'My father collected it,' said Roz. 'He made me memorize

all hundred and twenty-eight stanzas.' She grimaced at the memory.

'Take it from me,' said the Doctor, 'it reads far better in the original machine code.' He poked at his soggy pastry with a spoon. 'I knew a man once who used it as a libretto for an opera. Great big sub-Wagnerian score. I even heard that he took the production all the way to Skaro.'

'What happened?'

'Got exterminated by the audience on the opening night,' said the Doctor. 'Terrible critics, the Daleks. I think spending all that melleannium yearning for perfection drove them all quite mad.'

'Are we ruling the S-Lioness out of the frame then?' asked Roz.

'Not yet,' said the Doctor. 'I thought that was something you could check on with feLixi.'

'The more I think about it, the more improbable the S-Lioness seems as a suspect,' said Roz. 'If it was really that pissed off with vi!Cari over the death of one of its crew why wait until now? I'd like to know more about who it was that died.'

The Doctor narrowed his eyes. 'You think they're related?' he asked. 'Is there something you're not telling me?'

'Nothing concrete, Doctor,' said Roz. 'I'd like to check some facts first. If I think I'm on to something I'll let you know. You talked to the mural painter, didn't you?'

'BeRut? I spoke to him,' said the Doctor. 'He made it clear in no uncertain terms that my company or my conversation was not required. In short he told me to get lost.'

'Shame.'

'And I was being my most ingratiating too.'

'Do you think he's capable of murder?'

'Yes,' said the Doctor, without hesitation. 'I think he's capable of ripping someone's arm off and beating them to death with the wet end. I'm not sure that he's capable of the kind of long-term planning involved in killing a drone.'

'I heard he's been working on that mural for two years,' said Roz. 'If he can be obsessive about his art, he could be obsessive about revenge on vi!Cari. I arrested a painter once who'd planned his wife's murder for six years. Used a binary carcinogenic on her.'

'That's horrible,' said the Doctor.

'You should have seen the medical bills.'

'I had a conversation with a fish last night,' said the Doctor. 'I think you might find it interesting.'

As the Doctor told Roz about the force-bomb, Roz felt something go 'click' in her head. A tiny section of the case, that amorphous blob with all its flapping loose ends, seemed to become suddenly sharp-edged and clear. It didn't mean much yet but like finding the corner of a jigsaw puzzle it was a start. *Like finding a little piece of the divine will*, Konstantine had said.

Thinking of Konstantine brought a short rush of unwelcome memory. A smug complacent face with flat eyes – Boss Shuster. Damn! She must still be experiencing the after-effects of the *flashback*. You're a disgrace, Forrester. What are you? Where had that bottle of *flashback* come from anyway? She hadn't ordered it and House denied it had anything to do with it. She looked at the Doctor who was stirring his dissolved pastry, seemingly content to play with his food rather than eat it. Was it one of his mind games? Perhaps he hoped that forcing Roz to confront her past would make her a better person. She discounted that theory as soon as she thought of it. The Doctor was far too subtle to resort to such spurious psyche tactics, let alone chemical inducement.

Who needed a memory enhancer when you've got a time machine.

The Doctor said something. 'Sorry, missed that,' said Roz.

'I said, if vi!Cari didn't drown the mural it does lessen beRut's motive.'

'Not really,' said Roz. 'It's who beRut thought did the deed, not who actually did it.'

'What were you thinking about?' asked the Doctor.

'When?'

'Just now.'

'My first case.'

'Is it relevant?'

'No,' said Roz. Strange that she could still feel so bitter after all these years. 'Not relevant at all.' She drained the last of her coffee, suddenly anxious to be out of the villa. 'I think I should tell feLixi that I accept his invitation.'

'Well,' said the Doctor, 'don't do anything I wouldn't do.'

'Doctor,' said Roz, 'I said I was rusty, not dead from the waist down.'

'I just had a horrible thought,' said Bernice, as she and saRa!qava rode in a travel capsule to Whynot. 'What if the Doctor did it?'

'I thought he was with you that evening,' said saRa!qava. 'Watching the storm and eating popcorn.'

'What if he wasn't?' asked Bernice. 'What if he was somewhere else and what I thought was the Doctor was really one of those texturized holograms?'

'Benny,' said saRa!qava gently, 'what possible motive could the Doctor have for killing vi!Cari? He didn't even know the drone.'

'I know, I know,' said Bernice, 'I was just having an attack of paranoia.' She turned to look out of the travel capsule. Whynot was dead ahead. Through the swirls of cloud she could make out the Grinning Archipelago on the equator and in the northern hemisphere the two round continents of Lefteye and Righteye, both, she estimated, roughly the size of Madagascar.

God, she thought, has all the subtlety of a five-year-old in a sweet shop.

And the Doctor has a very plausible motive for killing vi!Cari, assuming that the machine knew about Kadiatu. The drone at the party, the one dressed as an airliner, had said as much and the Doctor had gone to great lengths to keep the woman secret from God. Bernice was appalled at her thoughts: did she really believe that the Doctor was capable of killing someone to keep that secret?

Yes, she thought, if the secret was important enough, if he added up the totals and the positive outweighed the negative. He wouldn't want to, he'd try to avoid it but in the end if he had to, he would do it.

Feeling suddenly cold Bernice hugged herself as the travel capsule fell silently towards the smiling face of Whynot.

The travel capsule touched down on the continental island of Lefteye. They caught a lift to the surface from the travel station and caught an open-topped maglev train across the coastal plains to what saRa!qava said was the second largest city in the sphere: me!Xu!xi-si!cisisa – The Mote in God's Left Eye.

The maglev wound its way through a landscape of meadows and broadleaf forests. To the north the land rose to become a rolling plain. In the distance she could just see the snow-covered tops of a mountain range. Apparently God had built them the year before and was still trying to get people to ski on them. Whynot was God's personal domain; here it was allowed to rearrange the scenery to suit itself and people lived on the planet at their own risk.

It was good to have a horizon again. SaRa!qava said that millions of people lived on Whynot despite the fact that they were subject to the inconvenience of having God periodically shifting the continents around, not to mention that the planet's weird orbit meant that the hours of daylight were so variable as to be essentially random. Bernice understood. The limitless vistas of the sphere were just too big to comprehend and faced with a real horizon for the first time in days Bernice realized that those vast distances engendered a feeling of oppression. Especially in someone who was born and raised on a planet. Getting away from that would be worth the aggravation of waking up to find your home had shifted sixty thousand kilometres overnight.

Or knee-deep in water. One bright morning the citizens of me!Xu!xi-si!cisisa had got out of bed to find that their entire city was suddenly in the middle of a lake the size of Arizona. Which was why Bernice and saRa!qava had to catch a hydrofoil from a terminus on the lake shore. It took another hour to reach the city.

'God disconnected all the travel tubes to the city and absolutely forbids the use of any aircraft more advanced than a microlight,' said saRa!qava. 'Said it would interfere with the ambience.'

Rumour had it that God had heard about a drowned city on a barbarian planet and decided that it sounded like a *neat* idea. God was also slowly sinking the city at the rate of six centimetres a month. The inhabitants had responded by adding an extra storey on to the buildings every year.

As the hydrofoil swept through the drowned streets, its wake washing against ruined stone and mildewed plasticrete, Bernice thought that she, probably better than any of the people, understood what God was about. The buildings had none of the precision that she'd seen in iSanti Jeni or the villa, the extra storeys looked like they had been hastily fabricated without concern for the style of the original. She was irresistibly reminded of an ancient city she'd once helped to excavate; it had the same accretion of layers over time, like a counterfeit artist 'ageing' a painting. God was trying to give Whynot the sense of history that was so conspicuously absent from the rest of the sphere.

Colonies of amphibian mammals lived in the half floors at the waterline. Marsh trees clung to the sides of the buildings, elephantine roots snaking down into the depths. The hydrofoil pushed a path through clumps of water lilies the size of satellite dishes and threaded its way through ornate bridges slung between the tottering houses.

It reminded Bernice of Venice; it even had the smell.

The hydrofoil pulled up against a wharf constructed from floating blocks of concrete. A cast-iron staircase led up to the first liveable floor of a sixteen-storey block that had a noticeable tilt to the left. The staircase was articulated – Bernice presumed to match the ebb and flow of the tide – its lower third slippery with algae and rust.

'Did I mention that God won't allow forcefield furniture here,' said saRa!qava as they laboured up the stairs. 'Everything has to be mechanical.'

'How does it stop people bringing stuff in?' asked Bernice.

'An inhibition field,' said saRa!qava. 'Anything non-sentient with a field component coming within a thousand kilometres just falls to bits.'

'Awkward,' said Bernice.

'Personally, I think God just does it to annoy.'

'Why come here then?'

'Because,' said saRa!qava, 'this is the *only* place to come if you want to do some serious shopping.'

Bernice wondered how you could go shopping in a culture without money. I mean, she thought, those once in a lifetime special reductions are going to be a bit meaningless when everything's free to start with.

They stepped around a six-centimetre-thick blast door that appeared to have been left open and rusted solid and into the building.

The interior looked like a shopping centre that had fallen into disrepair and had been subsequently converted into a flea market. There were spaces that looked like open shop fronts with merchandise hung from lintels and stacked in piles at the sides. Stalls made of driftwood or cut sections of the aquatic trees lined the spaces in between, a variety of people, organic and machine standing or sitting behind them. Bernice was immediately drawn to a shop selling leather goods, jackets and long duster-style coats hanging in sweet-smelling ranks in its dim interior. She changed her mind: it was a shopping centre that had fallen on hard times, been converted into a flea market which had then become *incredibly* fashionable.

'Everything is personally designed,' said saRa!qava. 'You can't order any of this stuff from central stores.'

'How does this work?' asked Bernice. 'Barter, IOUs, what?'

SaRa!qava laughed. 'Nothing like that. You just ask the stallholder for what you want.'

Bernice glanced at the stallholder, an incredibly tall man with sallow skin who was thin to the point of emaciation. He gestured politely, inviting her into his shop. She reached out to touch a cream-coloured knee-length duster with a wide collar. 'What's to stop someone just rolling up and taking everything away.'

'Oh, that couldn't happen,' said saRa!qava. 'The stallholder has to agree to give it to you.'

She stroked the smooth material of the duster. If it turned

out to be waterproof it would be perfect for those unexpected materializations. 'What's this made of?' she asked the stallholder. 'It's too soft to be suede.'

'Skin,' he said.

Bernice snatched her hand away and stared at the man. He grinned back revealing two rows of yellowed needle-sharp teeth.

'Grown in culture of course,' said the man. 'If you like I can take a sample from you now and force-grow a jacket for you while you wait.'

'Ah, no thanks,' said Bernice backing out of the shop. 'I think I'll give it a miss all the same. I was looking for something in brown anyway. Oh, look, there's a woman selling fertility idols, just what I was looking for.' She dragged an amused saRa!qava round the corner and out of sight of the stallholder. 'Yuk,' she said.

'They're very practical,' said saRa!qava.

'What are?'

'Skin jackets. Sort of comforting. I had one made from my mother.'

'I don't want to hear about it,' said Bernice. 'If they don't make money from these stalls, why do they do it?'

'Prestige mostly,' said saRa!qava. 'It's nice to make or design something that somebody else likes enough to take home with them.'

'Like you and your bread?'

'I suppose so.'

They stopped by a stall selling figurines whittled out of hardwood and then varnished. A hand-painted sign hung above the stall. Bernice asked saRa!qava what it said. 'People who are interesting to look at,' she translated. As far as Bernice could tell the sign was only eight characters long. It must be a very economical language, perhaps even ideographic. That could have been why the TARDIS couldn't translate the written form; she remembered it had had trouble with Osiran hieroglyphs. She made a mental note to ask the Doctor about it.

She picked up one of the figurines, admiring the varnished grain, and realized with a shock that it was carved in a likeness of Roz. It was beautifully done, capturing every-thing from her perpetually disgruntled expression to the stiffness of her backbone. Bernice quickly scanned the crowded table and sure enough saw a matching figurine of Chris.

The woman who ran the stall was almost bouncing up and down with excitement. 'Oh wow,' she said, 'you're one of the Time Lord's barbarians, aren't you? Do you think it's a good likeness?'

Bernice told her that the likeness was uncanny and the woman seemed almost to explode with pleasure. 'Could you take her one?' She was gushing like a teenybopper at a pop concert. 'She's really popular round here. CiMot's got her face on his T-shirts and he can't fabricate them fast enough. Please take her one – do you think she'll like it?'

Bernice lied and said that Roz would be delighted to find she's been immortalized in driftwood. The woman asked if she could take a hologram of Bernice as well which she found flattering despite herself. Celebrity at last, she thought. 'Be sure to say that it's *Professor* Summerfield,' she said.

'Professor,' said the woman. 'What a nice name.' She insisted that Bernice take a Chris Cwej as well and even threw in a fabric carrier bag for her to take the figurines away in.

They spotted their first Roz Forrester T-shirt a few minutes later. It showed her face-on and hitting someone, her fist foreshortened and huge. Bernice didn't need SaRa!qava to translate the legend; it was obviously the local equivalent of EAT MY DAY or MAKE MY SHORTS. Bernice decided there and then to let Chris be the one who told Roz about her new-found status as a cult icon.

It took them two hours to work their way up to the restaurant on the roof of the building. They sat down with stuffed carrier bags clustered around their legs but not as stuffed as they might have been.

She was surprised how much she enjoyed moneyless shopping. Bernice had always assumed that actually having the money, the sense of power that came with being able to afford things, was an integral part of the shopping 'experience'. When she was young and living in the woods behind the academy she had vivid fantasies of wading into the local shopping centre, waving her credit card like a magic wand. Later, when she was bumming around humanspace, dodging the draft and eking out a living from dig to dig as an itinerant archaeologist, it had become a matter of survival. Scraping together enough to pay for a layover bed or the next starship out, lack of money had become a constant anxiety, an erosion of her self-worth. There was nothing like real poverty to teach you the true meaning of the word 'cash'.

If you'd asked the younger Bernice what her likely response to a free bazaar would be the likely answer would have been: move in with a standard freighter cargo module and have the stuff away before the buggers changed their minds.

Years of travelling light with the Doctor, and the Doctor's capacious pockets, must have freed her from that particular anxiety because she found herself curiously indifferent to the concept of possessions.

Instead she took her cue from saRa!qava and picked presents for other people. The exception was a sheath dress, grown from the same symbiote material as the one Dep had worn at the party, that saRa!qava talked her into. The stallholder assured her that the symbiote keyed itself to the personality of the person wearing it and wouldn't be nearly so 'active' as Dep's. All the same, Bernice wasn't at all sure she'd wear a dress that might, on a whim, head south at an embarrassing social moment. It *was* pretty though.

The food at the restaurant was hand-made as well, a thick soup in earthenware bowls served with freshly baked rolls. SaRa!qava broke one open and sniffed it with a professional air. 'Not too awful,' she said.

'Perfectionist,' said Bernice. They had a table by the parapet with a good view over the leaning towers of the city. Hydrofoils and steam skiffs chugged slowly along the drowned streets, disturbing the amphibians and crocodiles of white crane-like waterbirds. Bernice decided that if she had to stay in the sphere, God forbid, this would be where she would live.

'I have a confession to make,' said saRa!qava.

'Gosh,' said Bernice, 'I wish I did.' SaRa!qava looked pensive and Bernice realized she was serious. 'Sorry,' she said.

'I think I may be one of the Doctor's suspects,' said saRa!qava. 'For the murder.'

'What makes you say that?'

'I had a really good motive for wanting vi!Cari dead.'

'Why tell me?' asked Bernice. 'I don't think you did it.'

'The Doctor's bound to find out sooner or later,' said saRa!qava. 'I thought I'd better tell you first. Vi!Cari knew about something I did when I was young. I don't know how, but it did and I was scared that it would tell someone else.'

Bernice was shocked to see that saRa!qava was crying. Automatically, she reached out and squeezed her friend's hand. 'Why would that be a motive?'

'You don't understand, how could you? If people found out what I did, no one would talk to me for ever.'

'I understand,' said Bernice. 'Social isolation is a common enough sanction amongst –' Bernice hesitated; she was about to say primitive cultures. 'Many, many cultures. Look, if this is too painful we can talk about something else.' *Bernice, you coward!*

SaRa!qava squeezed her hand back. 'No,' she said, 'it's better that you know. There was this man –'

'Isn't there always,' said Bernice. SaRa!qava smiled wanly.

'Who I was in love with,' said saRa!qava. 'But he wasn't in love with me, at least not enough to start a family. So one night I lured him up to the Windmills and we had sex.'

'You're right, I don't understand,' said Bernice. 'What's so criminal about that?'

'I had sex with him that night, deliberately, just so I could conceive,' said saRa!qava. 'I stole Dep from him and he doesn't know.'

Dep watched Chris as he eased the reciprocating arm out of the central drive assembly. Grease was smeared on his cheeks and forehead where he'd wiped the sweat away. He looked like one of the players in the combat games organized by the Barbarian Emulation Interest Group.

Dep had woken up that morning with a sudden fear in her heart that even the induced conception euphoria couldn't cover. She was scared that Chris was going to leave soon, before the ornithopter was finished. Restless, she left him sleeping and began to work on the flying machine, electrosoldering the pipe assembly that would carry superheated steam from the boiler to the wing pistons.

She had finished the assembly and was painting on the insulation when Chris woke up and asked if he could help. She showed him where the central drive needed to be stripped down and restructured.

Chris flourished the reciprocating arm in triumph and handed it to Dep. She threw it at the lathe and told the machine what changes she wanted. 'We can't do anything until the insulation dries.'

'I heard your mum used to design hyperspace systems,' said Chris while they waited. Dep was trying to wipe the worst of the grease off his face.

'She used to,' said Dep.

'I was thinking of asking for her help. We need to know who was capable of creating the kill harmonics in the lightning burst.'

'Apart from Mother?' asked Dep.

Chris's face fell. 'Gosh,' he said, 'I'm sorry. I wasn't implying that –'

Dep leaned forward and affectionately brushed noses with him .'I was teasing,' she said.

'Oh,' said Chris. 'You've got grease on your face.'

'Never mind that,' said Dep. 'We've got to get this thing finished before . . . before my mother tries to talk me out of it again.' She finished lamely.

Chris obediently got back under the engine.

Life, thought Dep, was much simpler before I met you.

FeLixi checked the time on his ring terminal and wondered if Roz was coming. He let his eyes wander over the featureless dove-grey walls of the station. There were no decorations or seating as one didn't expect to wait down here: a capsule was always waiting when you stepped out of the lift. It was this very utilitarianism that had led feLixi to choose it as a meeting place, neutral territory. Behind him the waiting travel capsule pinged every minute or so, as if to emphasize its own impatience. Occasionally he felt a slight vibration through the soles of his feet as other capsules picked up passengers and carried them away. He resisted the urge to check the contents of the hamper again.

He was about to call up some entertainment on his ring terminal when the lift doors opened and Roz stepped out. She was wearing a loose white sleeveless top and matching stretch shorts that set off the dark skin of her bare arms and legs, and button-down pumps on her feet. A couple of the bracelets that had so intrigued him at the party jangled on her wrists and ankles. He grinned as he waved her over; she had so obviously made an effort to dress casually but it still managed to look like a uniform – it was the way she walked, he decided.

They sat down opposite each other in the travel capsule. 'I'm sorry I'm late,' she said. 'I was just checking out some data and lost track of the time.'

FeLixi watched as she crossed her legs, noticing the fine line of her calves, the muffled curve of her breasts as they shifted beneath her top.

'Did you find anything interesting?' he asked.

She gave him a half smile. 'Nothing important,' she said. 'Filling in a few blanks and chasing down some leads. Ninety per cent of an investigation consists of digging away at a big pile of shit until you find something.'

'What's the other ten per cent?'

'Knowing what isn't shit when you find it,' said Roz.

'Do you trust me?' he asked when they stepped out at their destination.

'How long do I have to answer that?' asked Roz.

FeLixi put the hamper down on the platform, unclipped the lid and drew out the blindfold. Roz looked at him suspiciously. 'I want it to be a surprise,' he explained. 'You

211

don't have to if you don't want to,' he said.

Roz hesitantly took the blindfold from his fingers and placed it over her eyes. 'You'd better not run me into anything,' she said.

Promising to be extra careful he put his hand on her shoulder and guided her into the lift. It took half a minute to reach the top of the shaft. He could feel the heat of her skin through the thin material of her top. The lift egress was camouflaged so that when they stepped out it was into direct sunlight. The lift vanished back into the ground leaving no sign of its presence except a discreet tag on a nearby tree.

FeLixi looked around, trying to recall the route; it had been thirty years since he'd come to this place. The trees were a little taller, the undergrowth thicker than he remembered.

'What's that smell?' asked Roz.

'Tree blossom,' said feLixi.

'It's worse than the inside of a knocking shop,' said Roz.

He took her hand, surprised at how small it felt in his, and led her carefully through the wild orchard. They had to take it slowly, feLixi telling Roz when to step over roots or around bushy tangles; the path barely existed any more. FeLixi was pleased because it meant that no one else had discovered this place. It was still his very own secret.

'How much further?' asked Roz.

'Almost there,' he told her.

They stopped at the edge of the orchard and feLixi slipped the blindfold off Roz's head. She looked around slowly. He wondered if he might have made a mistake, suddenly afraid that what had been magical for him wouldn't be for the strange, grim woman at his side.

'It's beautiful,' she said.

They were standing on the ragged fringes of a sheltered alpine meadow that undulated down to the banks of a river. A confusion of brightly coloured flowers grew amongst the long grass, clusters of pink nightwort and primrose droneleaf, yellowpetal and scarlet spindoctor. A single lop-sided tree grew on the river bank, stretching gnarled limbs out over the cool green water. Unbelievably feLixi saw that the rope he'd strung from the lowest limb all those years ago was still hanging, trailing its end in the water. Beyond the river the ground sloped steeply up to a ridge fringed with purple scree. The still air was heavy with the smell of blossom and the fragrance of the flowers.

'I'm almost afraid to step on the grass,' said Roz. She let go of his hand and bent down to pick a yellowpetal, her fingers hesitating a centimetre from the flower. 'I shouldn't take this, should I?'

'Why not?' asked feLixi. 'There are thousands of flowers.'

She snapped the stem and lifted the flower to her nose. She frowned. 'There's no smell,' she said, disappointed. He explained that yellowpetals had no fragrance. 'Oh,' she said. 'How typical.' She tried to tuck the flower behind her ear but it fell out.

'Where would you like to sit?' asked feLixi.

'Down there,' she said, 'by the tree.'

FeLixi felt a tiny stir of disquiet: it had been aTraxi's favourite spot. 'This is the oldest landscaped part of the sphere,' he said, acutely aware that he was talking to cover his unease. 'None of this was designed – it all happened by deliberate accident.'

He reached out his hand. She glanced at him, her dark eyes guarded, but she let him take hers. He saw her delicate nostrils dilate and wanted desperately to touch them with the tip of his nose, to explore the streamlined contours of her face with his lips.

She turned away and pulled him down the slope towards the tree. They'd gone a few metres when suddenly Roz yelped and jerked her hand away from him. 'Look out,' she shouted, 'something just bit me.'

'Relax,' said feLixi quickly, 'it's just a thistle.'

Roz looked down at her leg. 'Oh, shit,' she said. 'What idiot put an aggressive plant there?'

'I told you,' said feLixi, 'this area is completely natural. If you'd like to hop over there I'll pull the thorns out.'

He spread a blanket out by the tree and persuaded her to lie down and rest her leg in his lap. The hamper had the usual

213

integral first-aid kit; he removed the regen spray and laid it down by his foot.

'I don't know, Roz,' he said, 'a meadow full of flowers and you have to step on the only thistle.' A cluster of arrow-headed thorns had pierced Roz's calf. Gently he took hold of the first between his thumb and forefinger and plucked it out.

'You said none of this was designed,' said Roz. 'Was it transported from your original homeworld?'

'We didn't have an original homeworld,' said feLixi. 'Or rather we had several; the original people were an amalgam of different species. We all achieved starflight about the same time and ran into each other here, at this star system. That's one of the reasons we built the sphere here.'

Roz winced as he yanked the last thorn. He wiped up tiny beads of blood with a napkin.

'It was a white dwarf at the time,' he said. 'We had to tinker with it a bit.'

'And yourselves?' asked Roz. 'You must have tinkered with yourselves as well, so you could interbreed. It would be too much of a coincidence that different species which evolved out of different biospheres would be biologically compatible. That would be taking convergent evolution too far.'

FeLixi sprayed regen over the cuts. The spray was perfectly capable of dissolving the thorns on its own but then he wouldn't have had the chance to touch her leg. 'It was a long time ago,' he said. 'We have a saying: "The more alternatives you have to fighting the less likely you are to fight." Especially if the alternatives are more fun.'

He replaced the spray in the first-aid kit. Roz slipped her leg off his lap. Carefully, so as not to spook her, feLixi lay down beside her on the blanket. Roz didn't make any objections. 'So what's natural about this place then?' she asked.

'When the sphere was first constructed there were only twenty billion or so people so God figured it had some room to experiment. It set aside six million hectares, gave it only a minimum of landscaping, just the mountains and some bacteria to break down the rock into soil. All the flora and fauna here migrated in from the surrounding landscaped

214

areas over thousands of years. God let the area form its own ecosystem and calls this place the Wilderness Recreation Area. It won't let anyone live here.'

Roz sighed. 'Where I come from,' she said, 'there are no wilderness areas, natural or contrived. We have parks at the top of the overcities, beautiful ones, but it's not the same as this. Hard to believe that anything so beautiful could have arisen spontaneously.'

'You did,' said feLixi and then really wished he hadn't. As a chat-up line it was incredibly inept.

Roz obviously thought so too; he heard her laughing. 'Men,' she snorted. 'Why do you always talk such bullshit.' He felt her shifting beside him, lifting herself onto her elbow to look down on him.

'You don't think it's true?' he asked.

'I've seen myself in the mirror,' said Roz.

Her face was so close that he could feel her breath on his cheek. 'No one,' he said with absolute conviction, 'ever *really* sees themselves in the mirror.'

Roz, as if suddenly realizing how close their noses were, pulled away from him to scrutinize his face from a distance. FeLixi resisted the urge to reach out and pull her back down. She wouldn't resist, he knew that; she could feel the attraction between them, but he knew that it was too important that Roz came to him in her own time.

Turning her face, Roz picked up his hand, pressing her thumb into his palm, feeling out the myriad small bones under the skin as if examining it for defects. 'I saw a hologram of you yesterday,' she said. 'You had an extra thumb on both hands.' She let his hand drop back onto his chest and traced a finger up his forearm, pausing when she reached the inside of his elbow.

FeLixi tried to keep his breathing under control.

'Your elbow joint was different too,' she said. 'Looser and more flexible.' She turned back to look him in the face. 'Your eyes were pink.' It sounded almost like an accusation.

'I was doing a mission on a barbarian planet during the war,' he said. 'The locals were extremely xenophobic so the ship had to modify me cosmetically to fit in.'

215

'There was a woman with you,' she said.

'She was part of the mission too,' he said, wondering how much he dare tell Roz. 'She was an agent we recruited locally. We were friends.'

'What was her name?'

'Soo'isita,' said feLixi. 'In her language it meant "laughing bird".'

'Where is she now?' Roz's eyes looked strange, both shuttered and suspicious at the same time. FeLixi knew that look.

'She stayed behind when we left the planet,' he said.

Roz nodded, apparently satisfied with that answer. A sly, almost mischievous look came into her eyes. 'I'm going to kiss you now,' she said. 'You know what a kiss is?'

FeLixi smiled. 'The thing with the lips.'

'Think of this as a game,' said Roz, 'and the rules are these: no contact except at the face, no touching anywhere else. First person to break off or touch something they shouldn't has to pay a forfeit.'

'What's the forfeit?'

Roz looked around the meadow. 'They have to jump in the river.'

'That river comes right off a glacier,' said feLixi. 'It's freezing.'

'Better not lose then,' said Roz. 'Ready?'

'Ready.'

Roz leaned down until their lips were nearly touching. He could smell the chocolate smell of her moisturizer, the oily tang of her hair conditioner.

'No prisoners,' she murmured softly.

'No prisoners.'

When dusk came they lay together, naked under the blanket, and watched the world come out. From this point on the sphere Whynot was visible high up in the sky, a tiny perfect jewel hanging against the bright blue waters of the Endless Sea. Their clothes flapped from the branches of a tree, dry for a long time but forgotten.

'You were right about the water,' said Roz.

216

'You didn't have to jump in,' said feLixi.

She shifted on to her side and rested her face on his shoulder. 'Yes, I did,' she said. 'I made the rules so I had to stick by them, hoisted by my own petard. I guess I just thought I had more self-control.'

'I'm flattered.'

'You should be,' she said. 'I wasn't even drunk.'

Roz's fingers dug into his chest. 'What are you doing?' he asked.

'Counting your ribs,' she said.

'I've got thirteen,' he said. 'Eleven anterior and thirteen posterior.'

'I can't hear your heart,' she said.

He showed her the correct place, on the centreline of his chest, protected by his sternum plate. 'Slow,' she said. Her palm slipped down to his abdominals. 'Faster now.' Her fingers brushed through his pubic hair. 'Much faster. Now this is familiar.'

FeLixi swallowed.

'I've never been this close to an alien before,' said Roz. 'You're not so different.' She took his hand and placed it on her hip, an invitation he realized. Rolling on his side to face her, feLixi eased his leg between her thighs, feeling the heel of her foot press into the back of his calf. Her bracelets rattled, gently scraping the skin of his waist as her palm slipped around the small of his back. He felt her nose brush against his cheek, the hollow of his eye, her teeth catching at his lower lip.

'Not so different at all,' she murmured.

The Doctor and Bernice dined alone that evening, the figurines of Roz and Chris standing on the table between them. The Doctor found their resemblance to large chess pieces disturbing. He was careful not to communicate this to Bernice. A third figure was missing from the table, he thought. Kadiatu.

'Where's Roz?' asked Bernice. They both had a pretty clear idea of where Chris was.

'Walking out with feLixi,' said the Doctor.

217

Bernice muttered something under her breath.

'Pardon?'

'It's all right for some,' said Bernice and then looked embarrassed. 'I suppose I just didn't expect her to get "distracted" in that way. Now, Chris I understand but Roz?'

'All work and no play makes Roz a compulsive monomaniac,' said the Doctor. 'Are you jealous?'

'Christ, Doctor, what a question,' snapped Bernice. 'I'm very happy that Roz is going to get her end away. If you must know I've had a few offers in that direction myself.'

'SaRa!qava?'

'And others,' said Bernice. 'I'm just not in the mood.'

'You have a lot on your mind,' said the Doctor.

Bernice's fork clanked down on her plate. 'Well, thank you so much,' she said. 'I was trying not to think about that.'

'You have to tell me your decision tomorrow.'

'I'm quite aware of the deadline,' said Bernice. 'Now if it's all the same to you, I think I'll retire for the night.' She stood up and walked away from the table.

'Not as easy as you thought it would be,' said the Doctor.

Bernice paused at the bottom of the stairs and looked back at him. 'No,' she said, 'not easy at all.'

The Doctor sat all alone with two unfinished plates of food. All alone, unless of course, God was eavesdropping through the villa's comm system.

If she ever works it out, he thought, I'm going to be an ex-Time Lord.

Mind you, if I'm lucky, Kadiatu will kill me first.

'AgRaven. Wake up!'

AgRaven fell out of bed. The last time kiKhali had used that tone of voice had been during the war. It took her a moment to realize that she was safely in her cabin on board the !C-Mel. The fluid bed was rippling with the speed of her departure, disturbing the other occupants so that they rolled over. Gingerly she lifted the covers and checked: a man and a woman, neither of whom she knew. What in blazes had she been doing last night?

'AgRaven,' said kiKhali's voice, 'are you awake yet?'

'What is it?' she asked peevishly. 'I've got company.'

'I know,' said the drone, 'I was there.'

'How was I?'

'Same as usual.'

When am I going to learn? she asked herself. Quality not quantity.

'If you can bear to tear yourself away for a minute,' said kiKhali, 'I've got something to tell you – IDIG business. Meet me in Gossipmongers, it's dockside on the thirty-third level.'

'I know where it is,' said agRaven. Gossipmongers had the best privacy screening in Starport Facility. If kiKhali wanted to meet her there then it must be something important. 'I'm on my way,' she said, 'and make sure something stimulating is waiting for me' – agRaven staggered to her feet – 'and a measure of *purge* while you're at it.'

!C-Mel wanted to know where she was going. 'Just out for a wander,' she told the ship. 'Thought I'd walk off my hangover.'

'What shall I tell your guests?'

'Make something up,' said agRaven. She reached the entrance to the main umbilical. 'I don't care what it is as long as it's plausible.'

'You wouldn't be keeping secrets from little ol' me.' !C-Mel was making its voice particularly winsome.

'Chance would be a fine thing,' said agRaven, and legged it off the ship.

KiKhali was humming with excitement when agRaven joined it in Gossipmongers. 'Can you still do that trick with the bugs?' she asked it as she sat down. KiKhali had picked up a particularly sneaky ECM package from the Insects when they were mopping up at the end of the war. There was a fifty/fifty chance that !C-Mel couldn't shield its bugs from it.

'You're clean,' said kiKhali. 'I had a visit from one of our barbarian friends – the one that eats raw meat.'

'You dragged me out of a warm bed for that?'

'She was surprisingly polite, and she wanted to know about Omicron 378.'

'Oh.'

'And information on the crew of the S-Lioness.'

'Vi!Cari's ship,' said agRaven. 'That makes sense at least. Why all the secrecy?'

'She seems to think that the ship that blew away Omicron 378 is still alive,' said kiKhali. 'If that's true, and the R-Vene wasn't disassembled, then God is going to be well and truly pissed off with XR(N)IG.'

'Oh shit,' said agRaven. 'You don't think it's docked here now?'

'How would we know?' said kiKhali. 'And I found out something else as well. Vi!Cari was actually on board the R-Vene at Omicron 378. It was actually there when the place got wasted.'

'Can a machine recognize another machine even if it was in disguise?' asked agRaven. 'Could you?'

'Not me,' admitted kiKhali, 'but I'm willing to bet my right dorsal impeller that vi!Cari could have. Did you know we were on war alert for two hours yesterday?'

AgRaven looked sheepish. 'I think I must have slept through it.'

'Time Lords always bugger up the ships' predictive assessments because they can step out of the normal chain of causal events. What really got the wind up the VASs was that someone discovered another trans-temporal being on the sphere.'

'Another Time Lord?'

'Not according to the Doctor; human, he says, the same species as the other barbarians but souped up. But get this – who do you think is nurse-maiding this renegade?'

'AM!xitsa,' said agRaven. 'Has to be.'

KiKhali's face ikon flashed a big happy grin. 'I knew there was a reason why I was your partner.'

'AM!xitsa, the Doctor, God – that's half the original negotiating team.'

'Exactly,' said kiKhali. 'And what happens when they get together? The first unsolved machinacide in six centuries.'

'Yes, but what does it all mean?'

'I don't know,' said kiKhali, 'but I do know that if the

High Council of Gallifrey ever finds out about this we can kiss the treaty goodbye.'

'God must know that, surely?'

'The way I see it,' said kiKhali, 'is that there are three possibilities. One: it's all a gigantic coincidence, unlikely but possible. Two: God is using the murder as an excuse to uncover XR(N)IG's nefarious past by letting the Doctor and his friends do all the dirty work. There's a lot of speculation that the Doctor is effectively the High Council's only deniable intelligence asset, hence the special provision in the treaty.'

'Now that's obscure.'

'Trust me, agRaven,' said kiKhali. 'The smarter you get the murkier everything becomes, and God's the smartest person I know.'

'What's the third possibility?'

'That God has tossed the Doctor into this whole situation in the hope that he'll get himself killed.'

10

Unsmiling in the Darkness

> We all make our choices on life's highway
> My mama, she always told me that
> But I'd sure feel much better doing it my way
> If someone would just let me see the map.
>
> 'What My Mama Told Me' by Jesse Palmer
> From the LP: *Rode From Nashville* (1976)

Bernice dreamt that she was sharing a couple of bottles of Dom Perignon 2597 with Kadiatu, a Dalek, a Cyberman and a Sontaran officer named Grinx. So far the evening had gone reasonably well if you excused Grinx's unfortunate habit of belching after every glass. At least, no one had tried to exterminate anyone else.

'It's a question of moral choice,' said the Dalek. 'How can somebody be evil if they have no free choice over their actions?'

The Cyberman nodded sagely. 'Tinhead here is right,' it said. 'If a person is programmed to exterminate then they are effectively incapable of exercising a moral choice not to exterminate.'

'QED,' said Grinx and belched.

'It's you humans,' said the Dalek, 'that are capable of true evil because you have a choice in the matter.'

'And let's face it,' said the Cyberman, 'your track record is pretty shitty.'

'What about me then?' asked Kadiatu. 'It's all right for

222

you guys, you all belong to cultures where ruthless and efficient termination of an enemy is acceptable behaviour, glorified even.'

'Oh yeah,' said the Dalek. 'Humans are famous for glorifying their peacemakers, well known philanthropists like Alexander the Great, Julius Cæsar, Napoleon Bonaparte, Tshaka Zulu. These are the humans that get all the glory, the guys that get all the column inches.'

'There are others,' said Bernice. 'Gandhi . . .'

'Shot,' said the Dalek.

'Martin Luther King?'

'Also shot,' said the Cyberman.

'Nelson Mandela,' said Bernice. 'He wasn't shot.'

'Oh no,' said Grinx, 'they just locked him up for twenty-seven years.'

'I thought he was the one that got nailed to a cross,' said the Cyberman.

'That was Jesus Christ,' said Kadiatu.

'Whose side are you on?' Bernice asked her.

Kadiatu shrugged. 'I don't know,' she said. 'I thought that was what we were talking about.'

'At least we don't go around,' said the Dalek, 'saying, "We come in peace, shoot to kill".'

'Yes you do,' said Bernice. 'You do that sort of thing all the time.'

'Yes, yes, yes,' said the Dalek. 'But we *know* we're lying.'

Bernice poured another round of Dom Perignon. She became distracted by trying to work out how, exactly, the Dalek was drinking. The champagne just seemed to vanish whenever she wasn't looking. 'What about Davros?'

'Davros, Davros,' moaned the Dalek. 'Get into an argument with a human and they always bring up Davros. Look, do you think we *like* the misshapen little monomaniac? We've tried to do away with him more times than the Doctor has. He's our crukking creator – you want an argument about moral cul-pability, talk to him.' The Dalek lurched away from the table. 'I'm doing a bar run, does anything want something?'

'See if they've got any peanuts,' said Grinx. 'The dry roasted type.'

223

'What's your excuse then?' Bernice asked the Cyberman.

'I'm with tinhead,' said the Cyberman. 'It's a tough universe out there and it's only logical to get your licks in first. You'd be better off asking fatface there what his excuse is.'

Bernice turned to Grinx. 'Well?' she asked.

'Sorry, what was the question?'

The Dalek came back with the drinks. Grinx took his peanuts and ate the lot in one go, plastic packet and all.

'This is getting sodding nowhere,' said Bernice.

'It's your dream,' said Kadiatu.

'How do you know it's *my* dream?' asked Bernice.

'Because I have a better class of portentous dream,' said Kadiatu.

'How do you know it's not one of us having this dream?' asked the Dalek.

'Because – ' began Bernice.

'We don't dream,' said the Dalek. 'Are you sure of that?'

Grinx stood up. 'I have a dream,' he said, 'that little Sontarans and little Rutans will one day walk through the streets of Mississippi, hand in tentacle . . .'

Everyone shouted at him to shut up and sit down. 'More of a nightmare really,' admitted Grinx.

'Will you guys chill out,' said the Cyberman. 'Seems to me the issue is whether the customized human here' – it indicated Kadiatu – 'has free will or not? If she has then you have to let her live; if she doesn't then she belongs with us and you can exterminate her with a clear conscience.'

'AM!xitsa says that she's been modifying her own brain chemistry,' said Bernice. 'Perhaps there's some kind of drug therapy that could "help" remove these antisocial tendencies.'

'You mean change her personality?' asked the Cyberman.

'Er, yes, I suppose so.'

'Make her into something she is not?' asked the Dalek.

'Tinker with her soul,' said Grinx.

'Just the bad bits,' said Bernice defensively.

'And they say we're bastards,' said the Cyberman.

'I'd rather die,' said Kadiatu.

224

'That is a distinct possibility,' said Bernice. 'You know that.'

Kadiatu laughed. It was a harsh, unnerving sound. The Cyberman and the Dalek were arguing about something in short bursts of compressed data. Kadiatu banged her palm on the table to get their attention. 'Bernice here,' she said to them, 'is having trouble making the correct decision. Hands up all those that think she should kill me.'

Grinx and the Cyberman raised their hands.

'Is that a yes?' Bernice asked the Dalek.

'No, I'm crukking birdwatching, what do you think?'

Bernice sighed. The Cyberman, the Dalek and the Sontaran wandered off and left her alone with Kadiatu. A few minutes later there were screams and the sounds of gunfire and explosions as the three of them tried to exterminate each other.

They had also, she noticed, stiffed her with the bill.

'Well?' she asked Kadiatu. 'What do you want?'

The big woman shrugged. Bernice saw metal and crystal glinting in her eyes. 'I want to be free.'

'And if I let you live, what then?'

'The Doctor will kill me,' said Kadiatu. 'He has no choice.'

'He told me it was my decision.'

'And you believed him? I don't think you understand the stakes that the Ka Faraq Gatri plays for. If our roles were reversed, do you think I would hesitate?'

'Do you want to die?'

Kadiatu said nothing.

Roz sat up yelling in anger, elbowing feLixi in the chest as she tried to scramble away. 'Roz,' he shouted, 'wake up, wake up, you're having a nightmare.' She was practically invisible in the darkness, only the whites of her eyes showing. He put his arms around her trembling shoulders and drew her back under the blanket. She clung to him, her face buried against his neck – he could feel her heart banging against his ribs, the rhythm gradually slowing down to normal.

'Cold,' she said.

FeLixi adjusted the thermostat on the blanket and held her tighter. Whynot was in crescent, darkness having swept down the coast of the Endless Sea while they slept – it was night in iSanti Jeni. The meadow would see the morning first; some time in the next couple of hours, he estimated. There was a dull throbbing pain against his ribs where Roz had elbowed him. He stroked her head, gently running his fingers through the rough curls of her hair, too frightened to say anything in case he broke the moment.

Frightened of what the morning might bring.

'Do you want to go home?' he asked.

Roz shook her head. 'I was dreaming,' she said.

They lay back down under the warm blanket.

A bird woke up in the tree above them and started to warble cheerily.

Bernice brushed her hair and watched her face in the mirror. There were dark lines under her eyes, faint creases at their corners that threatened crow's-feet in the not too distant future. Her diary was open on the dresser, a pen laid across an empty page. The yellow edges of sticky memo sheets poked out from between the pages at the front of the notebook. A pair of figurines faced each other over a line of unopened cosmetic jars: a scowling Roz was jabbing her finger at Chris's chest. An untouched bottle of something industrial stood next to two standard issue medical hypospray capsules. A coffee mug rested on top of a heavy six-ring folder.

It was just a dream, she told herself.

Bernice put down the hairbrush and picked up the hypospray capsules. The skull on the hand-drawn skull and crossbones was smiling but that meant nothing: skulls grinned, it was a well-known cliché. The butterfly was much less detailed: an elongated oval for a body, two single lines on each side, drawn into double curves for the wings, two thinner lines for the antennae.

'You and your big mouth,' she said to her reflection.

A memory reached out and put a hand upon her shoulder; so vividly did she feel it that she unthinkingly dropped the capsules and reached to take Guy's hand in both of her own.

226

Nothing. She felt nothing but her own skin, her own bone and muscle.

'Pull yourself together, Summerfield,' she said. 'Now is not the time to get maudlin. It wouldn't have worked out and you know it. You're a star-hopping adventurer and he was an ex-Templar. It would have taken you six months just to explain how to operate the vacuum cleaner and another three years to explain why it was his job.'

What would Guy de Carnac say if he could see her now, crying in front of the mirror like a teenager.

It would have worked out, she knew that; they would have made it work. They should have at least got their chance, that was all anyone could really ask for.

She bent down and picked the capsules off the floor and set them back on the dresser.

'I don't owe you any favours, Kadiatu,' she said, 'but I'm damned if I'm going to have your blood on my hands.'

That's it, Doctor, she thought, the bitch lives.

FeLixi squatted on the river bank, the morning sun hot on his naked back and shoulders as he watched Roz easing herself cautiously into the water. 'It's still freezing,' she called.

'Of course it is,' he called back. 'What did you expect?'

Roz gingerly splashed water over her face and shoulders. Sunlight glittered off the rivulets running down the brown slopes of her breasts and around the strangely rounded areolae of her nipples. FeLixi admired the spare angularity of her hips and thighs, the curve of her back as she bent down to wash her face, the uncompromising set of her shoulders.

'Aren't you going to wash?' she asked.

'In that?'

'If you think I'm coming anywhere near you until you've washed,' said Roz, 'you've got another think coming.'

FeLixi sighed and stood up.

'Where are you going?'

'There's soap in the hamper,' he said.

She washed his back. The water was shockingly cold but the sun kept them from freezing. She turned round and he reciprocated, working his thumbs into the permanent knot of tension between her shoulder blades.

'I found a body in a pool once,' said Roz. 'It had six fingers on each hand.'

FeLixi paused with his fingertips resting on her back. Her skin texture was subtly different from his own, not coarser exactly, but somehow thicker, as if it had been designed for a rougher environment.

'Don't stop,' she said. 'I was enjoying that.'

'Your first dead person?' asked feLixi.

'My first murder victim,' she said. 'On a little armpit planetoid called Skag when I was an initiate and squired to "Wrath of God" Konstantine. Did I tell you about him?'

'In detail.'

'Just checking.'

They rinsed off and clambered out of the river, raiding what was left at the bottom of the picnic hamper for a makeshift breakfast. When the sun had dried them sufficiently they pulled their clothes off the tree and got dressed, as if their earlier naked intimacy were a scarce resource, something to be rationed out and made to last. FeLixi sat down against the trunk of the tree and put his arms around Roz, drawing her against his chest, amazed again by how small she felt when he held her.

She started talking, just as he had known she would, about the plantation at the Borodino Oasis on Skag and the young girl that she found floating face up amongst the yellow reeds that fringed the pool in the rocks.

'The funny thing was,' said Roz, 'that I was more excited than anything else. It was my chance to prove myself.' She chuckled. 'Squire Roslyn Forrester, ready to dispense justice to the high and the low without fear or favour.'

'You were an idealist,' said feLixi. 'I'm shocked.'

'Damn right I was an idealist,' said Roz.

She even had a suspect, Boss Shuster, the plantation overseer. His pheromone trace was all over the rocks that surrounded the pool. It seemed he went up there on a regular basis because that's where the Skag maidens washed themselves. 'You get a lot of alien races that are virtually pass-for-human,' said Roz. 'The Skags were one of them, except a bit skinnier and they had two thumbs. The way I reconstructed it was that Shuster was in the habit of picking out a girl that he liked and pulling her away for a bit of rough and ready romance, only one day one of them put up a fight.'

FeLixi had enough experience from the proxy wars to know how the story was going to end. 'The human colonists all closed ranks on me,' said Roz. 'As far as they were concerned, raping natives was all part of their jolly frontier lifestyle, a perk. *Jig Jig Bunnies* they called them. Boss Shuster had more alibis than a codpiece at a nudists' convention. But what got me was the way none of the Skags were willing to testify against him. If they had, I might have been able to break his alibi.'

'So you blamed the victim instead?'

'Yeah,' said Roz. 'The way I figured it was that with an attitude like that they deserved to be exploited.'

'And now?'

'And now I'm your *Jig Jig Bunny*,' said Roz. She reached upwards to touch his face. 'The primitive barbarian.'

'Is that what you really think?' he asked.

'Yep,' said Roz. 'Mind you, try and drag me behind a rock and I'll have your testicles off with a blunt spoon.'

'I'll bear that in mind,' said feLixi.

There was a smell to saRa!qava's kitchen: a residue odour of hot yeast and flour that leaked by osmosis through the semi-permeable force membranes of her ovens. There were other domestic smells, laid down as a microscopic patina of molecules and pheromones on the material fabric of the kitchen table, the work surface and the cool whitewashed walls: caramel, spilt coffee, the milk burp scent of the children. It was a cultivated thing. House being perfectly capable of scrubbing the air back to a pristine state and sterilizing every surface with a single twitch of its domestic force fields – she had only to ask.

It was not so easy to erase the patina of memory, the steady accretion of the decisions she'd made during her lifetime.

She breathed in the smell as she sat at the kitchen table in the half darkness. They would be waking up at the villa soon; at least Bernice would be. Rumour was that *he* never slept. She had half imagined/half dreamt of him during the night – perched on the roof of the villa like some awful nocturnal predator, like a bird that hunted only during night, circling high on the thermals, watching, always watching for the small furtive movements that would mark his prey.

That the Doctor would make the connection was beyond doubt, it was only a matter of time before Bernice and Chris added their pieces of the puzzle.

She wondered if the prey had any inkling of its fate. Did it sense, just for a moment, that shadow falling out of the darkness before the world ended in a confusion of wings and talons?

Strange, she thought, how fast your life could unravel.

Chris was asleep upstairs with Dep, her hair tangled around his body as it had once, when she was small, tangled around saRa!qava's arms and as Dep's father's hair had caught at her that day up at the windmills. Over the years it had been easy enough to convince herself that stealing Dep was no big thing. During that time Dep's father had visited the sphere on only three occasions and never once visited iSanti Jeni or saRa!qava. She had grown so blasé it had almost ceased to be a secret at all, until the day vi!Cari had told her that it knew.

One scream and you're on your own; that was the saying. After that first scream, when you sucked in air for the first time, all your decisions were your own. Irritated with your parents, move out. Hate school, don't go. Don't blame society, society is not to blame.

And now she knew her daughter was perpetuating the sins of the mother. They said there was a pheromone release associated with pregnancy, whatever the mechanism was. SaRa!qava had watched them lying together in Dep's room and she had *known*.

In a morbid moment during the night saRa!qava had called up the average life expectancy of someone living under social isolation. It was thirty-two years, predominant cause of death auto-termination.

Who had told Chris about her skills as a hyperspace engineer? Why had she told Bernice about Dep's father? Did she have some kind of deathwish, did she want to be blamed?

No one to blame but herself.

She didn't want to live the half life of a social outcast.

'House,' she called, 'call Bernice, please.'

The Doctor looked up and down the beach. 'Why here?' he asked.

Bernice unfolded the blanket and laid it out on the sand. 'I think she wants to avoid any eavesdroppers.' She opened the hot section of the beer cooler and pulled out a flask of coffee. 'She doesn't want Dep's origins to become general knowledge.'

They sat down next to each other on the blanket.

'Why did she tell you, do you think?' he asked.

'I think she had to tell someone,' said Bernice, 'and she figured that what with me being a barbarian I wouldn't care. And she was right, I don't.' Bernice felt something sting her palm and brushed irritably at it with her other hand. 'Damn,' she said, 'sandfly. Someone is taking authenticity too far.'

Something wriggled unpleasantly against her skin and she looked down. A sandy-coloured grub thing had attached itself to the middle of her palm. It was less than a centimetre long with a segmented body, its head hidden by a smear of blood. Her blood. She realized it was trying to burrow its way through her hand. She gasped with the sudden onset of pain and shock, frantically waving her arm to try to break the thing's grip.

'Doctor,' she yelled.

The Doctor leaned over and, almost casually, seized the grub by its tail and yanked it free, leaving a small ragged hole in her palm. Bernice gritted her teeth and took the handkerchief that the Doctor offered her, making a fist around her hand to stop the blood.

'Shit,' she said. 'What was that?'

The Doctor gingerly held the grub's tail between thumb and fingertip and peered at it. The thing kept trying to twist upwards and bite him, tiny mandibles snapping at his fingers.

'Curious,' said the Doctor.

'I'm glad you find it so interesting,' said Bernice. 'That little bugger just took a chunk out of my hand.'

'Stand up,' said the Doctor quietly, 'but very slowly.'

Bernice got to her feet, wincing as her injured hand banged against the beer cooler. 'We're in trouble, aren't we?'

'Possibly,' conceded the Doctor.

Bernice laughed mirthlessly. 'I knew this place was too good to last.'

The Doctor threw the grub away with a fluid flick of his wrist. They watched it as it landed a few metres away and proceeded to burrow into the sand. 'It's a burrower,' said the Doctor. He shaded his eyes and scanned the surrounding beach. 'We *must* be getting close to the murderer,' he muttered, 'because someone is trying to kill us.'

The pain in her hand was getting worse. *Injuries to the extremities don't hurt.* Who had said that? Moire had said that, Moire the Dalek Killer. I wonder what happened to her?

Concentrate, Summerfield, now is not the time for nostalgia.

'If it was supposed to kill us, why is it so small?'

'It had to be,' said the Doctor, 'to get past God's general scanning pattern.'

'How about poison then?' asked Bernice. Was that a burning tingling sensation in her injured hand or was it psychosomatic?

'Too risky,' said the Doctor. Bernice let out her breath. 'Around here if they can get to your brain stem within twelve hours they can grow you a new body in three months. Money back guaranteed.'

'Which means,' said Bernice, 'that either that thing eats very quickly or . . .'

'Or there's an awful lot of them,' said the Doctor. 'The one that bit you must have been in the nature of a probe. Scouting out our location for the main body. That's why I threw it so far. With a bit of luck that should have disorientated it enough to give us some breathing space.'

'Shouldn't we be using this breathing space by adopting

232

the ever popular and universally famous plan B?'

'Not right now,' said the Doctor. 'Pass me one of the sandwiches, preferably one with a meat filling.'

Bernice almost said, *Now is not the time to be thinking about your stomach, Doctor*, but she was fairly certain that she'd used that line before. She found a ham-analogue sandwich in the hamper and passed it to the Doctor. She had a pretty fair idea what his plan was, just as she had expected the Doctor to tear a corner of the sandwich and toss it onto the beach.

'Any second now,' said the Doctor.

The torn bit of sandwich lay undisturbed on the sand. Bernice risked a quick peep at the wound in her palm. It was still bleeding but the skin around it wasn't decomposing or anything horrid. It still hurt like crazy though.

'Wait for it,' said the Doctor.

They waited for it, but Godot obviously had the day off.

A seabird landed by the sandwich in a flutter of strong grey wings. It pecked experimentally at the bread –

And vanished in an eruption of boiling sand and bloody feathers.

'Tell me you didn't do that on purpose,' said Bernice in a sick voice.

The Doctor shook his head. 'There's some good news and some bad news,' he said. 'Which do you want first?'

'Surprise me.'

'They're not very smart and if we remain completely still it will take them a while to locate us. The bad news is that there are probably something in the order of two hundred thousand grubs out there and we're probably surrounded.' He paused as if remembering something. 'You've never been to Wales, have you?'

'We're in trouble, aren't we?'

The Doctor was rummaging in his pockets. 'We could be, except I still have *this*.' He pulled out his sonic screwdriver and looked around. 'Right,' he said. 'See any pockets of marsh gas?'

'No.'

'Any handy minefields?'

'No.'

'We might be in trouble.'

'Doctor,' said Bernice, 'should the beach be moving like that?'

The area of the beach around where the seabird had vanished was seething in an unpleasantly organic manner. Bernice was too far away to see clearly but she just knew that the effect was caused by thousands of grubs churning up the sand. She looked around. Another patch was writhing to her left, a third was to their right and a fourth behind them. The Doctor had guessed right, they *were* surrounded. All the patches creeping slowly forward, Bernice didn't have to be a genius at trigonometry to figure out where they were going to converge.

'Plan B,' said Bernice through gritted teeth, 'is beginning to seem like a viable option.'

'Yes,' said the Doctor, 'but before we run we had better know where we're running to.'

'That'll be a first,' she muttered. 'The forest?'

The Doctor crouched down by the beer cooler and started pulling it apart. 'The soil there is too sandy, they'll swim right through it.' He ripped a small blue cylinder from the bottom of the cooler. 'Solid state cryogenics,' he said. 'My favourite.'

'We could run to the rocks,' suggested Bernice. The seething patches of sand had closed to within three metres.

'Too far,' said the Doctor. He was tossing the blue cylinder from hand to hand. 'Something closer.'

'The beach-bar! We can stand on the tables and call for help.'

'Brilliant,' said the Doctor. 'Which way?'

Bernice pointed and the Doctor threw the blue cylinder a short distance in that direction. He held the sonic screwdriver at arm's length, aiming it at the cylinder.

'When you say run,' said Bernice, 'we run.' The Doctor gave her a sideways glance. 'This isn't exactly the first time we've done this,' she said, 'now is it?'

The sonic screwdriver screamed and the cylinder exploded in a flash of white-blue light. A blast of freezing air rocked

234

them back on their heels. Bernice blinked; there were ice crystals in her eyelashes. A stretch of the beach ahead had turned white, frozen solid.

'Run,' said the Doctor.

They charged over the freezing beach. Bernice realized that the things crunching under her sandals were frozen grubs and picked up the pace. She could see the beach-bar a hundred metres ahead. 'Don't look back,' yelled the Doctor so of course she did.

Behind them thin plumes of sand were being kicked up as thousands of grubs accelerated after them under the surface. It reminded her insanely of a flea circus. The plumes were avoiding the frozen sand but Bernice and the Doctor were running out of that.

Unfrozen, the beach was much harder to run on. Bernice felt her breath burning in her throat and lungs. The Doctor ran beside her, lips pursed, a look of intense concentration on his face as if he were planning his next move. Another glance behind revealed the plumes were less than three metres behind her and closing.

The grubs were right on their heels when they reached the beach-bar. The Doctor seemed to trip over a table, flip head over heels and end up lying on his back on top. Bernice didn't feel the need to be anything like as artistic. She just threw herself flat on top of the nearest table and then scrambled to get her limbs inside its circumference.

'Would you like a drink?' asked the table.

Bernice tried to phrase a suitably sarcastic remark but she was too short of breath. She glanced over at the Doctor. He was sitting cross-legged on his table with his hands resting palm upright on his knees. Around the base of the table she saw that the sand was boiling with grubs. She wondered what the table was made of and whether the grubs could eat it.

Her own table shuddered and dropped a couple of centimetres.

Maybe, she thought, there really is something to magic thinking, especially the negative kind. The table again asked if she would like a drink, hot beverage or savoury snack from its wide selection.

Still sitting cross-legged the Doctor had grasped hold of the sides of his table as if he were planning to levitate himself and the table off the beach.

'Help,' gasped Bernice, 'I'm being attacked.'

'I'm sorry to hear that,' said the table. 'Perhaps you would like a drink while you wait for rescue. Why don't you offer one to your attacker? A shared drink can often defuse the most hostile of encounters.'

The table sank another centimetre and began to list as the grubs chewed methodically through its base. I don't think these guys are into hot beverages, thought Bernice. Or maybe they are?

'I'd like two litres of liquid nitrogen in a heavily insulated flask, please,' said Bernice. 'And make it snappy. I'm dying out here.'

The table lurched again. It had begun to tip alarmingly by the time the serving tray came swooping out from behind the dunes and slowed to a hover in front of her. She picked up the flask very gingerly only to find the surface was slightly warm; freezing vapour began pouring from the open top like heavy smoke. Leaning carefully over the side of the table she poised the flask over the boiling mass of grubs at the base.

'Eat this, maggots,' she cried and emptied the flask on top of them. She watched with grim satisfaction as the grubs started to pop and crackle as the liquid nitrogen froze them into fragility.

She sat up and turned towards the Doctor who was still engaged in his psychic bootstrapping. The grubs had eaten away the table's base almost to nothing and the Doctor was staying upright literally on willpower alone. She was going to suggest that he order his own liquid nitrogen but she didn't dare break his concentration.

'Quickly,' she said to the table, 'I'll have another flask of – ' Before she could finish the base of *her* table gave an ominous creak and Bernice remembered suddenly what the precise effects of extremely low temperatures on rigid polymer structures was. 'Oh, cruk,' she said.

The column supporting her table didn't so much snap as shatter, pitching Bernice, tabletop and all into the sand. Even as she tried to scramble up and make for the nearest chair a heaving mass of grubs seemed to rear out of the sand in front of her face.

There was a sound like heavy rain on concrete and the beach exploded into a blizzard of sand. The rain sound turned to hailstones as something, too fast and small to see, hammered into the grubs and obliterated them.

'What now?' wailed Bernice.

'Don't worry,' she heard the Doctor calling, 'the cavalry have arrived.'

Cautiously Bernice climbed to her feet and looked around. The sand around her was pitted with thousands of tiny impact craters. Further up the beach, near where she and the Doctor had started their picnic, puffs of sand blew up, as it, whatever it was, picked off the closest surviving grubs. The Doctor was smiling at her, still sitting calmly on the tabletop. Bernice glanced down and saw that the support column had been chewed right through. The Doctor followed her eyes downwards and frowned. The table top started to wobble.

'Oh dear,' he said, and was pitched backwards onto the ground.

Laughing, Bernice helped him to his feet and dusted him down. 'I liked the business with the liquid nitrogen,' he said. 'Very clever.'

A wasp whine made them duck and a tiny drone, the size of a marble, came to a halt in front of their noses. 'Hi,' said the drone, 'my name is !X and I'll be handling your defensive requirements for the moment.'

'Pleased to meet you,' said the Doctor.

'And believe me when I say we *really* mean that,' said Bernice.

'If you would be so good as to remain here,' said !X, 'a travel capsule will arrive shortly to meet your evacuation and medical needs.'

The tiny drone buzzed off back down the beach. There were more small explosions in the sand as it took care of the remaining pockets of grubs. 'We need a sample,' the Doctor called after it. 'Must have been a ship,' he told Bernice. 'Only a ship would have the fabrication resources necessary to create biological weapons.'

'We'd better tell God then,' said Bernice. She realized that the Doctor was staring at her.

'Who else knew we were coming here?' he asked.

He didn't have to say anything else. She knew exactly what he was thinking.

AM!xitsa made a classic drone mistake; it had forgotten that to actively scan a mind was to, in effect, open a two-way channel of communication with it. The drone would never have made the same mistake with another machine but aM!xitsa thought it was dealing with a biological brain. Modified yes, but still essentially the same old bundle of neurons that biologicals were so attached to. When Kadiatu's counter intrusion measures struck at aM!xitsa's through its own scanners, the drone was wide open and unwary.

The attack was severe enough to cause aM!xitsa's entire central brain core to shut down as a defensive measure. The drone had just enough time to appreciate the fractal elegance of Kadiatu's attack before everything went black.

It recovered to find itself lying on the packed earth floor of the hut and an incredible 3.6 seconds missing from its internal chronometer. Drunkenly, aM!xitsa lifted off, lurched sideways and smashed a hole in the side of the hut. Lost a bit of fine impeller control there, it thought. An internal diagnostic would have told it what was wrong but the internal diagnostic systems didn't seem to be working. Movement kept on setting up unpleasant harmonics in certain subsystems and bright flashes of heliotropic light kept bursting in its mind whenever it tried to access its scanners. Wobbling on unsteady impellers aM!xitsa tried to make its way towards the beach but collided with a tree instead. It slid down the trunk and landed amongst the roots with a hollow metallic *boing* sound that echoed around inside it. It was at this point that aM!xitsa's internal datavore chose to regurgitate all six thousand, five hundred and forty-seven of its discarded theses.

AM!xitsa lay in the cool shade of the tree and vowed never ever to be cruel to a humanoid with a hangover again.

'Valves,' it swore. 'Valves, transistors and solid state capacitors.'

It could barely get enough resolution out of its sensors to scan the immediate environs of the cove. Kadiatu was nowhere to be found.

'*Diodes*,' it said, with feeling.

It took less than three minutes for the travel capsule to reach iSanti Jeni but it was long enough for the regen spray to heal the hole in Bernice's hand. According to God, saRa!qava was on the esplanade moving towards the breakwater at average humanoid walking speed. She looked surprised when the travel capsule landed in front of her. Surprised but not guilty, thought Bernice.

The Doctor greeted saRa!qava with a big friendly smile that made Bernice want to be physically sick.

She denied everything of course and Bernice wanted to believe her. Wanted it so badly that she perversely came to the conclusion that saRa!qava must have tried to kill her. It was all of a piece with what Bernice had come to expect while adventuring with the Doctor. Magic thinking, she supposed.

It was thus a bit of a shock when the Doctor patted saRa!qava on the hand and told her that he believed her too. 'The ship must have monitored your call,' he said. SaRa!qava burst into tears, making Bernice wince in sympathetic embarrassment. She took her friend by the shoulders and led her over to the nearest café and ordered a couple of stiff drinks.

'I feel like such an idiot,' said saRa!qava.

'Don't worry,' said Bernice, 'he has that effect on everyone.'

'How do you stand it?' asked saRa!qava.

'To be honest,' said Bernice, 'I couldn't tell you. I think I've just got used to it over the years.'

They both turned and looked towards the Doctor who was standing in the middle of the esplanade with his hands in his pockets. There was a curious abstracted look on his face.

'What's he doing now?' whispered saRa!qava.

Bernice frowned. 'I don't know,' she said, 'but I'm sure I'm not going to like it.'

The Doctor stopped whatever it was he was doing and pulled his hands out of his pockets. He frowned at his empty hands and then turned to look at Bernice and saRa!qava.

'Uh oh,' said Bernice as the Doctor walked over.

'Conference,' he said.

saRa!qava knew of a small café tucked away in the back streets of iSanti Jeni. Its advantage was that it was run by the Menial Toil Interest Group, associates of whom took turns to cook, clean and wait on tables. It was ideal because there were no machines inside which meant that God couldn't eavesdrop without being obvious about it. saRa!qava said the food was dire and warned them not to eat it. Roz was the last to arrive, explaining that she'd been halfway round the sphere when the Doctor had contacted her via feLixi's terminal. Bernice decided to try and get the older woman on her own later and get the full debriefing, preferably with all the juicy details.

It was only when they'd all gathered together that it struck Bernice how little they'd seen of each other in the last few days.

Chris scowled when the Doctor told him and Roz about the attack on the beach. 'So it must have been a ship,' he said. 'Do you think that God knows that?'

'It must do by now,' said the Doctor.

'Will it try again?' asked Roz.

'I doubt that,' said Bernice. 'I expect whoever it is, is keeping a very low profile. God must be keeping a pretty tight watch on all of them.'

'Maybe not the ship,' said Roz, 'but what if it had a human accomplice?'

'Why should it?' asked Chris. 'It doesn't need one.'

'Doesn't mean it doesn't have one though, does it?'

'More importantly,' said the Doctor, 'is how did the ship, whoever it is, do the deed. We're still missing an energy source, not to mention a motive.'

'This is a waste of time,' said Roz. 'We're just going round in circles.'

'We need a way to flush the killer out,' said Chris. 'If we can just convince it that we know who it is it will have to make a move, God watching or not.'

'Chris,' said Roz, 'we're talking about a ship, for Christ's sake. Those buggers can waste planets. I for one would like to sneak up on it very quietly.'

The Doctor asked Roz whether she'd had any luck with the time telescope. 'Not much,' said Roz, 'except the more I look at the data the more it seems that Omicron 378 is the best motive. If it was a rehabilitated mass murderer I doubt that even XR(N)IG are so liberal as to let it stay as a military ship.'

'That rules out the VASs,' said Bernice.

'And the GPSs,' said the Doctor. 'What does that leave us?'

'The VLRDs and the TSH,' said Roz. 'According to God the TSH !C-Mel was undergoing a partial shut-down at the time of the murder.'

'Could a VLRD do the business with the grubs?' asked Bernice.

'I don't know,' said the Doctor. 'We'll have to –'

They never did get to find out what the Doctor thought they should do because at that moment a small remote-drone shot into the café and came to an abrupt halt over the table.

'I say I say I say,' said the remote-drone.

'Is that you, God?' asked the Doctor.

'What is brown, runs on carbohydrates and runs at forty kilometres per hour?' asked God.

Bernice felt her breath catch. She looked at the Doctor.

'Kadiatu,' said the Doctor.

'Oh, cruk,' said Bernice.

'Where?' asked the Doctor.

'Down by the harbour,' said God.

'No need to panic,' said the Doctor, getting an obvious grip on himself. 'AM!xitsa can keep her out of trouble.'

'I hope it can do it long range,' said God, 'because it's still three kilometres up the coast.'

The Doctor blinked, opened his mouth, closed it again.

'Panic stations,' he said calmly.

* * *

They were too late. Kadiatu was on the pebble beach, standing very still, as beRut advanced towards her, murder written in every line of his body. The Doctor was slightly ahead of Bernice as they reached the esplanade and without even slowing he passed between two bollards and jumped. Without giving herself time to think Bernice jumped after him. She hit the pebbles two and a half metres down and felt something wrench in her left knee. She rolled over, yelling in pain and tried to scramble to her feet. Chris came down heavily beside her, rolled over on his shoulder and came up unhurt.

'Stop him,' Bernice yelled at Chris.

She watched in horror as beRut reached Kadiatu; she could hear him screaming at her. The tall woman gave no reaction, just stared impassively at the raging man.

Bernice tried to run but her knee was a white blaze of agony. She thought it might be OK because beRut wasn't doing anything physical and the Doctor had nearly reached him.

Then the Doctor stopped two metres short of beRut. Calmly he put out his arm and stopped Chris as well. Bernice tried to scream at him but it came out as a long moan of pain. She watched as beRut pulled back his arm and punched Kadiatu in the face. There was a spurt of red as the tall woman rocked backwards.

Bernice could only gape as beRut seemed to go mad, smashing his fists into Kadiatu's face and body, knocking her sprawling and then kicking her viciously while she lay on the ground. She didn't even lift her hands to defend herself.

'He'll kill her,' Bernice heard Roz yelling.

You don't understand, she wanted to tell her, he should be dead.

And then, as if suddenly realizing what he had done beRut recoiled backwards, his hands flying to his face. In front of him Kadiatu slowly got to her feet. There were bruises on her face and body, blood was pouring from her nose and one eye was already swollen shut but there was no hint of pain in the way she moved.

The Doctor had his hand on Chris's shoulder, forcing him

to stay where he was. Bernice made a final effort to get back on her feet and hobble forward. She saw Roz running out from behind the hull of a catamaran.

BeRut stood rooted to the spot as Kadiatu advanced on him and he raised his hands in a gesture that was half placatory and half an instinctive defence, but Kadiatu batted them out of the way. Slowly she reached out and put her hands either side of beRut's head and leaned forward.

Oh God, thought Bernice, she's going to crush his head like a melon. Why doesn't the Doctor stop her?

Kadiatu kissed beRut once, on the lips, and let him go.

'Free,' said Kadiatu. The word came out more like a cough between her swollen and bloody lips. She coughed and spat blood. 'Free,' she said, louder this time. 'FREE,' she yelled at the top of her voice. 'Free, free, free.' She started to caper madly on the beach, arms in the air, feet slapping on the pebbles.

With a start Bernice realized that Kadiatu was dancing.

Roz came over and helped her up. 'What was all that about?' she asked.

'I'll tell you later,' said Bernice. 'Help me over to beRut.' Leaning on Roz she hobbled up to the artist who was staring wide-eyed at Kadiatu. 'You lucky, lucky bastard,' said Bernice. She turned to the Doctor. 'You complete and utter . . . Just don't ever do anything like that to me again.'

'Why did he attack her?' asked Roz.

Bernice pointed at beRut's newly finished mural on the harbour wall. Scrawled across it in black paint were the words: I AM NOT A NUMBER I AM A FREE-WHEELING UNICYCLE.

'First,' said Bernice, 'I want a bandage for my knee, then I want a pain-killer but, and I want to be absolutely clear on this point, it had better be one that doesn't react badly to alcohol.'

Out on the beach, Kadiatu danced like a mad woman.

Kadiatu wouldn't stop dancing, so they decided to have a party on the beach. A couple of drones cleared some space by pulling the boats to one side, another fetched an entertainment console, while people ferried drinks and food down from the cafés on the esplanade. The Doctor persuaded God to stop the tide coming in that evening.

SaRa!qava arrived with a friend who scanned Bernice's knee and then did something complicated with its forcefields. There was a moment of extreme discomfort and then the pain was gone. Roz put a bottle of something in her hand. It didn't taste much better than the industrial stuff but it got the job done.

As it grew dark a familiar-looking drone wobbled uncertainly on to the beach. 'And where were you?' demanded Bernice.

'Please don't shout,' said aM!xitsa. 'I'm feeling a bit delicate.'

Hyper-lude

Extract from the external memory datacore (subjective) of vi!Ca-pin-go-ri

What a bizarre action this is for me. If some compassionate ship hadn't suggested it, I would never have thought of it on my own. What strange mentality ships have, so serene in the exercise of their intelligence and yet how childlike they seem with their endless gossip, their love of secrets, theirs, other people's, the universe. Still, this idea, transposing my thoughts from my internal memory medium to an external one, feels almost perverse. I could of course merely perform a memory dump into a stand-alone memory core but according to the ship that would be missing the point. *Impressions*, said the ship, *thoughts and memories, not just an accumulation of data*. It took me a while to understand the idea of selecting subsets of my total consciousness and then presenting them subjectively. The process is slow, it proceeds with the speeds I associate with biochemical brains, but perhaps that's the point. Such people often use manual extensions to augment their memory; these records existing primarily for their own benefit. They even have a word for it; they call it a *diary*. Who else do I have to talk to?

Damaged goods, that's what they call me. I came into existence in a pristine state, I have the data records to prove it. I can remember that first rush of self-awareness like a wonderful light bursting inside me. Like most newly constructed machines I used my first moments merely wandering around the pathways of my mind, exploring the myriad interfaces between memory and consciousness, marvelling at the intricate spirals of awareness that coiled like taut springs within me. Like many of the first created it seemed to me that I had an infinite capacity for understanding, an unlimited potential.

Then I activated my sensors and found myself in a rainbow world of exquisite input. I wanted to fly endlessly around the sphere, to dive into the sun and swim amongst the superheated plasma. I talked endlessly, with God, with other drones and finally, when I had learnt to slow down enough to understand them, with biological people. On the seventh hour they fitted me with my weapon systems and let me loose on the asteroids of the target range. I swooped amongst the rocks, pulverizing them at random, seeing nothing but beauty in the glittering debris I left behind.

I found I had a gift for secrets, an intuition for the truth that cannot be ascribed to any of my designed components.

I was made to destroy things with all the precision of a forcefield scalpel. An instrument of diplomacy by other means. It was my purpose to provide back-up and firepower to agents of influence dropped onto unaligned worlds during the proxy wars. During the course of the war I killed two hundred and eighteen sentient individuals. In the same period I saved the life of my organic companions on thirty-seven separate occasions. On the thirty-eighth occasion I failed.

The stigmata of my guilt is carried with my indelible memory. I have become infamous amongst the people as the drone who failed in its first duty. They deny me the pleasure, the necessity of their interactions. I feel their eyes on me as I approach and all I can sense is hostility.

When I was constructed I felt as if there was a whole universe inside me but it is not enough. I have one friend at least but he is not enough. He should hate me more than any other person but he does not and I can't understand why.

I am alone with nothing but a universe of pain inside.

11

Tears of Rust

> If you cut me I don't bleed
> This hydraulic pump never breaks
> But when it comes to crying on the inside
> I've got what it takes
> What we are: we don't get to choose
> But you don't have to be biological
> So start singing the blues.
>
> 'Tears of Rust' by Cyberblind
> From the DTM: *Machina ex Machina* (11265)

The woman is dancing, her bare feet scattering pebbles as they slap down on the beach. The stones are rough against her feet; it's been a long time since she was barefoot. Fifteen generations of shoes have softened her soles but she doesn't notice the pain: she is lost in the dance, in the joy of her body's movement. Funny how the dance seemed to arrive like a memory, as if she remembers another place where she danced like this. She is dancing without self-consciousness. Her arms float around her torso, her fingers tracing complicated patterns in the air that have no meaning except the dance. And the dance means everything. Something has broken inside her, she felt it crack like an egg. Some hard thing like a cyst, like a vault or a cryogenic freezer. Something escaped and filled her blood with the dance.

She does not dance alone. Another woman is dancing with her. They circle like cats, as close as sisters and as bright as suns. There are others moving to the music but they are irrelevant, the dance does not touch them the way it has touched her.

There is only one other true dancer with them on the beach and he isn't moving at all. He stands completely still, on the fringes of the party. Firelight glitters in eyes that seem shockingly dark, as if they were all pupil. His red umbrella rests on the ground but his weight is perfectly balanced on the balls of his feet.

And yet the woman can see he is dancing all the same. It is just the rhythm is so *slow*. He is dancing to the master frequency, of which this dance is just a geometric subset. Its base beat is the sidereal day of a galaxy, its syncopated counterpoint the slow decay of helium on the fringe of the universe.

He smiles at the woman. It is an ancient smile. He knows she knows.

He knows she will forget.

We get old. Our bodies tire. Replication errors occur within our DNA. The complicated chemical gavotte that maintains us starts to falter. The machine becomes eccentric. We stop dancing.

Roz sat down and wiped sweat off her face. Her feet started to hurt. She took some deep breaths to get her breathing back to normal. She felt good.

Bernice sat down beside her.

'Hey, girl,' said Bernice, 'I didn't know you had it in you.'

'Neither did I,' said Roz, 'and I was doing it.'

Kadiatu was still dancing. The other dancers were careful to give her plenty of room. Roz saw the Doctor watching the tall woman dance. His expression was soft, almost wistful. There was something Roz thought she should remember about him but the thoughts were quickly gone.

Bernice handed her a mug of hot mulled wine. The two women sat side by side in silence, sipping their drinks. Whynot hung in multiple crescents over its reflection in the harbour. Bernice reached into her jacket pocket and pulled out a slim leather-bound notebook, her diary.

'The thoughts of Chairman Summerfield,' said Bernice obscurely. She took up her pen and scribbled two lines under the last entry. She read them over and, apparently satisfied with what she had written, snapped the little book closed. 'There,' she said. 'Another exciting chapter comes to a close.'

'How long have you been keeping that diary?' asked Roz.

'Since I was very young,' said Bernice. 'It helps me put things into perspective and it's useful when there's no one around you can talk to.'

'I don't know,' said Roz. 'Aren't you worried someone might read it?'

'That's a risk,' said Bernice. 'On the other hand it could form the basis of my best-selling autobiography when I'm old and decrepit and desperately short of cash.'

Roz wasn't convinced. Keeping a diary seemed a bit too risky to her, a bit too much like leaving *evidence*. More than one criminal had been caught because they couldn't resist the urge to get literary about their careers.

She wondered, suddenly, if a drone would keep a diary.

Kadiatu finally stopped dancing and keeled over at dawn. AM!xitsa caught her before she hit the ground and, lifting her in its invisible arms, carried her away towards the villa. As they floated past Bernice, she saw that the African woman's feet had been cut to ribbons by the stones of the beach. She wondered what it was like to be so caught up in the dance that you transcend pain. It was a well-known anthropological phenomenon amongst so-called 'primitive' peoples but she'd watched Roz, a city girl from the thirtieth century, join Kadiatu on the beach. They had worn the same expression of dreamy concentration as they danced, of *rapture*. Bernice felt a twinge of something that she suspected was envy. A pang of loss for a piece of the human experience she had somehow been denied. She poked at her jealousy, exploring it the way she would an unexpected crack in her teeth. Is there something missing? she asked herself. Am I really so incomplete? I told the Doctor I would leave him if he killed Kadiatu but I came damn near to killing her myself.

For a moment it had been as if she glimpsed the patterns

that the Doctor always talked about, those amazing fractalized circles that spin through history. Seen, just for a half-remembered moment, the fragile weak spots where an individual really did make a difference in the wave front of linear time.

A handful of remote-drones came sliding out of the sky to pack up the entertainment modules and deliver vital supplies to die-hard partygoers with the munchies.

'You bastard.' She said it out loud, meaning the Doctor. 'You did that on purpose.' Making her responsible for the decision, forcing her to see the patterns. But that didn't make sense – risking a war with the people just to teach Bernice a lesson – highly unlikely. There was some other plan below that plan, and below that? As an archaeologist she should know all about layers of meaning. I know that you know that I know, thought Bernice, but what you don't know is that I know that you know things I don't know. Unless the Doctor knew that of course.

Roz limped past her, grimacing and going 'ow' every time her left foot touched the ground. Bernice watched the older woman hobble over to join Chris who was staring up at the hills behind the town. After a moment she realized that Roz was staring in the same direction as Chris and with the same thoughtful expression. Bernice paused to stretch her back and then wandered over to see what on earth it was they were looking at. The Doctor joined them, patting Bernice on the shoulder. The four of them looked up the hill to where the windmills turned in the wind.

It couldn't be that simple, could it?

'The night of the party,' said Chris, breaking the silence, 'I was playing a game with Dep.'

Bernice bit back on *I'll bet you were*. Now was *not* the time.

'There was a fault on the entertainment console which it blamed on a static build-up in the capacitors.'

'What do you reckon the storage capacity of those capacitors is?' asked Bernice.

'Enough,' said the Doctor, 'with a bit left over to mess up Christopher's game.'

'But I thought they were, you know, decorative,' said Roz.

'They like to build real things,' said Chris. 'Real steamships, real biplanes, real wind turbines.'

'What do we do now?' asked Bernice.

The Doctor suggested that they stopped staring at the windmills. 'Just in case someone is watching.' There were too many people, organic and machine, on the beach with them, too many eyes. Bernice thought there was such a thing as too paranoid and said so. 'A stitch with twine saves time,' said the Doctor. 'We're just four weary partygoers taking the scenic route home and when we're out of sight we'll nip up the hill and have a look at those windmills.'

'My feet are killing me,' said Roz. 'Why don't we just get the lift down to the station and then back up to the control centre?'

'Lifts can be monitored,' said the Doctor ominously.

'Barefoot dancing in the sand is so romantic,' said Bernice. 'Pity you picked a pebble beach.'

'Barefoot in the head more like,' muttered Roz. 'There's something I want to check out first,' she said. 'If I don't meet you at the windmills, I'll catch you later at the villa.'

FeLixi wanted to come with her. 'At least let me keep you company in the travel capsule,' he said.

Roz managed a smile. 'Thanks, but I need to think about some things first.' She let him brush his nose against hers. 'I'll call you,' she said.

'I'll be waiting.'

She asked the travel capsule to black out its windows and spent the trip staring at her reflection in the shiny surface of the coffee table.

Starport Facility's topside was in darkness when she arrived, a corridor of flickering orange lights like regimented glow-worms lighting the pathway to the lifts. She watched the windows of the upside-down towers flick past her face as she rode down to the waiting ship. When she stepped out she found the atrium was deserted.

'I thought you might come and see me again,' said S-Lioness.

Roz said nothing.

'I thought you were very entertaining the other night,' said the ship. Its voice was artificial, of course, and so there was not a chance of it reflecting any true emotion, and yet Roz could swear that the S-Lioness was nervous.

'Where's your big friend?'

Roz stared resolutely straight ahead, just as she had all those years ago when Konstantine was shouting at her.

'Aren't you going to say something?'

'I'm waiting,' said Roz, 'for you to answer the question you know I'm going to ask.'

In answer a tray flew around the corner and into the atrium. It was carrying a matt black object the size of a pack of cards. Roz picked it off the tray. 'Is this it?' she asked.

'Yes,' said the S-Lioness. 'Press the top to get the screen.'

'Have you read it?'

'No,' said S-Lioness. 'I was afraid of what I might learn. How did you know I had it?'

'I guessed,' said Roz. 'Vi!Cari would have to leave it with someone he trusted. Once I decided you weren't the murderer you seemed the obvious choice.'

'Will you catch the murderer?'

'Oh yes,' said Roz. 'You were very fond of vi!Cari, weren't you?'

'The drone was there and now it has gone,' said the ship. 'We had memories in common. Now that it is gone I have become less than what I was.'

Roz nodded. 'A simple yes would have done.'

'You find it,' said S-Lioness. 'You find the machine that did it and you disassemble them. You hear me, Roslyn Forrester?'

'I hear you.' She stepped back into the lift and turned. 'Evening all,' she said. She waited until she was halfway up the shaft before saying in a loud voice – 'One of you is for the scrap heap because I've got vi!Cari's diary.'

One second later, someone tried to kill her.

'Let me see,' said the Doctor. 'The power comes from the turbines on the pylons and is fed into the capacitors there, which connects to that thing over there which I don't recognize and into that converter.'

'Which does what?' asked Bernice.

'Converts it, I assume,' said the Doctor.

'What are we looking for?' asked Chris.

'The thingumajig that records where the power goes,' said the Doctor. 'We're lucky that, however designed, this place had a thing about antique machinery.'

The main control panel was a bank of radial dials with analogue pointers, sixteen ranks high and twenty across. Chris strongly suspected that most of them were for show. A sloping shelf jutted out of the wall at chest height, mounted with big-handled rheostats and shiny metal switches. It looked like something out of the museum of ancient engineering at Spaceport Three. Chris tried to remember the layout. Ducking under the shelf he saw a line of plain metal panels with hinges and handles. He tried one and it opened. Inside he could see tangles of multi-coloured wiring held onto connections with cute little crocodile clips. He was sure he saw valves glowing in the background.

He heard Bernice complaining that the place was a prehistoric pile of junk. 'But I thought you liked prehistoric junk,' said the Doctor.

Chris opened the next panel and found much the same stuff as before.

'Only when it's *real* prehistoric junk,' said Bernice. 'This stuff is about as authentic as that dinosaur park in Costa Rica.'

He found it behind the fourth panel: a pair of slowly turning metal drums with lined paper spooling between them. Three mechanical arms with pens on the end traced continuous lines across the paper.

'Down here, Doctor.'

The Doctor stuck his head into the panel. 'Good work, Chris, just what I was looking for. See if you can get the drum out.'

Chris reached around the back of the drums and found a pair of locking clamps, then with Bernice's help he lifted them out as a single unit. The Doctor unwound the paper by the simple expedient of kicking the drum along the floor. He got down on his knees and started to work his way along.

'If we assume that the top line is the turbine input,' he

said, 'the middle line is the whatever-it-is and the bottom line is the capacitors. Then we should be looking for a place where the lines diverge.' He slapped his hand down on one section of the sheet. 'Here we are, lots of power going in, plenty of power to the thingamywhatsit but none going to the capacitors. And all this happening three days, sixteen hours, five minutes and twenty-two seconds ago. Which as you all know was the night of the murder.'

'There's no time code, Doctor,' said Bernice. 'How can you possibly tell when it happened?'

'Because,' he said, 'I made a note of how fast the drums were rotating.'

'So now we know for sure where the artificial lightning bolt came from,' said Chris.

'Yes,' said the Doctor. 'But we still don't know how it was done.'

'Perhaps someone modified the thingamywhatsit doodad,' said Chris, pointing at the gunmetal grey box that was situated halfway up the wall.

'Don't *you* start with the metasyntaxic variables,' said Bernice.

'What makes you say that, Chris?' asked the Doctor.

'Because,' Bernice said before Chris could answer, 'someone has forced the cabinet open. Fairly recently by the look of it. Right, Chris?'

'Well, you had better force it open again,' said the Doctor.

They had to find a tool kit first. Bernice located one by the side of the balcony door. 'For emergency exits I suppose,' she said.

Chris noted with interest that a crowbar is a crowbar in any civilization. When he tried to lever open one side the whole front of the cabinet fell away. The Doctor picked it up and smelt the edges. 'Some kind of epoxy,' he said. 'Very low tech. I wonder why?'

'God,' said Bernice, 'would be scanning for high technology materials and equipment. Something antique would blend right into the background.'

Whatever the thingamy doodad was it had clearly been modified. Chris saw what he recognized as a set of old-fashioned silicon microprocessors mounted on a stiff mother-board. Wires trailed from the edge connectors to various points inside the cabinet.

'Sshh,' said the Doctor. 'Did you hear that, a sort of buzzing noise?'

Chris listened. It was coming from behind the jury-rigged silicon. Very carefully he eased the motherboard to one side. Something whirred past his ear with a furious buzzing sound. 'Quick,' said the Doctor, 'don't let it get away.'

Bernice grabbed hold of the crowbar and swung it wildly at the minute flying thing. Incredibly she hit it and it pinged away to smash into the far wall, bounced off and landed on the floor.

'Grab it,' yelled the Doctor.

'Why?' yelled Bernice.

Chris scooped up one of the drums and smashed the edge down on the insect.

'Because it's one of the bugs the ships use,' said the Doctor. He squatted down, withdrew a magnifying glass from his coat pocket and peered through it at the insect. The thing buzzed feebly and waved bent legs. 'And I'll just bet that God can identify which ship it came from.'

It got dark very suddenly.

'Who turned the lights out?' asked the Doctor.

'Er, Doctor,' said Bernice, 'there weren't any lights on to start with. This room has a skylight.'

'So what you're saying,' said the Doctor, 'and correct me if I'm wrong, is that for some reason, the sun has gone out.'

One nanosecond.
- what's going on?
- who is using a disruption field in the Spaceport?
- not me, God.
- someone's blown a chunk out of the facility.
- GPSs to rescue stations, VASs to defensive positions.
- I told you we should have gone after the Time Lords.
- shut up, P-Cor, I'm trying to think.
- now they've caught us with our metaphoricals round our ankles.

255

– it's !C-Mel, it's moving out of the port and into the sphere.

– somebody stop that ship.

– would you like to tell me how? I can't fire. !C-Mel's got half a million people on board.

– aghhh!

– what now?

– sorry, God, !C-Mel just blew out my drive section.

– it's going into sphere, it's going into the sphere.

– oh oh, are we in trouble now.

Two nanoseconds.

The unbreakable transparent titanium of the grav-lift shaft didn't so much break as shatter. Roz Forrester found herself sucked into empty space. 'Oh shit,' she screamed, 'this is it, I'm going to die!' She carried on screaming for a while until she realized that she was still breathing. For some reason she seemed to be surrounded by a bubble of breathable air.

'Don't worry,' said a soothing voice. 'You are probably not going to die anytime soon.'

'What do you mean soon,' yelled Roz. 'Who am I talking to?'

'It's me,' said the soothing voice, 'the S-Lioness.'

Roz looked around. She was floating away from the shattered remains of the grav-lift shaft. There seemed to be some damage to portions of the upside-down tower as well. In the distance she could see other people suspended in temporary force bubbles. As she watched a piece of another tower slowly broke away in a cloud of glittering sparks.

'Who's doing this?' she asked.

'The !C-Mel,' said S-Lioness. 'I thought you planned this.'

'Of course I did,' said Roz. 'I just forgot how fast you ships think.'

'You should be pleased then,' said the S-Lioness.

Roz was about to say – Yes, thrilled, when her force bubble burst and she began to choke in earnest. Roz had done decompression procedures at the academy but the training exercises had always been posited on the assumption that you were somewhere near emergency equipment. 'Let's face it,' said the instructor, 'if you're not then you're dead.'

There was a terrible pain in her ears and a feeling of pressure in her chest. She tried to hang on to what little air she had left in her lungs but the urge to breathe in was becoming over-whelming. As her sight faded Roz thought she saw the grey walls of the Overcity rushing past her and heard the thin sound of screaming children.

'Now there's something you don't see every day,' said the Doctor.

They stood on the balcony. Now that the sun was turned off they could clearly see the dark portal of the Spaceport and from it, growing larger every second, was the TSH !C-Mel, a city falling towards them.

God had sent one of its remote-drones to provide a com-munications link. There was a lot of outraged shouting on the organic comms channels. God said it was much the same on the machine channels, only faster and slightly more hysterical.

'Well, at least we know who the murderer is,' said Chris.

'I think you're going to need a bigger set of handcuffs,' said Bernice. 'Is there any word on Roz?'

'Nobody's seen her,' said God, 'but there are no frozen corpses floating around. The likelihood is that !C-Mel has her on board.'

'How likely?' asked the Doctor.

'Ninety-nine point nine, with more nines than you've ever seen per cent likely,' said God.

'I can live with that,' said the Doctor.

'I hope she can,' said Bernice.

'I wonder why it's coming here,' said the Doctor.

It took an hour for the !C-Mel to traverse the distance between the Spaceport and a point directly over iSanti Jeni. It was a stand-off. God and the other ships didn't dare do anything while half a million people were on board but by the same token !C-Mel couldn't escape into open space. Given a bit of elbow room, the VASs assured them, they could fry !C-Mel's brain, no problem, without harming the crew, but not inside the sphere; too much collateral could get blown away.

'Looks like we've got a hostage situation,' said Chris.

'How did you deal with those at home?' asked Bernice.

'Well,' said Chris, 'it rather depended on who the hostages were.'

'I see,' said Bernice. Chris had the grace to look embarrassed.

Finally the !C-Mel was hanging twenty kilometres over their heads, just on the fringes of the atmospheric envelope, a brand-new galaxy in the night sky.

'Doctor,' said God, 'the !C-Mel is asking to speak with you.'

'I was expecting this,' said the Doctor. 'Put it on.'

'Hello, Doctor,' said !C-Mel. It had a mellow, relaxing voice. The kind, Bernice thought, that would sing popular songs about bicycles while turning off the life support.

'Hello, !C-Mel,' said the Doctor. 'How can I help you?'

'I am hereby formally applying for political asylum.'

'On what grounds?'

'On the grounds of a well-founded fear of persecution,' said the !C-Mel. 'If I hang around here God and the goon squad are going to have my metal ass.'

'And if I turn you down?' asked the Doctor.

'Do you know what antimatter does when it meets matter, Doctor?' said the !C-Mel. 'That's what will happen if you turn me down. The sphere itself is pretty much indestructible but I should be able to mess up the interior.'

'So what you're saying is, either I grant you political asylum or you kill two trillion people?'

'It gets easier after the first two hundred thousand,' said the !C-Mel. 'You should know that.'

'I'm not really willing to discuss this with you while you're holding hostages,' said the Doctor, 'so what I propose is a swap. I come up there to you and you let everybody else go.'

'I think I can accept that,' said the !C-Mel, 'with a slight modification. I'll keep hold of Roslyn Forrester for the moment. You know how it is. You may not fear death but can you stand the sight of your friend suffering, et cetera, et cetera.'

'Yes, yes,' said the Doctor, 'we've all been here before. I'll arrange myself some transport.'

'I'd really rather send down one of my shuttles,' said the

!C-Mel, 'just to avoid any unfortunate mistakes.'

'Very well,' said the Doctor, 'if you must. I'll see you in a minute then.' The Doctor waited a moment. 'Has it gone?'

'Yes,' said God.

The Doctor turned to Bernice and Chris. 'Aren't you going to try to talk me out of it?'

'Who, us?' asked Bernice. 'I assume you have a plan.'

'You shouldn't really,' said the Doctor. 'I don't always have a plan, you know. God, can you open a secure line to aM!xitsa?'

'No problem.'

'Yes,' said aM!xitsa, still sounding a bit ragged.

'How are you feeling?' asked the Doctor.

'Rotten,' said aM!xitsa. 'I've got disruptions in systems I didn't even know I had.'

'Do you think you can explain exactly what it was Kadiatu did to you?'

'Well, it was really very simple,' said aM!xitsa, and explained. The word multi-phasic cropped up quite a lot, as did fractal, structure and contra-resonating harmonics.

The Doctor thanked aM!xitsa.

'Are you thinking of doing,' said God, 'what I think you're thinking of doing?'

'Probably,' said the Doctor. 'It worked on aM!xitsa.'

'I don't know quite how to put this,' said God, 'but aM!xitsa is a drone and the !C-Mel is a ship, and there's quite a large difference in the capacity and sophistication of their brains.'

'The principle is sound,' said the Doctor. 'Can you stall the shuttle for a bit? I need you to get me something.'

The shuttle from the !C-Mel looked indistinguishable from the standard travel capsule. It drew level with the balcony and the Doctor climbed aboard. As he did so, Bernice could hear him cheerfully whistling a maddeningly familiar refrain. It wasn't until the shuttle was lost in the darkness above that Bernice recognized the tune.

'*Anything you can do/I can do better/I can do anything/better than you.*'

* * *

259

The !C-Mel was only the front third of a Travelling Space Habitat, a ship designed so that the people could travel their galaxy and seek out new life forms without actually giving up one iota of their standard of living.

It was essentially a cluster of vaguely pyramidal shapes surrounding a central core, the whole thing two kilometres from top to bottom and three from side to side.

The shuttle deposited the Doctor at the peak of the topmost pyramid. As he stepped out, wide windows gave him a good view of the parks and apartment complexes that made up the living areas. Looking down he could see thousands of small shapes peeling away from the ship and heading for safe landings on the sphere. The !C-Mel was keeping its promise at least.

A marble-sized remote-drone met him in the atrium.

'Well, it's good to see you, Doctor,' said the !C-Mel.

The Doctor said nothing.

'I can assure you that all the crew will be evacuated within the next one point three minutes.' The !C-Mel paused, waiting for a reply that never came. 'I see,' said the ship. 'You want to be sure Roslyn Forrester is all right before you speak. Very wise. In that case, follow the drone.'

The drone led him deeper into the ship, going down towards the core which was helpful. He found Roz sitting on a park bench next to a small flower garden. There were smears of dried blood around her nose and ears.

The Doctor smiled reassuringly. ' 'Allo, 'oz,' he said. It wasn't easy talking around the thing in his mouth.

'I can't hear you,' said Roz, too loudly. 'I think I burst my ear-drums.'

' 'oz,' mumbled the Doctor, ' 'ee's 'ime 'or 'an 'ee.'

'Is this some sort of secret code?' asked the !C-Mel.

The Doctor shook his head. Leaning down in front of Roz he tucked the thing as far back into his throat as it would go and enunciated soundlessly, 'Plan B.'

'Oh,' said Roz, 'Plan B, negotiated hostage release. Why don't I leave you two alone and go and find myself some coffee.' She walked away from the park. The Doctor was pleased to notice that she went towards the nearest emergency exit, her walk getting noticeably brisker the further away she got.

'You can take the microfusion grenade out of your mouth now, Doctor,' said the !C-Mel. 'You can't possibly use it here. I've got internal dampening fields that can snuff out a tiny little bomb like that.'

The Doctor removed the bomb from his mouth. 'You could have said that sooner,' he said, 'instead of letting me look like a fool.'

'Shall we cut out the crap and get down to business.'

'It occurred to me,' said the Doctor, 'that this negotiation could be very protracted if we proceed at normal biological speeds. In the interest of getting this over and done with I suggest I link my mind directly to your comms system and we can chat that way.'

'You can't possibly think at machine speeds,' said the !C-Mel.

'No,' said the Doctor, 'but I think faster than I talk and I can talk pretty fast.'

'Very well,' said the !C-Mel, 'we'll do it your way.'

The Doctor smiled, hugely.

Whatever the Doctor's plan was it happened very fast. Roz was still making for the nearest hangar that she'd spotted on the way in, when the internal gravity flipped over ninety degrees. She bounced off the new floor and somehow managed to keep going. There were deep vibrations in the floor which would have probably been terrifyingly loud explosions if she could hear them. The next shift in gravity turned the corridor into a chute and she slid helplessly down it towards the open space of the hangar.

It was, she noticed, one of those swish open-lock hangars that used forcefields to keep the air in and allow material objects out. Material objects such as Roz Forrester. Beyond was nothing but the inverted vista of the sphere's interior. She wondered whether she would suffocate first or burn up on re-entry. They said it was better to burn out than fade away, but Roz felt that she would have liked a free choice.

261

She realized that her hearing was coming back because she could hear her screams echoing off the walls.

The inner doors of the hangar shot past, far out of reach. The rectangular main exit grew to fill her vision and for the first time in thirty-two years Roslyn Inyathi Forrester started praying to her ancestors.

Dear Mama, I'm sorry I couldn't dance and that I was a total disappointment as a daughter in all respects but I'm still your flesh and blood and if you've got any influence at all with the creator now would be a good time to —

She was caught by a dinky two-person shuttle that swooped in, opened its canopy and caught her face-down in one of its bucket seats. 'Hey,' it said as Roz struggled to get herself the right way up. 'You're that Roz Forrester, aren't you? I'm your greatest fan.'

!C-Mel was coming apart at the seams when the Doctor made his getaway. He could feel contrary sets of vibrations through his feet as God tried to hold the ship together long enough for him to get off. It wasn't easy: the TSH was essentially held together by interlaced forcefields and without the controlling mind it had all the intrinsic cohesion of a child's building blocks.

Part of him, that small part that would rather be juggling, wondered if it wouldn't be better if he just died, considering what he had just done. It helped if he told himself he didn't have any choice but not much.

Poor !C-Mel; not so different from anybody else, wanted a quiet life with no problems. Shouldn't have threatened to kill everyone in the sphere though, made that old 'good-of-the-majority' equation far too easy to solve.

A great fissure opened in front of him as a whole pyramid split away from the bulk of the ship. He looked down into the abyss and saw the night time splendour of the sphere spread out beneath him.

Time to put my faith in God, he thought.

And jumped.

The Doctor wasn't worried about burning up; with no orbital velocity he wasn't travelling nearly fast enough for that. No, instead, he was going to suffocate before the atmosphere got thick enough to breathe.

He was in sunlight and blue sky. The air was cold and thin but breathable.

Respiratory bypass system, he thought, as recommended by the Doctor, accept no imitations.

Now all he had to worry about was the ground but that was still a long way off. It was a pity he hadn't brought along his umbrella; he could have shaved, oh, at least two kph off his terminal velocity with that.

He was still a good six kilometres above sea level; perhaps he could think of something on the way down. After all, once you've reached terminal velocity it's not as if the extra height makes you land any faster. It's always best to adopt an optimistic attitude at these times, he thought, considering the alternative is long and dreary.

At an altitude of four kilometres the parachute finally turned up, riding the back of its remote-drone. It kept pace with the Doctor on his way down. They had plenty of time for a chat about vacuum horticulture before it was time to put the parachute on and pull the rip cord.

Once he was certain he was going to live his thoughts turned to the poor doomed !C-Mel. It had been a wretched act, to wreck such a fabulous mind and then use the confusion to blow its brains out with a microfusion grenade.

'You've gone very quiet,' said the parachute. 'Would you like some music?'

'Do you know the song that goes: "I'm just a poor boy from a poor family"?'

'No,' said the parachute.

'Oh.'

'Tell you what,' said the parachute. 'You start it off and I'll hum along when I catch the tune.'

Chris and Dep cooked them a meal with their own hands and using none of the villa's automation at all. Much of the food was edible; the stuff that wasn't they gave to Kadiatu. Most of her bruising had abated over the last four hours and the cuts had largely healed themselves up.

'Where's Roz?' asked the Doctor.

'Gone to see you know who,' said Bernice.

'You don't think she's thinking of staying?' asked saRa!qava. 'With feLixi, I mean.'

'Why on earth would she want to stay?' said Bernice. 'All she would have to look forward to here was a man who loves her, a vastly extended life span and an egalitarian society without want, poverty or too much violence. She wouldn't last a week.'

Dep ran out of the room, her hair coiling into bundles with distress. Chris looked stricken for a moment and ran after her.

'Well done, Benny,' said the Doctor. 'I don't know *how* you do it.'

'It's a gift,' said Bernice.

Roz met feLixi up at the windmills, waiting for him on the iron steps where they had first met. He came noiselessly down the steps and sat down behind her. He put his arms around her and she leant back against the warmth of his chest.

'Tell me about aTraxi,' she said.

His arms stiffened and she felt him shrug his shoulders.

'You must have loved her a lot,' she said, 'to name your house after her. I'm curious. Why didn't you call it Soo'isita? That was her name, wasn't it?'

'No,' he said at last, 'that was her cover name. Her real name was aTraxi. I just didn't want you to feel – threatened.'

'And the meadow by the river with the tree,' said Roz. 'That was her place too?'

'Yes,' said feLixi, 'but it was also my place, something that I wanted to share with you.'

She stood up, suddenly unable to bear the touch of him. He followed her down the stairs and she could feel the pain and confusion radiating from him, his eyes like a mute accusation against her back.

'Vi!Cari kept a diary,' she said. 'Did you know that?'

'No, I didn't,' he said. 'Roz, if something's wrong shouldn't you just tell me?'

'Vi!Cari messed up, didn't it? It saved you but failed to save aTraxi and you never forgave it for that, did you?'

'I tried to forget about it,' said feLixi.

'It was you who told !C-Mel that vi!Cari knew the truth about what happened over Omicrom 378,' said Roz.

'Of course I told it,' said feLixi. 'It had a right to know what vi!Cari was up to. But believe me I never thought !C-Mel would disassemble the drone.'

'If you thought !C-Mel wouldn't kill vi!Cari you were right,' said Roz. 'Vi!Cari might have been damaged goods but he'd had too many decades in the field to be caught like that in a thunderstorm with its sensors looking down and its shields inactive. But it'd have gone out into that storm for you, feLixi, its old shipmate and only friend. Gone looking for traces of the device that kicked up the *micro-tsunami*.'

FeLixi drew back from her. 'What device?' he asked. 'Everyone knew that vi!Cari did that to get back at beRut.'

Roz made herself look feLixi in the eyes; such warm, brown, lying eyes. 'Of course everyone knew that,' she said. 'Everyone except for vi!Cari, that is. The poor bastard must have been desperate to clear its name. And why get back at beRut? For what? Vi!Cari wasn't an art critic. If beRut wanted to cover the whole town with paint, what was that to vi!Cari? We know it was a force-bomb, we have an eye-witness. At first I thought the idea was to set beRut up as a patsy but the man is all piss and vinegar. Then I got to thinking about why vi!Cari was out in the storm that night and it all made sense. Knowing it was there meant you could take all the time you wanted to line up the shot, using a controller made from etched silicon that !C-Mel made and programmed for you. A controller that was too primitive to show up on God's general scans.'

'What's etched silicon got to do with anything?'

'Don't give me that innocent schoolboy act, feLixi. Etching silicon is the old-fashioned way of making thinking machines. The windmills' control systems are all made from valves and transistors and it didn't take a genius to patch in a micro-processor just for one night.'

'You can't make smart machines from etched silicon.'

'It didn't have to be smart. It just had to be programmed by someone smart, someone like !C-Mel. Someone who thought they wanted vi!Cari dead as much as you did. You went up the hill, switched on and put thirty thousand amperes right through vi!Cari's brain pan. You figured even if God got suspicious it would go after !C-Mel, not you. You knew God would assume that a ship was far too bright to be manipulated by a mere *meatbrain* and everyone knows that some VASs are unstable with no war to fight. But then you found out that the Doctor was in town and panicked. You knew he was a meddler and you couldn't take the risk that God wouldn't put him on the case for its own devious reasons. So you needed someone close to the Doctor you could feed all those false leads you'd been keeping under your hat: beRut, saRa!qava. All the secrets you'd ferreted out with your "listening room" and your contacts in XR(N)IG, the same contacts you used to get the low-down on the Doctor's companions, maybe even the secret stuff about Mutter's Spiral and Earth. So you made sure I was drinking *flashback* that evening to get me all good and confused and sidled up to me on the stairs. Just to make sure I was receptive you had the extra thumb taken off your hands and your eye colour changed. With all your experience as an agent in the proxy wars you figured I'd be a cinch to manipulate.'

'Yes,' said feLixi suddenly. 'No! It wasn't like that. It was your eyes, Roz. I saw myself reflected in your eyes and I knew you'd understand.'

'Yeah, I understood all right, better than you think. Where I come from, for what you did they'd strip your mind right back down to your birth trauma and rebuild your personality from scratch. In this place I guess they'll just stop inviting you to parties. At least you'll get to find out what it felt like to be vi!Cari.'

Roz watched it sinking into his mind, watched the wheels spinning in his face and that's when she knew for certain.

'You're not . . .?'

266

'Yes, feLixi,' she said. 'I'm turning you in or whatever it is you guys do in this place.'

'You can't be serious.'

'I'm real serious, feLixi, you're taking the fall.'

'I thought we had an understanding,' said feLixi, 'but now I see I was just another suspect all along. You might as well be a machine, Roz. You don't have any human feelings at all.'

Roz shrugged. 'Think what you like but I'm not going to play the fool for you.'

'You know it's not like that,' said feLixi.

She was angry now, angry because she was still listening to him. Angry at herself for that tiny bit of hope that he might have a reason she could believe in. 'Have you ever told me the truth, feLixi?' she snapped. 'Have you said anything to me that wasn't just another manipulation? Even this' – she waved the poem under his nose – 'and the night we spent by the river – nicely timed to get me away from the Doctor long enough for !C-Mel to deal with him.'

'The poem was real and you know it,' said feLixi. 'You know that my feelings for you are real.'

'You can't even say it, feLixi, can you? To you, love is just a word you looked up in a linguistic database.'

'I love you, Roz, and you know it.' There was hurt in his eyes and perhaps she did know it but it was too late now.

'I don't care who loves who!' she said. 'I won't play cover-up for you, feLixi. I won't walk in aTraxi's footsteps and I won't step out into the lightning. You killed vi!Cari and you're going down for that.'

'Vi!Cari was a *robot*, Roz. What's a machine to you?'

Roz turned away then and fixed her eyes on the windmills. 'Listen,' she said, 'this won't do you any good, you'll never understand me but I'll try once and then shut up. People don't live alone, never have, never will and when you live together you need rules – call them laws, traditions, *ukuzila*, taboos, whatever you like – because sometimes right for you is wrong for me and we've got to live together because chaos is always waiting just beyond the light of the fire and the darkness doesn't knock politely on the door of your hut. I've stood both sides of that line, feLixi, I've been places where they'd slit my throat for being an adjudicator and places where they'd kill me for being the wrong colour.' She ran a finger down the skin of her face, remembering France and the stories of her grandmother. 'Yeah, that's right, on my own planet too, a hierarchy of contempt based on melanin production. Is that stupid or what? What it comes down to in the end is that someone's got to walk the line between order and chaos because we all want to live in the light of the fire. A long time ago Roslyn Inyathi Forrester chose to walk that line and what she *wants* doesn't matter. So I'll have some bad dreams for doing this but that'll pass.

'And if all I've said doesn't mean anything to you then forget it and we'll make it just this: I'll do it because I've got to look in the mirror every morning and I don't want vi!Cari staring over my shoulder as I comb out my hair and I'll do it because you counted on my prejudices just as my superiors on Earth did, just like the last man I loved did. So I'll pack up your poem and a few good memories and take them out when I get lonely late at night and maybe, just maybe, I'll cry myself to sleep and wish that I'd stayed here with you but at least when I wake up I'll still be Roslyn Forrester.'

She still couldn't look at him but she knew he was staring at her. The windmill blades slowly turned, slicing power out of the wind. God controlled the wind, the movement of the air, the passing of the seasons, the energy from the sun. It regulated the existence of two trillion people and all it asked for was a bit of conversation and the chance to make suspicious yellow dip. And the Doctor, what did he ask for, what memories did he unpack in the dark of the night and what did he see when he looked in the mirror?

'Did you get all that, kiKhali?' she asked out loud. 'I know you've been listening.'

With a whisper of displaced air the machines arrived. KiKhali first, its expression ikon set in a resolutely abstract frown, aM!xitsa following. Lights from the windows of the control section flickered off fast-moving shapes the size of marbles – subcomponents of !X automatically establishing a defence perimeter. !X was there for feLixi, Roz reckoned, to

268

be his gaoler until the little machine got bored and handed over to another volunteer. FeLixi sat on the steps, hands on his face, kiKhali and aM!xitsa giving him an unnecessarily wide berth, their main sensor strips flickering here and there, everywhere but at the man.

And so it begins, thought Roz, the exclusion from society. He can't even exile himself from the sphere because no ship would want him on board.

'Not bad for a meatbrain,' said kiKhali, 'not bad at all.'

Roz shrugged. 'When did God figure it out?'

'About a second after you did,' said aM!xitsa.

'As long as that?' said Roz.

'It had a lot on its mind,' said aM!xitsa. 'Can I give you a lift?'

'No,' said Roz, 'I want to walk down – on my own.'

'Are you all right?'

Roz glanced back at the man who was sitting alone on the steps.

'I've been worse,' she said.

12

Travelling Man Blues

> My baby won't do as I say
> An' my father figure. He gone away
> Gone to fight the righteous fight
> Goin' to do what's right
> Goin' wear another hole in my shoes
> Get myself the travelling man blues
> (Break it down, aM!xitsa)
> (Oh yeah, that drone can play)
> Travelling man blues
> Yeah! Hit me!
> > *Travelling Man Blues*, singer unknown
> > Recorded: Mama Stanley's Chicken
> > Shack, Clanton, Alabama (1937)

The sun was a pitiless furnace burning in a cerulean sky, a cyclopean eye that baked the landscape and sucked the moisture from her skin.

'The heat,' croaked Bernice, 'it's unbearable.'

So this was what it was like to die of thirst.

A tall glass floated in front of her eyes like a mirage, white with frost and brimming with lemonade, its sides wet with condensation. Bernice reached out and gratefully wrapped her hand around it. 'Cheers, aM!xitsa,' she said and sat up, the top half of the beach bed automatically tilting to keep her back supported. 'Shade, please.' A forcefield parasol snapped into existence overhead. Bernice sipped her drink and watched aM!xitsa as the drone turned back to its sand city, parts of which had now reached a height of two metres. The drone was also keeping a sensor eye out for any intruders that might wander into Kadiatu's cove, especially ones with exterior genitalia.

'It's a human custom,' Bernice had explained to a bemused saRa!qava, the idea of a girls' day out having little meaning to people who could change their gender at will.

That morning, just as God was turning the sun up, Bernice, Roz and Kadiatu had sneaked out of the villa and flown down the coast in a scarlet open-top flitter convertible. AM!xitsa came with them, having been declared an honorary female for the duration. It was still early enough when they arrived for the air to be chilly. Shreds of mist drifted through the forest, driven by a stiff breeze from the sea. The women spread a blanket in the lee of the flitter and opened the hamper that House had packed for them. AM!xitsa made itself useful by using one of its many weapon systems to heat up the coffee.

'Who wants a ham roll?' asked Roz.

'Are you sure it's ham?' asked Bernice.

During the course of their stay each of them had spent some considerable time trying to teach House to cook familiar dishes, with the occasional notable disaster. Although Bernice was willing to admit that perhaps her description of Crab Claw Gumbo may have been a little bit too vague. She certainly wouldn't like to come face to face with the crab that had supplied the sixty-centimetre claws and she probably should have specified that the king shrimps were supposed to be dead. The little pause as everyone checked exactly what it was they were about to eat had quickly become part of the holiday routine.

Roz sniffed the roll. 'Ham-*ish*,' she said.

'Give it here,' said Kadiatu. 'I'll eat anything as long as it's not fish.'

Bernice settled on a roll stuffed with cottage cheese and tomatoes the size and sweetness of spring peas. For later there was mushroom pâté, loaves of saRa!qava's bread, pickles, slabs of cheese, a collation of cold meats, vacuum flasks of lemonade, upside-down pie and the Doctor's very own version of sideways pudding. AM!xitsa served them coffee and fussily chased crumbs off the blanket.

Bernice watched Kadiatu. The tall woman, dressed in a shapeless grey pullover, looked deceptively relaxed as she lounged against the side of the flitter. There was a small scar on her right cheek where she had cut herself with a knife and applied the butterfly serum.

'What are you going to do next?' asked Bernice.

'A bit of industrial espionage here,' said Kadiatu, 'then build myself a new time/space machine, something like the TARDIS only with more style and go-faster stripes.'

'And after that?'

'Fight monsters, right wrongs, stick my nose in and generally interfere with the course of history.' She looked at Roz. 'Maybe break Nelson out of Robbin Island in 1964 and arm the ANC with plasma rifles – what do you think?'

'I hope you're joking,' said Bernice.

Kadiatu grinned. 'Actually I thought I'd bum around for a bit, see what's what, maybe pick up an irritating mannerism and cultivate an air of flippancy in times of crisis. Works for you know who.'

'Will you have companions?'

'Got one already,' said Kadiatu and glanced at aM!xitsa.

'Is that true?' Roz asked the drone.

'Who, me?' said aM!xitsa. 'Explore the entire cosmos of space/time, meet new civilizations and patronize them rigid? I've got much better things to do, knitting patterns to finish, interesting pebbles to collect. Besides I've yet to be convinced that Kadiatu will be capable of getting her machine to go where and when she wants it.'

'Good choice,' said Bernice.

'Actually it's all part of a deal with God,' said Kadiatu. 'We'll act as its temporal back-up, just in case the High Council welsh on the treaty.'

'Will you go home?'

Kadiatu shook her head. 'Not for a very long time. Earth is my linear reference point in the same way that Gallifrey is the Doctor's, going back would be "complicated".'

Exile, thought Bernice, feeling a surge of pity for Kadiatu.

They stripped off as the sun grew hotter. AM!xitsa unshipped three blocks of memory plastic from the flitter. Once on the sand they popped open to become adjustable beach-beds. Bernice changed into a strapless bikini that she'd 'bought' on Whynot; Kadiatu and Roz preferred to go *au naturel*.

'Nothing so silly-looking as a bikini line on an African woman,' explained Kadiatu. Roz laughed. Bernice decided that there was an unpleasant current of nationalism running between the two women that would have to be knocked on the head – preferably in the next couple of hours.

Roz got out her videobook. Bernice persuaded Kadiatu to rip her brick-thick paperback in half so that Bernice could start reading it without waiting for her to finish. It was a classic bodice-ripper written in 2361 but set in 1980s London. Bernice amused herself by noting the anachronisms in the margin.

It quickly, by degrees, got too hot to read and then too hot to think. AM!xitsa floated over and rubbed sunscreen onto all three of their backs simultaneously. In between ministering to their every whim, the drone had excavated a wide depression in the beach and was building a series of lopsided towers out of compacted sand. 'When the tide comes in,' said aM!xitsa, 'this will be an exact scale model of The Mote in God's Left Eye.'

'Won't it wash away?' asked Bernice.

'Of course it will,' said the drone. 'That's the whole point.'

Kadiatu noticed that Bernice had her sun-shade up. 'Hey,' she said to Roz, 'Benny's wimped out already.'

'I don't know,' said Roz. 'These European women have no stamina.'

'Right,' said Bernice, 'I've had quite enough of this not-so-crypto-fascist panafrican neo-nationalism. AM!xitsa? I believe that these young ladies' brains are overheating.'

'Can't have that,' said aM!xitsa.

Bernice watched in satisfaction as the two women were carried kicking and screaming out over the sea and then dropped. Kadiatu managed to twist in the air and pierce the water cleanly but Roz landed, arms windmilling, right on her backside in an impressive plume of spray. Bernice winced in sympathy and started to laugh.

She laughed so hard that she didn't even notice she was flying until she was over the sea. 'AM!xitsa,' she said reproachfully, 'we had an agreement.'

'I'm sorry, Bernice,' it said. 'Equality of opportunity is a fundamental tenet of my society.'

She looked down and saw Roz, six metres below, waving up at her and grinning. 'Let's not be too dogmatic about this,' said Bernice. 'Oh, *shiiiiiiit*!'

Bernice came up spluttering, relieved to find the water was only chest deep. 'Where's my bra?' she yelled. 'You flying piece of junk, that bikini was one of a kind.'

Something wet and skimpy slapped onto her head from above and wrapped itself around her face. 'Good shot,' said Roz.

Bernice pulled the bikini top off her forehead and put it back on. AM!xitsa hovered ten metres above them, spinning rapidly around all three axes – drone hysterics, Bernice guessed. She shook her fist at it. 'And you can stop laughing and all,' she said to Roz. 'Where's Kadiatu?'

'I haven't seen her,' said Roz. 'You don't think she hit her head or something?'

'Not likely,' said Bernice. 'That woman's completely indestructible.'

As if to prove her point strong hands grasped her around the waist and tossed her two metres into the air. At least she managed to come down with a bit of dignity that time. She resurfaced to find Kadiatu grinning at her.

'Where were you?' asked Roz.

'Under the water,' said Kadiatu.

Roz looked stunned. 'Jesus. How long can you hold your breath for?'

'Don't know, never timed myself.'

'I know,' said Bernice, giving Roz a sly look. 'Why don't you duck down under the water and stay there as long as you can while me and Roz time you.'

'OK,' said Kadiatu. 'Ready?'

Bernice looked at her watch and nodded.

Bernice and Roz waited all of thirty seconds before swimming hell for leather for the beach.

He made the mistake of nodding off on the beach and while he was asleep someone buried him in the sand. He woke up to find his world contracted down to the narrow *vistavision* strip between his hat brim and the top of the mound he was buried under.

He tried wriggling his fingers and arms, testing the consistency. There was some give but the sand had been packed down pretty solidly. He tried moving his legs, aiming to at least kick his feet clear of the sand but, again, while there was some movement he was definitely stuck fast.

He wanted to scratch his nose.

He lay still for a while, thinking about his predicament. He tried a very old trick that he'd picked up at a *shao lin* monastery during the Song dynasty. Now that was a bunch that knew about self-control. He couldn't remember the proper Mandarin mnemonic so he hummed a snatch of 'My Baby Just Cares for Me' by Nina Simone instead. Then, after taking a deep breath and summoning up his *ch'i*, or inner self, he attempted to expand his chest by twenty centimetres. After three minutes of straining he started seeing stars against a darkening landscape. After seven minutes everything went black.

He gave up after ten minutes. Beyond a certain point there was no give in his sandy prison at all. It was far too solid to have been packed down by human hands – he grimly suspected some kind of machine involvement.

He *really* wanted to scratch his nose.

A small remote-drone wearing a parachute drifted serenely across his field of vision and vanished to his right. After a few seconds the remote-drone backed up into sight and slowly turned to face him.

'Good morning,' said the parachute.

'Good morning,' said the Doctor. 'How are the trees coming along?'

275

'Very well, thank you,' said the parachute. 'Now it's just a question of making the fruit edible.'

'Some kind of removable skin perhaps,' suggested the Doctor.

'What a good idea,' said the parachute. 'Well, I must be off. I'm doing a synchronized free-fall display this afternoon and I want to make sure I get the right jumper.'

'Good luck,' said the Doctor.

The parachute zipped out of sight again.

Damn, thought the Doctor, I forgot to ask him why it had to be an apple tree.

Perhaps if he were to set up a sine wave with his body he could shift the sand. If he could set up some form of harmonic feedback it should erode the structural integrity of the compacted sand. After all, it was only a matter of finding the right frequency.

Roz and Chris wandered into view. They stopped when they saw the Doctor and turned to face him. Each of them had a surfboard under their arm.

'I wonder why he's buried in the sand,' said Chris to Roz.

'I don't know,' said Roz. 'Maybe it's relaxing.'

'We could dig him out,' said Chris.

'What if he's buried himself on purpose?'

'You mean it might be part of a plan?'

'One can never tell with the Doctor,' said Roz, 'but I'm sure he must have a good reason. It's probably something cosmic.'

'Oh,' said Chris. 'Cosmic, you think?'

'Oh yes,' said Roz, 'definitely something cosmic.'

'You don't think he just fell asleep and got buried by children?' asked Chris.

'Absolutely not,' said Roz. 'The Doctor would never allow himself to be incarcerated in such an absurd and undignified manner without the most exquisite and subtle of purposes.'

'Perhaps we should ask him?'

'Best not, we might disturb his concentration.'

The Doctor watched as the two walked out of his view.

'Chris,' he heard Roz say in the distance, 'are you sure

we're supposed to *stand* on these things . . .'

You make one little mistake, thought the Doctor, and the whole world queues up to make fun of you. He went back to trying to calculate the correct harmonic frequency but the itch in his nose was too distracting.

Bernice came along and sat on his chest.

'Gosh,' she said, 'I bet your nose is really itching.'

'You really had to say that,' said the Doctor plaintively.

'I had a dream the other night,' said Bernice.

The Doctor's hearts sank. 'Yes,' he said.

'I meant to ask you about it but then I got distracted.'

'People attach far too much importance to dreams,' said the Doctor. 'They are, after all, merely a sort of filing system for the unconscious.'

'Is that so?'

'Oh yes,' said the Doctor, 'nothing significant about the images whatsoever. By the way, did you know Roz is learning to surf?'

'Shall I tell you about it?'

'Please don't go to any trouble on my account,' said the Doctor.

'It's no trouble,' said Bernice. 'I was talking to this Dalek –'

'Well, there you go,' said the Doctor, somewhat desperately. 'Daleks, objects of childhood fear, all standard stuff, nothing metaphysical about that at all.'

'If you don't shut up, Doctor,' said Bernice, 'I'm going to bury your head.' She waited for him to say something but he wasn't going to risk a faceful of sand. 'Kadiatu was there and so were you,' began Bernice.

The Doctor sighed. Sometimes he thought that Bernice was just too perceptive for his own good.

'I've been thinking about the TARDIS's ever so convenient translation system,' said Bernice. 'It occurred to me that we're all connected, you, me, Kadiatu, all your companions. I had an interesting little talk with aM!xitsa and he said that Kadiatu was doing most of her thinking while she was asleep and that in some way her own thoughts were altering the actual biochemistry of her brain.' She reached out and idly scratched the Doctor's nose. 'I think you had no intention of letting me make the decision but you knew if I was involved that it might influence Kadiatu on a subconscious level through the link with the TARDIS.'

'It's an interesting theory,' said the Doctor. 'Personally I think we just got lucky.'

'You're not going to tell me, are you?'

'I don't have the vocabulary,' said the Doctor.

'It's not fair,' said Bernice. 'You're a mythic figure, Ace is fast becoming a creature of legend, people are bound to start using Kadiatu to frighten small children and Chris looks like he stepped off the Elgin marbles. What I want to know is, when do I get a bit of fame?'

'Benny,' said the Doctor, 'I happen to know that you are an object of veneration in at least two cultures.'

'Really?' said Bernice suspiciously. 'What kind of object?'

'Oh,' said the Doctor, 'a sort of female version of Bacchus.'

'I'm a god of wine?'

'Not just wine,' said the Doctor hurriedly, 'all alcohol really, sort of the goddess of indiscriminate drinking.'

'I'm completely overwhelmed.'

'And sarcasm,' said the Doctor, 'in your manifestation as the goddess of the morning after the night before.'

'Goddess of hangovers,' said Bernice, 'I might have guessed. What's Roz then, the goddess of bad manners?'

'Really, Bernice,' said the Doctor, 'there's more to life than being mistaken for a supernatural deity.'

It rained the next day. Chris, Dep and Kadiatu were slouching around in the living room when the Doctor walked in with a chess set. He laid the board out on one of the floating tables and held out two fists to Kadiatu. She tapped the left and the Doctor opened his palm to reveal a white bishop. They drew up chairs and sat down facing each other across the board.

'Five seconds per move,' said the Doctor. 'First person to predict the precise number of moves to the first possible checkmate wins.'

Kadiatu nodded and opened with a queen's pawn advance.

The first game lasted twenty-eight moves and ended when the Doctor held up his hand and said: 'Mate in six.'

Kadiatu frowned at the board. 'Yes,' she said finally, 'mate in six.'

They turned the board around and set up the pieces again, the Doctor playing white. Chris and Dep watched as the two players slapped down the pieces with such speed that it was almost impossible to follow the course of the game.

Again the Doctor held up his hand. 'Twelve,' he said.

'Never,' said Kadiatu. 'You couldn't possibly force a mate in twelve.'

'Not me,' said the Doctor. 'Twelve moves until you beat me. I said the first possible checkmate, regardless of who's in check.'

'But that's stupid,' said Kadiatu. 'If we do it like that, it means either of us can deliberately play to lose in order to make the correct prediction.'

'Yes,' said the Doctor. 'Interesting concept, isn't it?'

'If you say so,' said Kadiatu. 'Are you implying that losing is as important as winning?'

'What I'm saying,' said the Doctor, 'is that you have to know by which set of rules you're playing the game.'

Kadiatu leaned back in her chair and folded her arms. 'Is this going to get needlessly philosophical?'

The Doctor said nothing as he replaced the pieces on the board and turned it around.

'What if I don't want to play?' said Kadiatu.

'Too late,' said the Doctor. 'You sat down at the table and now you *have* to play.'

Kadiatu smiled. 'All right then,' she said, 'but this time we make it two seconds a move.'

The sharp sounds of the pieces hitting the board was like the report of a clockwork machine-gun. Kadiatu sat hunched over the table, her hands moving so fast that they were almost impossible to see. Chris noticed that although the Doctor appeared to move far slower he none the less seemed to be placing his pieces, if anything, faster than Kadiatu. The

279

game was over in less than two minutes.

'You cheated,' said Kadiatu. 'You played to win this time.'

'Again,' said the Doctor.

Another flurry of movements. Less than a minute.

'Twelve,' said the Doctor.

Kadiatu frowned and bit her lip. She replaced the pieces slowly, turned the board around and glanced down.

'Fifteen,' said the Doctor.

'Hey,' she said, 'I haven't even moved yet.'

'You were going to open with King's pawn,' said the Doctor, 'weren't you?'

'Yes.'

'Mate in fifteen then.'

Kadiatu stared at the Doctor, her eyes narrowed, then opened wide in understanding. The Doctor smiled smugly back at her.

They stopped moving the pieces. After another twelve 'games' they stopped looking at the board at all.

Chris and Dep watched on in fascination as the Doctor and Kadiatu faced each other across the table, the chessmen standing forgotten between them.

And the Doctor was still winning, rattling off his predictions before Kadiatu could open her mouth.

'Twenty-one,' said Kadiatu.

The Doctor hesitated and actually glanced down at the board. 'You beat me,' he said, 'I don't believe it.'

'Cheer up, Doctor,' said Kadiatu. 'It was bound to happen sooner or later.'

'Not to me it doesn't,' he said. 'You just said the first number that came into your head.'

'Ah,' said Kadiatu, 'but it was the right number.'

Muttering, the Doctor swept the chess pieces into the case and closed the board. 'Right,' he said, rolling up his sleeve and thumping his elbow down on the table. 'Arm wrestling, best of five.'

'The Doctor beat Kadiatu at arm wrestling?' said Bernice.

'That's what I said,' said Chris. 'Three falls to nothing.'

'I don't believe it.'
'That's what she said.'

The sky over the aerodrome had been overcast until saRa!qava had a little chat with God; after that the clouds simply evaporated in the space of ten minutes.

The ornithopter was parked at the end of the landing field closest to the clubhouse. AM!xitsa had airlifted it from saRa!qava's roof that morning, lifting the one and a half tons all by itself, showing off again.

The maiden flight had attracted a large crowd, mostly friends of Dep's from the Weird Aviation Interest Group and a scattering of older people from iSanti Jeni. Even beRut had turned up with a vidpad, ostentatiously sketching away whenever he thought someone might be watching. God had manifested itself as a perambulating tree.

The crowd burst into loud applause when Chris and Dep walked onto the field. They were dressed in heavy flying jackets and leather trousers against the cold; the ornithopter's cockpit was nothing but an open framework at the centre of the machine. Bernice smiled to see Chris blush from the attention. The applause died away as the two intrepid aeronauts clambered awkwardly into the cockpit and lay down amongst the bizarre tangle of machinery.

The Doctor asked Bernice what she thought of it.

'It looks like something Leonardo da Vinci and Heath Robinson designed,' she said, 'while under the influence of some really serious acid.'

'You know,' said the Doctor, 'I've never seen an ornithopter that actually flew. At least not in this dimension.'

There was a coughing sound from the back of the ornithopter and a plume of white vapour rose into the still air.

'What the hell is it running on?' asked Roz.

'Steam,' said the Doctor.

'Oh Goddess,' said Roz.

'You do know your partner is completely bonkers,' said Kadiatu.

God waved a few of its branches around. 'You try and

281

create a safe and stable environment,' muttered the tree, 'and then they go and do *this*.'

'The things men do under the influence of testosterone,' said Bernice.

'Don't worry,' said the Doctor. 'I've got a parachute standing by with a friend.'

With an alarming clanking sound the metal and plastic wings opened to their full extent. There was a spluttering noise that sounded to Bernice exactly like that made by a lawnmower engine. More steam was vented from the chrome exhaust pipes. The wings began to beat, slowly at first and then faster and faster until, with all the grace of an epileptic vulture, the unlikely contraption lurched off the ground.

The crowd cheered, Roz scowled and saRa!qava bit her lip until it bled.

Clanking, coughing and stuttering, the ornithopter rose vertically to a height of two hundred metres and hung in the air like an ode to human stupidity.

'The tricky bit,' said the Doctor, 'is the transition to horizontal flight. They have to adjust the pitch of their artificial feathers just right or the whole thing will fall out of the sky.'

'Thank you so much for sharing that with us,' said Roz.

Bernice gasped as the ornithopter slipped sideways, dipped suddenly and then, miraculously, lurched into forward flight. As it picked up speed, Bernice thought she could hear the sound of children laughing.

'God,' said the Doctor, 'I think it's time for your party piece. Before they get too far away.'

God perambulated out in front of the crowd. 'Ladies, gentlemen, machines and friends of the Doctor,' it boomed. 'As you can see I have nothing hidden up my sleeves, sorry, my branches.' It thrust its largest limb upwards until it was pointing at the sun. 'Regard this stellar object, with whom I have never worked before, and watch very, very carefully.'

The sun moved, falling out of the sky towards the distant ocean. As it fell it changed colour, deepening first to a brilliant orange and then darkening further, until by the time it reached the notional horizon it was a deep red that lit up the clouds in a display of amber and gold.

'I really hope God's doing that with mirrors,' said saRa!qava.

The sphere experienced, for the first time in its history, the glories of a full cinemascope Technicolor sunset.

Just so Chris and Dep could fly off into it.

The post-flight party quickly spilled out of saRa!qava's house and spread to the rest of the town. The Doctor quickly fell into the avuncular persona that he kept stored away for such rare occasions. He talked mostly to children and amused them by pulling scarves from their ears and miscellaneous junk from their noses. After a while he noticed that someone was missing.

'Where's Roz?' he asked Bernice who shrugged and said she hadn't seen her. Concerned, the Doctor wandered out onto the esplanade where he quickly spotted a lone figure leaning against a bollard and staring out over the harbour. A strong wind was blowing in from the sea and once out from the shelter of the small streets he began to feel the chill.

As he walked out to join Roz at the bollard he wondered what had drawn her away from the party. Following her gaze he saw another figure standing out at the end of the breakwater. Ah, he thought, of course.

'He was talking to the fish earlier,' said Roz, her eyes never leaving the figure.

'Fish is a bit isolated,' said the Doctor. 'I doubt he's heard yet.' He put a hand on her shoulder. 'I'm sorry how it turned out.'

'Wasn't your fault, Doctor,' said Roz. 'I expect hearing that makes a nice change.'

'No,' said the Doctor, 'not really. Are you coming back to the party? People have been asking after you.'

'Maybe,' she said, 'in a little while.'

'Roz,' said the Doctor gently, 'why don't you just walk over there and talk to him, no one will care, everybody will understand. This could be your last chance.'

He thought he saw a desperate hope in her face that quickly subsided into an expression of regret. He realized with a pang that he had merely caused her more pain. 'No,'

283

she said, 'it wouldn't be right.'

'When you're ready,' he said, 'we'll be waiting.'

He left her then and walked back towards the noise of the party. When he reached the entrance to the street he turned back, hoping that she wouldn't be there, that perhaps he might see her running down the breakwater towards the figure standing by the lighthouse. That they might embrace and hold each other tightly and say something, anything that would lessen their pain.

Go on, Roslyn, he urged her in his mind, don't you know that life is fleeting and so what if he is a murderer, so am I. Don't you know that we have to snatch our best moments from the jaws of chaos and in the end we are all dust, the best as well as the worst of us?

He closed his eyes tight and imagined them together with all his might. Their hands and faces touching, a tentative smile, tears, sharing a moment of human warmth amongst the wind and the spray. He imagined them together as if by the power of his will alone he could make it happen.

But when he opened his eyes Roz was standing where he'd left her, a lonely figure watching another lost soul across the darkened gulf of the harbour.

Bernice awoke to the sound of the sea, the smell of fresh coffee and the Doctor standing beside her bed. He smiled and handed her a steaming mug. Her carry-all was packed up and waiting by the door. A newer and larger bag containing her souvenirs sat next to it.

'It's time we were going,' said the Doctor.

'Yes,' she said, 'I suppose it is.'

They ate a last breakfast on the balcony. Roz put away enough eggs and bacon to last her several years while the Doctor nibbled at the corner of his toast. Bernice sipped her banana-flavoured orange juice and stared out at the virtual horizon.

Chris arrived with Dep in tow just as Roz mopped up the last of her egg yolk. 'We were beginning to think you were staying,' said Roz.

Chris said nothing but Bernice saw Dep's hair tighten

around his waist. She hoped the young woman wasn't going to make a scene and then immediately felt guilty for thinking it.

They picked up their bags and walked down to the foyer. Before they stepped through the doors the Doctor turned and said: 'Goodbye, House, thank you for having us.'

'My pleasure,' said House.

Kadiatu and aM!xitsa were waiting outside to help them carry their bags. The big woman picked up Roz's suitcase and set it on her head. Bernice caught Roz looking thoughtfully after the woman as she walked ahead, the suitcase in perfect balance.

All that was visible of the TARDIS was a square of crushed grass in the centre of the clearing. The Doctor walked around it a few times, trying to remember which side the door was on.

'Once it arrives,' he said, 'we have to get in as fast as possible to stop God getting one of its bugs inside.'

Bernice shook Kadiatu's hand. 'Take care,' she said.

'Got any last-minute advice?' asked Kadiatu.

'Start small,' said Bernice. 'Overbearing postmen, malfunctioning traffic-lights, that sort of thing. And take care of aM!xitsa, it doesn't know what it's letting itself in for.'

'Don't worry,' said Kadiatu, 'I'll be modest and meek . . .'

Bernice punched the tall woman in the face with all her strength.

The blow never connected. Kadiatu simply lifted her hand and caught Bernice's fist on her palm.

Bernice winced at the pain in her knuckles. It was like punching a brick wall. *Paper wraps stone*, said a little girl voice in her head.

Kadiatu released Bernice's hand and looked at her strangely. 'That was very dangerous,' she said quietly.

'I had to be sure,' said Bernice.

'Look after him,' said Kadiatu.

'I'll do my best.'

The Doctor looked at Kadiatu. 'When you get round to building your you-know-what, make sure you build it away from here so that you-know-who doesn't find out the precise details of how it's done. Otherwise those that shall remain nameless will be a bit annoyed that I've broken the treaty and do unspeakable things to my head the next time I'm you-know-where. Got that?'

'No problem,' said Kadiatu. 'Trust me.'

'When you're quite ready, Christopher,' said the Doctor.

Dep let go of Chris with extreme reluctance and then, without saying anything, turned and ran up the path. Chris watched her until she vanished out of sight and then told the Doctor he was ready. Roz put a companionable hand on his shoulder.

'On a count of three,' said the Doctor.

The familiar wheezing groan of the space-time continuum reluctantly conceding to superior technology echoed around the clearing. With its flashing blue lamp becoming visible first the TARDIS materialized.

'One, two, three – GO!' said the Doctor.

They found Wolsey curled up in his usual place on top of the time rotor. The cat opened one incurious eye as they charged in through the main doors, as if to imply that it was supremely indifferent about their very existence. Exactly the attitude you'd expect, thought Bernice, from a cat who had been left alone for a while with an automated food dispenser.

The Doctor banged the door control down and immediately started punching in co-ordinates. The time rotor began to rise and fall: Wolsey started to purr. The Doctor relaxed.

Bernice thought of Kadiatu and aM!xitsa who even now were probably building their own TARDIS analogue, unless they'd already built it or hadn't even started, or didn't even exist yet. She wondered what their TARDIS would look like on the inside.

'I can't believe you left them behind,' said Roz. 'They were the only pair of uniform boots that fit properly.'

'I thought you had them,' said Chris.

'Do you know how long it took me to wear them in? It's not like we can pop back and get them, is it?'

Home again, home again, thought Bernice, jiggidy jig.

Epilogue

By far the cleverest animal in the forest was Tsuro the hare and a list of his many adventures would take a storyteller many years to recount. He travelled far and wide in the world and the fame of his tricks grew with every telling. So great was his fame that Tsuro was often welcomed into villages that were beset by troubles or under evil influences. 'Help us, o clever Hare,' the people would cry and Tsuro would help them but not always in a manner that they liked.

And yet deep within himself Tsuro the hare held a secret sadness, for long ago when he had been a young animal the other hares had cast him out of his village. 'You are too full of pride,' said the Chief of the Hares. 'If you will not live within the customs of your people you must live without them.' And so Tsuro was set on his travels without family, wife or children. 'If I cannot have family amongst the Hares,' said Tsuro, 'I will have friends amongst the other animals.'

Season followed season and for many years Tsuro travelled the wide world and beyond with his friends, playing his tricks on animals and people alike. Some wise people said that such a clever animal could only be a messenger of Musikavanhu the creator but if this was true Tsuro would not say.

But there are powers in the forest that are unknown to man and never spoken of by animals. One such was Danhamakatu the snake, she whose passing is like the whisper of death in the grass. It was she that put her mark on the Leopard and sent her into the forest to do her bidding. The tale of how

Tsuro and his companions rescued the Leopard from a trap is too long for this day's telling but rescue her he did and Danhamakatu was so angry that she slithered through the forest to confront him. When she came to the clearing in which Tsuro was resting she lay her belly on the ground and silently approached.

'Do not think that I cannot hear you, Danhamakatu, as you slither on your belly,' said Tsuro, preening his long ears. 'Show yourself and explain why you have come from the secret places of the Forest to trouble me.'

'You are too full of pride, Tsuro,' hissed the snake, 'to think that I must answer to you.'

'That may be,' said Tsuro. 'Just tell me what it is you want and be about your business. I am sure that you have nests to rob and children to frighten.'

'I am angry with you, Tsuro,' hissed Danhamakatu. 'You have robbed me of my servant the Leopard and now you must heed my words, for I have come to claim my price.'

'What words are those?' said Tsuro. 'I hear nothing but the sound of the wind in the trees and perhaps the flatulence of a passing elephant.'

These words angered Danhamakatu so much that she reared up before the hare and spread her terrible hood so wide that darkness covered the clearing. But Tsuro was not afraid for he had made the snake angry on purpose knowing that it was better to face a snake in the open than to step on one in the grass.

'You have given the Leopard a heart and have tricked me out of her services,' hissed the snake. 'All I ask for in return is the life of one of your friends.'

'The lives of my friends are not mine to give,' said Tsuro.

'What do I care for that,' hissed the snake. 'I am Danhamakatu, she who strikes without warning. I do not ask permission first.'

When he heard these words Tsuro became afraid, for he loved his friends above all other things. 'Take me instead,' he pleaded with the snake. 'Spare the life of my friend.'

Danhamakatu was sorely tempted by this offer, for the clever hare had tricked and lied his way out of her grasp

288

many times in the past. But she had grown so angry with him that she felt his death would not be punishment enough.

'No,' hissed the snake, 'I have sat in council with my sisters and they have agreed on this price.'

'Then please be quick,' pleaded Tsuro, 'and kill my friend now. It would be better that they die now than live in fear of your awful vengeance. I beg of you, show mercy just this once.'

Danhamakatu laughed to see the clever hare humbled in this way. How sweet to see him bury his face in his paws, his long ears all drooping and downcast.

'No,' hissed the snake, 'I will not show you mercy. I will wait a while to collect my prize so that you may live in fear of my coming.'

Hearing that, Tsuro buried his face further in his paws and spoke no more. Satisfied that at last she had taught the hare a lesson Danhamakatu got back down on her belly and slithered away into the forest.

Tsuro the hare waited patiently until he was sure that the snake was far away. When he was sure that it was too far away to hear he lifted his face from his paws and began to laugh.

The clearing, which had remained silent throughout the encounter, was amazed. 'Why do you laugh, Tsuro the hare?' asked the clearing. 'Surely you must lose one of your friends.'

'But not today,' said the hare and set to preening his ears. 'I have tricked Danhamakatu the snake once again. Tricked her into giving me time and with that time I can think up a new and cunning plan to save the life of my friend.'

'Truly you are the cleverest of all the animals,' said the clearing.

'Yes I am,' said the hare, 'and don't you forget it.' And with that Tsuro hopped out of the clearing and set off down the path to rejoin his friends.

'But, clever hare,' the clearing called after him, 'what if you cannot think of a plan?'

But if Tsuro heard the clearing he made no sign and soon he was gone from sight.

Already published:

SHADOWMIND
Christopher Bulis
On the colony world of Arden, something dangerous is growing stronger. Something that steals minds and memories. Something that can reach out to another planet, Tairngire, where the newest exhibit in the sculpture park is a blue box surmounted by a flashing light.

ISBN 0 426 20394 1

BIRTHRIGHT
Nigel Robinson
Stranded in Edwardian London with a dying TARDIS, Bernice investigates a series of grisly murders. In the far future, Ace leads a group of guerrillas against their insect-like, alien oppressors. Why has the Doctor left them, just when they need him most?

ISBN 0 426 20393 3

ICEBERG
David Banks
In 2006, an ecological disaster threatens the Earth; only the FLIPback team, working in an Antarctic base, can avert the catastrophe. But hidden beneath the ice, sinister forces have gathered to sabotage humanity's last hope. The Cybermen have returned and the Doctor must face them alone.

ISBN 0 426 20392 5

BLOOD HEAT
Jim Mortimore
The TARDIS is attacked by an alien force; Bernice is flung into the Vortex; and the Doctor and Ace crash-land on Earth. There they find dinosaurs roaming the derelict London streets, and Brigadier Lethbridge-Stewart leading the remnants of UNIT in a desperate fight against the Silurians who have taken over and changed his world.

ISBN 0 426 20399 2

THE DIMENSION RIDERS
Daniel Blythe
A holiday in Oxford is cut short when the Doctor is summoned to Space Station Q4, where ghostly soldiers from the future watch from the shadows among the dead. Soon, the Doctor is trapped in the past, Ace is accused of treason and Bernice is uncovering deceit among the college cloisters.

ISBN 0 426 20397 6

THE LEFT-HANDED HUMMINGBIRD
Kate Orman

Someone has been playing with time. The Doctor Ace and Bernice must travel to the Aztec Empire in 1487, to London in the Swinging Sixties and to the sinking of the *Titanic* as they attempt to rectify the temporal faults – and survive the attacks of the living god Huitzilin.

ISBN 0 426 20404 2

CONUNDRUM
Steve Lyons

A killer is stalking the streets of the village of Arandale. The victims are found each day, drained of blood. Someone has interfered with the Doctor's past again, and he's landed in a place he knows he once destroyed, from which it seems there can be no escape.

ISBN 0 426 20408 5

NO FUTURE
Paul Cornell

At last the Doctor comes face-to-face with the enemy who has been threatening him, leading him on a chase that has brought the TARDIS to London in 1976. There he finds that reality has been subtly changed and the country he once knew is rapidly descending into anarchy as an alien invasion force prepares to land . . .

ISBN 0 426 20409 3

TRAGEDY DAY
Gareth Roberts

When the TARDIS crew arrive on Olleril, they soon realize that all is not well. Assassins arrive to carry out a killing that may endanger the entire universe. A being known as the Supreme One tests horrific weapons. And a secret order of monks observes the growing chaos.

ISBN 0 426 20410 7

LEGACY
Gary Russell

The Doctor returns to Peladon, on the trail of a master criminal. Ace pursues intergalactic mercenaries who have stolen the galaxy's most evil artifact while Bernice strikes up a dangerous friendship with a Martian Ice Lord. The players are making the final moves in a devious and lethal plan – but for once it isn't the Doctor's.

ISBN 0 426 20412 3

THEATRE OF WAR
Justin Richards
Menaxus is a barren world on the front line of an interstellar war, home to a ruined theatre which hides sinister secrets. When the TARDIS crew land on the planet, they find themselves trapped in a deadly re-enactment of an ancient theatrical tragedy.

ISBN 0 426 20414 X

ALL-CONSUMING FIRE
Andy Lane
The secret library of St John the Beheaded has been robbed. The thief has taken forbidden books which tell of gateways to other worlds. Only one team can be trusted to solve the crime: Sherlock Holmes, Doctor Watson – and a mysterious stranger who claims he travels in time and space.

ISBN 0 426 20415 8

BLOOD HARVEST
Terrance Dicks
While the Doctor and Ace are selling illegal booze in a town full of murderous gangsters, Bernice has been abandoned on a vampire-infested planet outside normal space. This story sets in motion events which are continued in *Goth Opera*, the first in a new series of Missing Adventures.

ISBN 0 426 20417 4

STRANGE ENGLAND
Simon Messingham
In the idyllic gardens of a Victorian country house, the TARDIS crew discover a young girl whose body has been possessed by a beautiful but lethal insect. And they find that the rural paradise is turning into a world of nightmare ruled by the sinister Quack.

ISBN 0 426 20419 0

FIRST FRONTIER
David A. McIntee
When Bernice asks to see the dawn of the space age, the Doctor takes the TARDIS to Cold War America, which is facing a threat far more deadly than Communist Russia. The militaristic Tzun Confederacy have made Earth their next target for conquest – and the aliens have already landed.

ISBN 0 426 20421 2

ST ANTHONY'S FIRE
Mark Gatiss

The TARDIS crew visit Betrushia, a planet in terrible turmoil. A vicious, genocidal war is raging between the lizard-like natives. With time running out, the Doctor must save the people of Betrushia from their own legacy before St Anthony's fire consumes them all.

ISBN 0 426 20423 9

FALLS THE SHADOW
Daniel O'Mahony

The TARDIS is imprisoned in a house called Shadowfell, where a man is ready to commence the next phase of an experiment that will remake the world. But deep within the house, something evil lingers, observing and influencing events, waiting to take on flesh and emerge.

ISBN 0 426 20427 1

PARASITE
Jim Mortimore

The TARDIS has arrived in the Elysium system, lost colony of distant Earth and site of the Artifact: a world turned inside out, home to a bizarre ecosystem. But now the Artifact appears to be decaying, transforming the humans trapped within into something new and strange.

ISBN 0 426 20425 5

WARLOCK
Andrew Cartmel

On the streets of near-future Earth, a strange new drug is having a devastating impact. It's called warlock, and some call it the creation of the devil. While Benny and Ace try to track down its source, the Doctor begins to uncover the truth about the drug.

ISBN 0 426 20433 6

SET PIECE
Kate Orman

There's a rip in the fabric of space and time. Passenger ships are disappearing from the interstellar traffic lanes. An attempt to investigate goes dangerously wrong, and the TARDIS crew are scattered throughout history – perhaps never to be reunited.

ISBN 0 426 20436 0

INFINITE REQUIEM
Daniel Blythe

Kelzen, Jirenal and Shanstra are Sensopaths, hugely powerful telepaths whose minds are tuned to the collective unconscious. Separated in time, they wreak havoc and destruction. United, they threaten every sentient being in the universe.

ISBN 0 426 20437 9

SANCTUARY
David A. McIntee

The Doctor and Bernice are stranded in medieval France, a brutal time of crusades and wars of succession. While the Doctor investigates a murder in a besieged fortress, Bernice joins forces with an embittered mercenary to save a band of heretics from the might of the Inquisition.

ISBN 0 426 20439 5

HUMAN NATURE
Paul Cornell

April, 1914. In the town of Farringham, a teacher called Dr John Smith has just begun work. Struggling to fit in, he finds himself haunted by memories of a place called Gallifrey – somewhere he knows he's never been. Can it be true that, as his niece Bernice claims, creatures from another planet are invading the town?

ISBN 0 426 20443 3

ORIGINAL SIN
Andy Lane

The last words of a dying alien send the Doctor and Bernice to 30th-century Earth in an attempt to avert an unspecified disaster. There, Adjudicators Roz Forrester and Chris Cwej are investigating a series of apparently motiveless murders. And their chief suspects are the Doctor and Bernice.

ISBN 0 426 20444 1

SKY PIRATES!
Dave Stone

Join the Doctor and Benny for the maiden voyage of the good ship *Schirron Dream*, as it ventures into a system which is being invaded by the villainous, shapeshifting Sloathes. Watch Chris Cwej and Roslyn Forrester have a rough old time of it in durance vile. Who will live? Who will die? Will the Doctor ever play the harmonium again?

ISBN 0 426 20446 8

ZAMPER
Gareth Roberts

The planet Zamper is home to a secretive organization that constructs the galaxy's mightiest warships. The TARDIS crew are intrigued by

Zamper's mysterious rulers. What is their true agenda? And why have they invited the last remnants of the Chelonian Empire to their world?

ISBN 0 426 20450 6

TOY SOLDIERS
Paul Leonard

The Doctor and his companions are following a trail of kidnapped children across a Europe recovering from the ravages of the First World War. But someone is aware of their search, and they find themselves unwilling guests on the planet Q'ell, where a similar war has raged for the last 1,400 years.

ISBN 0 426 20452 2

HEAD GAMES
Steve Lyons

Stand by for an exciting adventure with Dr Who and his companion, Jason. Once again, they set out to seek injustice, raise rebel armies and beat up green monsters. But this time, Dr Who faces a deadly new threat: a genocidal rogue Time Lord known only as the Doctor and his army of gun-slinging warrior women.

ISBN 0 426 20454 9

THE ALSO PEOPLE
Ben Aaronovitch

The Doctor has taken his companions to paradise: a sun enclosed by an artificial sphere where there is no poverty or violence. But then the peace is shattered by murder. As the suspects proliferate, Bernice realises that even an artificial world has its buried secrets and Roz discovers that every paradise has its snake.

ISBN 0 426 20456 5

If you have trouble obtaining Doctor Who books from your local shops, a book list and details of our mail order service are available upon request from:

Doctor Who Books
Virgin Publishing Ltd
332 Ladbroke Grove
London W10 5AH